Pippa Roscoe lives in Nor[t]
and makes daily promises t[o]
the day she'll leave her com[   ]
walk in the countryside. She can't remember a
time when she wasn't dreaming about handsome
heroes and innocent heroines. Totally her mother's
fault, of course—she gave Pippa her first romance
to read at the age of seven! She is inconceivably
happy that she gets to share those daydreams with
you. Follow her on Twitter @PippaRoscoe.

Canadian **Dani Collins** knew in high school
that she wanted to write romance for a living.
Twenty-five years later, after marrying her
high school sweetheart, having two kids with
him, working at several generic office jobs and
submitting countless manuscripts, she got The
Call. Her first Mills & Boon novel won the
Reviewers' Choice Award for Best First in Series
from *RT Book Reviews*. She now works in her
own office, writing romance.

TWIN CONSEQUENCES OF THAT NIGHT

PIPPA ROSCOE

THE SECRET OF THEIR BILLION-DOLLAR BABY

DANI COLLINS

MILLS & BOON

First published in Great Britain 2024
by Mills & Boon, an imprint of HarperCollins*Publishers* Ltd,
1 London Bridge Street, London, SE1 9GF

www.harpercollins.co.uk

HarperCollins*Publishers*, Macken House, 39/40 Mayor Street Upper, Dublin 1, D01 C9W8, Ireland

Twin Consequences of That Night © 2024 Pippa Roscoe

The Secret of Their Billion-Dollar Baby © 2024 Dani Collins

ISBN: 978-0-263-32000-8

03/24

This book contains FSC™ certified paper
and other controlled sources to ensure responsible forest management.

For more information visit www.harpercollins.co.uk/green.

Printed and Bound in the UK using 100% Renewable Electricity
at CPI Group (UK) Ltd, Croydon, CR0 4YY

TWIN CONSEQUENCES
OF THAT NIGHT

PIPPA ROSCOE

MILLS & BOON

For my incredible niece, Izzi.

You are such an inspiration,
and it has been nothing but a joy
to watch you become the woman you are today.

Your strength, conviction, sense of adventure
and sense of humour are boundless and wonderful,
and I'm lucky to be part of your life.

All my love, always,

Auntie Pippa

xx

CHAPTER ONE

NATE WAS IN his sister's flat. It looked the same, but certainly didn't feel the same. There was a glass of wine in his hand, but he couldn't remember how it had got there, and nor could he smell the rich fruity scent of what he was sure would be a Beaujolais. His vision was fuzzy at the edges and his sister was saying something, but he couldn't hear it. Sound was muffled, as if his head was wrapped in a blanket. His vision was tunnelled and her eyes widened in alarm, her mouth opening in shock, just as he was drowned in blackness...

'Mr Harcourt, can you hear me? Mr Harcourt?'

He was being shaken roughly, pain slicing into his head. Something was wrong. His sister was sobbing. Begging.

'Please help him. Please do something.'

His body rolled viciously and he landed on a bed with a thud. A light shone in his eye, blinding him, but he couldn't close it. He tried to smack the hand away, but his arm wouldn't move.

'His left pupil's blown.'

Words like 'CT', 'angiogram', 'bloods' swam as he tried to find his sister, but he couldn't move a muscle. He was in hell, his body on fire. He felt everything: each needle-stick, each poke and prod, the knuckle against the arch of his foot. But his body wasn't reacting. Nothing.

Numb, but not numb.

'What's going on?'

Hope sounded so scared that it terrified him. He knew that fear, the incomprehensible touch of death come to steal away loved ones, and he wouldn't inflict that on her. He couldn't.

The high-pitched moan of the monitor screamed until it descended into irregular pips.

'You're going to be fine, Nate. I promise. The best doctor is flying in right now to do the operation.'

What operation? What had happened?

'Nate, you're going to be fine,' his sister whispered into his ear. 'I promise.'

The cabin door on his small private jet slammed shut, yanking him from the nightmare that wasn't a nightmare. Nightmares were baseless fears: terrors of the unknown, irrational monsters dredged from the unconscious. What Nate had just experienced was a sleeping memory. Events that had been real and had happened more than two years ago, the night he'd returned from the disaster that was the Casas deal. The night a headache that had started in Madrid had ended with him collapsed on the floor of his sister's London apartment.

Of course, it had never crossed anyone's mind to announce to the world that Nathanial Harcourt, English billionaire, had suffered a cerebral aneurism. It hadn't even required discussion. It was imperative not only for Harcourts, but also the three businesses that he owned personally, that news of such a weakness not threaten the financial bottom line.

It had been somewhat bitterly amusing to Nate that the idea that he was taking a self-indulgent journey of discovery in Goa was favourable to a near death experience to his board members and the public. So it had been kept secret because of vultures, economics and public perception.

All of it: the successful operation done in London that very night, the medical flight to the private Swiss hospital where he would not only receive round-the-clock medical attention, but also intense and expert rehabilitation until he could return with absolutely no evidence of any mental or physical incapacity.

Only his sister and his grandfather knew that instead of sunning himself on a beach he'd been learning how to *'make pain his friend'*.

Bugger that.

The initial operation had been a walk in the park compared to the long-term fallout. He might have been in the best private medical facility that money could buy, but it didn't mean a thing. The rehab, the fatigue, the headaches, the clicks he heard whenever he moved, the hearing loss, the jaw pain, the back pain, the slowed reaction times? These were untenable to a man who had been raised to see weakness as anathema, an abomination to be rooted out, cut out like a cancer before it could impact stock share prices and public perception.

They were daily reminders, taunts, cruel and constant, in those first twenty months, reminding him that he was not the man he'd once been. That he needed to be careful, watchful of his health, his diet, his exercise…his stress levels. For a man who'd rarely denied himself a thing, his life had become about strictures and rules: scheduled medications and vitamins, check-ups booked in the diary years in advance.

And his grandfather refusing to meet his eye.

'You should consider reducing your workload. Considerably.'

For more than two years, Nate had worked harder than he ever had before to get back to where he could resume his life seamlessly, so that he *didn't* have to reduce his workload 'considerably'. He had grown his hair out a little—attributing it to his self-indulgent adult 'gap years' and not down to the fact that it now hid a scar line. He had lost weight which, according to the latest headlines, was from partying too hard rather than a loss of appetite from diminished aptitude for taste and smell.

But the impact on reactions, his decisiveness, the things that had made him a truly excellent businessman? Utterly devastating. It was as if he were constantly wading through liquid amber: holding him back, slowing him down, making it hard to think and breathe sometimes.

He saw it in the faces of his staff, his sister, his grandfather. The confusion, the doubt, the frustration with his slowness... He just wasn't the same as he'd been before. The doctors insisted that it wasn't *'a cause for concern'*. That it would *'go away with time'*. And he could see it; they just didn't understand. Didn't get what it was like to have your whole life change with the flip of a switch. A switch that had flipped the moment he'd returned from that damn business with the Casases.

'Flight time to Madrid is just over two hours from London, Mr Harcourt.'

Nate nodded to acknowledge he'd heard the air stewardess making her way towards him. He closed his eyes, hoping to relieve the ache left by the nightmare that wasn't a nightmare, and leaned back against the headrest.

'And if there's anything,' she continued, 'at all,' she said, pressing a hand on his shoulder, his eyes opening quickly enough to see a flash of fire engine red talon against his white shirt, 'I'd be very happy to oblige.'

If there had been any doubt about the intent of her words, it was obliterated by the lascivious look in her eyes.

A little over two years ago Nathanial Harcourt would have smirked, caught her wrist, pulled her into his lap and given her, in vivid Technicolor, her heart's desire, uncaring of what the captain and his co-pilot did or didn't see.

Back then, he'd been in his prime, the *enfant terrible* of the British business scene. He owned three companies personally and was the CFO of his family's business, Harcourts—a brand and name synonymous with luxury, exclusivity and opulence. The international department store had been in his family for generations, and he was hotly tipped to be the next CEO. After all, he'd been groomed to lead it, first by his father and then, after his parents' death, by his grandfather. But in order to prove himself to the board, he'd been on his way to Madrid to secure a deal with a Spanish fashion conglomerate, Casas Fashion. And success had been within his reach…

Until he'd met Gabriella Casas.

Nate looked down to find his hand fisted on his thigh and the air stewardess still waiting for him to respond to her invitation.

'Thank you, darling, I'll take a whisky,' he said, purposely misunderstanding her, his voice full of a gravel dragged from bitterness the air stewardess was utterly oblivious to.

She withdrew her hand from his shoulder and, masking her disappointment, disappeared towards the jet's impressive galley.

Nate looked out of the small round window, seeing the moon painting clouds in an unearthly glow.

Gabriella Casas.

Even now his body betrayed him, reacting to the memory of her in ways that he couldn't control. Erotic tension teased him into an arousal he didn't want. His stomach clenched as the small private jet taking him back to Madrid hit an air pocket and dropped him back into the first time he'd laid eyes on her, when he'd not known her name. When he'd arrogantly thought it wasn't even important.

She was, simply put, the most beautiful woman he'd ever seen. And Nathanial Harcourt, who *never* made the first move, had been completely unable to stop himself. Large, startlingly hazel eyes locked on his and he felt as if he'd been punched in the solar plexus. He'd spent years thinking over every single moment of that night, unpicking where he'd gone wrong, where he'd failed to spot the warning signs. Wondering if the cerebral aneurism had perhaps already started affecting him even then.

'Would you like a drink?'

'I don't want you to get the wrong idea.'

'I only asked you for a drink—nothing more.'

Nate could still feel the heat of her gaze on him, seemingly as unable to look away as he'd been. He, who had seduced countless women in countless countries, had been utterly seduced by what he thought was an innocent.

'I want to talk to you.'

'And I want to hear everything you want to say, but first... I need... I want to do...this.'

He hadn't been able to stop himself. He should have asked first, but the sheer shared desire he could feel between them made the air so thick with want it was almost impossible to think. A kiss…just a touch of lips, that was all he'd intended. But he hadn't realised, hadn't known that he'd not be able to stop at that. And even then, he'd wondered whether he'd be able to spend the rest of his life without her in it. It was like heaven, just before it turned into hell.

The next morning he'd opened his eyes to an empty bed and he'd been shocked. A cynical part of himself now mocked the irony mercilessly. The number of beds he'd sneaked away from hardly stacking up to the single time it was done to him. He'd sat up, looking around at his clothes strewn about the floor, each one a sensual memory and a censure at the same time.

He'd caught sight of a small glittery clutch beneath the side table and reached for it. With no compunction whatsoever, he'd opened it, looking for some sign of who he had spent the most spectacular night of his life with. No phone, no ID, just a credit card and a room key: *G Casas*.

He'd stared at it numbly for moments while his usually rapid-fire brain made sluggish connections it didn't want to make. Anger poured through his veins and he dressed with furious, jerky movements.

After he'd realised who he had spent the night with, he'd paid his investigators more than triple their rate to find out whatever it was that had been missed the first time, because he'd known that they must have missed something. That was when he'd discovered the depths of Renata Casas's treachery.

Gabriella Casas had been, he could only presume, sent by her mother to seduce him, probably because her own

stomach-churning attempts to do so had failed spectac-
ularly. He should have paid heed to the gleam in Renata
Casas's eye as he'd informed her they would be keeping
things strictly professional. But he hadn't expected her to
send her own daughter to distract him from the fact that
they were trying to fleece him out of millions by selling
him shares in a company they didn't own.

But confronting Renata and Gabriella Casas that afternoon had been a mistake. That was the conclusion he'd
come to after reliving the events of that twenty-four-hour
period over and over again through the merciless sessions
of physio and rehab.

*'Get her out of here. I never want to look at her ever
again. She's no better than a whore.'*

Gabriella's mother's words stung like a vicious slap.
And he'd hardened himself against the image of Gabriella standing there shaking, her eyes full of pleas, regrets, apologies.

Lies, it was all lies.

Renata had illegally tried to sell him shares she didn't
own in a business that wasn't hers. Her *son's* business.

*'Lady, you're crazy. My lawyers are going to go
through everything with a fine-tooth comb and when
they're done...'*

He'd left them with that threat and returned straight to
his sister's apartment in London. And then a small blood
vessel had ruptured everything he'd ever known.

Nate knew that it was irrational to link the two together—emotional rather than evidentiary. But he kept
telling himself that once he was done with Casas Textiles, his whole life would get back to normal. Just like
it was before.

Which was why, two years later, he was flying to Spain

to be a key witness in a fraud and embezzlement trial against Renata Casas. Nathanial Harcourt never made a promise he didn't keep and now he was here to make good on it.

Renata Casas and her daughter would rue the day they'd tried to make a fool out of Nate Harcourt.

'Are you okay in there?' Gabi's brother worriedly called through the toilet door. Javier Casas was worried about the idea of her giving evidence at her mother's trial, but that wasn't why she was hiding in the bathroom.

'Yes, just a minute,' she replied.

She stared at herself in the mirror. The long dark tresses that she had once taken so much pride in were now pulled back in a chaotic bun—not artfully designed by a stylist, but thrown back with little time or care. Clothes that had once been so much of her focus—fabric, colour, style, cut, *design*—were now chosen by cleanliness level and, even then, the top she wore betrayed a spatter of tomato sauce from lunch. Cheeks that had once been flushed pink with youth and excitement were now thinner, cheekbones pronounced from lack of opportunity rather than diet or contour. She looked pale, putting it kindly, she thought as she skirted over the thumbprints of darkness smudged beneath her eyes.

She'd spent too long staring at the newspaper she'd sneaked in here with her. The words had long ago become blurred and the only thing she could see clearly was the eyes of the still handsome man she had spent one spectacular night with, a little over two years ago. The picture was black and white, but she would have sworn she could see the espresso-rich depths of his gaze, staring straight at the camera—staring straight at her.

Nathanial Harcourt.

He'd grown his wheat blond hair out. That night, it had been short, efficient. She remembered the feel of his scalp beneath her nails, the way he'd unfurled beneath her as she'd done that while they'd kissed. Her breath caught as she remembered the feel of his tongue, his touch, his need for her. The way his skin had pebbled as she chased the goosebumps with her kisses, fascinated by his reaction to her all the while he was trying to distract her with her own responses. She blinked back tears, remembering how they'd laughed, how he'd let her get things wrong. He'd let her explore him, learn the feel of things, of them together, the way her heart pounded, passion sighed, her legs trembled, her hands fisted, the way she had gasped, the way he had growled. The way that—

No!

She swiped at a tear with one hand as the other curled the paper beneath her fingers, clenched and furious.

No. She'd tried to reach him every day for nearly two years.

Every. Day.

Emails. Phone calls. If she'd had a fax number, she would have tried that too. At one point she'd been half convinced that there was a conspiracy, that people were actively trying to keep her away from him. She'd tried everything she could think of, bar getting on a flight, and the only reason she hadn't done that was that she simply hadn't been physically able to. She'd reached out to contacts in the fashion industry, anything to get a message to the CFO of Harcourts department store. She'd even gone to the Spanish flagship store in Madrid and they'd eventually called security. And the shame! The shame at abasing herself like that had laid fresh hurt over old scars in her battered self-confidence. And all that time he'd been sunning himself on a beach in South Asia.

But now he was here. In Madrid. Having been called as a witness in the trial of the century, if the gossip rags were to be believed.

No one had thought that Nathanial Harcourt would actually do it, least of all her mother. But apparently the last thing he had done before disappearing on his extended 'sabbatical' was file charges against Renata for what she had done.

Gabi hadn't been surprised though. She'd realised what would happen the night she'd met him—the fateful night that had changed the entire course of her life. And no, she could never bring herself to regret it, not for a second. But so much had happened because of it.

That night, her mother had sent Gabi to Nate with every intention of having her daughter seduce the rich English businessman in order to distract him from her illegal wrongdoings. Instead, for Gabi it had been the final straw. She had gone there to tell Nathanial Harcourt that her mother didn't have the ability or permission to sell shares in her son's company and that he should leave without looking back.

She'd wanted to tell him, but she'd been so stunned by him, by his apparent interest in her, she'd been struck silent. She tried, several times, but it was as if she couldn't say it and he wouldn't hear it. His flirtation had undone her, and her innocent responses had strangely delighted him, and for just one night she'd thought she'd found someone who had seen her, understood what was at the core of her. Otherwise, she never would have done what she did.

But when he'd tracked her down at her mother's house

the next day, after she'd fled the hotel, the betrayal she'd seen in his eyes before the mask came down was the first of many blows her heart would receive that day.

'You send her after me like some Mata Hari and now you want to get rid of her?'

'Why would I want her? She's no better than a whore.'

The vicious shock of her mother's accusation had struck another blow. And when Nate had refused to even look at her, defend her, argue that what they'd shared had been more, it had scattered those broken pieces to the four winds.

'Sweetheart, are you okay?' Emily whispered, gently knocking against the bathroom door. Her sister-in-law's concern finally nudged at her conscience. Gabi shook off her thoughts, gave herself a stern *pull yourself together* glare in the mirror and opened the door into a familiar, loving, chaotic mess.

'Mamá! Mamá! Mamá!'

The sound of little feet running down the long hallway towards her lifted her heart at the same time as bringing a damp heat to her eyes. Her babies, Ana and Antonio, with matching grins, pink cheeks and dark mahogany gazes, raced towards her on feet only just becoming steady.

She crouched down to meet them and took them both in her arms, and after letting the moment soothe the ache in her heart, she reached to tickle them both until they all descended into giggles. She bent her head to their crowns and inhaled the sweet smell of her children and then gently pulled back.

'What mischief are you two up to then?' she demanded.

'They understand that? In English?' Javier asked in Spanish, leaning against the doorframe, wiping his hands from washing up after lunch.

'They know that while we're here we speak English,' Gabi replied in English.

Emily slipped beneath her husband's arm, carrying her own daughter, Lily, a pretty curly-haired one-year-old, and for a second Gabi's heart ached. She breathed past the hurt of the sight of her brother with his arm around his wife and child. It was the family unit that she'd always wanted but had never had, not only for herself but for her children.

'I'm fluent now in Spanish if it's easier?' Emily offered.

Gabi smiled and stuck to the lie that she wanted Ana and Antonio to be bilingual for their sake. Javi, her brother, had never pushed Gabi to tell him the name of the twins' father. She was sure that he had figured it out, but he'd never said anything. Their relationship, so much better since she had left her mother's, had involved a lot of support and a lot of work, and so much of it was built on trust. Trust that when she needed to she'd tell him. Trust that he would be there when she did.

Her brother had given Gabi absolutely everything—he'd needed to, because when she'd left Renata's house she'd left with nothing but what she'd been wearing. She'd not gone back since the night of the argument between Nate and Renata. There was not a single thing in that house she'd wanted. And while Javi wouldn't have it any other way, there was a huge part of Gabi that wished she could find some way of being independent.

'Cara, you have twins. They should be your focus, not worrying about money or housing. Especially not when I can give those things to you.'

She knew that what her brother had said made sense. She would *never* deprive her children of any kind of shelter or support just because of her own stubborn desire to provide for her family herself. But still…it cut her deep.

It hadn't been easy—discovering she was pregnant just when she had lost everything she had known. Realising that the father of her children wanted absolutely nothing to do with her. Becoming a mother at the age of twenty-three and losing what few friends she did have to partying and clubbing and travels around the world. Watching the hopes and dreams she'd had for her fashion designs slip through her fingers had closed something off within her.

But no matter what imaginary future she'd once dreamed of, the moment that she'd held both her babies in her arms, she knew—*knew*—that she'd never have had it any other way. She would protect these two innocent children with every single fibre of her being. She would love them so much that it would make up for any lack of father figure. These two children would not have the same upbringing that she had. No matter what she had to do to make that happen.

'Is it the court case?' Javi asked, the concern etched across his features in frown lines. 'You don't have to be a witness for the prosecution, you know. They've got enough evidence and even if they didn't—'

'It's fine,' Gabi dismissed, easing herself up from the floor and watching her twins run off into the sitting room of Javi's apartment in Madrid. 'It's the right thing to do,' she said with a simple shrug. And it really was. She wouldn't shy away from the horrible truths about her mother. 'I'm just sorry it meant uprooting everyone from Frigiliana to come here.'

Emily shushed her with a wave. 'I've been wanting to come back into town for ages.'

Gabi smiled at Emily's use of 'town' for Spain's capital

city. Her Spanish was almost perfect now, but the Britishisms she used still identified her as a foreigner. Emily, who had been estranged from her brother for five years at one point, was now almost as close as a sister. But there were still some things that Gabi needed to keep to herself. And one of those things was Nathanial Harcourt.

The same Nathanial Harcourt who was due to give evidence. The prosecutor had assured her that they wouldn't meet as they were scheduled at different times for the day. He'd explained that the delays court cases often experienced meant that it was highly likely she'd be pushed back to the next day anyway.

But Gabi wasn't so sure. She couldn't shake the feeling that, having put him firmly from her mind and life when the twins turned one, a reckoning was upon her, one way or another.

CHAPTER TWO

NATE PEERED UP at the courthouse as he walked towards the entrance. He paused at the top of the steps, taking a breath, buttoning his blazer and smoothing down his tie. He was finally ready to put this whole entire mess behind him. He'd leave here after giving testimony against Renata and her attempt to defraud him and steal money from him, and then liquidate his remaining shares in Casas Textiles.

They were worth next to nothing, thanks to the publicity surrounding Renata's arrest and trial, but he didn't care. It was rumoured that Renata's brother was propping her up financially, and Nate didn't care about that either.

He pushed through the building's doors, gave his name at the court's reception and waited for the prosecutor's assistant. He disliked the way that his pulse had risen and the nervous energy that coursed through him. Before the aneurism, he would have thrived from it, used it, but now every change in his body could be a warning sign of something terrible.

He shoved that thought to the back of his mind. Nate had recovered. It was the only reason he'd come back six months ago. He would never have returned if he couldn't have done it seamlessly. His reaction times were only a little slower than before, but he was still healthier than most.

'Mr Harcourt?'

Nate turned to find a suited man with glasses peering up at him.

'Señor Torres?'

The man smiled. '*Sí*. It's nice to finally meet you.'

Nate nodded in acknowledgement. He didn't need nice. He needed this done.

'It will all be very simple. The prosecutor will ask you to state what happened, the defence lawyer may have a go at putting a twist on things, but really, with the corroborating witness statements…' Torres punctuated his sentence with an expressive shrug that implied it would be nothing short of impossible for Renata to wriggle out of this.

Nate listened as he scanned the faces of the people gathered in the large foyer.

'Are you looking for someone?'

Nate paused for a beat. He had been and hadn't even realised it. 'More like hoping to avoid someone, but I doubt they'll be here.'

'I can check if you like?' Torres offered.

'No, that's okay. They'll be a witness for the defence.'

'Then there is no reason that you will see them today,' Torres reassured him. 'This way?' It was an invitation Nate couldn't refuse.

The courtroom was situated off a long bright hallway, down which people stalked with businesslike efficiency. That focused energy was familiar to him and he used it, harnessed it, before he entered the room.

In his mind he'd always imagined his confrontation with the Casases taking place in a London court, with all the grandeur of rich mahogany, green leather, black robes and grey wigs. So the overwhelming use of pine in

the small Madrid courtroom left him feeling a little disappointed. Led quietly to a seat near the door, he stared
at the back of Renata Casas's dark hair, her shoulders
drawn in a line of barely suppressed tension. He glanced
at her hand where it rested, white-knuckled, on the pale
wooden desk before her.

No, not tension. Anger.

He huffed out a laugh. The audacity of this woman
was absolutely outrageous. Conversations between the
lawyers and the judge in Spanish washed over him as
he took the time to observe her. Occasionally she would
lean towards her lawyer and say something and he would
nod. Nate wondered how much of that was staged. He
looked back over their encounters, and wondered how
he'd missed it. How he'd been so taken in, first by her
and then by her daughter.

And if his pulse spiked at the thought of Gabriella he
chose to ignore it, because his thoughts had flown to that
familiar doubt. Had the aneurism already been affecting his actions then? He'd been assured by doctors that
it hadn't, that it wasn't how aneurisms worked, but Nate
was a man utterly used to, and dependent on, trusting his
instincts, trusting only himself.

He'd had to be. Because after his parents' death when
he was twelve, after his grandfather had separated him
from his sister, he'd been sent away to boarding school,
where he'd only had himself. After only days in the cold,
feral environment of boys cut from their families too
soon, where weakness was a vulnerability to be exploited
and grief was something to be repressed, he'd learned
that lesson hard and fast.

In the last two and a bit years, that core sense of inner

strength had been in question and now it was time to get it back.

'Mr Harcourt?' Torres gestured for him to take the witness seat.

Gabi's heels clicked along the hardwood corridor outside the courtroom where her mother was standing trial. Thankfully, the press that had swarmed like flies on carrion at the start were currently distracted by a politician who had been caught having an affair with a younger colleague and Gabi had managed to arrive unscathed.

She took a breath, trying to level her breathing. She'd meant what she'd said to Javi—she was ready to give evidence against her mother. But she couldn't help that for more than the first two decades of her life, Gabi had clung to the belief that one day, just one day, her mother would explain that she hadn't meant to be so selfish, that she hadn't meant to behave so badly...that she *did* love her.

Gabi had been waiting for something that would never come. And eventually all the tantrums, the way everything had to revolve around her had become so intrinsically part of Renata that she had started to do illegal things, thinking she could get away with it. But in the end it was the emotional manipulation that had hurt the most. Her mother had made Gabi feel that she needed her, that only Gabi could understand her, only Gabi could help her. So she'd stayed, she'd tried. But even that hadn't been enough for Renata's insatiable selfishness.

Gabi wondered if things might have been different if her father had remained in the picture. If he hadn't remarried as quickly as possible and begun a new family—one that suited him better. If she'd had his support, maybe she'd have been able to defend herself against her mother before that terrible last day. But she hadn't.

Gabi turned at the end of the corridor, bending the direction of her thoughts away from such painful meanderings and instead checked her watch. Emily had taken the kids to the museum. A small smile pulled at the curve of her lips. At eighteen months, they were probably a tad too young to take it all in, but she desperately wished she were there with them, rather than here.

But it was time. Time to put it all behind her. For so long, the court case, the fear that she might bump into *him*, had been hanging over her like the sword of Damocles. She'd half expected him to drop into her life and cut it in half. Because beneath her worry about giving evidence against her mother, what had really been chipping away at her nerves, her appetite and her sleep had been the fact that here, finally, was the opportunity to let Nate know that he was a father.

Gabi pressed a hand to her stomach just at the thought of it. She'd wanted him to know for so long. But she'd been alone the whole way through her pregnancy and then when the twins were born. She'd been alone when she'd held them for the first time, seeing the utterly incredibleness of them and not being able to show him. She'd been alone when she'd looked at her children sleeping beside each other and realised what they were: the two pieces of her heart.

The hand against her stomach turned into a fist. She'd been alone on the long, lonely nights when both the twins were crying inconsolably, and she'd been alone when she'd *needed* him, and she'd still tried to reach him. But on their first birthday she had drawn a line, promising that she wouldn't open them up to the same devastating rejection that she had experienced herself.

But now that Nate was here, in the flesh, could she keep that from him? It made it different, didn't it? She *had* to tell him now.

Señor Torres opened the door to the courtroom and peered around, smiling when he found her. He beckoned her towards him and Gabi refocused. One thing at a time. It was how she'd managed to survive the twins' first year. And now their second.

One thing at a time.

Gabi entered the courtroom and took the seat at the back that Señor Torres indicated for her, keeping her gaze low while her pulse raced, terrified of meeting her mother's eyes. She hadn't seen Renata since that night. They'd had no correspondence, her mother unwilling and Gabi simply unable to face the mother who had called her such horrible things. The terrifying *jealousy* her mother had revealed that night, even after intending for Gabi to 'sway' Nathanial Harcourt to blindly hand over money for shares Renata couldn't provide. The hatred. *That* was what she'd seen that night. Her mother had hated her. Gabi struggled to take a breath around the emotion clogging her throat.

'Thank you for explaining the minutiae of the accounting details,' one of the lawyers said in English, snapping Gabi's gaze up from the floor to the man in the witness chair. 'For the purposes of understanding the emotional impact this had on you and your business, can you describe how the incident made you feel?'

Gabi's heart thumped once, hard, and then stopped— as if it had utterly exhausted itself at just the sight of Nathanial Harcourt. She took in his appearance as he paused to collect his thoughts before answering the lawyer's question. And in that time her eyes saw things that she felt soul-deep—her children's gaze, her son's forehead, the spark of determination her daughter would get...

But there was something slightly different about him. The way he held himself, perhaps? He'd lost weight, but he wasn't gaunt—*lean*. The sense of restrained power beneath the sophisticated handmade suit was irrefutable. The pale blue tie served only to contrast with the rich golden honey of his skin tone. Memories of the night they'd shared pressed at her from all sides until Nate finally answered the lawyer's question.

'This whole situation has been deeply unpleasant. To have my name brought into such a scandal, the name of my family linked with fraud and embezzlement? Untenable. Devastating. If I had thought it a mistake, then of course I would have tried to find a reasonable solution, but the sheer intent, the meticulous and devious planning that went into defrauding a foreign businessman? It should be the shame of Spain and if I never meet another Casas as long as I live I'll die a happy man.'

Every single word struck a blow, severing the fragile hope Gabi had nurtured secretly in her breast. She knew, categorically and without a doubt, that there was no way this man would ever show her, or their children, a kindness and she just wouldn't risk it. She had promised to protect her children at all costs, and if that included protecting them from their own father—then so be it.

When Nathanial Harcourt decided to go all-in, he went all-in. It was imperative that he resolved this situation conclusively. Because only once this was resolved could he finally begin to get the rest of his businesses in order.

Yes, he could almost feel it. Things slotting into place, peace being restored.

And then he looked up to the viewing seats and caught sight of Gabriella Casas and his entire world turned on its head.

He watched the blood drain from her face, leaving behind two streaks of red across cheekbones sharper than he remembered, making him feel like a bastard. He had, obviously, been directing his statement towards Renata Casas. But while he couldn't, didn't, know how involved her daughter had been in the fraudulent plans, he could see that his words had affected her greatly.

'Thank you, Mr Harcourt, you may leave,' the lawyer concluded in English this time.

Nate stood, unable to take his gaze from Gabriella, who, it seemed, was equally unable to look away. Helpless. She looked helpless, he thought as he crossed the bright wood floor, utterly uncaring of the conversation passing between the two lawyers and the judge behind him. He ignored Renata utterly, instead taking everything in about the woman who had bewitched him over one single night—the *only* woman he had let his guard down for.

Oh, he might be world-renowned for the company he kept on his arm and in his bed, but that was a long time ago now. Gabriella was the last woman he had been with and at the time he'd been taken in by what he'd thought had been honesty. He was so lost between his memories of that night and the way that Gabriella was looking at him now, he was completely ignorant of the commotion building behind him.

All he could see was her large eyes, reminding him of labradorite, watching him walk towards her, the slashes of shame and something else making a mockery of the way she had flushed with pleasure, the sprinkle of freckles he remembered across her nose dimmed by her pallor. Her glorious hair, silken strands he'd fisted in his hands to bind them together, was hidden, pulled back harshly from a make-up-free face. She looked diminished, less than, and something in him roared in denial that he might have had some part to play in that.

No, it was a ruse, he told himself. As he drew closer, she rose from her seat to meet him and if there was something awkward about her movements he didn't notice it, because he was lost in the memory of how perfectly they had fitted that night. How he'd let himself think, believe, that for once he'd found someone who might actually understand him. Might actually want him not for his money or his status, but *him*.

He opened his mouth to speak when he suddenly heard a cry behind him.

If the last few years had taught him anything, it was how to differentiate the sounds of pain. There were cries of agony, hurt, frustration, fury, injustice and desperation. But the sound that Renata Casas had made was none of those things. It was indignant. Selfish. Outraged.

Before turning around to see what had caused Renata to make such a noise, he caught Gabriella paling even more, closing her eyes as if warding off a wave of pain. Frowning, he glanced back to find Renata Casas glaring at him and her daughter, together, just before she collapsed into the most dramatic and ridiculous faint Nate had ever seen.

The court had been adjourned for twenty minutes when Renata's defence lawyer insisted that his client be assessed by a medical professional. The prosecution and the judge seemed to have very little patience for the entire thing, but agreed with the need to determine that the defendant was at least legally fit to continue.

Señor Torres had ushered Nate and Gabriella back out into the hallway to wait until a decision on how to proceed had been made. Gabriella had immediately taken out her mobile phone and started to type furiously back and forth with someone and, while her phone was on silent, the increasingly frustrating sound of its vibration was beginning to grate on Nate's nerves.

Was it a boyfriend? A lover?

He pulled himself up short, startled by the sting of jealousy burning its way up his spine. He turned on his heel to face her, unable to hold his curiosity back any more.

'What are you doing here?' he demanded.

She bit her lip, but kept her gaze firmly on the screen of her mobile. 'I'm here to give evidence.'

He braced his hands on his hips, staring at her, willing her to look up at him. 'But it's the prosecution's turn for witnesses.'

'Yes.'

'Yes, what?' he demanded. Why was she being so difficult?

Finally, she looked up at him, her gaze clear of the anger and frustration he felt pouring out from him.

'I'm giving evidence against my mother.'

'What?' Shock cut through him.

'I had thought,' she said carefully as she put her phone away, 'that you were much quicker than this. Maybe your...' she trailed off, her hand gesturing in the air as if looking for the right words '..."sabbatical" has affected you somehow?'

He ground his teeth together to prevent the angry retort on his tongue from emerging. Her words had hit a
little too close to home. This woman was *nothing* like
the sweet, funny, guileless girl he thought he'd met. She
might be giving evidence against her mother—she might
be helping his cause—but that didn't mean she was innocent of any of this. He *would* find out her intentions here.

Gabi's pulse was racing and her blood was boiling. How
could she have *ever* spent a night with this man? He was
arrogant, presumptuous, *estúpido*. The only satisfaction
she'd had from their encounter was seeing that her reference to his slow wits had hit home. She was pretty sure
that not many people managed to get a strike against Nathanial Harcourt.

Her phone vibrated in her hand.

We're outside.

She stood, suddenly desperate to get herself and her
children as far away from Nate as possible.

She nodded at him. 'Mr Harcourt—' and half fled
down the corridor.

'Is that it?' he called after her. 'Really?' he practically yelled.

Really.

Señor Torres would message her to let her know when
she'd be needed, but Gabi knew her mother. Knew what
had driven her outburst today too. She hadn't missed the
way Renata's eyes had widened in realisation as she'd
seen the two of them together, what that meant for the
grandchildren she knew about but had never met. But,

more importantly, what that meant she could use for her trial.

A hand tightened around her stomach, warning her that whatever had happened today wasn't over. There would be repercussions, she was sure, but for now Gabi just wanted to hold her children and take them all as far away from here as possible.

She practically ran down the stone steps, unable to shake the feeling that something was catching up with her, gaining on her. But as she burst out into the sunshine and onto the pavement, the fresh air blew through the sense of claustrophobia. She gathered herself quickly, refusing to let the twins catch on to how rattled she'd been, not only seeing her mother but also their father.

'Mamá! Mamá!'

She turned, instantly recognising her son's voice, and swept Antonio up into her arms. She adored the way he loved her, unrestrained and uninhibited. She cradled his head to her neck and looked to Ana, so much more stubborn and independent than her brother, but just as loving. Her heart swelled. She didn't need anything more than what she had, she told herself. Not Casas Textiles, not her mother and certainly not Nate.

'I'm sorry, I kept them away as long as possible,' Emily said, her daughter in a sling nestled against her chest. 'But Antonio wouldn't settle.'

'That's okay. Thank you so much for taking them in the first place,' Gabi said, settling Antonio on her hip and reaching for Ana's mop of curls.

'Did something happen? You're out earlier than I—'

Gabi saw the concern in Emily's gaze before her sentence trailed off and turned to see what she was staring at before she could stop herself.

Nathanial Harcourt stood at the top of the steps, his jaw clenched, his jacket open and riffled by the breeze. The thick blond swathe of hair shadowed his brow, but nothing could mistake the intensity of his gaze as he observed Gabi with her children. Even from here, the taut lines of his body were forbidding, and Gabi had the sudden urge to flee.

'Gabi?' Emily asked.

'It's fine. We just need to go. Now.'

For six hours Gabi felt as if she were on the verge of a heart attack. Panic had taken up residence in her chest and only when she got back to the little villa that was nestled in between Nerja and Frigiliana did she finally feel that she might have outrun her past.

She had opened all the windows in the villa and filled the fridge with the food she'd bought on their way back from the small airfield Javier's jet had landed in. She'd begged off spending the night with her brother and sister-in-law, just needing a little alone time with her babies. Just needing a little alone time for herself.

As it was, Ana had started to cry the moment they'd walked away from their little cousin Lily and it had taken nearly two hours and four books, all the kisses and cuddles feasible, to calm her down. And even then Gabi was half convinced that she'd just exhausted herself to sleep. Thankfully, Antonio had recognised that his mother was at the end of her tether and kindly suppressed the desire to mirror his sibling.

After putting a wash on, and grabbing a few paltry mouthfuls of *tortilla*, *jamón* and *Monte Enebro*, she tackled the washing-up, brushing the tendrils of hair back from her face with suds-covered hands.

She'd made it home without him knowing. The relief, so strong and so sure, swept her concerns finally away, so that when the knock on the door sounded she genuinely thought it might have been Javi checking up on her, or one of her neighbours, who often took in parcels for her.

But when Gabi opened the door to see Nathanial Harcourt standing, with one hand braced against the stone arch and the other fisted at his side, dark eyes bright and sparking with dangerous gold flecks, she was utterly and completely stunned.

'What are you doing here?' she asked, finally finding her voice.

Nate glared at her with a flinty gaze. He opened his mouth as if to answer her question and slammed it shut again before he could.

Gabi's body shivered as goosebumps scattered over her skin. He looked…incredible. Perhaps it was because earlier, back in Madrid, she'd been expecting him, prepared for the sheer might of his presence. But here? In her little home, her sanctuary, it hit her with full force.

He drew from her the kind of response she'd only read about in story books, seen on TV and felt in person only once in her life—the night they'd spent together. It started with a rush that flooded her from head to toe, like a wave that crested over her skin, drenching her in a heat that burned but didn't leave a mark. It prickled her hair like static and snapped at her fingers like firecrackers. And she'd have thought she were going mad if she wasn't almost one hundred percent sure that he felt exactly the same way.

'How did you find me?' she asked, forcing herself to speak again to break the inexplicable connection that had formed between them.

'I have people for that.' His voice scraped gravel over her sensitised skin.

'What do you want?' she asked, her voice trembling. It wasn't a physical fear—not for a minute did she think she was in physical jeopardy—but there was a threat here and it was very real.

He barked out a laugh, as if something she'd said was funny, and she knew. She knew without knowing, she knew despite her heart still hoping. He had taken one look at Ana and Antonio and he'd known.

'Lie to me and tell me they're not mine,' he commanded. 'Do it, and I swear you'll live to regret it.'

CHAPTER THREE

NATE WAS HOLDING on by a thread.

Three things had happened when he had watched Gabriella on the court steps earlier that day.

First, he'd realised that he might have been wrong about Gabriella's involvement in Renata Casas's machinations, though he couldn't be entirely sure that the fact she had been due to give evidence against her mother wasn't just another Casas ploy to escape punishment.

Second, he'd registered with a shocking twist of jealousy and a terrible sense of loss, that Gabriella was now a mother. And he couldn't account for why he suddenly felt as if something precious had slipped through his fingers without him even realising it.

But then, third, when he'd seen the second child, when Gabriella had turned to look up at him, he'd seen fear and secrets in her eyes. She hadn't wanted him to know about her children. *Twins.* A girl and a boy, with eyes just like his and his twin sister's.

The shock had left him standing like a statue on the courthouse steps, long after Gabriella, her friend and the children had gone. With shaking hands, he'd punched in his lawyer's number and ordered him to pull up everything they had on Gabriella Casas, calling himself all kinds of stupid for not doing so before. While his lawyer was doing that, he'd ordered his driver to take him back to the airstrip where his private jet was waiting. Because he didn't have to wait until his lawyer called back. He *knew*, without needing confirmation. He didn't even need to be told the age of the children. Because it was Gabriella who had given herself and their children away.

By the time he arrived at the private airstrip, he had Gabriella's address, a detailed biography and some highly illegally obtained files on her two children. Nate hadn't asked for it, and wasn't sure he even wanted to look at those files, but he couldn't stop himself from staring at the pictures taken by the private investigator hired by his lawyers as early research for the court case against Gabriella's mother.

The short flight south from Madrid to the private airfield near Nerja took less than an hour. Which was precisely how long it took for an atavistic, primal need to see his children to take root. Because when he'd first seen the tiny children it had been as a stranger and now, powerful and driving, terrifying in its intensity, he needed to see them with a father's eyes.

With a start, he realised he'd arrived at the same private airstrip two years ago and directed his driver straight here, ignoring how that made him feel. And now, as he looked down at Gabriella, he was barely holding on. He could see the concern in her gaze, fear even, but honestly, in that moment, she wasn't his concern.

They were.

'I want to see them,' he ground out from between clenched teeth.

She shook her head, sending long curled tendrils of hair flying. 'They're asleep.'

'I don't care,' he snapped.

But the effect on Gabriella was instantaneous. Drawing herself up to her full height, her hazel eyes gleamed. 'They are asleep and I will not wake them. It took hours to get them down.'

'Why? Is something wrong?' he demanded urgently.

Gabriella frowned. 'No. They are just...*tired*,' she stressed.

Ready to dismiss her concern, he stepped forward, only to meet a firm hand against his chest, stopping him.

Gabriella took a visibly shaky breath. 'We have things to talk about, yes. But you do not come into my house with this much anger. I won't have it around my children.'

'*Our* children,' he practically seethed. She didn't respond. That didn't make him feel any better, but he did see her point. He turned away to gather himself, unable to do it under her watchful, determined gaze.

He was getting this all wrong. He knew he was. But how to explain it? This feeling flooding his body like adrenaline, fear and love all at the same time? The fear that something could have happened to them without him knowing, without him being able to prevent it. The fear that something still might.

He turned back, needing to know. 'Would you have told me? Would you have ever told me?'

Everything about her changed in a heartbeat; her pallor turned red as blotches appeared beneath the delicate tan of her skin. Her eyes, glittering shards of defiance, turned dark and forbidding.

'Is that a joke?' she spat.

Nate reared back in shock. Gabriella, as if a red haze had descended around her, stepped forward seemingly without realising it.

'I asked you a question. Is. That. A. Joke?'

'No,' Nate said, holding his hands up as if to ward her off, shocked at the vehemence in her tone.

'I tried to reach you for nearly two years.'

Oh, God.

His stomach dropped the moment he realised what must have happened.

'Every single day, I sent you two emails, I called you on the number that you gave my family three times. I reached out to colleagues who might be able to get a message to you. I reached out to every single one of your companies on public emails, contacts through contacts, uncaring of how utterly delusional it made me look. At one point I thought people were actively trying to conspire against me.'

Nate wanted to bury his head in his hands. They had been, in a way. She had tried to reach him for almost the same amount of time that he'd been sequestered in a Swiss hospital. So no, she wouldn't have been able to reach him. Of course she wouldn't.

'Nate, for the entirety of my pregnancy and the first year of my children's lives, I tried to tell you in every single way possible.'

He clenched his jaw, the muscles aching and throbbing in protest.

'Where were you?' Gabriella asked, the anger diminishing as she ran out of words, leaving her feeling drained and shaky and strangely vulnerable. 'Where were you?' she asked again, and this time she felt tears press against her eyes as she swallowed them back. *When I needed you.*

Does it even matter? she asked herself. Was there any excuse that could make up for how alone she had been for all those days, and the months that had followed?

Nate's entire demeanour had changed. There was sorrow and guilt in his gaze. He reached for her, but she turned away. No. He had missed his chance with her. She had promised herself that she would never go seeking what wasn't there to be found. She'd learned that lesson directly from her father. So no, Nate didn't deserve her understanding. But, she thought, taking a trembling breath, he *was* the father of her children and he did deserve to see them. She knew that much at least.

'If you have calmed down, you can come in, you can see them but, *por favor*, don't wake them.'

She felt Nate follow behind her, uncomfortably aware of the space that he took up in her home. He was tall and broad, and although she vaguely remembered thinking that there was something different about him, it didn't seem to have affected the impact he had on her.

She led him through the living area and kitchen, doubtful that he'd be impressed with what he saw. Javier had wanted her to have more, but Gabi argued that this small villa was enough. She had refused his largesse, but had welcomed the riot of plants and pictures Emily had insisted would survive a single mother's lifestyle. They had become the bits and pieces that had made this small but perfect villa a home for her and her children.

A home without a father.

She led him to the twins' room, where the door was already open a crack. She turned and found Nate looking almost terrified, and fought the ridiculous urge to reassure him. He had brought this on himself as much as she had. And then she felt bad for her uncharitable thought. She placed a finger to her lips and gently pushed the door open wider.

A nightlight glowed warmly, warding off complete

darkness, and Gabi tried to see what Nate saw when he looked at his sleeping children. Long dark lashes spread shadows across round cheeks. Little perfectly formed mouths looked like drawings from a fairy tale and tiny hands flexed in dreams as their chests rose and fell with beautiful regularity. Antonio snuffled a little and Ana was out for the count, as always. Her deep sleeper. It had saved Gabriella's sanity in the months when Antonio was restless and miserable.

Her heart had hurt at the time, and she'd never been able to shake the feeling that even then, even utterly unconscious of how the world should be, Antonio had known that out there was a father who wasn't with him.

Gabriella clenched her fist as she watched Nate stare at his children with something like awe, like love. Was it that easy for him? To come in here after all this time and just be a father? Gabi hated the twist of resentment and tried to turn away.

'Which…' Nate swallowed visibly. 'Which…'

Anger turned to pity in an instant. 'Ana is on the left. She sleeps like the dead. Her hair is just a shade lighter than Antonio's, though you'll not be able to see it now. Antonio, he's the light sleeper. He'll wake up if a pin drops,' she said around a smile, her whisper dropping to an even quieter level, in case she conjured him from sleep. 'Ana is stubborn and determined. Antonio is happy and easy-going, but…'

'But?' Nate turned, his head close to hers, closer than she'd realised.

'But a little more delicate,' she said, suddenly worried that he might not like that about his son. Might want to mould him in ways that went against the beautiful little boy he was. And, just like that, she realised how dangerous it was to bring a stranger into their lives. A stranger who had power and money that she simply didn't have.

Nate nodded, the darkness of the room preventing her from seeing how he had interpreted her descriptions of their children. *Their* children.

Suddenly she wanted Nate to leave, wanted to put space between him and the twins. She turned away, hoping that he would follow. He seemed reluctant, but at last he came back out into the hallway and followed her into the large kitchen.

'Would you like a drink?' she asked as she saw that he registered the baby monitor plugged in by the fridge, the half-done washing-up. Signs of a life that had been perfectly fine until he'd shown up.

'Whatever you're having,' he replied tonelessly.

'Well, I'm having a herbal tea, so—'

'That's fine.'

His tone, the absence of one, grated on nerves so frayed she could barely stand it. She wanted to know where he'd been, what he wanted. Was he planning, even now, to take her babies away from her? Did he have that right? Surely a court would side with her.

Sí, cierto.

Gabriella Casas—the daughter of a woman currently on trial for embezzlement and fraud. Fraud that her mother had tried to implicate her in, determined to shift the blame away from herself.

She hated it, being so vulnerable to him, but there was no doubt in her mind that she wouldn't be able to stop him if he decided to turn against her. Everything she had done in the last two years had been for her children. Everything she would do for the rest of her life would be about them, about ensuring that they were raised in a better environment than she had been. And she would do whatever it took to keep that promise, but...

'Nate...' she turned, her heart in her throat, her eyes filling with unshed tears '...please don't take my children from me,' she begged.

As he'd looked at his children—*his children*—a wave of something entirely foreign, other, but all-consuming had washed over him, changing him on an almost cellular level, so it took him a beat to register Gabriella's words.

'I... That's not why I am here,' he said eventually. And it wasn't. As someone who knew how devastating it was for life to change in an instant, he would never do that to his children.

Not immediately and not without knowing more, at least. Because although he'd spent one incredible night with a stranger who'd become pregnant with his children, he still couldn't trust Gabriella Casas at all. She had lied to him about who she was—or...at least hadn't actually told him. She had apparently tried to reach him, but what evidence did he have? He knew nothing about her as a mother and if she proved in the least bit neglectful then he'd have absolutely no compunction about removing the children from her care.

But the entire house spoke its own truth. There were child gates across open arched doorways, safety plugs over sockets. There were toys everywhere, softness and love. There were pictures on every single wall. Of Ana and Antonio, of her with them, of her brother and sister-in-law and their little daughter. Pictures *without* Renata Casas, or Gabriella's father—Lautaro, he remembered from the file.

Or himself, he realised with a thud of his heart.

And even if he hadn't been able to take all that in, the report from the PI had been thorough. Gabriella was frugal with her brother's money, had no external income, and had lived life as a single mother, utterly and totally orientated around the twins. She took them to a local playgroup once a week, seemingly just to socialise the children. Had coffee with the other mothers occasionally and, aside from Javier and his wife, Gabriella rarely left the house. Her life revolved around her twins.

Their twins.

Christ. He was a father.

It was something he'd never wanted or intended. He'd never planned on having a family or a generation coming from him—he'd always imagined leaving that to Hope. It wasn't the pressure or the responsibility—he was the CEO of three businesses and the CFO of an international conglomerate.

It wasn't just an innate mistrust of the female sex and what they wanted from him. It went deeper than that. It went to the heart of what family meant to him—the need he'd have to protect, to safeguard his family and the fear of what would happen if he failed. If he failed in the way that he and his sister had been failed after his parents had died.

But now? It wasn't just some hypothetical *What if?* He *was* a father. And it didn't matter what he had felt or feared in the past. He needed to draw a line between then and now. Because now he had to do better, be better. For them. His children. Children that Gabriella had raised, alone, for eighteen months.

'You are their mother, Gabriella. Nothing will change that. Ever.' He wasn't a complete bastard. 'But I'm their father and I *will* be in their lives.'

The darkness flickered back into her eyes. 'Now? *Now* you do?'

Unease settled in his chest as he realised that he couldn't afford to lie to her about where he'd been and why it had been kept such a secret. There was too much at risk. But admitting such a weakness? He warred with it until tension zipped through his body like lightning and the thunder of a headache rolled in.

'Can we sit?'

Gabriella looked at him for a moment and nodded, turning to pour water from the boiled kettle into two mugs, before leading him outside. She put the two mugs down on the table and retrieved a wireless monitor from her pocket, placing it where they could both see it. The wooden table filled the small tiled patio covered by stars, but Nate didn't care that galaxies filled the sky, where the moon was so big it bathed everything in a milky glow.

Where were you?

No one outside the Harcourt family was allowed to know what had happened. And if he had his way—if the plan he was making at the back of his mind worked— that would *still* be the case. Because only once she had agreed to his demand could he be sure that his children would be safe.

'The day after I returned from Spain…the day after the argument with your mother… I was visiting my sister when I collapsed.' His words necessitated an exhalation, but Nate still felt that tightness in his chest, anxiety pushing outwards at his ribs and lungs.

Gabriella frowned, but didn't say anything.

'I was rushed to hospital, where I was diagnosed with a ruptured cerebral aneurism.'

'A cerebral—?'

'A blockage in an artery in my brain burst, causing bleeding,' he explained a little simplistically. 'The doctors had to open my head—' he gestured to his head and Gabriella's eyes widened in shock '—and stop the bleeding. Which they did.'

Gabriella stared at him for a moment as if lost for words and then he could almost see it, all the thoughts crashing through her mind in the space of a single breath, flushing her skin.

'Was it because of my mother? Was it something she—'

The shake of his head cut off her words. 'It doesn't work like that. It could have been there for years and I could just as easily have lived the rest of my life without knowing about it,' he said with a shrug, despite the fact that, only hours before, he himself had half believed the opposite. He'd seen how much the thought of it horrified Gabriella and, in a strange twist of conscience, had wanted to spare her from that.

'Is it...' Concern had her nearly half out of her seat. 'Do we need to get the twins checked?'

He reached for her and gently tugged her back down into her chair. 'It's very unlikely that it is hereditary, but we will absolutely get the twins checked as soon as we can.' He didn't want to frighten her, but he had already spoken to his neurologist in Switzerland and been reassured by him that he didn't need to rush the children directly to him.

'Are you okay?' she asked.

The question surprised him, the genuine concern in her voice hard to ignore.

'Yes.' He gave her nothing more than that. He couldn't. Because he couldn't trust her yet. And because, if he were truthful, he'd tell her that nothing had been okay since the last time he'd seen her.

* * *

Gabi looked at him for a long moment, taking him in. She'd seen it—signs of what had happened to him—without realising it. Although he looked in the absolute prime of life, his skin glowing that pale honey gold of the British, lips an almost enviable shade of blush, she'd known.

She reached hesitantly across the table to the hair that had grown out in the more than two years, pausing when Nate tensed, but continuing when he didn't stop her. She gently pushed back the thick wedge of hair just covering his brow and beneath discovered the thin silvery shadow of a scar well healed. No one would notice it, probably even if they were looking.

He must have suffered so much—shock, fear. And he'd done it alone?

'Why did it have to be kept a secret?' Gabi asked, not out of anger and frustration at the obstacles that had kept them apart, but as a mother who would be heartbroken to know such a thing had happened.

Nate swallowed, the moonlight dancing across his throat as her gaze followed the movement. 'I'm in such a position, in such a family, that to show weakness would—and did—create a power vacuum that impacted my sister and others greatly.'

'Stock and share prices? Lack of confidence, leadership challenges...' Gabi guessed quickly.

Nate's brow raised into a wry question.

'Whatever you think of my mother—what *I* think of my mother—she was a businesswoman first and foremost for my entire life. I understand a lot more than you may imagine.' The last words were delivered frostily but she couldn't help it. She had always been known as Renata Casas's daughter, Javier Casas's sister, no one imagining that she had a fully functioning brain of her own, desperate to prove her own worth.

She shoved that thought aside and focused on the present. She needed to know where she stood—it was what she had made her anchor point after leaving her mother's house.

'What do you want, Nate?' she asked wearily.

A muscle pulsed at his jaw. Moonbeams danced across his cheekbones and his brow cast shadows across an unfathomable gaze. A patriarchal nose spoke of his rigid determination, stubbornness, but in it she also saw her children, heard their laughter. They had inherited their father's good looks.

'I want,' he said, his voice like gravel, 'my family to be safe.' And her heart eased for just a moment before his next words registered. 'I want—and *will*—be here, Gabi, a part of their lives. I doubt you'd have been able to put my name on their birth certificates in my absence,' he said—warned, even—but her mind had suddenly become sluggish, as if not wanting to understand what it already knew. 'So the quickest and cleanest way to ensure my rights as a parent, as a father, would be for us to marry. Obviously.'

Obviously.

It was a single thud of her heart. The swallow of her breath. She couldn't marry this man. Panic and fear crept across her soul. She stared into his eyes, hoping to see what he was thinking, but garnered nothing other than the impression of absolute determination.

'You could take them anywhere tomorrow and I would have absolutely no recourse, other than months, if not years, of legal wrangling,' Nate said. 'I think the Casas family has been through enough scandal already, don't you?'

Gabriella's stomach roiled and acid bit her throat. 'How dare you blackmail me?'

'Are the stakes not worth it?' he demanded. 'Are our children not worth absolutely anything I can do to ensure that I am there, that they are protected by me, my wealth, my name?'

Gabriella scoffed. 'Oh, this is about money, is it? If money was all a child needed then—' *Then I would have been fine*, she managed to stop herself from saying.

She bit her lip and gathered herself, forcing herself to think. Their emotions were running high, it was only natural. And Nate was at least right about one thing— their children were worth it.

'Children need more than money, Nate,' she insisted. 'They need emotional stability, emotional understanding. They need love and vulnerability and are you in a position to tell me that you can provide *that*?' She was shaking by the time she took a breath. His eyes, shadowed in the darkness, veiled his thoughts. *Mierda!* She took a shuddering breath.

'Of course they need those things,' he growled, 'and I'll try not to be offended that you seem to think me incapable of love and emotional understanding,' he went on, the red slash of heat across his cheeks speaking of his anger. 'But do they also not deserve to have both of their parents with them, both of their love, *as well as* the material support that I can provide?'

Nate's words cast a spell. For the twins' entire lives, she had walked the tightrope between trying to give them whatever they needed and what her conscience allowed her to take from her brother. Because Gabi had allowed her entire life—and finances—to become wrapped up in Renata and Casas Textiles, she had nothing. Her mother's

accounts and assets were frozen, and she knew there was
no point in approaching her father for help.

Her father. The man who had disappeared from her
life the first chance he'd got. Who had remarried and had
the perfect two-point-four family, who would all much
rather pretend that she didn't exist. Yet here was Nate,
telling her—warning her—that he would do whatever it
took to be a part of their children's lives. Her heart hurt
from being pulled in so many different directions.

'Yes, I want to give my children their every material
need, and yes, I want to give my children the kind of family unit that I didn't have growing up. But marriage? You
don't even *like* me,' she accused. 'And I don't know you.'

'These are not insurmountable considerations, Gabriella. And nothing that can't be resolved in time. If we are
united in our desire to love and protect our children, is
that not already a stronger, more long-lasting bind than
any mistaken assumptions about love?'

She hated that he was right. Hated that what he said
made sense to her. Hit by a wave of exhaustion, from the
day, from the months, from the years of doing this alone,
was it so bad to be tempted by the offer to share her load
and her love for these children?

'I need more than a good sales pitch, Nathanial. I need
to know what the rules would be, the reality of what this
would look like between us.' Gabriella had spent almost
her entire life second-guessing herself and her sanity because of her mother. Renata had demanded everything
on her terms, but her terms had changed with the breeze
and that kind of insecurity was untenable to Gabi now.

'Let me make one thing clear, Gabriella. There is no
us. Not in *that* way, even if we marry,' he warned.

She didn't have to ask for clarification. She knew what

he meant, even as shame and hurt crawled across her body, leaving angry red fingerprints on her skin. She nodded, acknowledging his words.

'This isn't a decision I can make right now,' she said, buying them both a little breathing space. 'I need time. And you need to meet your children. When they're *awake*.'

CHAPTER FOUR

NATE HAD LEFT not long after that for a nearby hotel and Gabi had stayed outside, beneath the canopy of stars decorating the night sky, wondering what they—who had seen so much—would advise her to do.

If she agreed to marry him, would she regret it? Or should she try to forge her own way ahead? She honestly couldn't tell. She knew what he'd said made sense, legally and practically, but emotionally it felt like insanity.

But whatever passed between her and Nathanial, her children did need to know their father. How she handled this would affect the rest of their lives and she would not, could not, mess that up for them. She used the number he'd put in her phone before leaving to let him know that they would start slowly with the children. His one-word response was quick and curt.

Agreed.

That night she dreamed of touches and caresses, of breathless sighs and pleasure only half-remembered, safe and secure in a dreamworld where reality could neither intrude nor harm. She woke up hot and flustered, but miraculously before the twins had woken.

She tiptoed across the hall and peered into their room, thankful that they were still asleep. If she was lucky, she might even squeeze in a quick shower. She turned just as a loud pounding sounded against the door, rousing the twins from their sleep with cries of shock and surprise. Gabi bit back a curse, placed a soothing hand on the chest of each of her babies, promising in gentle whispers that it would be okay, before leaving to answer the door, which banged ominously again.

She wrenched it open and hissed at Nate, 'Stop making so much noise! You've already woken the twins—can we let the neighbourhood get some sleep?'

With his hand pulled back, he almost looked comical. *Almost.* He certainly looked good, she thought resentfully, knowing that her hair would be pulled in a million directions, that her skin was still sleep-wrinkled, not to mention the fact she hadn't had a chance to brush her teeth yet.

She turned and let him decide whether he'd follow her or not, returning to the twins' room, where Antonio was showing off his impressive lung capacity and Ana looked on the verge of joining in. Deciding to cut the drama off at the pass, she quickly scooped up Antonio and dipped to place a thousand kisses all over Ana, causing her to giggle hysterically, the sound soothing Antonio's tears.

She looked up to find Nate filling the doorway, an intense look in his eyes. She hated that she noticed the breadth of his shoulders in his Egyptian cotton white shirt, the lean hips circled by a black leather belt, the expertly cut trousers that she could recognise as hand tailored. In her mind, she added just a few tweaks to their design to ensure that the soft material hugged his thighs a little tighter, his backside and...

'What can I do?' he asked.

'Coffee. Please,' she added when her conscience prodded her.

He stalked off towards the kitchen and she counted to ten. Her awareness of him was too much and it was something she was going to have to get over. He'd made that very clear the night before.

There is no us...even if we marry.

And she told herself that if she agreed to his proposal she wouldn't need anything more.

She settled Antonio on the ground, leaving him to cling to her leg as she retrieved Ana from the crib. Shaking off all her hopes of a shower, she took the twins into the kitchen, where Nate was making coffee, the rich, heady scent giving her a much-needed jolt. Antonio, still tugging on the white nightdress at her thigh, stared up at his father cautiously with eyes wide and so similar it made her chest ache.

She crouched down to his level, with Ana still in her arms.

'Ana, Antonio, this is my friend, Nate,' she said in English.

Nate's gaze flew to hers, the frown asking his question. 'I wanted them to be bilingual,' she explained, a strange heat on her cheeks at the response she tried not to read in his gaze, which became a flush of defiance and shame under his scrutiny.

But should she feel ashamed that he had missed so much of his children's lives? She had tried so hard to reach him, only giving up when it had started to take its toll. She had spent her entire life asking to be loved by people—she wouldn't waste her children's lives on the same. But that seemed like a very different matter now that he was standing here in her kitchen.

To her surprise, Nate crouched down to meet them low to the ground. 'It's nice to meet you, Antonio and Ana,' he said.

Antonio leaned to whisper in Gabi's ear, *'He sounds funny!'* and she smiled, a smile which froze on her lips when her son turned back to Nate and gave him one of his best smiles.

Father and son stared at each other and, in an instant, she knew, no matter how much she justified it, how reasonable it had been at the time, that her children had missed this, missed the opportunity to be with their father, and it would be a source of guilt and hurt for many years to come.

Nate felt the change in Gabi. She was beginning to soften towards him, and while that felt like a victory, he barely noticed it because he was so distracted by Antonio and Ana. He couldn't stop staring at them, taking everything in about them—their laughs, their moods, how much they looked like Gabriella. How much he had missed. It was an avalanche of emotion he knew would take time to wrangle into order.

Gabi had advised him to let them come to him. They'd let him know when they'd be comfortable with him picking them up, or how much attention they wanted. He hadn't missed the pleading in her gaze, begging him to give them time to adjust to his presence.

All the while, he was still struggling to adjust to *hers*. He'd valiantly tried to keep his eyes at face level that morning while she'd been dressed in what he was sure *should* have been a perfectly sensible white nightdress. The difficulty was that his memory had no problem adding in the details of what couldn't be seen. The early morning wind had pressed the nightdress against curves his hands remembered, skin his tongue had tasted, a woman his soul had recognised.

Until he remembered Gabriella's betrayal and a familiar anger twisted through him. But even that had gone completely out of his mind when she'd brought Antonio and Ana into the kitchen. And that was the last thing he remembered consciously thinking because after that it had just been pure chaos.

Breakfast had been an intense debate of bananas over blueberries, before a bowl of mashed up wheat thing that looked absolutely disgusting. Gabriella had set up the twins either side of her to give her maximum access and it was a system that seemed to work for the most part, if the state of the floor was ignored. Following breakfast, the children rained down mass destruction on the living area, before Gabriella marched them all off for a short walk and play outside before they went down for a nap. At last, he thought he might be able to talk to her, but she'd spent the entire time making lunch *and* dinner, putting on a wash, folding away dry clothes, then quickly hoovering and tidying the sitting room. He'd asked again if he could help, but she dismissed any attempts. He didn't think it was even conscious—it was just 'easier if I do it myself'. Then the twins had woken, and after changes of nappies, and drinks of water, it was lunch, and then more nappies, and...

It hurt his head just thinking about how she did all this on her own. That she'd *had* to do it all on her own took a chunk out of an already decimated conscience. Because the reality was, it didn't matter how that night had ended, whether he thought Gabriella had been working with her mother to defraud him or not, he should have known, or at least made sure, that there were no consequences...let alone twin consequences.

Yes, he'd been recovering from the operation, but physio and rehab hadn't kept him from a mobile phone or a laptop where an easy search or a single question could have provided him with whatever answer he'd needed.

He'd always been considerate of who he shared his bed with, their pleasure and protection as much a priority as his own. But he'd also always been aware of what drew the opposite sex to him. The name and the money: a gift and a curse. More than a few of his lovers had proved more interested in his wallet than him, so Nate had always kept those he shared pleasure with at arm's length.

Until the night with Gabriella—until the night he'd finally thought he'd found something different. *Someone* different. And it was the savage betrayal of that belief that had shut down his usually meticulous care. But no matter the reason why, it wasn't enough of an excuse. It could never be enough of an excuse to have behaved the way he had to her. Guilt filled his chest, even more so since reading some of the emails she'd tried to send him.

'Nate?'

Gabriella's voice pulled him back to the present and he came into the sitting room to find Ana mid-nappy-change and Gabriella jiggling a sobbing, hysterical Antonio up and down in her arms.

'Can you take him?'

'What? I thought—'

'I know, sorry, but Ana needs changing and Antonio won't stop. Here, just...' Nate wasn't quite sure how 'just' was supposed to cover the first time he was to hold his son as a screaming eighteen-month-old, but somehow he ended up with Antonio in his arms, staring up at him with glistening eyes, red cheeks and snot. Everywhere.

And, for a second, Nate had never felt anything like it. This was his child and for all his protests of not wanting children, not wanting a family—one that could be taken away in the blink of an eye, one that he could be taken away from—he understood. He got it. The connection, the bond, the sense of finding the thing that had been missing from his life.

Had his own father felt this when he'd held Nate and Hope for the first time?

And, from somewhere deep within himself, a tendril unwound and connected him to the parents he usually refused to let himself think of. A wet heat pressed against the back of his eyes and, just as he was about to take a shaky breath, Antonio let out the biggest wail and shoved a messy fist at his face as if to push him away.

'Antonio,' Gabriella chided, but Nate absolutely did *not* miss the vein of amusement in her tone.

'Your support is overwhelming,' he observed tartly, covering the startling moment of sentimentality.

'You're welcome,' she replied sweetly.

'I don't remember thanking you,' he sniped, and she laughed and suddenly everything stopped—Antonio's cries, Ana's fidgeting and his heart. Each one of them just stopped to listen to the sound of her laughter, pealing out into the room with such delight and joy that at first Ana joined in, then Antonio, and finally Nate did too.

Nate watched Gabi make her way towards the kitchen after putting the twins to bed that evening. She was unguarded and looked tired, and he felt like a bastard. He'd just finished reading the last of the emails that the acting CFO had deleted, thinking they were either a prank or from a stalker. When he'd been sent the first ones, last night, he'd promised that he'd read every single one of them. And now he had.

He called her name out gently, cautious of waking the twins, and she came to stand on the threshold between the living room and the patio. He wondered if she knew how beautiful she was, whether she was conscious of the impact she had on him or not. He wavered over the thought that would have been conviction only a day before: that she was doing it on purpose.

He nudged one of the glasses of wine he'd poured for them towards her and only when she saw that he'd brought the baby monitor out did she finally give in to his silent invitation. There was nothing but the sound of cicadas as she waited, unable to hear the loud, wild drumbeat of his conscience.

'I'm—' he started as the word caught in his throat and he had to clear it. 'I'm sorry,' he said, forcing the words through guilt that was thick and stuck to his every inhalation. He stared at his hands, too ashamed to meet her gaze.

'For what?' she asked cautiously.

'For not being there when you needed me to be,' he admitted, forcing himself to look up at her, to show her how sincere he was.

She frowned.

'I read your emails,' he explained.

'All of them?' she asked, clearly surprised.

Nate nodded.

'That must have been hundreds,' she hedged.

'Actually, you topped a thousand,' he said with no trace

of humour. 'Wouldn't copy and paste have been easier than individually writing each one?' He tried to joke, but it landed flat. He clenched his jaw. 'The acting CFO blocked them all, thinking they were a…scam. I never saw a single one of them until last night,' he tried to assure her.

'Checking up on my story?' she asked a little defensively and he looked away. He *had* been checking up on her. Because every single interaction they'd had until this moment had been either a lie or a misunderstanding and he was finding it hard to keep track.

'Can you blame me?' he demanded, his own frustration eating into his tone and dismantling whatever détente had settled between them that afternoon. He wished he could call the words back, but it was too late.

He could see it, the warring within her—the same hurt and the same anger. And now he remembered what he'd not been able to before: the devastation he had seen in her gaze when he'd confronted her and her mother. The hurt that made him wonder, hope, that he was wrong about her.

She looked away, taking a sip of her wine, and when she turned back her expression was determined, braced for the conversation they should have had years ago.

'My mother sent me to that hotel to seduce you,' she admitted, her gaze locked onto his.

He sat back in his chair, shocked. 'You admit it?'

'That it's what my mother wanted? Yes. Absolutely. But I wasn't going to do it,' she rushed on to say, leaning forward as if to argue her case. 'I wanted to tell you what she was doing. I wanted to warn you, but then you didn't recognise me and instead you…'

'I flirted with you,' he said, finishing her sentence. Remembering how *he* had approached *her*. How surprised he'd been by the fact she'd seemed almost reluctant to speak to him at first.

He shook his head, marvelling that once again this woman had turned his life on its head. Everything he'd thought for the past two years began to shift on soft sands, only to reassemble with new meaning and new direction. But was she really telling the truth? *This* time?

'Why didn't you tell me who you were?' he asked, his voice dark and heavy. 'Why did you leave in the morning?'

'Because… I didn't think I was blameless in all this. My mother sent me there to sleep with you and I…slept with you.' She shrugged as if it had been nothing to share her innocence with him, as if she thought why she had done it didn't make a difference to him. But it did. Because he wanted to believe her.

He searched her gaze, trying to see what she was hiding, but all he saw was shame and guilt.

'I should have told you who I was and why I was there, before anything happened…and then, after?' She laughed, the sound so helpless that a part of him wanted to reach out to her. 'How would you have believed me? How *could* you have believed that I wasn't part of her attempt to steal from you?'

He wouldn't have. He *hadn't*.

Because even now he could barely believe that the woman he'd met that night was as incredible as he'd first thought. As captivating and beguiling as she'd seemed. The integrity and sense of humour, even if somewhat reserved, he'd enjoyed enticing from her had been something miraculous to him. He'd *enjoyed* her.

But the sense of betrayal he'd felt when he'd discovered her identity—and then when he'd uncovered Renata's plan, it had all coalesced into a conspiracy theory that hadn't seemed that farfetched. And, in truth, it wasn't even that far from what he'd already experienced before from other lovers.

But Gabi Casas wasn't just another lover. She was the mother of his children, so, in truth, it didn't matter what had happened before. All he needed was to convince her to draw a line under the past and start afresh—by wearing his ring.

Gabi reached for her glass, but stopped when Nate next spoke.

'It doesn't matter now,' he dismissed.

It did to her, but she didn't think that Nate would believe her or even want to hear it.

'All that matters is Ana and Antonio.'

On that, they could at least agree. But marriage... The thought made her heart ache. Deep down, even though she had become a single mother with two children, she hadn't lost the hope that one day she might find love, that one day she might find a person to put her first, to be hers, someone who would want to spend the rest of his life with her.

But she would not have that with Nate—a man who wore his distrust of her like a suit of armour. She wouldn't have fancy words or endearments, caresses of affection, looks of lust and desire... No, if she married him, she would be denying herself the only thing she had ever wanted—to be loved for who she was.

But what her children would have, if she married him, was a father who she could see would put them first above all things, who would see to their every need, and who would protect them with the same ferocity that she felt.

A father different to her own.

'I want us to be better,' she said, putting the glass down on the table.

'Better?'

'Better than my parents,' she clarified. 'I want Ana and Antonio to have the best of everything,' she said, taking a breath. 'And that includes having both parents here together.'

She could practically feel the roll of victory that shimmered across Nate's body, even as he tried to leash it. She struggled, feeling as if she were handing herself and her children to him on a plate. But she wasn't. Because she was going to make sure that Ana and Antonio would have more than what little she had been given by her parents.

'I understand that you want nothing between us,' she said, looking away. 'But I have conditions too, Nate, and if you're neither willing nor able to agree to them, then we might as well stop this right now.'

'No,' he said quickly. Too quickly. 'I want to hear your conditions.'

'Whatever we agree, you will be in our children's lives, Nate. But if I agree to marry you, if you are going to be their *father*, their *parent*, then I need you here, present and committed to them one hundred percent. I mean it, Nate,' she warned. 'No business meetings that run over,' she said, remembering standing outside the headteacher's office after school for a mother who never came. 'You will be present at every school event, recital, performance.' Knowing the pain of endlessly searching the audience for her father's face, and never finding it. Knowing the hurt of that useless hope.

He shifted forward in his seat, his face coming into the light, holding her gaze with a sincerity that felt solemn, binding, soul-deep. 'I promise you I will be there.'

Dios, how she wanted to believe him.

'I also need you to agree to stay in this marriage until the twins are twenty-one years old.'

He frowned, as if unsure about the strangely specific stipulation.

'Ana and Antonio will be your only family until they are adults themselves,' she said, her teeth clenching at the end of her sentence to hold back the wave of hurt. She couldn't, wouldn't, let them be second-best for their father. She wouldn't let him place a second family over the needs of his first. The visceral pain that tightened around her heart had not dulled over the years. She had simply got used to it.

'Agreed,' he said—and she chose to believe that the understanding she thought she saw in his eyes was imagined. She knew better than to trust what she thought she saw in people. Renata had taught her that.

Every single day with her had been a lesson in caution, because with Renata she'd never known. And not knowing what she'd find in the next hour, let alone the next day, had created such a deep, intrinsic insecurity that she had only just begun to shake it off just as Nate had stormed back into her life.

'And I need one last thing.'

She could see he was willing to agree to almost anything, right then and there, and it eased some of the fear on her children's behalf. At least he was taking this seriously.

'If there's a problem, I need to know. If you're angry or upset, I need you to be clear because I spent *so* many years not knowing with my mother. Having to guess, having to watch, having to bend and twist and change whenever her mood did. And I can't do that again. I can't do it to myself and I won't do it to my children.'

'Of course. I will tell you and if you need to, ask. Any time.'

'The truth. You'll tell me the truth?'

'The truth,' he replied, and she nodded. 'Marriage would give us *both* legal protection, you know,' he said. 'It's not just for me. There will be no prenup and you would be entitled to half of everything I have.'

She waved it aside, missing the look of shock that passed across his features, as if the matter of a few billion pounds were nothing to her.

'It's about them, Nate. It's only about them.'

'So, you agree?' he demanded. 'We'll marry?'

Gabi nodded, wondering if she'd just signed her life away, before looking at the baby monitor and smiling sadly.

It didn't matter. As long as her children were safe.

CHAPTER FIVE

WITHIN TWENTY-FOUR HOURS Gabi was regretting her decision immensely.

'What do you mean, we have to move?' she asked the next day when he laid down his decree like an entitled king. She was giving the twins their lunch, Antonio shaking his head from side to side in a valiant attempt to avoid a spoonful of mushed broccoli.

'You can't expect us all to live here, surely?' he demanded from where he hovered by the doorway.

She looked around the little villa that had been her refuge for the last two years, seeing only memories of the children's first steps, the first time they'd slept through the night, all the firsts that had made her feel a sense of accomplishment as if she'd climbed a mountain.

'What's wrong with it?' she asked, seeing his demand only as a criticism. Of her. Of her as a mother.

'We need more space. And if we are closer to Barcelona then it will be easier for me—'

She dropped Antonio's spoon on the highchair's tray with a clatter, surprising both Nate and Antonio, and their faces were near mirror images of shock.

'No,' she said, her hand cutting through the air. 'No. That's it. I'm done. I take it back,' she said, walking away from the table and over to the sink. 'I'm not doing this any more. We're not getting married—'

'Gabriella—'

'Please stop calling me that. Your accent butchers it. *Gabi.* Just call me Gabi.'

She knew she sounded irrational, but she couldn't take it any more. Weeks of stress about the court case, months of stress about him and the babies. The only thing solid beneath her feet was this house, her routine. The playgroup once a week. Her brother and Emily.

'Gabi?' he tried, the word sounding even more awkward on his tongue. 'I'm going to clean up the children and put them down for a nap and we can talk.'

She nodded. 'Yes. Absolutely, Nate, because I'm sure you know how to change a baby's nappy, how to give a baby a bath and where to find the clean clothes.'

He took a visible breath, but she couldn't stop.

'If we go to Barcelona, because it's *easier for you*, and you take me away from my support network here, who will help me?'

'*I'll* be your support network,' he insisted.

'Oh, okay then,' she replied, refusing to hide the sarcasm she felt creeping into her tone. 'Let's try this. I have cracked nipples, some discharge from them. Is that—?'

'Stop! Okay!' he said, his words clipped, urgent and shocked. Finally, he nodded. 'Okay. You have a support network here. I get it.'

She nodded, watching him mentally backtrack.

'Did you…really have cracked…?'

'Do you really want to hear about it?' she asked on a half laugh.

'No-o-o…' He drew out the word, pressing down the front of his shirt as if he were in a business meeting as he sat down beside Ana, who had been gazing curiously between them. 'But kind of…' he said, his head tilted to the side, and it made him look nearly ten years younger. It reminded her of the night they'd spent together, before the misunderstandings and consequences. The night she'd laughed and joked with a man who had let her explore her innocent sexuality with both patience and fervour.

She wanted to laugh now, just as she had then, wanting to let the moment magic away all the anger and anxiety…and then Ana flung a spoonful of homemade tomato sauce across the kitchen.

And it went like that for the next few weeks, seesawing between panic that she'd done the wrong thing and Nate easing her mind.

One quiet afternoon, she and Nate told the children that Nate would be living with them from now, because Nate was their *papá*. They took it in as much as any eighteen-month-old would have, the conversation startlingly easy.

'Papá? Okay.'

They were too young for the emotional drama that would have come with age and experience, with hopes, disappointments and hurts meshed together. And they were young enough to adapt, to take their lead from her, so she forced herself to be as easy around Nate as possible. That didn't mean that there wouldn't be tears and tantrums as they all negotiated the new family dynamic, but she could only hope that she was doing the right thing. That Nate would stick to his promise and that he could be the father she wanted for her children. But only time would tell.

Eventually she'd had to concede that Nate was right

about the house. They did need a big enough space for the four of them. And when her conscience had wrangled her, just like it had with Javier, Nate had convinced her otherwise. He was their father; anything he did was for them and they would benefit from it. So when he'd shown her pictures of a gorgeous sprawling villa only ten miles from where they currently were, she suddenly understood what he'd meant. The villa was not only heartachingly beautiful, it had two double bedrooms, two children's rooms and two offices. There was a swimming pool— even with a children's area, unobtrusively gated and safe. The entire space was on a single level in a U shape, with floor-to-ceiling windows showing off the beautiful lush garden in the centre courtyard and hidden from sight was a pool house on the far end of the property.

Gabi smiled, knowing that Emily would fall in love with it immediately. And while there was so much for the children, she could see that there was also something for her in one of those offices and that maybe, just maybe, she might be able to find some time to resume her drawing and designs. It was the only thing that she missed about Casas Textiles.

Of Renata's court case, they'd received a message from Señor Torres, explaining that between the delay tactics of the defence regarding Renata's health and various rescheduling requirements, neither Nate nor Gabi would be required to give statements until at least the end of the summer. Two months at a minimum. In some ways Gabi had felt relieved, but in others she hated that it still hung over her, occupying too much of the time she should have been spending on plans for the wedding.

And now that it was only a few weeks away, her designs had been more and more on her mind. In truth, only one design. Over the years it had changed style considerably, but the wedding dress design she had worked on at college, the design she'd never shown anyone, came into her mind almost constantly.

But she thrust the thought aside. This might not be the wedding she had hoped for, but it would be her only wedding. Whether or not Nate took his vows as seriously as she did, there would be no other marriage for her. No other husband she knew as she looked out over the night sky. She hoped that one day she might get to see her dress, but she doubted it would be on her.

Nate was learning to compromise, perhaps for the first time in his life, and he was just beginning to realise how much his sister, Hope, let him have his way. He'd always been an expert negotiator, which usually removed the necessity for him to have to bend others to his will, but Gabriella—*Gabi*—was impervious to his sway.

He knew it would be difficult for them both to meet in the middle. Everything about this situation was entirely new to him, but he was a fast learner and he was determined. But Gabi seemed to resist him at every turn.

'She's going through a lot, Nate. You have to give her time,' his sister urged. 'As much as you should be giving *yourself* time,' she warned gently.

'I'm fine. I've recovered. I'm having check-ups. I'm doing what the doctor advised.'

Well, mostly, Nate thought to himself.

His doctors had advised that he halve his workload. At least. That had been part of his intention when he'd arrived in Spain—to at least remove Casas Textiles from his portfolio, but that had been put on hold the moment he'd met his children. And as for the other businesses, he was absolutely sure that he could handle them, despite what the doctors thought. He had overcome his aneurism and he had recovered. That was all that mattered.

'I can't wait to be there and meet my niece and nephew,' she cooed down the phone. She and Luca were trying for children, and although they hadn't shared much, Nate knew that it wasn't an easy road for them.

'We'll be there soon. Are you sure you've given Gabi enough time to prepare for the wedding?' Hope asked, and Nate smiled.

'She was the one who suggested the date and the time-frame, Hope,' he said, bristling at the suggestion that he was rushing things. That was certainly what his grand-father had suggested—he'd even had the audacity to ask if Nate had requested a DNA test.

'Okay. As long as you're not being difficult.'

'I'm not difficult,' Nate hotly denied.

'You're right. Not difficult. Just stubborn, autocratic and—'

'I'm hanging up now.'

'Luca says hi,' she called as he ended the call.

Nate smiled, putting his phone away. Luca Calvino had surprised him, but if he could have chosen anyone for his sister it would have been him. A man who could protect her from whatever she faced. Yes, he was glad Hope had someone like him.

Which was why he knew that when he met Gabriella's brother again he would have to tread lightly. They hadn't exactly had the best of starts and they were going to be in each other's lives for as long as he lived, because, no matter what anyone thought, Nate was taking his upcoming marriage vows seriously. Yes, he knew that there were practicalities that would have to be navigated. But they would all simply adjust, he thought, as if he could bend everyone to his will.

He looked over to where Gabi was introducing their children to the new house. She was dressed in a long patterned dress that skimmed across her body in rich ochres, reds and oranges that suited her. She picked up Ana and held out her hand to Antonio and she was beautiful. Utterly beautiful and seemingly completely blind to it. And when she turned to him and smiled, his heart pulled a beat and her smile froze, until Antonio tugged on her dress and she turned back to beam at him. His son pointed in his direction and *boom*, his heart pumped hard as his son looked at him with something close to joy in his gaze. The warmth that spread through him eclipsed all else and Nate knew with absolute conviction that he would do anything to make this marriage work. For them. To protect them. It was his only focus. It had to be.

Gabi fussed around the spectacular dinner table in a way that Nate had never seen before. They had moved into the villa only two days ago, but Gabi's seemingly endless, somewhat nervous energy had ensured that all the children's things were put in the right places and that her belongings were in her room. His room—in the same wing of the stunning U-shaped villa as hers and the children's—had been almost easy to unpack. Unlike Gabi's photographs and bedspreads and soft materials and large paintings and plants, Nate's room was brutal in its simple bare necessities.

Gabi's interior designer sister-in-law Emily had visited before they had moved in and had spent a day walking through the house and discussing all manner of things that Nate had left to them. But he couldn't argue with outcome. They had made the house a home in the blink of an eye. And while he'd ensured that there were assistants and removal professionals ready to help, Gabi had insisted on doing far too much herself. And the short, sharp put-down he'd been given when he'd asked if she might want to share the load with them had stopped any further suggestions.

But the nervous energy rolling off her in waves now as she looked at the candles and low lighting, the vases of flowers and the profusion of food so delicious it made his mouth water, was beginning to rub off on him.

She passed him to fuss over a napkin and he caught her wrist. Ignoring the shimmer of sparks that scattered across his skin from where they touched, he turned her to face him.

'Stop,' he commanded gently.

'But it has to be perfect,' she said worriedly.

'It doesn't. But it *is* pretty perfect from where I'm standing,' he said, hoping to ease her nerves. He could see how much this meant to her and, after everything that had happened in the last few weeks, he wanted that for her too.

He wanted to cup her cheek, reassure her with his touch, but he wasn't sure he had that right. Instead, all he could offer her was his word. 'I promise to try and make this as easy as possible. I will be on my best, most charming behaviour.'

'You want to try and charm my brother?' she asked, almost laughing. 'I'm not sure how well that will go down,' she observed sceptically.

'Then what do you advise? I will do whatever it takes. And I can be charming. Can't I?' he asked with utterly artificial concern, succeeding in making her laugh this time.

'You have your moments,' she admitted.

'This is important to you,' he observed.

Gabi nodded. 'It's…' The shudder that rippled through her breath was audible to him. 'It's the first time that *I'm* hosting them. Not my mother, or not me in her home, *their* home, but them in *my* home. I want it to be perfect.'

'Did you do that a lot? Host for your mother?' he asked gently, trying to get to the source of her anxiety.

Gabi nodded. 'Yes, but it was always—*This is wrong, that's bad, this should not even be here.* Things would get thrown or broken.'

'Thrown?' Nate asked, shocked at the idea.

Gabi shrugged. 'Renata enjoyed being dramatic. Even more so when it came at someone else's expense.'

'Gabi—'

The doorbell cut off what he was about to say and because she seemed almost relieved, he let it pass for now. But he realised that he really didn't know enough about how Renata Casas had behaved towards her daughter.

He and Hope had grown up with two perfect, loving parents. He'd had nearly twelve years with them and he remembered those times as a kind of idyll. His tall, focused father on the brink of becoming Harcourts next CEO. His mother, bright, beautiful and bold, her interior designer's eyes always sparkling.

The night they had been killed in a car accident had taken something from him. His and his sister's lives had changed irrevocably, in more ways than just from their loss. But at least he had known the warmth of their love, the security of it. Seeing Gabi, the determined mother, the insecure sister, the softness clashing with the steel, he wondered just how much her parents had hurt her.

* * *

Gabi hadn't been able to watch the posturing between her brother and Nate. And even as she reminded herself that her marriage was going to be nothing more than a co-parenting contract, she *still* wanted her brother and her husband to get on.

'I think it's going well,' Emily whispered, leaning into her shoulder as Gabi rinsed the wine glasses.

Gabi cast a furtive glance over her shoulder, where the two men were all but squaring off. 'This is what you call going well?' Gabi whispered back, wondering what on earth Emily would think going badly would look like.

Emily shrugged an elegant shoulder, her blonde hair falling down her back in gentle waves. 'Nate, he's English, so he's going to be a little more stilted than you might expect. But he's also a Harcourt.'

'What does that mean?'

Emily frowned. 'The Harcourts have been a household name for generations. The public interest in them is on a par with royalty, and I'm not exaggerating. And it only got worse after their parents' death.'

Gabi would never be able to forget the image of the two twelve-year-old Harcourts, each standing behind a coffin, especially given the frequency with which it was used by journalists whenever Nate or his sister were mentioned in the press. Her heart would fall each time, unable to comprehend just how much that would have shaped Nate's life.

'His sister, Hope, regularly gets vilified in the press, though that seems to have died down now that she's engaged again.'

Gabi was fairly familiar with the intrusive nature of the press, courtesy of her mother—but perhaps not on the same level as Nate had been. And she could only begin to imagine how the press would have presented Nate's cerebral aneurism if they had ever found out.

'Charming, though,' Emily continued, unaware of her thoughts. 'And good-looking too,' she observed wryly.

Gabi laughed off the insinuation, ignoring the way her cheeks heated.

'Gabs, Javier and I have been talking,' Emily said, leaning back against the kitchen sink.

She sounded serious and it caught Gabi by surprise, her heart suddenly rippling into a familiar anxious rhythm. 'Is everything okay?'

'What? Oh, yes, absolutely. It's just that…we would like to gift you your wedding dress. I know, or at least I can guess, that this isn't perhaps quite what you might have envisioned—'

'Oh,' was all Gabi was capable of saying in response. Having buried her dress design in a drawer, she had planned to go to a shop when she next had a free moment and buy something off the rack. She hadn't even thought to ask if Emily might want to come because… because she wasn't used to people wanting to be involved.

Suddenly she saw how, because of that, she had made her wedding seem somehow smaller, less important. Not because of Nate and what had motivated it, but because she had kept it small. The thought that Javi and Emily wanted more for her, wanted it to be something special, brought a damp heat to the backs of her eyes. And that made her brave enough to ask, to hope, that they might agree to her suggestion.

'Actually, I was wondering if I might have one of my designs made. It's nothing, really—'

'Absolutely!' Emily cried, cursing Renata Casas to hell

and back for the damage she had done to her children. Gabi had so much potential, but was only beginning to realise it when she'd discovered she was pregnant. Emily had watched as Gabi had navigated that with an emotional integrity and authenticity that would seem impossible to anyone who knew Gabi's mother. But she could only hope that her burgeoning sense of self wasn't lost beneath the powerful character that was Nathanial Harcourt. 'Do you have the designs here? I would absolutely love to see them.'

Gabi and Emily returned from the study, and the way Emily had gasped when she'd seen Gabi's design had given her a much-needed boost. Emily had refused to let Gabi consider anything other than getting the dress made. The Spanish lace was traditional but used in a modern way, the neckline and figure-hugging silhouette dramatic and impactful. But it wouldn't mean much until she saw it in person. Allowing the tenuous feeling of excitement about the wedding to grow as they returned to the dining table, her stomach dropped to find Javier and Nate standing with fists at hips, pointing accusingly, the air heavy with harshly spoken words.

'No. You have it completely wrong.'

'Me? You are delusional, Harcourt. Utterly delusional.'

'That's rich, coming from a man who thinks that—'

'What is going on?' demanded Emily, presumably before either of the two men could hurl any more insults that they couldn't take back.

'Nothing.' Javier shrugged, instantly his demeanour changing to confused.

'Nate?' Gabi asked, hoping for more clarification.

'What?' he asked, seemingly equally confused. 'We were just talking about football.'

'Football,' Gabi repeated. *'Football?'*

'Yes,' both men replied at the same time, as if it were Emily and Gabi who were being particularly dense.

'Football,' Emily said to Gabi, nodding, and grabbed a bottle of wine and two glasses and led her outside and out of the way of the male bonding session.

'Football?' Javier demanded the moment the women had left the room.

'Would you rather I tell them what we were really arguing about?' Nate bit back, pulling his tie a little looser.

'Probably not,' Javier growled. 'Look, Gabi's happiness is my number one priority in this. You, I couldn't care less about.'

'That, you have made painstakingly clear. And I'm fine with it, by the way,' Nate added with a pointed finger. 'But you should know that I feel the same way.'

'You won't tell me where you were for the first eighteen months of your children's lives?'

'I've told Gabi and that she's fine with it is all that matters,' Nate warned darkly.

Javier levelled him with a gaze, seemingly taking Nate's statement as good enough. For now, at least. The Spaniard fisted his hand and pressed it against his lips, seemingly at war with himself over his next words.

'Gabriella… She has been through a lot. It is up to you what she tells you of our mother—but you should know that Renata Casas has not one single maternal or unselfish bone in her body. The woman is a menace. You need to be ready for her.'

'Understood.'

'I'm serious.'

'So am I. You're not the only one with a difficult family, Casas.'

After a beat, something else came into Javier's gaze. Sincerity and something almost like a plea. 'She deserves to be happy, Nathanial. Safe and happy. If you can't give her that, then you should let her go. Now, rather than later.'

He heard Gabi's brother's words, took them in as much as any brother would, but also heard them as a fiancé and the father of Gabi's children.

'She will be. I'll see to it.'

'You better had,' Javier said, before heading out onto the patio to the long wooden table beneath the arched pergola. 'Emily, *mi amore*, pour me a drink and remind me never to try and teach an Englishman about football again.'

Nate chucked out a cynical laugh—he could respect the man, if not quite say that he liked him yet. But he was glad to see that Gabi had a brother as strong-willed and determined to protect her as Nate felt about Hope. Which was why he refused to simply dismiss Javier's warning as the behaviour of an overprotective brother.

Nate quickly fired off a message to his brother-in-law Luca Calvino—the owner of Pegaso, an international security company—asking him to find out everything about Renata Casas, including where she was. Now was not the time for lawyers. This was his future wife and he was taking no risks with her or their children.

Javier was right. From what Nate knew of her, they should be ready for anything. Putting away his phone, he watched Javier, Emily and Gabi talking and laughing amongst themselves, and found that he suddenly missed his sister. This was the kind of family unit that they would have had, had their parents lived, had they not been foisted off on boarding schools and a grandfather only interested in business and strength, might, money and power. In that moment, Nate made a silent vow. To Gabi, to his children. Never would they grow up the same way that he and Hope had. Never.

CHAPTER SIX

GABI LOOKED AT herself in the mirror, turning at every
angle to stare—not at herself, but at her wedding dress. It
was *beautiful*. It was the first and only of her designs to
have ever been made and it took her breath away. Javier
had found the perfect seamstress, who had been able to
perform a miracle in such a short space of time.

Gabi ran a hand across the wide scoop neck and down
the embroidered Spanish net lace that had been used to
delicately overlay the ivory silk that skimmed her figure
perfectly, so that, rather than being tight and confined, it
flowed across her skin in a caress.

With her hair piled up in a bun that was artfully messy
rather than accidentally, and the small touches of make-
up that accentuated the line of her eyes and the colour
of her lips, Gabi dared to hope that she looked suitable
to be the bride of Nathanial Harcourt.

But if she was suitable to be the bride of the father of
her children that would have to be enough for her, she
decided, ignoring the painful throb in her heart.

The dress's skirt fell out in a cascade to form a demi-
train at the back that could be pinned for ease of movement, but also to increase the shape. She pinned it up,
deciding that the train was a little too dramatic for the
simple wedding taking place in the gardens of the hotel

at the Viñuela Reservoir. She had visited here with Javier shortly after leaving her mother's house, not yet knowing that she was pregnant, and the incredible view of the lake and mountains, the serenity of it, had touched her deeply. When Nate had asked her where she wanted to get married, she'd known that it was here.

A knock sounded on the door behind her, Emily's voice coming through the wood. 'Gabi, are you decent?'

'Come in,' Gabi called, looking back to see both Emily and Hope Harcourt stop in their tracks with gasps.

'You look...' Emily started.

'Absolutely incredible,' Hope finished.

Gabi's chest swelled as she realised that neither of the two women were exaggerating. The blazing appreciation in their eyes soothed some of the doubts she'd developed from growing up under her mother's painful scrutiny.

'Whose is that dress?' Hope asked, her eyes flickering over the material and the design.

Emily smirked. 'It's hers.'

'Yes, I know that, but I mean—'

'No, it's *hers*,' Emily clarified.

Hope's jaw dropped. 'Really? You designed this?' she asked. 'I want it! No, wait, that didn't come out right,' said the blonde Englishwoman so similar and yet so different to her twin brother that Gabi was still getting used to it. 'As a buyer. I want it as— No,' she said, cutting herself off. 'I'm sorry, we can do this later. You look absolutely amazing,' she said, but Gabi had understood, had realised what her future sister-in-law had said. The CEO of Harcourts—an international, highly exclusive stockist of designer and haute couture—wanted a dress designed by her? 'But we're going to talk later,' she said, pointing a determined finger at her that reminded Gabi of her daughter, Ana.

Her children had been fascinated by Hope and Nate—as if sensing not only family but familiarity between the two adults and themselves. Just the thought of them made her heart race.

'Where are—'

'They're fine,' Emily reassured her before she could even finish.

'They're with my husband, Luca. It's good practice for him,' Hope said, 'and I promise they really couldn't be in safer hands. But I think I might just go and see them—not because I'm worried, but because my niece and nephew are the most adorable children I've ever met!' she cried, giving Gabi a quick kiss and a squeeze on the arm.

Gabi waited for Hope to leave and smiled at Emily.

'She's nice, I like her,' said Emily conspiratorially.

Gabi nodded. Hope and her husband, Luca, had flown in last night, apologising for not meeting her sooner, as if it had been their fault that they hadn't known about her. Gabi hadn't known what to expect, what Hope might have heard about Renata Casas's daughter. For all Hope knew, Gabi could have intentionally got pregnant in order to trap her billionaire brother.

Gabi had been braced for a barrage of questions and instead she'd got reassurances that her brother wasn't a complete arse. Gabi had seen so much in her eyes—hope that her brother would be happy, hope that they could make it work, instant love for the new members of her suddenly increasing family—that Gabi couldn't help but like her fiancé's sister almost immediately.

'And Javier?'

'Javier is with Nate, getting ready.'

'Making sure he doesn't run away?' Gabi asked wryly.

'Probably trying to pay him to run away,' Emily said, and they both descended into giggles.

'This is no laughing matter, Harcourt.'

'It's my wedding, and if I say that I want you to wear a boutonnière, then you should wear a boutonnière, no?' Nate said, greatly enjoying his future brother-in-law's apparent discomfort.

'But mine is *pink*.'

'Real men wear pink,' Nate said with a shrug.

The quick inhalation told Nate that his taunt had hit dead centre. Javier snatched the flower and shoved it rather indelicately into his buttonhole and, with a glare, stalked over to the room's bar and poured himself a whisky.

'Want one?' he asked.

Nate shook his head. He wanted to be completely clear today.

'Don't need the Dutch courage?'

Nate smiled. 'Not in the least. Did you when you married Emily?'

Something indefinable passed across Javier's gaze. 'When I—'

An urgent knock pounded on the door just as Nate's phone started to ring. Both men stared at each other for a second to process that something was wrong before Nate answered the phone and Javier the door.

'It's Renata Casas,' Luca explained. 'She's here.'

'How?'

'The guys I had on her say that she must have switched cars. They weren't expecting her to do so. It's not good enough, Nate. I'm sorry—'

'Don't be sorry, just don't let her anywhere near Gabi. I'll deal with this,' he said, hanging up on his brother-in-law and turning in time to see that Javier must have been given the same information if the furious look in his eyes was anything to go by.

'You coming?' Nate asked.

'Absolutely,' Javier growled.

They found her out by the entrance to the villa, the beautiful sunshine and stunning water feature speaking of serenity that was being utterly massacred by Renata's hysterics. Nate's Spanish was basic at best and he was half thankful he couldn't understand her from the look on Javier's face.

She was being held at bay by one of Luca's discreet security staff and one from the hotel, both attempting to prevent her from gaining any further ground than she already had.

'*Basta!*' Javier shouted, calling a stop to his mother's sudden hysterics. For a moment.

The look of relief on the two men's faces would have been comical if Nate hadn't been so furious.

'What are you doing here, Renata?' Nate demanded as the two other men stepped back to make space for him and Javier.

'I am here for my beloved daughter's wedding, of course,' she replied, apparently unable to keep the sneer of disdain from her voice.

'You are wearing *white*,' Javier spat, and for the first time Nate realised that Renata was dressed in what could conceivably pass as a wedding dress.

Rapid-fire Spanish passed between them, hot, angry and too quick for Nate to keep up.

He got between mother and son, gesturing for Javier to back up before turning to face Renata. He looked at her—really looked. The arrogance and disdain and fury dripping from every pore seemed to hit the ground between them like acid. The contrast between how loving, how nurturing Gabi was with their children, that she was even capable of such love, despite being raised by this *wolf*, was nothing short of miraculous.

'I am here for my daughter. A mother should be with her child on such a day as this.'

'You're right,' Nate said. 'Gabi should be surrounded by people who love her on this day. People who want the best for her, who want to celebrate her joy, her happiness with her,' he said, and even though he half wondered whether he himself was capable of giving her those things, he knew categorically that Gabi deserved them. 'People who will be there in her life as she moves forward as a mother, as a wife, and as a woman.'

'See? You understand.'

'I do,' Nate confirmed. 'Just as I understand that you are not, never have been and never will be, one of those people,' he said, stepping closer to her, his pulse pounding in his veins, barely contained fury driving him. 'And I will do everything in my power to make sure that you are never able to hurt her ever again,' he promised.

He stepped back and turned to Luca's man. 'Put her in a car. Take her home. And keep her there until this evening.'

'You can't do that—it's illegal. I'll call the police!' Renata yelled.

Nate nodded. 'You're right,' he said, turning back to the man again. 'Take her phone.'

He turned his back on Renata and ignored her screams

of frustration and accusations. He retrieved his own phone, called his lawyer and told him to expect a phone call from the Spanish police and to begin whatever passed for a restraining order in Spain. He also passed on the details of the hotel's security man for a witness statement.

'I'll deal with whatever consequences the police deem fit regarding Renata today, but right now, I have a wedding to get to.'

He ended the call and turned to find Javier assessing him with a steady gaze.

'Did you mean what you said?' Javier asked.

'I always mean what I say,' Nate dismissed, struggling a little more than he perhaps should be to get his racing heart rate under control.

'About Gabi?'

'Absolutely,' Nate replied without a second thought. She was the mother of his children. She would soon be his wife. She and they were his to protect and he would do whatever that took. Whatever.

Gabi found herself looking out at a lake that could be mistaken for glass it was so still, reflecting the majestic outline of the mountains in the distance. The water looked almost turquoise today, as if decorated just for her wedding. But it was the serenity that she most wanted in that moment.

Emily had come here yesterday and turned an already idyllic location into a magical wonderland with her interior designer's eye. A magical wonderland where even witches existed, apparently.

Luca, Hope's husband, came to stand beside her and she smiled sadly.

'You don't have to stand guard,' Gabi said gently.

'That's not what I'm—'

'She's here?' she asked. 'My mother?'

The Italian billionaire side-eyed her as if considering what to tell her before turning back to face the lake beside her.

'*Sí,*' he said.

Gabi sighed. She was not surprised. Not really. It had been like that for almost her entire life.

She nodded. 'On my sixteenth birthday, she was so insecure about having a "woman" as a daughter that she seduced the father of my best friend and was caught having sex with him in the downstairs bathroom by his wife,' she said, shuddering at the memory, and at the devastation of losing one of the few friends she'd managed to make at the private school that she'd hated. Humiliation, anger, resentment and genuine self-pity—that was what Gabi associated with the key moments in her life. So she had learned to wish them away. Learned not to have expectations. Learned not to hope.

'I wonder what she had in mind for today,' she said ruefully.

Gabi had needed time and support when she'd left her mother's house, staying for a while with Javier and Emily, finding a therapist who could help her navigate her mother's narcissism. Narcissism in the true sense rather than a misplaced character descriptor. It was as much beyond Renata's control as was breathing. It had to be about her, always, because there was nothing else of importance. Not even her children.

Gabi knew she should have continued with the therapist, but when she'd discovered that she was pregnant she'd switched her focus to them, ensuring that they would have a mother who put them first. Always.

'Nate and Javier are dealing with her. They will make sure she leaves.'

Gabi nodded. 'For now,' she amended. 'She'll leave for now.'

Luca murmured an agreement and there was a peaceful silence between them for a moment and she realised what was different.

'You didn't try to make an excuse for her,' Gabi observed.

Luca shook his head, his lips pulled down. 'I know about bad mothers,' he said simply. 'There are no excuses or platitudes for those. Most people look to reassure, to insist that there's some goodness to be found. But sometimes,' he said, looking at her directly, 'there is none. So, no. No excuses for bad parents,' he said, and Gabi wondered if he'd noticed that her father wasn't there either.

He'd sent flowers. A pretty bouquet with a bland printed note:

Wishing you the best on your special day

They could have been sent on her birthday, if he'd ever done such a thing.

What was wrong with her that her parents couldn't be like everyone else? she thought with a vicious twist of hurt. But wasn't that what Luca was saying? That she wasn't alone in the 'bad parent' stakes?

She liked Luca, he was near perfect for Nate's sister, a calm, grounding force that the other woman needed. Nate's family suited him.

'Family is what you make of it,' he said, turning back to watch Emily and Hope playing with the children as the few guests they'd brought together began to take their seats on rows of chairs with white bows tied at their backs. The officiant waited patiently beneath an arch of beautiful flowers and twisting ivy, the lake visible beyond. 'And, from the look of it, you have a rather spectacular one,' he said, and Gabi couldn't help but smile. 'There isn't a single one of them that would not die to protect those children or you, Gabriella,' he said, bringing her gaze back to his. 'And I know what I'm talking about.'

In the distance, Nate and Javier emerged from the building, wearing sunglasses and looking utterly devastating in their tuxes. Whether they knew it or not, they matched pace and looked for all the world like two mythological gods come to earth to play amongst the mortals. The wind pressed against them, showing them off at their best.

Nate was fiddling with a cufflink, but both his and her brother's attention were fixed on their destination at the top of the aisle. Nate's beauty—the natural power of him—called to her all the way across the courtyard. Handsome barely covered her soon-to-be husband. *This* was the man she had spent the night with in a hotel, *this* was the powerhouse that had confronted her mother in court, *this* was the father of her children and the man she would spend the rest of her life with.

A shiver ran through her at the thought of what kind of wedding night they could have had, and what they *wouldn't* have. But then the sound of her children's laughter was carried to her on the same wind that had pressed against Nate. It was a timely reminder of her reasons for being here today. The safety and security of her children, and the hope—the desperate hope—that they might have a better upbringing than she'd had.

'Shall we?' Luca asked, offering her his arm.

* * *

Nate pulled at his cufflink as they made their way towards the aisle, scanning the grounds for a sign of Gabi. He saw his children first, playing with Emily and Hope, his heart missing a beat when Ana looked up at him with large, almost green eyes and a bright smile, and waved at him.

Javier paused at the bottom of the aisle and Nate turned to look at him.

Javier smirked. 'You think I'm going up there with you?'

'That's my job,' Luca announced as he met them, Nate trying to look around him for Gabi.

Luca tutted loudly enough to bring Nate's attention back to him. 'You're going to want to wait to see her, man, seriously. Let's go.' He nodded to the top of the aisle, where a large, intricate flowered arch bowed over the officiant. Nate frowned, and tried to lean around Luca to see Gabi again before being not so gently nudged by Javier.

'Go on, get up there,' Javier said with a laugh, and Nate gave up, following Luca to the top of the aisle.

Shoving aside his frustration with his soon-to-be brother-in-law, he grimly smiled at the few guests he'd wanted and Gabi had gathered, not in the least bothered by how selective they had both been.

Luca passed by Hope and leaned in to give her a kiss, full on the lips, and batted a hand at the *oohs* and *ahhs* that came in response from the people around them. Nate felt an awkward pressure in his chest, witnessing the easy affection between his sister and her husband.

But they had what they had, and he knew what he needed with Gabi. He'd not lied when he'd told her that they couldn't be an 'us'. He simply couldn't risk it because, deep down, he knew that she would make him vulnerable in a way that he might not be able to survive. Yes, he had wants and needs, but that didn't matter. He could—and would—respect the sanctity of marriage, respect his *wife*, and not seek satisfaction elsewhere. But when the children were old enough? When they were twenty-one, he would let Gabi go wherever she—

At that precise moment, Nate caught his first glimpse of Gabi in her wedding dress and the bottom dropped out of his world.

His heart pounded so powerfully in his chest, he barely heard Luca taunt, 'Told you so.'

He could feel his skin flush beneath his suit, causing a bead of sweat to trickle down his back. He fisted his hands by his sides to stop himself from doing something stupid, like reach for her, pull her to him and—

'Sunglasses,' Luca prompted.

'What?'

'Sunglasses,' Luca hissed.

Nate pulled the sunglasses from his face and caught the moment that Gabi, meeting his gaze, paused ever so slightly mid-stride. He felt it, the arc of electricity that snapped between them, remembered it from the first moment he'd laid eyes on her in the hotel bar and thought for just a second that she'd felt it too, pulling at her, binding her to him just as surely as any vow or legal document. He'd never, no matter how many women he'd encountered before, felt anything like it.

Gabi was unique, the only one, obliterating all thought of anyone else and making a mockery of his determination to keep her at arm's length. She purposely looked aside, trying to sever the connection between them, smiling and nodding to their guests. But it didn't work.

She was utterly exquisite, her hair piled high in a bun with tendrils flickering in the breeze. Subtle make-up only served to accentuate her natural beauty—the tan of her skin highlighting the sea-storm hazel of her eyes. She wore no necklace, no earrings—not even an engagement ring. She didn't need to, because she was the jewel, he recognised in an instant. And while he could vaguely hear mutterings about the dress, *she* shone the brightest.

As she reached the top of the aisle she gave her bouquet to Ana and kissed Antonio, who fussed quietly next to where Emily carried their cousin in a sling.

Look at me, Nate urged silently. *Look at me.*

Because he wanted that feeling again. That thump to the chest as powerful as any punch, just to know he hadn't been imagining it. As a man who knew what it felt like to have two hundred joules thumped into his body to bring him back to life, Nate wasn't exaggerating the impact of just one look from her.

Look at me.

Finally, Gabi straightened, walked up the two small steps to join him, the officiant and Luca on the dais and turned to face him.

Christ.

He hadn't imagined it. He was hit with such force it nearly knocked him off his feet.

He barely took in a word the officiant said that day. Later, people would tell him how beautiful it had been, how touching the service was. But he only had eyes for Gabi. His ears only heard her words and if he'd had even the slightest whim of fancy, he'd have said that his soul only knew hers that day.

'Nate?' the officiant prompted.

'Mmm…?' he said, dragging his attention from Gabi to hear the gentle ripple of laughter that rolled across the guests.

'Your vows?' the man asked.

'Oh, yes. Vows.' More gentle laughter covered his moment of awkwardness as he came back into himself and what he needed to do. 'Gabriella…' he started, pushing beyond the sound of blood rushing in his veins. 'I could give you someone else's promises—to cherish you until death, to have you, to hold you, but those promises, said by so many people, don't feel right for you or for us,' he admitted, knowing that she would understand. Knowing that she also knew that to speak of love would be a lie, to speak of honour, when he had so little, and cherishing, when he'd promised not to do such a thing, felt like sacrilege.

'So, instead, I will give you this promise. I will be father to our children, I will be with you as we guide them to be the best versions of themselves they can be. I promise to walk beside you in all things, to encourage and help you in all that you do. I promise to talk to you, listen to you and care for you. Through whatever comes our way, I will be whatever strength, comfort, counsel or companion you need. Everything I am, everything I have, is yours, now and for ever.'

There was a moment of such silence he thought he might have lost his hearing, until every guest collectively let out a sigh. Someone laughed, someone clapped, one of the children cried a little before being hushed, but all Nate could see was the tears gathering in Gabi's eyes, and he could only hope that he'd said the right thing, *done* the right thing. Finally, the near stranglehold of anxiety loosened its grip from around his throat and he took his first deep breath of that day.

'Nathanial…' Gabi started, having to clear her throat before continuing. 'Like you, I didn't want to speak another's words today. Your promises suit me and they suit us,' she said, reassuring him a little. 'So here are mine for you. I will care for our children, with you by my side, teaching them right from wrong while allowing them to explore their creativity, self-expression and emotions without judgement or confinement. I will share my thoughts with you, my joys, my sorrows, and hope that you will trust me with your thoughts, joys and sorrows. In sickness and in health I will carry your burdens as my own,' she promised, and his heart flipped in his chest, 'as I know you will mine. Love comes in many forms—ours comes as a family,' she concluded, and the guests, perhaps slightly misunderstanding words intended for him, a meaning only shared by them, descended into rapturous applause.

The officiant continued the remainder of the ceremony and could have spoken Ancient Greek for all Nate knew, but the last sentence rang clear in his head like a bell of warning. One he had absolutely no intention of paying heed to.

'You may now kiss the bride.'

After such pretty words, after such sweet simplicity, the kiss should have been tender, sincere, innocent even. But it was nothing of the sort. He met Gabi in the middle, and any thoughts of the chaste kiss that he had intended fled the moment his lips met hers.

Heat burned the back of his neck, tension fisted his stomach, and it took everything he had not to reach for her arms and pull her against him, to hell with the guests watching on. In what must have been a state of equal shock, Gabi's lips parted in a gasp, inadvertently giving him access his body took full advantage of.

He felt her submit, almost melt against him, immediately creating an addiction in him that would never be satiated. Craving coursed through every fibre of his being and he couldn't let her go. His hands automatically drew her closer against him, and the thrill of victory cried in his breast as he felt her body press against his. It was only when the whooping cat calls from the audience finally cut through the pounding of his heartbeat in his ears that he paused.

Gently pulling back from her, Nate realised that he had completely obliterated the line he had drawn between them and he would never be able to put it back.

CHAPTER SEVEN

GABI WOULDN'T HAVE been able to say what had happened after the ceremony. Not until she finally found herself sitting at a long table, Ana and Antonio fussing between her, Emily and Hope. Her lips tingled, her heartbeat was erratic, her skin still felt flushed and over-sensitised. Nate had plunged her into a sea of sensation and she was barely able to stay afloat.

Her eyes tracked him wherever he went, her body felt him from across distances near and far. It was as if the kiss had forged an unbreakable connection between them. Not just legally or emotionally, but *physically*. Her body remembered their night together, the passion that had brought her not only so much pleasure, but two children. Through their presentation as a married couple, and the champagne toasts and canapés, she oscillated between memories of kisses, past and present, as if drugged.

Until they sat for the wedding breakfast and Ana put her arms up to Nate in the universal gesture for 'hold me'. Gabi's heart stopped when Nate, staring at his daughter as if she were the most precious gift he could receive, plucked her from Emily's lap and held her to his chest as if he might never let go.

Antonio crawled into her lap, Gabi's arms automatically coming around him as he leaned against her, and both parents looked at each other, their children in their arms, and knew that, no matter what had happened in the past or would happen in the future, they had done the right thing.

Nate came to sit beside her at the double seated head of the table, and she fought the urge to simply rest her own head against his shoulder. Her mouth wobbled in an attempt to prevent the yawn escaping, but Nate's focused gaze saw everything.

'You're tired.' It was a statement, not a question.

'I'm fine,' Gabi dismissed with a patient smile. 'We'll be home soon.'

Something flickered in his gaze, and she was about to question him on it when Javier tapped a fork to a glass and insisted on making a speech. She leaned back and gently rocked her son as her brother welcomed her new husband to the family, as Hope and Emily, and even Luca, looked on with emotion shining bright in their eyes.

'Family is what you make of it,' Luca had said.

Words to live by, Gabi realised. And while she had been utterly and irrefutably focused on making sure that she was the perfect mother for her children, the kind of mother she'd never had, she thought that perhaps it was time to ensure that their family was much bigger than her. She looked at Nate, could see the ferocity of his love for his sister, the need to protect those he considered *his.* But she wanted more for Ana and Antonio. And she was beginning to think that they might be able to make that happen.

Nate ended the call that had put the final part of his plan in place. It was an extravagance, for sure, but one that Gabi and the twins deserved. They *all* deserved.

'What are you doing out here? It's nearly time to say goodbye to the guests.'

He turned to find his sister walking towards him across the courtyard, a hand shading her gaze from the late afternoon sun. He looked at her, eyes bright, cheeks pink, and felt relief. He could see how happy she was, how much she'd enjoyed meeting her niece and nephew and the new members of their family.

As she drew closer, she narrowed her eyes. 'What are you scheming?'

'Nothing for you, *dear sister*. Just some honeymoon plans.'

'Honeymoon? I thought you were just returning to the house?'

'Not any more.'

'Well, you'd better be sure about it, *dear brother*,' she said, sweeping her arm around his waist, 'because Gabriella Casas doesn't strike me as a woman who likes having plans changed on her.'

'Gabriella *Harcourt*,' Nate replied with shocking possessiveness.

Hope turned as they entered the large barn where the wedding breakfast had been served, and smiled with something like pride. 'Yes, she is a Harcourt, isn't she.'

Nate looked up to find Gabi once again looking at him. Ever since the officiant had proclaimed that he could kiss his bride, it was as if an invisible thread had bound them together. It was something that pulled and pushed at his skin, wanting and waiting and not in the least bit patient.

He tried to shake off the feeling that Hope's warning was unnecessary as they said goodbye to the officiant and staff, as the last of the guests drove away from the stunning venue, and Gabi looked at him tiredly and said,

'Home,' with such longing he realised that he might have just made a very big mistake.

He winced. 'About that...'

Gabi was fuming. And it wasn't easy to fume on a speed-boat slashing through waves, holding onto your children as if their lives depended on it. Yes, they were wearing life jackets, yes, she knew that they were 'perfectly safe', as the pilot of the boat had told her repeatedly, and yes, much to her irritation, they *did* seem to be having the time of their lives. But *she* wasn't.

All she'd wanted was to go home. Where she could change, where she could get the children back into their routine, where there was familiarity and rhythm. She'd thought that she and Nate could spend the next few weeks settling into whatever it was their marriage would look like.

Gabi studiously ignored Nate as he cast nervous glances her way. The arrogant, presumptuous, *estúpido*... What use did she have for honeymoons and husbands? She'd been perfectly fine without him. And then she caught sight of Antonio wriggling in his father's lap, a look of sheer joy across his face as he cried happily into the wind, and bit back the thought. It was right that her children had both their parents—she just wished their father wasn't so high-handed, or handsome.

She hadn't wanted a honeymoon, because theirs wasn't a normal marriage. It wasn't about rose petals and ro-mance, champagne and diamond rings, she thought as she clenched her fist around a ring that was far too much for her, and far too much beyond her wildest imagination. She didn't want a honeymoon because she didn't want to make this longing for something *more* even worse.

The boat arrived at a small private island just off the coast of southern Spain. She'd visited some of the islands during some of her mother's infamously extravagant parties, but Gabi had never been to this one. It looked like a castle rising up from the sea, trees and large boulders simultaneously decorative and natural. She caught glimpses of chrome and glass embedded harmoniously within the wild landscape.

It was beautiful, she thought a little resentfully. It was where she would have wanted to come had she… Gabi bit her lip and forced a smile to her mouth when Ana cheered, looking up at the pretty island.

The boat's pilot guided them efficiently to a jetty and helped them offload as dusk began to descend. Little lights either side of the wooden deck led them up steps that took them towards a house that looked like a modern-day fairy tale.

'What about clothes?' she asked, pulling to a stop halfway towards the villa.

'They were packed and brought here earlier,' Nate replied, leading her on a few steps before she stopped again.

'And the things the children need? Like nappies and wipes, and bottles and toys and—'

'All here, I promise.'

Panic gripped her. 'And Antonio's blanket? He can't sleep without it,' she said, terrified by the hysteria that would ensue if Antonio didn't have his pacifier. 'And Ana, she needs her—'

'Both the blanket and Ana's squeaky clam are here, I promise,' Nate insisted. He held out his hand to her. 'Please, Gabi, just come and take a look. If it's awful, then we can leave first thing tomorrow.'

'Why did you do this?' she asked, unable to keep the utter defeat from her tone.

'Because…' He paused, taking a breath and shifting Antonio onto his other hip, completely unaware of how devastating he looked, dressed in a tux and carrying his son. 'I wanted to do something nice for you.'

With that, he turned and walked on ahead, leaving her to wish so very much that he hadn't.

But, as he had promised, Gabi discovered everything that the children and she would need for at least two weeks in the bags that had been left by unseen staff in their rooms. Ana's toy clam, Antonio's blanket—everything.

Dead on her feet, Gabi didn't even think about changing out of her dress as she put the children to bed, only realising she was still wearing it when Ana, almost asleep, thrust out her hand and patted the material on her arm and announced *'bonito'*. It was the highest compliment she could have received for a dress she had designed herself, she thought, backing out of the room and going to find Nate.

He was standing in front of the single floor-to-ceiling window that wrapped around half of the entire villa, looking out at the stunning nightscape on display. He had removed his tie and cufflinks, the sleeves of his shirt rolled back in such a carelessly attractive way it almost stung.

If Gabi could have slipped off to her own room and not seen him again she would have, coward that she was. But the one design flaw of her dress—one she promised herself to rectify—was that she couldn't get out of it without help.

He caught her gaze in the window's reflection and simply watched as she approached, waiting. She looked away, unable to hold his gaze. She knew she must have sounded utterly irrational and churlish, resenting such a gift from her *husband*—the word felt strange in her heart. But how could she explain? How could she find the words to tell him how much it hurt, wanting more than she was allowed to have?

'Can...?' She tried again after clearing her throat. 'Can you...?'

He turned. 'You need my help?' he asked.

Gabi nodded, startled when he let out a cynical laugh.

'Your dress? You need my help with your dress.' He nodded to himself as if angry.

Heat poured into her soul. 'Look, if you don't want to—'

He raised his hand, cutting her off. 'It's not about want, Gabi.'

'Nate,' she said, exhausted and done, 'I don't know what the subtext is here. I don't know why you're angry, when you changed all the plans that I knew, when you basically upended everything, just because you can—'

'I'm angry, Gabi, because you don't *let* me help.'

Gabi pulled herself up short and Nate shook his head as if in disbelief, as if realising she had absolutely no clue what he was talking about.

'You don't let me help with the children, you don't let me help *you*. I'm not allowed to make changes to your routine. I'm not allowed *in*.'

Shocked by the truth of his words, Gabi's own anger rose. 'I'm trying to navigate the convenient marriage you wanted and the parental role you need, Nate. It's not easy,' she snapped.

'There is nothing *convenient* about any of this.'

'On that, we can finally agree. I'll see you in the morning.' She turned, furious tears pressing against the backs of her eyes, determined to get to her room before he could see them fall.

'Your dress,' he called after her.

'I'll rip it if I have to,' she yelled, forcing aside the sob that filled her chest. She slipped quietly into the room next to the children's, hating the sight of the rose petals that she was sure Nate hadn't even seen, making a mockery of her wedding night. A bucket beside the bed held a bottle of champagne and melted ice water and she wanted to hurl it out of the window.

The tears came then. Silently, in the way she had learned as a child. Hot and hurting as they poured down her cheeks. She snatched at the zip behind her, clumsy fingers suddenly uncaring of the dress that had brought her so much joy, and tore at the material desperately, needing to get it off her body.

Eventually, with only a little ripping, she wrangled the silk and lace from her skin and sobbed, sucking in a lungful of the first clear air she'd taken that day. She scrubbed her make-up from her face in the shower, where her tears were nearly invisible, and from habit waited until she was sure that they had run dry before getting out.

She slipped between the satin sheets, ignoring the rose petals, but as she finally closed her eyes and tried to find sleep, she couldn't stop hearing his words in her head.

'You don't let me help... I'm not allowed in.'

A tear escaped from beneath her closed eyes, because she realised she had never learned to trust that, if she asked, help would be given. And she couldn't help but think how terribly sad that was.

An hour later, Nate gently prised open her door to make sure that she was okay. He stayed in the doorway, unwilling to wake her, watching her sleeping amongst the red rose petals, for enough time for the moon to pass overhead before turning away.

Nate clutched his espresso in a death grip, knowing it was his only lifeline to staying awake at that moment. Last night had hardly been the typical wedding night, but, for a man who had never intended to marry, he wasn't that surprised. He'd not slept a wink, tossing and turning between memories of their kiss, the wedding, the single night they'd shared more than two years ago, and his words to her. Words that had fallen from his lips out of sheer frustration and his own tiredness. He should never had said them. He'd been hoping that Gabi would adjust, would slowly start to give him more space, more responsibility, but she hadn't. Instead, it had almost been getting worse.

At around three in the morning he'd begun to fear that she didn't trust him. That she didn't think she could leave the children with him. That because of his aneurism— a weakness, a vulnerability—he was unreliable. Wasn't that why he'd not told anyone outside the family about what had happened to him? Knowing that the business world would not only smell blood in the water but take advantage of it too. But to think that it made her doubt him as a parent…

'Morning.' Gabi ventured quietly from the doorway to the kitchen.

He turned, hating the way that, after searching her face, he could see signs of her distress last night too. He looked around her but couldn't see Ana or Antonio.

'They're still asleep, miraculously,' Gabi said, correctly

interpreting his thoughts. 'Which is a good thing—' she sighed '—because I want to talk to you.'

Nate nodded, ready to accept whatever resolution she had come to, knowing that she had done so because of the way she carried herself. Determined, which he respected. Powerful, which he admired. Beautiful, which he couldn't deny.

She came into the room and sat at a gorgeous golden oak hand-carved table, warm from the gentle morning sun as it streamed through the windows. She looked like a summer fairy, Nate thought, before blaming the ridiculous thought on a considerable lack of sleep.

He took a seat opposite her and waited.

'I owe you an apology,' Gabi said, and he immediately shook his head in denial.

'No, you don't.'

She held his gaze. 'I do,' she said solemnly.

'Gabi—'

'Nate, *por Dios*, if you don't let me finish—'

'Sorry,' he said, raising his arms in surrender, biting back the urge to insist that she didn't.

She flexed her hands against the table. 'You were right,' she admitted. 'I didn't—*don't*—let you help. I can't. Because...' She took a breath. 'Because I grew up in a household where everything I had came with strings. Where if I was given something, it was either taken away later or used against me.'

The fury Nate felt towards Renata Casas increased with every word Gabi spoke.

'And where most of the time, when I asked for help, it was either dismissed or forgotten,' Gabi said, and Nate's heart pounded in his chest.

'When I couldn't get hold of you to tell you about the

twins,' she said, and Nate felt a fresh twist of shame un-
furl in his gut, 'I had to go to my brother. Javier, who had
already been so damaged by our mother. I... I know that
he would never say such a thing, let alone think it, but I
was afraid that I and my children were a burden to him
that he might eventually resent.'

Pink, painful-looking flushes appeared in patches beneath the gentle tan of Gabriella's skin. He had done that
to her. His neglect had done that and he needed to know,
needed to hear it all. Not as punishment, but so that he'd
never forget what she had felt because of his inaction.

'That was terrible for me because I...' Gabi struggled
to force the words through the hurt that had accumulated
over the years. But Nate knew he deserved to hear the
truth. The only way that they would be able to move forward, even remotely successfully co-parent, would be if
she was completely honest with him. 'I didn't want to get
used to his help, only to have it taken away.' His love. She
hadn't wanted her brother to take away his love...like her
parents had done. 'And then you came and... And signing a paper and wearing a ring doesn't suddenly make
me feel as if you will stay, because my father didn't,' she
said with a shrug, as if those words didn't beat against
her fragile heart with the strength of a battering-ram. 'He
didn't. He remarried and made himself another family.
And my mother? Well, she's been married three times,
so it's hardly something I see as reliable. And—'

Her words stopped when Nate reached across the table
and placed his hands over where her fingers were picking at each other. Suddenly Gabi felt both impossibly
young and terribly old, and, above all, utterly vulnerable.

'That will not happen here,' he vowed.

She tried to shake him off.

'Gabi, whatever happens, you will be taken care of, protected, financially at least.'

'It's not about finances.'

'No,' he admitted. 'It's not, but at least that is something that you can see on an account statement and know. The house is in your name. I have set up accounts for you and the children. I have no access to them. I cannot close them.'

His words did soothe something in her, but she also knew they were a patch, to cover her real need.

'As for parenting and supporting you? This is only something I can show you daily, until hopefully you don't have to question it any more. If you let me. If you *trust* me.'

Gabi wasn't deaf to the plea in his voice, nor the urging of her heart. She knew that she needed at least to let him try—let herself try.

'But Nate, you can't just make decisions that directly impact me and the children without me knowing. You've been in our lives for five minutes—'

He opened his mouth to speak but she knew what he was going to say. 'I know that's not your fault, but it is fact. And there are things you don't know about the children. What if they'd been terrified of the water and you didn't stop to ask? What if Antonio had nightmares sleeping away from his bed, or Ana had allergies?'

Nate stared at her, understanding swirling in his gaze, and at least had the grace to look a little ashamed.

'We need to be able to talk, Nate. Share things,' she concluded, 'before decisions are made.'

Like we promised in our vows, she thought.

He looked back up at her, sincerity shining in his eyes as if he'd heard her silent plea. 'Agreed.'

Eventually she nodded.

'Gabi, I need to tell you. Your mother—'

'Was there yesterday,' she said with a sad smile. 'I know.'

Nate frowned, clearly having believed that he'd kept it a secret. 'I didn't want it to spoil the day.'

Gabi let out a huff. 'I think we did that well enough ourselves, don't you?' she asked ruefully. But she could at least realise that he had tried, in his own way, to protect her.

'Do Ana and Antonio know about her—Renata?'

Gabi looked down at her hands and shook her head. 'I left her house the night you visited and have never been back. She never tried to reach me, and I didn't want to speak to her. I didn't see her again until court... And grandparents have never come up around them because...'

Because she and Javi had only ever referred to her as Renata, and because there had not been any other grandparents in their lives for them to ask about her mother. Because, as she knew, his parents had passed.

'Let's start again,' he said, slapping his hands on the table determinedly, but whether he was trying to avoid the topic of his parents or something else she couldn't tell. 'There are staff here, a chef and a housekeeper. Let's make the most of the next two weeks, to take it as easy as possible. Find a new routine for us and the children, with no stress or worries. Together, as a team.'

'A team?' Gabi tried the word out for size, beginning to allow herself to hope. To wonder what she could do if she had more time, if she let other people in to help. If she *trusted*. 'A team,' she repeated with a little more determination.

* * *

And they did just that.

It wasn't easy, Nate discovered, working out how to manage the twins together, especially when they were already so quick to adapt and test the waters with them each separately in order to get their own way. But it brought Nate and Gabi closer much more quickly, forcing them to be a united front against the sheer might of their children's strong and fascinating personalities. Having someone else to cook and clean—things that he now realised Gabi had done herself in order to lessen the financial debt and burden she felt she owed Javier—was an absolute godsend.

It gave them time to spend together as a family, but it also gave Gabi less to do and within days he could see how the dark circles he'd only just realised were there were beginning to fade. They lounged around a shallow children's pool, perfect and safe for Ana and Antonio, who were proving to be utter water babies. They were getting used to him now, and were beginning to interact with him so much more. Ana had been hard won and definitely the last holdout, but it had only made Nate more determined to earn her trust. She took her cues from her mother and was a lot more watchful than Gabi realised, Nate thought.

In the evenings, after the twins had been put to bed, dinner would be waiting for them out on the terrace, where the heat of the day had gentled and the cover of night brought the flowering scents of bougainvillea and the sound of cicadas.

And he didn't miss England one bit, Nate realised. All the while he'd been in Switzerland, recovering and rehabbing, he'd missed his desk, his sleek bachelor pad, with an almost obsessive fixation. But since coming to Spain, since meeting his children, since marrying Gabi...he'd not even thought of it once.

They quickly settled into the routine of sharing dinner, a glass of wine and anecdotes of their childhoods. Nate was determined to listen, and if Gabi noticed that he didn't quite share as much as she did then she didn't say anything. Slowly, day by day, he felt himself beginning to relax, only having to turn his attention to a few work-related matters for the duration of his honeymoon.

And when he had a spare moment he was beginning to consider whether it was sensible to liquidate his shares in Casas Textiles after all. Perhaps there was something there for Gabi? But only if Renata was utterly and completely removed. He thrust aside thoughts of his mother-in-law because when he did so he felt the pressing of a headache against his brain in a way that he neither liked nor wanted to know about.

Gabi laughed at a story she was telling, and once again he was struck by how incredibly beautiful she was. And she had absolutely no idea. Everything about her seemed connected in a way that was both natural and sensual at the same time. He'd seen her in her wedding dress, her bikini, her hair soaking, her skin damp and wrapped in a towel, and he'd had to retreat to his room before he embarrassed them both. So, while he should be celebrating his victories with her as a parent, he couldn't help but feel that he was utterly failing in his own attempts to keep this marriage out of the bedroom. Because in bed, alone, each night he dreamed only of her.

CHAPTER EIGHT

A WEEK AFTER returning from their honeymoon and Gabi was already missing the staff. Nate had made several offers to employ help, but Gabi was resistant. Resistant, reluctant and resentful. She'd been managing just fine by herself before he'd come along—shouldn't they need *less* help with an extra pair of hands? But somehow she was even more exhausted.

In truth, she didn't want strangers in her house. She didn't want people there to judge her if she got things wrong or made a mistake. She knew she was a good mother. She knew she was, but she couldn't help feeling that having help would be like admitting she couldn't cope.

Nate had flown to London that morning and promised to be back later that evening, and deep down she'd been looking forward to it, hoping that the reprieve from his presence would lessen the anxious yearning that had built since the wedding. She'd blamed the time spent by the pool on the honeymoon.

It was one thing seeing a man in his prime, broad shoulders, toned, *defined*, but seeing that same man play so lovingly and patiently with his children? It was a level of attraction she hadn't experienced before. A level of possession and ownership buried deep within the desire she felt for him, because that was her *husband*. And then she remembered his edict: convenient. Name only. Co-parenting. And seesawed back to miserable yearning again.

Gabi poured herself a glass of wine and sat down on the sofa, staring out at the night sky through the open French windows. She promised herself that she'd grab something more substantial than the bowl of peanuts she'd brought with her into the sitting room. She had a basket of washing still to fold, and had planned to make a start on sauce for the children's lunches, but she just needed five minutes to herself.

The scent of honeysuckle and bougainvillea slipped in on the breeze and it soothed her thoughts. Her mind finally settled enough to wander a little and, in her imagination, she saw wisps of material, the line of a dress, a vibrant colour from a flower that had caught her eye on the island where they'd honeymooned, the way the petals were layered, making her think of skirts and...

Her fingers reached for a pencil, wanting to get the images from her mind onto paper. It had been so long since inspiration had struck, her confidence cruelly decimated by her mother, her time utterly consumed by her children. She'd begun to fear that it might have gone. She might have lost it for ever, if she'd ever had it in the first place. But her wedding dress, the comments, Hope's praise, they'd given her a push in the secret part of her that still cherished the hope to make her dreams come true one day.

She debated for a moment. She really should get on to the housework. But the desire, the need, to channel this moment of creativity was so strong it wouldn't be denied. She grabbed a pen and some paper from beside the landline and gave herself five minutes. Just five and then she'd get back to the laundry.

Nate checked his watch as he put his key in the door and winced. It was nearly two in the morning. The meetings had run on and had left a strange tension in his neck that even now, rolling his shoulders, didn't quite shift. He didn't like it, and he didn't like what it made him feel, what it made him fear, so he pushed it down and shook it off.

At least he'd achieved what he'd set out to do, he thought as he put his briefcase down in the hallway and went to the kitchen to pour himself a whisky. Another thing he shouldn't be doing. He knew it was bad for him, the doctors had recommended a very healthy lifestyle to follow, but Nate clung to the glass as if it were his act of defiance, his proof that things were back to normal, the way that they had been *before*.

Which was why, despite the opportunity to sell one of his companies to a consortium based in Norway, he'd decided against it. He was managing just fine, no balls were being dropped, because he was better now. He didn't need to compromise his dreams for the future from *before*. That was why he'd spent so long in Switzerland after all. Making sure he was back to normal. Working at full capacity and—

He stopped in the doorway to the living room, finding Gabi asleep on the sofa. She was surrounded by bits of paper and a half-drunk glass of wine had been discarded next to a bowl with a handful of nuts still left in it. Was that all she'd had for dinner? He hadn't noticed any pots or pans in the sink, or the food she would often leave for him in the fridge.

Even from here he could see the dark smudges beneath her eyes were back. And he had to wrangle his frustration with the stubborn woman. She was working herself to the bone—had been ever since the twins had been born, he imagined. Why wouldn't she accept his help?

You know why.

Yes, her mother had been a monster, her father little better by his absence. But didn't Nate have some responsibility to bear? He'd promised to show her that she could trust him to help, and had he? Had he really?

He frowned, putting the glass of whisky down and making his way towards the sofa. He picked up one of the pieces of paper left on the coffee table beside the wine and stared. He might not be a fashionista, but he had grown up in an international department store, specialising in luxury items from household to fashion and everything in between. He didn't have his sister's eye, nor his mother's, but he knew what would sell, and as he stared at the dress design on the page he knew it was good. Not just good, but *really* good.

He picked up a few more pieces of paper. He could tell the early ones had begun with less confidence, a little less daring. But, as she had gone on, the lines became firmer, stronger, more determined. At some point she must have grabbed coloured pens from the children's box, but even then she'd tempered and blended the garish primary colours into splashes and lines of colour that gave just enough of an idea of what it could look like.

Without thinking, with his phone he snapped a few pictures of some of the stronger designs and sent them to his sister with 'What do you think?' as a message. It was a running joke between them, because most of the time they knew exactly what the other would think.

He perched down on the edge of the sofa beside Gabi's feet and sighed. She was running herself ragged, leaving not even a minute for herself, and it had to stop. Tomorrow, he would fix it, but tonight he needed to get her off the sofa and into her room.

Unwilling to wake her, even for that short walk, he stood and scooped her up into his arms. And, just like that, the world shifted. She settled against his chest, her hand coming up to press near to a heart that leapt beneath her touch. The subtle floral perfume that he associated only with her rose to tease his senses. The way her body pressed against his sent him straight back to the night they'd shared in Madrid...and memories of what they'd shared, the delicious, heady pleasure that had made him half sure he'd fallen in love before he'd felt absolutely sure he'd been betrayed. So much confusion and so much emotion around that night, but even now he still felt a magnetic pull to her. To be with her.

But things were so new and precarious between them, he couldn't risk giving in to his base desires. Forcing his body's wayward reaction back under control, he walked towards her room, pausing only to briefly look in on the children as they passed. He pushed the door to her bedroom open as Gabi's hand reached up from his chest to curl around his neck, gently grasping the hair at his nape. His pulse picked up, the accidentally sensual contact tearing at the fine thread of his control. Despite the gentle breeze through the open window, here in her bedroom, the scent of her, the sense of Gabi, was so much stronger.

He walked to her bed and carefully laid her down, needing to retreat before he did something unconscionable. But as he began to pull away, the hand around his neck tightened and he looked down to find Gabi staring up at him, eyes open, awake and full of the same yearning he felt deep in his bones. Heat poured over his skin, settling into every atom and fibre of his being.

Gabi's skin flushed, her eyes sparked and her mouth opened as if to say something and he wouldn't, couldn't, hear it. Coward that he was, he gently removed her hand from his neck and backed away from Gabi's bed, unable to turn away from the longing in her gaze until he reached the corridor and closed the door behind him.

It wouldn't have taken much for Gabi to convince herself that what had happened last night had been a dream. It had that kind of quality in her mind. But she knew herself well and if it had been a dream, Nate wouldn't have left her. So, embarrassed and a little confused and very tired, she dragged herself out of bed and into the shower, before heading to the twins' room.

But their beds were empty. She knew that they were okay, realised in an instant that they were probably with Nate, but adrenaline was a sharp painful spike through her chest as she hurried towards the kitchen.

There she found Antonio staring up at Nate with banana and soggy wheat all over his face, clapping furiously as Ana tried to put her feet on Nate's shoulders as he held her above him, laughing.

'Ana, *basta*!' he teased. 'I'm not a climbing frame,' he said, his voice different to what she'd heard before, gentler. 'No, you can't do it!' he gently mocked.

'Yes, Papá, yes, Ana do it!' she said, clearly enough for them to understand.

Nate froze—just a moment, not enough for Ana to notice, but Gabi caught it, caught the way his entire being resonated with some indefinable emotion, because she'd known it too, the first time her children had called her Mamá. In that instant he caught sight of Gabi in the doorway, his eyes so full of parental love, the utter intensity of it, that she couldn't help but smile and nod, understanding that he needed to know that she'd heard it too.

'Ana, Ana, Ana,' he cried, dropping her down into his arms, sneaking kisses on her belly and making her scream with laughter. Antonio looked between Nate and her, cheering and not seeming to feel even remotely left out, but enjoying his sister's happiness.

Gabi pressed a hand against the swelling of her heart, knowing that, no matter what attraction she felt for Nate, she wouldn't dare risk *this*, their family, for something as dangerous or selfish as her wants. So when she looked back at Nate she told herself that last night *had* been a dream, and forced whatever feelings that remained so deep she would hopefully forget them.

By the time Gabi returned from putting the twins down for their late-morning nap, Nate had a coffee waiting for her on the garden table. She eyed it warily and Nate realised that this had become their 'discussion' routine whenever they had something they needed to talk to the other about.

'What is it? I've got to get lunch ready.'

'It's about that, actually,' Nate said, sitting down to show that he wasn't going anywhere. She eyed him suspiciously, but he gestured to the seat opposite him.

'It's time.'

'What's time?'

'It's time that we hired some help,' he said, trying not to roll the tension out of his shoulders.

'We don't need it, Nate. We're perfectly fine—'

'You're exhausted,' he said quietly, aware of the precarious line he was treading. She'd told him enough about her mother, about her need to give their children the opposite of what she'd had, that he knew how delicate this needed to be. 'I'm tired just looking at all you do around here. I'm helping, I know, and you're letting me, but... wouldn't it be easier, better, if you had more dedicated time to focus on the twins?'

The moment the words came out of his mouth, he knew they had struck wrong and he tried not to wince at the shiver of hurt that cut through her gaze.

'Are you implying that I don't give them enough attention?' she demanded, her accent getting a little thicker with the strength of her emotion.

'No!' he cried. 'I'm not. I'm *really* not. I know how much you do for them, how much you give them and...' he tried to choose his words carefully '...and I think it might be too much.'

She frowned and he used her moment of confusion to push on. 'You're exhausted,' he said again. 'But the thing is, you don't have to be. We can have a housekeeper, someone to help with the cooking and cleaning. And we can have someone to help with the children. There are two of them, Gabi. Twins, and I know from personal experience just how draining we can be. You need a minimum of two pairs of hands just to keep them breathing half the time. But that's them. This is about you. Don't you want more than just being a mother?' he asked, thinking of the inspiration he'd seen in her drawings. Hating the fact that he hadn't known that she'd designed her wedding dress until he'd spoken to his sister late last night. 'You are an excellent mother,' he stressed. 'Don't you think having a little time for yourself will only make that even better?' he probed.

'Nate, if you can't handle them—'

'This isn't about me, and I *can* handle them,' he growled, frustration tipping the tension towards a headache and getting the better of him. 'This is about making sure that the mother of my children doesn't break herself by exhausting herself needlessly and sacrificing her own wants and needs.'

Gabi pulled back from the table as if she'd been slapped and half of him wished he could take back the words while the other half knew they needed to be said.

'I know I've only been here for a few months now, Gabi, but I can already tell that this is a marathon, not a sprint, and that we should take all the help we can get in order to make sure that the time we spend with our children is as easy and carefree as possible. I also know that the time we spend as individuals rather than as parents is just as important,' he said, pulling her design from last night from his pocket, unfolding it and passing it to her across the table.

'You owe it to yourself as much as those children to follow your dreams, Gabi. Having help means that you can. And the way the children are growing and learning, it's even just basic safety to have someone to help *and* it's good socialisation,' he said, knowing that he sounded like the parenting books he pored over in secret whenever he got the chance. He felt like a bastard, but he knew that using the twins' safety and benefit would win her over far more easily and quickly than for her own sake.

'Can I think about it?' she asked, and he nodded, getting the sense that he might have finally swayed her towards the idea.

* * *

Gabi had warred with the decision, even though she'd known he was right. She'd forced herself to push past her own fears to see that it was best for her children. Their children. So she agreed to hire not only a housekeeper but someone to help with the children, knowing that it made the most sense. But the person she chose surprised everyone, most especially Nate. And Gabi decided to enjoy every minute of it.

'I'm not sure about this,' Nate said, closing the door on her favourite applicant.

They had been interviewing for two days and she knew that it had tested his patience. She had rejected the English nanny because no one could convince Gabi that the woman knew how to smile. Nate had vetoed Anna-Marie, the eccentric woman from Órgiva, when she'd told him off for drinking coffee. Names and faces had passed through the two days of interviews, all of whom had been *fine* but not good. Until now.

'Bilingual in Spanish and English, a degree in child education, *five* years' experience, with first class references. What is there to complain about? Unless you're being sexist.'

'I am *not* sexist.' Nate's quick and outraged retort made her hide a smile.

'Wonderful. Because he's starting next week.'

Gabi had to turn away before she laughed at the sight of the flickering muscle at his jaw. Oddly, she'd known there wasn't any true heat to his objection, she could feel it. Just as she could feel that Jorge would fit in perfectly. The twins had loved him on sight, and she'd been touched by how his entire focus revolved around them as soon as they came into the room. Children noticed things like that. She had as a child.

Jorge had asked what *her* concerns were about the process. He'd been the only one, as if he had the emotional sense or intelligence to see that this was hard for her. She also knew that he'd impressed Nate, despite his grumbling, and was looking forward to when he moved in.

The villa's small pool house at the back of the estate was perfect for him. He'd explained that his parents lived close by and that was why he'd wanted to stay in the area, which demonstrated how perfect he was to help her care for her twins. From the moment he arrived, Jorge fitted in to their days seamlessly, having fun with the new housekeeper who, despite being nearly thirty years older than him, he flirted with shamelessly.

The change for her was almost instantaneous. Not in the typical structure of the day; mornings and breakfast remained her and Nate's responsibility, at her request, as was putting them to bed. But it was during the day that she realised she had more time. Not having to cook, the laundry and cleaning being done for her. She oscillated between feeling guilty and a huge sense of relief. She'd pick up a book to read, just because she *could*. But still her old sketches and pens and pencils, all her university work, waited untouched in the study she'd claimed as her own. As if she wasn't quite sure that she'd earned it yet.

But it was about two weeks after Jorge started that she began to realise how much Nate had been juggling too. A little less tension showed around his shoulders, a tiredness she could only identify now that it was not there in the shadows beneath his eyes. He started taking some meetings in his office during the day.

'Are they asking more from you now?' she'd asked out of curiosity once as he'd headed towards another meeting.

He'd looked blankly at her, then frowned. 'No?'

'It's just that you seem to have a lot of meetings.'

He blinked. 'I can take them during the day now.'

This time *she'd* frowned, only realising what that meant as he'd shrugged and left the room. He'd been spending his days with them and while she'd been sleeping he'd been running several empires. Guilt pricked painfully at her conscience.

She had been relying on herself for so long that she'd started *thinking* only of herself. Or perhaps it had just been survival mode, doing what needed to be done. But she couldn't let that happen again because they were a team.

She was letting herself enjoy the evenings they spent together too, as their conversations developed from discussing the children to hopes for the future, things that made them laugh, experiences that either differed from each others' so greatly they were fascinating, or were so similar it was startling.

An ease began between them, creeping slowly closer to something more. Touches were so fleeting she thought she might be imagining them. Eyes lingering just a little longer than necessary. A heat simmering gently beneath their interactions, something so vastly different from the incendiary night they'd shared so long ago that it took Gabi a while to realise it was there. She tried to ignore it, to push it away. Because for the first time in so very long she was happy, she realised. Genuinely happy. Her children were the joy of her heart, but Nate was providing a peace and a stability she'd never known. And she felt a tentative trust in him beginning to form.

She was looking out at the sunlight dancing off the pool in the garden when her watch alarm pinged to let her know to wake up the twins. She gently pushed open their door and peeked in. Ana was standing up in her cot, her eyes glistening and cheeks pink.

'*Qué tienes, mi amor?*'

Ana pointed at Antonio. Gabi turned and leaned into his cot, gently rubbing Antonio's belly.

'Antonio,' she whispered, but he barely lifted his eyes. Concern snapped through her like lightning, but she forced herself to be gentle. 'Antonio,' she said, louder, trying to rouse him. She felt his forehead and it was burning up. Beneath her hand, his stomach felt almost solid.

'Nate!' she yelled. 'Nate!'

She picked Antonio up gently, feeling horror almost incapacitate her.

Nate rushed into the room, his words dying on his lips as he took in the sight of her, terrified and clutching their child to her chest.

'I don't know what's wrong...' She looked up at him helplessly. 'I need you. I don't know what to do,' she whispered.

'What do you want to do?' he asked, as if he trusted her completely.

'I want to go to the hospital.'

'Then we go to the hospital.'

CHAPTER NINE

NATE'S HEART SEEMED to stop beating and he wasn't sure if it was ever going to start again. Gabi passed Antonio to him and picked up Ana. In the background he heard Jorge run into the living area as the housekeeper yelled and cried.

Ignoring them all, he rushed out to the car, cradling his son, and when he turned Gabi was by his side. Just over his shoulder he saw Jorge now with Ana, and Gabi told him they'd follow. He gave Antonio back to Gabi and opened the door for her, before rushing round to the driver's side.

'Forget the car seat,' he told her before she could even ask. 'We don't have time.'

Nate drove as fast as he could, not caring about laws or speed limits, only safety, only his child.

He called his assistant from the car's hands-free system.

'Mike, I need you to call the nearest hospital and tell them that I'm bringing in a barely conscious twenty-month-old child with a fever and a firm abdomen. Tell them I want their top paediatric consultant to meet us in the emergency room. When that's done, call Dr Brunner and tell him to call me. If he can't get through, just tell him to keep trying until I answer.'

He barely heard his assistant respond before hanging up the call as he overtook a truck winding too slowly around the turns in the road.

'Sorry,' he said to Gabi, impossibly conscious of every jolt or movement to her and their precious cargo.

'I don't care,' she said, her lips resting on the superfine hair on Antonio's head. 'Do whatever you have to,' she commanded, and he hit the accelerator.

His neck ached from flicking his gaze from the road to the seat beside him, unable to stop himself from covering the hand Gabi had wrapped protectively around Antonio with his own, in between changing gear.

Nate counted down each painful, worrying minute until they pulled into the emergency room, abandoning the car in a doctors' parking space and running around to open the door for Gabi, while shouting for help.

He felt his phone vibrate where he'd shoved it into his top pocket, but ignored it as several staff members dressed either in scrubs or white coats came running.

Gabi hurled Spanish back and forth with the staff so quickly that all he could do was make space for the gurney they brought to them. Gabi looked up at him, torn between needing to share the information and wanting to translate for him, but he shook his head. 'Do what you have to.'

She nodded once and continued her conversation with who Nate had decided was the lead doctor. He stood back and looked down at his son's small body as people crowded around him, hooking up monitors and trying to flash a light in his eyes.

His chest ached as if someone had cleaved it in two and he didn't care that tears pressed against the backs of his eyes. His attention snapped to the entrance when he heard Jorge calling his name loudly and clearly above all the commotion. He turned and beckoned the young man, who looked both competent and scared for them at the same time.

Without a word, Nate opened his arms for Ana, who was crying and saying 'Papá!' over and over again. He held his daughter to his heart and tried to soothe her even though it felt as if the world was coming apart at his feet.

His phone buzzed again and he held Ana, kept his eyes glued to Antonio and Gabi and answered his phone.

'Nathanial.'

'Dr Brunner.'

'Where are you?'

'The hospital in Nerja, southern Spain.'

'Okay. Hold on.'

Nate heard muffled voices and tapping on a keyboard, thankful that the no-nonsense physician who had overseen his medical treatment was ruthlessly efficient and knew him well enough to understand what he needed.

'Your son is twenty months old, with a fever, abdominal stiffness and lethargy.'

'Yes.'

'Okay. The hospital you're in has an excellent reputation. Well-trained staff and no red flags.'

'But?' Nate demanded, sensing the other man's professional hesitation.

'I still want to send my colleague down to you. I trained with him and I'd have him care for my children if I had them.'

'Done.'

'Okay. I would, in no other circumstances, speculate with such limited information, but I want you to first know that this is not presenting as an aneurism—as I'm sure that's where your mind is going right now.'

Nate wanted to drop to his knees and weep. It was such a shocking sensation, he hardly noticed that Jorge pressed him into a chair beside the bed where they were assessing Antonio.

'It is probable that this is a UTI—a urinary tract infection—but I would like to speak to the physician when he has a moment to confirm his thoughts. I'm fluent in Spanish so the language won't be a problem. Do you have someone you can pass the phone to, until that happens?'

'Yes,' Nate said, clearing his throat, his mind half full of words of thanks, but mostly still full of fear.

'Go be a dad, let me be a doctor. I'll stay on the line until I speak to the treating physician and then I'll speak to you again and tell you what I know.'

Nate turned to Jorge, told him what Dr Brunner had asked, and entrusted the phone and the task to the young man and turned back to watching Gabi nodding and shaking her head, answering the multitude of questions the medics had for her.

Knowing that she was doing everything in her power to get Antonio the right treatment, Nate fixed his gaze on his son and willed him to be okay.

Shortly after they had been admitted, they were moved to a private room on a floor higher up in the building. It was spacious with a sofa where Gabi, Nate and Ana were huddled together and a chair that was alternately occupied by the housekeeper and Jorge.

At some point the head of paediatrics had come in with another doctor and spoken to both of them, along with a translator provided by the hospital so that they could both understand and so that Gabi didn't have to do it herself. Before they'd left, the doctors had asked for a word with Nate and Gabi had barely noticed, returning to her vigil beside Antonio. Jorge had offered to take Ana home if they'd wanted, but neither she nor Nate had wanted to be away from either of their children for even a moment.

By the time that she had been reassured that her son was in neither a critical condition nor likely to get worse, she checked her phone and saw the seventeen missed calls from her brother. Nate had encouraged her to call him back. She knew without a shadow of a doubt that Javier and Emily would be here in a heartbeat if they could, but they were currently in Sri Lanka.

It took nearly twenty minutes to convince them that there was no point coming back to Spain, and she was able to say with absolute conviction that she had all the support she needed in Nate. He'd been a rock, completely and utterly. And it was only when she put the phone back in her bag that she realised that he was still holding her free hand. It had been that way, off and on, for both of them since arriving at the hospital. A near constant need to touch, to know, to reassure and to seek assurance. Giving and taking passing between them like the ebb and flow of a tide, when needed and when able to provide.

She'd asked him if he wanted to call Hope, but Nate shook his head and explained that he'd wait until he knew they were home safely, not wanting to worry her. Gabi wanted to point out that that wasn't the reason to call his sister. It wasn't about sharing information, it was about sharing the burden, but she could see he would not welcome such advice, certainly not now.

Ana was asleep on his chest, tears clumping her long lashes together and still red-cheeked, but soothed enough to sleep. Antonio was hooked up to an IV bag of anti-biotics and monitors since the tests had come back and confirmed that he was suffering from a UTI. Nate had accepted the information with a grim nod and returned his focus to his son.

When Gabi had fretted that she'd done something wrong, that she should have seen it earlier, that she could have done something to prevent it, Nate had pulled her into his side and gently shushed her with reassurances. She had gone to him, used him, relied on him and he had been her strength. No, he hadn't taken away her fear, but he had weathered it with her, been there to lean on, to reassure her, to care for her. As he had promised to do on their wedding day.

She must have fallen asleep on Nate, because his arm was around her, gently waking her. 'Gabi, he's up.'

It took only seconds for her to regain her senses and spring to his side, but there he was, her son, a little red-cheeked and seemingly utterly furious with the IV fluids.

'The antibiotics work quickly with infections like these,' said a nurse, smiling. 'You should be able to take him home in a few hours.'

The relief Gabi felt was near euphoric. She looked to Nate beside her and saw exactly the same thing reflected in his gaze, felt the sudden and intense need to kiss him, to have that closeness with him, to draw that energy from him, but wavered. As if he'd sensed her thoughts, he pulled her gently to him and pressed his lips to the top of her head. She told herself it was enough. It had to be.

Three hours later, the housekeeper threw open the door for them and welcomed them home. Gabi was bone-deep tired and reluctant to let either Ana or Antonio out of her sight. But even she could see that she needed to let them sleep and standing in the doorway and watching them wouldn't help anyone.

Jorge had offered to stay in the room, just in case, and even Nate had been touched by the offer, but he was happy that the monitor was enough. He sent Jorge off to the pool house to get some much-needed rest and thanked the housekeeper for making dinner before she left for the night, sniffing and cooing about how happy she was that the little ones were home safe.

Gabi watched in awe as Nate handled everyone with perfect calm and patience, leading her out to their table beneath the bougainvillea, where neither he nor she seemed to have any appetite for the food their house-keeper had lovingly and carefully provided.

'You were amazing today,' she admitted, falling back against the chair with exhaustion.

'Me?' he scoffed. 'You were the one who talked to all the doctors, told them that they needed to diagnose Antonio and quickly. Christ, Gabi. You were incredible.'

She felt a blush rise to her cheeks. 'I couldn't have done it without you. I was terrified.'

'So was I,' he admitted.

'Really? You just seemed so in control.'

He huffed out a bitter laugh. 'I thought my world was ending.' He put a hand to his chest as if even now his heart needed soothing.

It struck her then that it hadn't been that long since he'd been in hospital himself. And she hesitated to ask, but then realised she wanted to know. Needed to know.

'Did it bring back bad memories for you?' she asked.

Nate looked at her, the gentle dusk falling around them a time for sharing intimacies and secrets. 'It brought back bad fears perhaps, rather than memories. I thought…' He seemed to waver. 'I thought that it might have been an aneurism, like mine.'

'Oh, Nate,' she cried, reaching for his hand across the table. 'I didn't even think,' she said, horrified that it hadn't crossed her mind.

He shook his head. 'My doctor told me that it was incredibly unlikely, but I spoke to the paediatric consultant at the hospital, who agreed that when things settle down we should think about getting both Ana and Antonio in for a scan, just in case.'

'Why wait?' she asked, not sure why they would.

'The diagnostic tests aren't pleasant, and they're young, it could be scary. But I agree, we need to know, just in case. If that's okay with you.' Nate deferred to her, knowing that he wouldn't do anything without her agreement.

Gabi nodded quickly and determinedly, but the clouds were still in her gaze. 'Still, that must have made this entire thing so much worse for you.'

Nate shrugged, trying to dismiss it, but he couldn't shake the image of Antonio limp in her arms. He'd genuinely thought for a moment that he might lose his son and feared it might have actually broken something in him.

He didn't talk about his feelings, he wasn't used to or even comfortable with sharing such things, but Gabi had been vulnerable with him. She had trusted him. Perhaps it was time for him to do the same.

'I hate hospitals. I *hate* them,' he said, surprising himself with the vehemence in his voice. 'The smell, the noise, the hushed whispers of considerate nursing staff and the brash booming voices of consultants whose jobs are so important they don't care who hears them. But it's the patients. It's quiet in some and loud and selfish in others, but it's all the same. Desperation. Regret,' he said with a shrug, as if he hadn't felt those things himself.

'Yes, there are successes, yes, there is hope and there are miracles performed almost daily, everything—from someone learning to breathe on their own to the all-clear from cancer. Bloody miracles, like me—being able to live again, despite a damn bomb going off in my head,' he said bitterly, knowing that he probably sounded like a madman, angry and ungrateful.

'But all those people, all those miracles, they don't really prepare you for the fact that your life has completely and utterly changed. It will never be the same. You might get used to it for a while, a new pattern, a new routine, cut out meat and dairy, stop drinking alcohol, get regular exercise, the pain will go eventually and you'll get used to it.'

The words were pouring out of him, from where he couldn't tell, otherwise he'd stop them. Because he couldn't see Gabi any more, he could only see a montage of the two years of his life following his collapse. 'People watching and assessing in case you have a relapse, in case you show symptoms of another aneurism, or my sister asking me questions that test my memory, as if she was making sure it wasn't damaged. My grandfather watching me as if I might still ruin his empire one day,' he said, gripping the edge of the table with white-knuckled fingers.

He barely registered that Gabi had come to sit beside him, but he felt her presence like a balm, pushing back some of the anger at the depth of his hurt.

'And me. Not knowing if and when it might happen again, despite the quarterly scans and check-ups. Doubting myself, wondering what if...'

'Did you ever speak to Hope about it?'

Nate shook his head.

'*We aren't weak, Nathanial. We don't have that luxury.*
The first time my grandfather said that to me was minutes
before my parents' funeral. And within two days my sister and I were shipped off to separate boarding schools,'
he said, shaking his head. 'I always suspected that he'd
done that on purpose. To toughen us up. The Harcourt
version of "big boys don't cry".'

And while he knew that the Swiss centre's counsellor
had tried to help him see how damaging that had been, it
hadn't really registered until now, how that mentality of
silence, of doing it alone, had cut him off from the support network that Gabi had managed to tentatively build
around her in her brother and sister-in-law.

His entire life, from the age of twelve onwards, had
been founded on the belief that you couldn't talk about
your feelings, you couldn't show emotion, that if you
hurt you hid it, learning only how to be a broken man.
Wasn't he still that?

'Some people,' he said, clearing the emotion from his
throat, 'when they recover from something like this, become daredevils, tempting fate and death, having escaped
it once. Others seem to double down on who and what
they were before.'

'And you?'

'Me? I don't know. I just don't know,' he admitted.

She reached out and gently loosened his fingers from
their grip on the table, threading her own through his,
her palm gently pressing against the back of his hand,
smaller, but somehow so much stronger.

'Your life changed in a single moment and nothing
you knew would be the same again. And now you are

putting one step in front of the other and looking for the right path to take,' she said.

He looked at her beneath the veil of darkness, the understanding in her eyes shining brighter than the night sky. 'Like you did? When you found out about the twins?' he realised.

She smiled. It wobbled a little, but it was there. 'Yes,' she admitted. 'Nothing stays the same, Nate.'

Her words were quiet in the unsettled air between them, and she wondered whether they sounded as prophetic to him as they did to her. She wished, so much, that things could have been different for him as a child. It sounded brutally cold and emotionally desolate. She hurt for him the same way that she'd hurt for herself—a soul-deep ache that only love could heal. But that kind of love took years to develop, she believed.

She inhaled deeply, letting the night air revive her, tuning in to the sounds and feel of it wrapping around her, suddenly aware of just how physically close she was to Nate, the heat of his body radiating out to dull the nip of cold on the gentle breeze.

She shivered, not from the drop in temperature but from awareness.

All those touches, throughout the day, earlier and now, they had slowly layered one over the other until she couldn't deny it. If she hadn't thought Nate was aware of it too, wanted it too, then she wouldn't have dared. But she felt it, that same heady intoxication that had urged her to follow him that night in the hotel, when she'd been so innocent and naïve. And yet, even now, knowing everything that would happen, and not just because of her babies, she would make the same decision all over again.

Because something connected her to this man, something primal, instinctive, otherworldly. Some part of her soul recognised him as if they had lived these lives before and would do so again.

The silence that built between them was steady but not uncomfortable. It was *expectant*. He gazed at her with such longing that it pulled at her pulse like the moon pulled the tide, drawing her to him with an unstoppable force that she couldn't fight, even if she'd wanted to.

Goosebumps scattered across her skin from where his thumb rubbed over the back of her hand. Such an innocent, simple touch, but one that had a seismic impact. Because he'd done it that night too. He'd laughed at himself and accused her of making him horny. She hadn't understood what he'd meant by that word, and had later looked it up to understand.

She'd been nervous when she'd got to his room, and he'd taken her onto the balcony and they'd talked beneath the stars, just like they had been doing the last few months, she realised with a sudden jolt. He'd eased her nerves and removed any kind of pressure. She'd told him she was leaving and he'd walked her to the door. He'd looked at her as if she were the world that he'd wait for, and that was why, instead of leaving that night, she'd turned into his arms and kissed him. She'd chosen to stay, not because she'd had a drink, not because her desires and herself were out of control, but because she'd known *him*.

'The last couple of years have changed us both, I think,' she said, finding the right words as she slowly stood from the seat, not quite letting go of his hand yet. 'And we aren't the same people we were that night.'

He looked up at her from the chair, his body seemingly relaxed, but she knew. She could see the line of tension that ran through his body, the sudden alertness, the watchfulness, a predator restrained only because he chose to be.

'This would change things again,' Nate warned.

'Everything changes all the time,' she informed him gently.

'But I need this not to change things,' he said, quietly but steadily. 'There's been too much—'

'Okay.'

'Okay?' he asked, as if trying to clarify what she wanted.

Gabi's lips curved into a sad smile in the darkness. She understood why he needed that sense of control, could see that he was trying to give her what he could. And for tonight, for now, that would be enough. Because she needed him. She needed something hot and passionate and real to surround her.

Antonio's illness had made her feel so cold, almost numb, and it had terrified her. So she was using Nate to make that disappear, to make her feel something again. Because when he touched her she felt *alive*, she felt beautiful and wanted and honoured, and tonight, of all nights, she needed those things.

'Take me to bed?' she asked and waited, breath held, to see what he would do. Seconds ticked by, minutes maybe, and she was about to give up...when he moved.

He leaned forward from the chair, not once taking his eyes from her, slowly, smoothly, bringing himself to his full height so that she had to crane her neck just to keep that connection.

He stared at her as if memorising this moment, as if half afraid that it might never happen again. Or was that her? she wondered. She gazed up at him, his broad shoulders filling out the white shirt that glowed in the moonlight, open at the chest so that she could see the dusting of hair that had delighted her that night.

Clouds shifted across the moon, his face a study in chiaroscuro as he closed the distance between them with a step. But it was when the clouds finally passed across the night sky that she saw what was in his gaze and her heart snapped.

In his eyes she saw nothing but raw hunger.

CHAPTER TEN

'TAKE ME TO BED?'

Gabi's question roared through his veins, hurtling at a speed that navigated his body in the space of a heartbeat. Longing. He felt it in every inch of his being. He had done all that he could to keep his distance from her. He'd stepped back at every moment he could have stepped forward, refusing to trespass over the line he'd drawn between them. But now Gabi was asking him to and he didn't have the strength to deny her.

She looked up at him, her dark hair streaming down her back in gentle curls, her eyes glowing like labradorite in the moonlight with a desire that was different to what they'd shared in the hotel.

Then it had been nervous, excited, *illicit*. At the time he'd thought it just spending the night with a stranger, but now he knew the real risk that she had taken that night and somehow that made it more precious to him.

He shoved thoughts of the past away. Gabi was right. They had changed, but he told himself that what they *had* didn't have to. It *could* stay the same, if he willed it so. Because he couldn't lose them.

He couldn't. He'd only just found them. His *family*.

Strangely, that didn't chasten his desire for Gabi, but increased it. *Mine*, he realised. A possessive passion caught fire, immolating him where he stood. He breathed through the flames, relishing the burn as he swallowed, knowing that Gabi was the only balm that could soothe him now. Because it was a fire that came from her.

Now, when he looked at her, there were no nerves, no hesitation, just raw desire and a hunger that matched his own.

She swayed towards him at the same time as he leaned towards her, his hands already moving—one to cup her neck beneath the waterfall of her hair, the other cradling her cheek, not so that he could angle her face to meet him, but just so that he could get his damn hands on her.

Home.

When his lips met hers his entire being both relaxed and tensed, an exquisite torque that spun his heart and his head in different directions. She opened her mouth to his on a sigh and he took full advantage, finally slipping the leash of his restraint.

More.

He wanted more. To feel more, to touch more, to taste more. He walked them backwards without breaking the kiss, not with a destination in mind but a need. A need to feel her pressed beneath his body—and the bedroom was too bloody far away.

She came to an abrupt stop as her back hit the French window lightly, the gentle glow of illumination from the living room outlining her with a halo of gold. There was no fear in her eyes, just that same spark of more. A dare, a challenge.

Show me what you've got, her eyes were saying.

Please, the whimper that fell into his mouth begged.

He let his hands trace her body, caress her curves, fist the skirts of the dress she'd changed into when they'd got back from the hospital. Memories from earlier clouded his gaze, but Gabi cupped his jaw and pulled his gaze back to hers.

'Stay with me. Stay here,' she commanded like a goddess he wanted to worship.

He nodded, placed a carnal kiss to her lips, his tongue prising her mouth open and plundering all she had within. His heart raced, pounding as if trying to escape his chest, his fingers flexed against her hips as he pulled her against his powerful erection. She gasped again and it felt like a craving on his tongue.

He reluctantly pulled back from the kiss, not because he wanted to, but because there was something he wanted more. His lips curved into a smile as he saw the momentary disappointment in her eyes until he pressed openmouthed kisses down the centre of her chest, his hands unable to resist the lure of her breasts, the perfect fit against his palms. His thumbs flicked over taut nipples and her body came alive beneath his, writhing with as of yet unsatisfied arousal.

He dropped to his knees as his hands reached her thighs, and his fingers ruched the material of her dress. Gabi's legs quivered and he heard the back of her head thunk gently against the glass. The thought of her naked and pressed up against that glass fired such an intense burst of need through his body that he missed a breath.

He looked up at her, meeting her gaze. She was biting her lip in a way that only increased his need for her.

'May I?' he asked, feeling the thrill of wicked desire catch light and the sparks in her eyes respond.

She nodded, a smile curving her lip from beneath the teeth that had it pinned. 'You may.'

That was all the permission he needed as he pulled her

panties down her hips, thighs and one foot after the other, before placing them in his trouser pocket. His thumbs massaged her hips, soothing the quivering juncture, and he inhaled slowly and deeply, wanting to know this moment for ever. He parted her restless legs gently, her folds carefully, but, unable to resist any longer, he pressed his mouth to her in the most intimate of kisses.

The moan of pleasure that Gabi made was the most erotic thing he'd ever heard in his life. He swept his tongue across wet heat, unable to stop himself from pressing his mouth deeper against her, his thumb teasing her entrance as he sucked at first gently, then more firmly, on her clitoris, drawing—as he'd wanted—gasps and pleas from her. The sound of her begging thrilled him, not because she was surrendering to him but because she had surrendered to her own pleasure.

He felt it come for her, the power of it thrilling him nearly as much as her, as she trembled and writhed and bucked beneath his mouth and hands, her moans utterly mindless now as she reached higher and higher, a peak that eluded her again and again until finally it found her.

Nate was her sexual awakening and her sexual undoing. All the seams and ties and stitches that had held her together since he was last with her flew apart, leaving her open and exposed to his every touch. It took for ever to gather the scattered pieces of herself back together again, her body pulsing to a rhythm that she had barely learned once, but remembered and had missed so very much.

She shivered, not from the cold but by the shocking sensitivity he had wrought from her, her legs trembling until Nate rose from the floor and swept her up in his arms, encasing her in a warmth and protection that made her feel safer than she had ever felt before in her life. Unconsciously, her hand rested against his heart, searching for the strong, powerful beat that soothed her own.

Quietly, they passed the twins' room and he wavered, as if unsure whether to take her to his room or hers. She reached to pull him into a kiss, easing the momentary confusion in his eyes and reigniting a hunger that hadn't yet been satiated for him. He shouldered her door open, closed it behind him with a gentle press of his heel, before crossing to the bed and laying her gently down.

He stood back, staring at her long and deep.

'You are so beautiful,' he whispered as if conscious of the sleeping twins across the hall.

His words warmed her cheeks, but it was his care for the twins that made her want him more. From the bed, she held out her hand and when he took it she pulled him down against her body, welcoming him with a kiss that was already on her lips.

Yes, she was still reeling from an orgasm so intense it was still humming through her body, but it hadn't soothed the craving for *him*. The need to feel *him*, deep within her. The need to know whether she had imagined how it had felt to be so deeply connected to him. Her legs shifted against his and she realised that they were still clothed.

She started tugging impatiently at his shirt and he laughed quietly, his hands coming to stall her fumblings and take over. Unable to look away from him even for a moment, their gazes locked as they slipped buttons from loops, shucked clothes over heads, casting them aside, until they faced each other, naked and wanting.

She might have been self-conscious if she hadn't been able to clearly read his desire for her in the red flush slashed across his cheekbones, the glittering in his gaze, the twitch in his fingers hanging at his sides as if restrained from reaching for what they wanted: *her*.

The power she felt in that moment, the power that he had given her, was near euphoric. The vulnerability he showed as he revealed his want for her shifted something in her heart that she forced aside for the moment. Because his desire reignited hers and she couldn't wait any longer.

They came together in the middle, a tangle of limbs and sighs and kisses and touches. Sensation skated across her skin, her heart beating loud and strong, and wanting more.

'Gabi, wait—'

'No,' she returned. She'd waited long enough. He couldn't make her wait any longer!

'Gabi…' He drew her name out in the air between them like a prayer, and only then did she reluctantly pull back from her exploration of his chest.

'Protection,' he whispered regretfully, and she realised that he probably didn't have any. They'd had no need of it before.

She bit her lip. 'I'm on the contraceptive pill. To regulate my periods after…' She trailed off, stupidly embarrassed despite the intimacy they were about to share. 'I was tested when I was pregnant, and everything came back negative, obviously,' she whispered, wanting the world to swallow her up.

His thumb lifted her chin, slowly raising her gaze to his. 'I've not been with anyone since you,' he confessed, her heart soaring shamelessly at his words. 'And we are about to share our bodies,' he whispered gently, 'which means that there is nothing you can tell me about yours that I would not want to hear.'

'Like cracked nipples,' she whispered to herself, remembering from before, and Nate threw his head back and laughed. She was so shocked by the sound it took her a moment before slapping him on the arm and shushing him, biting back the laughter that had sprung so beautifully between them.

This was what she'd remembered from their night together. This was what they had shared. Why was it that laughter had somehow brought them so much closer than passion? Why was it that which had forged such a deep connection? She had been devastated when it had been lost, broken apart by savage misunderstandings.

Nate collapsed beside her on the bed, unaware of the lump forming in her throat. One that she ruthlessly pushed aside as she leant back beside him, trying not to read too much into the way he pulled her against his side, the press of his erection still delicious to her.

She wanted to bury her head in the space between the mattress and his chest, to burrow down and hide, not her embarrassment—because he'd been right, they were about to share their bodies and there shouldn't be any. But to hide her love for him. Because she knew without a doubt that it would scare him away.

Just like it had scared so many other people in her life.

'Hey,' he said, pulling her face up to him, delighted as he placed a kiss against her lips. 'Where did you go?'

'Well, I got a little bored of waiting, so—'

Her words ended in a scream as his arms swept around her, pulling her to him, and he rolled her beneath him in one swift move, pinning her wrists beside her head.

'You're not going anywhere. I'm not letting you out of my sight ever again.'

Was it real? Could he really feel like that?

He kissed the column of her throat, his teeth gently nipping at her skin, sending shivers of pleasure across her chest and shoulders. Kisses turned to touches, turned to explorations and turned to sighs and moans of pleasure as his hands slipped between her legs and played with her some more.

Throbbing and wanton, she pulled him in for another drugging kiss, thrilled by the press and possession of his tongue in her mouth, the invasion only a suggestion of what he was capable of. And then finally, *finally*, he lay between her legs and guided himself into her, slowly, carefully, but so fully that she realised in a single breath what she'd been missing since she'd fled that hotel room.

The other half of herself.

Nate held himself deep within the heaven that was his wife—his *wife*—for as long as possible. Even when every instinct within him roared for more, he stayed there, making sure that Gabi acclimatised to the intrusion of him so deep within her.

He'd known she was a virgin before they had sex the first time and had done everything in his power to make that as pleasurable an experience for her as possible, but that had been more than two years ago. His only thought was for her—her comfort, her pleasure. His own release could wait.

But surrounded by the gentle grip of her muscles, skin to skin, his mind was a kaleidoscope of images of what he'd missed. Gabi round with their children, the flush of blooming health on her cheeks, all those firsts and all those joys…

She leaned to press a kiss against his forearm, anchoring him back in the present, and when he flexed his hips just slightly she threw back her head in bliss and all he wanted was more. She tucked her pelvis and gasped as he slid in just that little bit deeper, his arms beginning to shake with the pressure of restraint.

'I want it all, Nate. Please, can you give it to me?' she asked. And he cursed himself for making her beg.

He nuzzled the sensitive spot behind her ear and whispered, 'Anything you wish,' biting his teeth together before he could add, *my love.*

Urged on by her, each thrust took them to places he'd thought impossible to reach. He lost seconds, minutes, hours in the sounds of her gasps and pleasure, the racing of his heart tied to each slap of his body against hers, the slick and slide of their need so utterly erotic that he had never been so hard, half scared that he might remain there for ever in a near excruciating pleasure pain pinnacle, unable to cross the threshold of his orgasm.

Again and again, he forced them to the brink and back, an exquisite form of torture, desperate to make this last, desperate to make this perfect, desperate for her to feel him in her for hours, even days to come.

Pleas in a heady mix of Spanish and English filled the room, his name in a husky voice speaking of how much she had cried her need that night. Her fingers gripped him where she could, holding on or urging on, it didn't seem to matter. They were both shaking with the sheer force of holding back an orgasm that started deep within Gabi but ended with him.

They came together, pulsing and breaking in time to a rhythm that had been set nearly two and a half years ago, Nate inhaling as Gabi exhaled, creating an internal tide where she was the moon and he was the sea, destined to wash back and forth against a shore for ever, while a star-studded eternity looked on.

He pulled her close to him and rolled onto his back, unable and unwilling to break the connection between them just yet. His last thought before he closed his eyes was that she fit perfectly against him, as if she had been made for it.

Shocking pain tore through his head as he jerked awake, drenched in a cold sweat, heartbeat racing and body locked in tension so severe that he was paralysed. Forcing his reeling mind to focus, he could just make out Gabi's sleeping form on the other side of the bed. Thank God he hadn't woken her.

He sucked air in through his nose and waited for his muscles to relax enough to move, purposely trying to release each one consciously, despite knowing that no amount of willpower would work until the sleep paralysis passed from his body. Each second felt like its own infinity, each one showing him a new fresh hell of his own fears.

Something happening to his children, to Gabi, to Hope. The faces of his family, new and old, passed before him as if in some macabre reenactment of the old Dickens book, each seemingly warning of what had or could come to pass.

Fear spiralled and unwound, reforming into a new reel and starting all over again. Nausea gripped his stomach on the final fear…of two children mourning the death of their parents…and he lurched out of bed and was nearly sick.

He made it to the en suite bathroom without waking Gabi and he splashed cold water across his face, even while every single muscle in his body protested the pain and ache of the tension that had turned them into stone. His pulse raced, his breathing erratic, but he knew he had to calm down, he had to control his body. He had to.

He gave up using his hands and put his lips to the tap, sucking in mouthfuls of water to lose the acrid bite of nausea. He sank onto the floor beside the shower, the hard tiles cool but a blessed relief from the burning that had overtaken his body.

He wiped his mouth with the back of his hand, staring at nothing while his mind hurtled at a hundred miles an hour. The headache, the tension… He knew the odds of a recurrence of the cerebral aneurism were low, less even than a single percent, especially after the type of treatment he'd received. But they weren't non-existent.

Eventually, he hauled himself off the floor and peered back into the bedroom, where Gabi was still sleeping. A fist seemed to squeeze his aching gut, seeing how delicate she was, how wronged she'd been and how much better she deserved.

He closed his eyes and counted to ten. Sucking in a lungful of air, he turned on the shower, thankful that it was super quiet, quickly washed off the horror and fear from his body and, after drying himself thoroughly, he crept back into bed.

As if nothing had happened.

Gabi woke in an instant, her eyes springing open as her consciousness broke through the barrier of sleep. Bed. She was in her bed. A delicious ache threaded through muscles and skin that felt sensitised and warm but shivery too, even now, just from the memory of last night.

She pinned her bottom lip with her teeth, a lip that was slightly swollen and a chin that was just a little pinker, she'd imagine, than it had been yesterday. *Gracias a Dios!* Nate didn't have stubble. She was about to get up when an arm sneaked around her waist, pulling her back against a hot, hard body.

'Where do you think you're going?' Nate demanded in a voice thick with gravel and desire.

Gabi squeaked in surprise. It hadn't even crossed her

mind that he would still be here, half convinced she remembered waking last night and finding the bed empty, being disappointed that he'd not stayed with her. But it must have been a dream, a projection, because Nate was most definitely still here in bed with her. His skin was warm and smooth against hers, surrounding her in an almost blissful heat that she never wanted to leave.

She burrowed back against him, but when he shifted, sliding his knee between her legs, she felt the ridge of his arousal against her and unconsciously arched into him. His hands began to wander, smoothing over sensitive skin, her hips, between her legs, her breasts, all beginning to flush beneath his attention.

'Good morning,' he whispered in her ear, bringing a smile to her lips.

'Morning,' she whispered back, the word turning into a moan as he delved between her legs, seemingly very interested in the damp heat he found there.

'We shouldn't—'

'You have somewhere else you'd rather be?' he asked, half laughing, not stopping his exploration even a little.

'No, it's just that I should… I should wake the twins,' she said as her body shuddered beneath his touch. Her nipples hardened and her skin ached for more.

'Actually, Jorge and I are going to look after the twins today.'

'What about me?' she said around a gasp as Nate managed to hold onto the conversation as if he were not playing a sensually torturous game with her.

'You are going to spend some time with your sketchpad. Whether that's in your office or out in town, or at a coffee shop… Anywhere you need to be, our driver will take you.'

His hands fell back as she pulled away to turn and look at him. 'But—'

'No buts. We're starting again. And this time you are going to make sure that you are as much of a priority as they are.'

'And I'm doing this with a sketchpad?' she asked, confused.

'Yes, Hope wants to see six designs by the end of the month.'

'What?' she demanded, her body going stock still in shock.

'Yes, didn't I tell you?' Nate asked innocently, as if he didn't know.

She leaned across the bed, grabbed a pillow and tried to hit him with it. 'No, you didn't tell me!' Her task was made harder because he was behind her and using her own body as a shield, while laughing.

'Well, now I have. But right now I don't want to talk about my sister, Gabi,' he said, his tone suddenly serious and utterly sexy. He was looking at her as if he were starving and it wasn't for breakfast.

'The kids…' she tried again meekly, knowing that she wanted nothing more than for Nate to feast on her.

'The kids are still asleep and will be for at least another thirty minutes.'

'Thirty minutes?' she queried.

'I can do a lot in thirty minutes,' he replied, cocky and confident in a way that made her want to know exactly what he meant.

'Show me,' she commanded.

And he did.

Twice.

CHAPTER ELEVEN

GABI HAD RUN the gamut of emotions in the last month and it had left her exhausted…but so fulfilled. At first, she'd been utterly delighted with the idea of time to spend on her designs, and although she'd not actually been able to spend Antonio's first day home with her sketchpad as Nate had suggested—unwilling and unready to be away from her son just then—she did slowly begin to take time for herself. An hour here and there turned into two, then three.

But the first time she'd taken herself away to spend a full day on her work had been an utter disaster. Nothing had come. Well, nothing but self-doubt and negative thinking. She'd stared at a blank page, thinking, *Six designs…six designs for Harcourts' CEO*. It didn't matter that Hope was her sister-in-law, she just couldn't channel *anything* onto the page. In her mind, instead of the creative muse, she heard her mother's voice.

'*It's sweet that you try, mija. It means so much that you want to be involved in my business…*'

'*It's pretty, but it's just not* good. *I'm sorry.*'

'*I would make it in a heartbeat, Gabriella, but who would buy it?*'

Each one had cut a fresh wound over old scars and by the time she'd returned home she been a wreck. Nothing was worth feeling like this, not even her designs. She'd wanted to burn her sketchpad and had been ready to tear out the few new ideas she had forced out onto the page.

Nate had come to find her, watched her while she paced back and forth in the study.

'This was silly. A waste of time,' Gabi said, her thoughts still a jumble and feeling embarrassed. Why had she thought that she could even do it? Let alone produce six designs. 'I should be here with the kids,' she said and she meant it too. It had been a transition as gentle as it could have been, but she missed them when she wasn't with them, worried that they were missing her, worried that they saw it as a rejection. A rejection she knew so well.

She sat on the chair and put her head in her hands, pressing at her temples. It was all so much—too much of a mess. She should just stop. They'd give Jorge a good reference, he'd find more work in no time and she could come back to looking after the twins.

Nate leaned against the large drawing desk he'd fitted her office with.

'What happened?' he asked carefully.

'Nothing happened. Nothing at all!' she groaned, embarrassed to admit it. 'Look, I know you put a word in for me with Hope, but I think it was a mistake.'

'I didn't,' Nate said quietly. 'Hope has always been the one with an eye for fashion. I've always had a talent for numbers,' he said, shrugging. 'She came to me. But I'll let her know you're not interested.'

Gabi looked up. 'I *am* interested. Oh, God, I want it so much, Nate. But I'm just not good enough,' she admitted helplessly. 'I couldn't draw a thing today. Not a single thing. And the designs I do have are mediocre at best, bland. Just bad. Pathetic,' she ended on a whisper, knowing that the disdain in her voice was her mother's, not her own.

Nate squinted at her as if he could tell, as if he knew. 'Who told you that?'

'I don't need anyone to tell me that,' she said.

'Oh. So you told yourself that?'

She glared up at him, resenting what he was getting at. 'I don't want to do this right now,' she said, getting up, but he caught her by the wrist and gently pulled her in front of him.

'Who told you that?'

She shook her head, but still said, 'My mother.'

He nodded sadly, pushing a long, lazy twist of hair back from where it had hung over her shoulder. 'I'm sorry that she said those things to you. She shouldn't have.'

Gabi bit her lip, feeling hot, heavy tears press at the corners of her eyes. Nate cupped her jaw, his thumb smoothing over her cheekbone, and she couldn't help but lean against the warmth and comfort he was offering her.

'Can I say something that might hurt, but also might help?' he asked.

She bit her lip, unsure whether she could take any more hurt right now, but eventually she nodded.

'Your mother wasn't there today. She hasn't seen those designs. She didn't say those things to you. Those words were echoes of the fear you feel. That fear is stopping you from *enjoying* your creativity. If these designs go to my sister, great. If they don't, who cares?' he said with a shrug. 'But stifling your creativity, stopping yourself from doing something you *enjoy*? That's not okay. And you know that's not okay, because you would never allow your children to give in to their fears like this.'

Nate was right. She hated that he was, because it meant she had said those things to herself. But realising that it was her and not her mother meant that she could control what she said to herself, that maybe she could accept and move through that fear...

And *that* gave her power.

A power she used, bit by bit, the next day and the days that followed. She kept going back to her designs—they weren't always perfect, but she was persistent. And eventually she delved deeper and deeper into that inner core of creativity. She created designs *she* wanted to see and feel against her skin, textures and colours that were sometimes just functional, for a mother or a working woman, and other times daring, for a woman embracing and enjoying her sensuality.

Because if Nate had been determined for her to rediscover her creativity, then he was ruthless in his pursuit of her sensuality. Her nights were filled with passionate exploration and wondrous discovery of her own pleasure, and his. She could tell, she could sense it, that he had never been as connected to anyone as he was to her. Otherwise, there was no way that she could feel what she felt for him, surely.

Which was why she knew that there were times when he withdrew from her. An hour in an afternoon, two on the occasional morning. Sometimes she would wake to find the bed empty and he'd explain it away with an urgent meeting in a different time zone. There would always be an excuse. But she couldn't help feeling that, even as they drew closer, they were falling further apart. And even if she tried to tell herself it was nothing like Renata, that he wasn't manipulating her like her mother had, she couldn't help but feel that he was keeping something from her, and that was the one thing that could break them apart.

'Okay, Nathanial. You're booked in on the twelfth, the day after tomorrow, at three p.m.,' Dr Brunner confirmed.

'Okay,' was all Nate could say, finally having caved and called his neurologist.

'And is Gabi going to be joining us?'

Nate swallowed. 'Not this time.'

'Does she know?' Dr Brunner asked, as always more perceptive than anyone would credit. 'Have you told her?' he asked again in the midst of Nate's silence.

'I don't want to worry her,' Nate said, irritated with his own show of defensiveness.

'Nathanial, her support is a vital part of your recovery.'

'You call this a recovery, Doc?' Nate bit out through clenched teeth. In the last month, his headaches had become worse. His palpitations would come on at any time during the day. There was no rhyme or reason to the episodes and it had become near impossible to keep them from Gabi.

'We don't know what this is, it could be nothing to do with your medical history. That is why you should have her support.'

Nate felt the censure in the doctor's words, but Nate knew what he was doing. Gabi was just beginning to find her feet again after the confidence wobble at the beginning of the month. Nate trusted his sister's judgement implicitly and even if Hope hadn't insisted that Gabi's designs were excellent he'd have encouraged Gabi to follow her desires because, honestly, it seemed that absolutely no one had until now.

She deserved the time she now carved out for herself,

rather than utterly sacrificing her own wants and needs for her children or, worse, him. Which was why he didn't want to worry her. He had absolutely no doubt that she'd drop everything for him and he didn't want that.

He was more than capable of handling his episodes himself. He would have to make some decisions when the test results came back, he knew that. And he would. But, until then, he just wanted to enjoy this. One last day before he left for Switzerland.

He came to stand on the threshold of the patio. He looked out across the mountain range in the distance to where it fell into the sea. It was so very different from the sleek London skyline that could be seen from his apartment in Mayfair. In just months, his entire life had changed and, God, he was thankful for it.

He looked to where Gabi, in a turquoise and fuchsia striped swimsuit that showed off every single beautiful curve of her body, tried to smooth sunscreen over wriggling little bodies desperate to get into the pool. Ana's laughter filled the air as Antonio screamed just before a splash of water so great that it slapped against the hot tiles surrounding the pool. Clapping hands, truncated Spanish, giggles and the heat of the sun surrounded him as he closed his eyes.

Nate could have laughed. Until Gabi, his life had been entirely numbers and boardrooms, grey suits, white shirts and pleasures that he'd thought enough. But he'd had no idea. Gabi had brought a world of colour, emotion and feeling to him and what would he give her in return?

He clenched his jaw and the images and fears crashed through him, as if clouds had passed over the sun. The pain, the agony, of standing by his parents' grave, Hope's hand in his, beside a grandfather who had refused to permit even a single tear. A fist punched a hole in his gut as the past became his children's future and his heartbeat pounded painfully in his chest.

In his mind, it wasn't *him* that suffered in silence, but Antonio and Ana. It wasn't him who was cut from the gentle, loving home his parents had created and sent away to share a room with six other boys, and subjected daily to either the bullying of older children or the tight-lipped meanness of teachers, but his children. *They* were the ones who forced their hurts and hopes and love behind a stony façade because they were a vulnerability that could be exploited. *They* were the ones who learned that no one would come for them, that they had to do it alone, that they had to do everything alone.

A savage pain cut through his heart, so powerful he nearly gasped.

'*Estás bien?*' he heard Gabi ask through the rushing of blood in his ears. Forcing a smile to his face, he nodded and waved her off, slowly turning back into the house before making his way to the bathroom, where he closed the door and collapsed. The sooner he got to Switzerland the better.

Gabi checked her watch again, hating herself for it. Nate wasn't just a few hours late—he was a day late. A whole day. She'd left messages for him on his mobile, email. She'd even called his assistant, who had repeatedly assured her that he was passing on his messages. But she hadn't heard from him since he had left for his business meeting in London two days ago.

She was scared. Scared because he hadn't done this before. Scared because it made her question how well she knew him. Scared because it reminded her that she had been here before with him, nearly two and a half years ago now. Scared because she couldn't stop the avalanche of old fears of rejection and abandonment from crashing down over her head.

Gabi paced the room, unable to let out the growl of frustration coursing through her body. Pinpricks of fear and doubt covered her skin in a thousand cuts, and her body heat fluctuated between cold sweats and hot flushes. She couldn't do this again. She couldn't live like this— with another person who hid things from her, kept their feelings under a mask. She needed honesty, she needed truth. And she knew that Nate wasn't being truthful with her. But it was more than that. It was the twins.

That morning, trying to put the children down for their nap had been awful. Ana had refused to sleep without seeing Nate. She'd been utterly inconsolable. 'Where's Papá?' she'd asked again and again. 'I want Papá.' Nothing Gabi had done, or could have done, had stopped her tears. Cheeks painfully red from crying, dark brown eyes red-rimmed, hot and desolate, Gabi had only been able to rock her back and forth as Ana cried herself to sleep, wanting her father.

Gabi knew that she would never forget that moment. It had struck too close to home for her, for her own inner child, who had felt exactly that same pull, that same need. The need for a parent, for the comfort that only a parent could provide, only to discover that they would never come.

Gabi's breath sobbed in her chest as she came to a halt in front of the French windows of the villa. She'd barely survived the absence of her father and the absolute hysteria of growing up with someone who couldn't see beyond their own needs. And somehow, in one single moment, Nate had come to embody both things.

She couldn't do it. She couldn't do this to her children. She'd made him *promise* to be here. *Promise* to tell her what was going on. And he had failed that promise. Her heart was shattering at a painfully slow pace. It was as if she could feel each tiny piece breaking off as every second passed and he still wasn't here. She loved him. She had given herself to him. She had shared her children with him and he was gone.

A small part of her wondered whether this was too much. All she was feeling…was it too much, too soon? She needed space, time. She needed to hear what he had to say. But too many years of trauma and self-doubt crashed over her like a wave she struggled to surf. She was drowning in past hurts and gasping for breath, for a lifeline when there was none.

Her mobile rang, cutting into her thoughts, and she swung between relief and fear as she looked at the name. It was Hope.

'*Sí,*' she answered, forgetting her English for a moment.

'Oh, Gabi, isn't it wonderful news?'

Gabi's mind crashed to a halt, Hope's words both confusing and unexpected. But, before she could question her, Hope pressed on. 'It must be such a relief. I mean, I know the doctors have always said that the recovery would be up and down, but honestly! This time I could actually have cried. An all-clear. It's just fantastic.'

'Yes,' Gabi replied, forcing the words out through numb lips. 'It is.'

'I'm so glad I caught him, he'd just turned his phone back on after flying back from Switzerland, so he should

be with you soon. I just wanted to maybe add to the cel-
ebrations a little—'

Gabi was aware that she was making non-committal
noises, but her mind was racing as quickly as her heart.

'Because I've looked over the designs, Gabi, and they're
marvellous!'

'Thank you,' she said woodenly, not really sure what
Hope was talking about.

'Look, obviously now is not the time, but I wanted to
let you know as soon as I could, and I want you to think
about where you want to go from here. I'll call in a few
days to set up some proper, official time to talk, but in
the meantime, just know I love them and I want more!
Okay? Anyway, love you, bye.'

Gabi stood in the centre of the living room, the phone
hanging loosely in her hand, trying to process what she'd
just heard.

Nate hadn't been in London? He'd been in Switzerland? The doctors had given him the all-clear? So he'd
been worried about his health and not telling her? He'd
kept that from her and lied about where he'd been?

A white-hot blade cut through all the hurt and pain
she'd felt before Hope's call. All the doubt, the questions,
the agony…the love. All of it. Cut through, clean, and
now she felt nothing. Absolutely nothing.

In minutes she'd decided what to do. In less than half
an hour the twins, sleeping through the entire thing, were
on their way with Jorge to her brother and sister-in-law's
and by the time Nate walked through the front door she'd
packed everything that he'd need for the immediate future. If he didn't retrieve the rest of his belongings by the
end of the week, she'd burn them.

That was how cold her fury was.

In the past it was hot, hurt, devastated. But now she was older, now she had learned, *now* it was about ensuring that her children were treated better than she had been. And that made her focus as finely edged as any sword. Sharp, focused and determined.

Nate walked through the door, exhausted after an intense seventy-two hours. He'd barely had time to eat, let alone sleep or even make the call to Gabi that he'd known he should have. But what he wanted to say, he wanted to do in person. The last three days had changed everything for him and all he wanted to do was hold Gabi, kiss his children and...

As he walked into the living room he caught sight of Gabi, standing in the middle of the room, looking out through the open French windows.

'Gabi? Is everything okay?' he asked, a sudden rush of adrenaline sparking through already shorted circuits around his body.

She turned to look at him and all he could think was hollow. She looked hollow. Empty.

'What happened?' he demanded, rushing towards her, only stopping when she put up a hand between them.

She looked at him blankly for another second and then something strange came into her eyes.

She shrugged. 'Happened? Nothing happened, I don't think. Obviously, you would tell me if something had, no?'

Unease unwound like a thread from a spool, tying itself into knots and loops.

'No, I—'

'Nothing?' she asked. 'Nothing comes to mind?' she asked, her lips pursed, colour gone from her cheeks. 'Okay,' she said with a shrug, twisting her fingers together.

No. Not her fingers. Her wedding ring.

Dread pooled in his gut.

'Gabi—'

'My name is Gabriella. To you. Now—' she nodded as if to herself '—now it is Gabriella,' she confirmed firmly, twisting the ring from her finger and putting it down on the table.

She looked up at him, meeting his gaze, steady, but cold. And, no matter what had passed between them, Gabi had never been cold.

He didn't know what to say, he didn't know what the rules were in this situation. He didn't know where to start, because he wanted to tell her *everything*. He knew he'd made a mistake the moment he'd got the results from the doctors. He knew he shouldn't have kept her in the dark.

'I'm glad you're okay,' she said woodenly. 'I *am*,' she insisted. 'But you can go now.'

'What? Go?' he demanded, confused. Clearly, she knew about his trip to Switzerland and he could only imagine how terrible that must have made her feel, but—

'Yes. You can go now,' she said, slowly enunciating the words as if English were his second language.

'Gabi, stop.'

'I didn't ask you for much before we married, but I told you my terms. That you were present for the children until they were twenty-one and that you told me what was going on with you.'

Colour began to leach back into her cheeks, as if she were struggling to push back an immense anger and hurt. He could only imagine, because he knew how much he was feeling in that moment. He could feel his family slipping through his fingers. He'd spent so long trying to protect them from a pain that was in the future, he'd not realised how much damage he was causing in the present.

'Gabi, wait. I need to explain,' he said, dropping his bag on the floor and closing the distance between them. If he could explain, if he could just touch her, hold her, she'd let him.

She took a step back.

'What was it?' she demanded. 'Why did you go to see the doctors?' She glared at him, daring him to lie to her.

'I was getting migraines. Palpitations. Chest pains,' he confessed, his mind racing as quickly as his heart, hoping to see a way through this, other than the impending doom he felt himself hurtling towards. A doom entirely of his own making.

'For how long?'

He clenched his jaw, the muscles aching in protest. 'About a month.'

Gabi's hands fell to her sides and she let out the most painfully cynical laugh. 'That long?'

He wished he could deny it. He wished he'd done things differently, but he hadn't. And only now did he realise the cost.

'I asked you. Time and time again. How many lies have you told in that month? Twelve? Thirteen? No, it must be more than that. Once a day?'

Her voice was rising towards a shout and he looked to the corridor towards the children's bedroom.

'They're not here,' she explained, following his gaze. 'Jorge has taken them to Javier and Emily's.'

Anger and loss cut through him like lightning splitting a tree trunk, but he forced himself together with sheer brute strength. He inhaled slowly, knowing that she was watching his every move. But the moment he saw the sheen of tears in her eyes he decided, restraint be damned. He closed the distance between them, reaching for her arms, but she twisted from his grasp.

'Please, Gabi. I need to explain. I thought it was back. The aneurism. I thought—'

'I don't care.'

'I know that's not true,' he insisted. 'I know you care. It's the most important part of you, your heart. It's so big—'

'It's broken, Nate,' she said, interrupting him again. 'You broke it. You. Broke. It,' she repeated, each word punctuated by a sob that slashed across his heart.

The tears fell then, rolling down her cheeks, each one causing him more pain, one after the other.

'Our daughter cried herself to sleep today for you. For hours she cried for you.'

Her words twisted his heart into painful dimensions.

'So, no. There are no explanations, Nathanial. You lied. And I *knew*! I knew you were lying to me these past weeks. But we had an agreement, so I thought, no, surely he'd tell me if something was wrong. But you didn't.'

She looked up at him, as if pleading, wishing for him to tell her that it was all a mistake. That he hadn't done it.

'You made me question myself. You made me doubt myself and you made your children cry for you. So now, you go,' she said, pulling herself together.

'No,' he said, shaking his head, panic gripping him with a tighter fist than he'd ever felt. He couldn't leave her like this. He couldn't leave, knowing he'd made her feel those things. Why wasn't she letting him explain? If he could, then she'd understand, but she wasn't letting him.

'Don't make this harder than it needs to be,' she said.

'This deserves to be hard, Gabi. It shouldn't be easy

to do,' he said, realising the truth of the words as he said them. 'It should be absolutely the hardest thing ever,' he implored. 'This is our family, our children. It should take absolutely everything we have.'

'I've given everything,' she cried. 'I did. *Me*. But you? You kept it in, kept it all to yourself. Unwilling, or unable, it doesn't matter.'

'Of course it matters. But you won't let it, will you?' he said, finally catching on to what was going on, furious that nothing he could say would change things. 'Because I was never going to be good enough, was I? You were just waiting for me to fail—as a parent or a husband. And if it hadn't been this, it would have been something else, wouldn't it?' Nate demanded.

Gabi shook her head, refusing to accept what he was saying. That cool calm that she had needed to get this far was beginning to shatter. Too many emotions were breaking through while she was trying to hold onto the lifeline of control that she needed to survive this night.

'No. That's not true.'

'It is. I can't deny that I messed up, Gabi. I lied. I was scared. I thought...' He slammed his mouth shut, as if unable to bring himself to say what he'd thought might happen to him. What the migraines might have meant. 'But what you want from me? The perfection you need from me as a father? What you want from *yourself*? It is impossible. We're not perfect. We're going to make mistakes. And so are our children.'

Outrage slashed through her. 'Of course they're going to make mistakes. *They* don't have to be perfect.'

'But *we* do? *That* is the standard you are teaching your children. No matter what you say to them, it's what they will see,' he threw back at her. 'That they have to be perfect. That it's not okay to make mistakes.'

Anger and fear had her trembling from head to toe. 'The only mistake here, Nate, is you. Now, leave. Please. Right now.'

He levelled her with a look so full of hurt and anger, but she knew he saw exactly the same thing reflected in her eyes. He waited, as if hoping that she might change her mind, take back the angry, painful, bitter words, but she didn't. She couldn't. And it was only when the door slammed behind him that she collapsed to the floor, crying just like her daughter had only hours before, for the man who had broken her heart.

CHAPTER TWELVE

NATE STARED OUT across the town of Frigiliana from the hotel room's balcony, trying to pick out the villa where his wife and children were. The cost of the room had been extortionate but anything other than a hotel room spoke of a permanence he simply couldn't accept yet.

A banging sounded against the door and he half expected to see Gabi's brother, ready to tear him limb from limb, but it was worse. It was his sister.

'What the hell do you think you're doing?' Hope demanded as she barged through the door. 'I mean, I'm glad you're okay,' she continued, looking up at him with genuinely sorrowful eyes. 'I'm glad you're not going to die,' she said, reaching for his shoulder, smoothing the sleeve of his shirt, before shoving at him and saying, 'but I could kill you right now.'

Then she stalked into the living area without sparing it a glance and turned, pinning him with a look. 'Is Gabi okay? I'm so sorry. I shouldn't have called her and said... all that. But why didn't you tell her?' she demanded. 'Why didn't you tell *me*?'

'Are *you* okay?' he demanded of his sister who, even for her, was acting...

'Oh, it's the hormones,' she confessed miserably, and

Nate felt like a bastard. He'd completely forgotten that his sister and Luca were going through IVF.

'Hope—'

'Oh, God, don't you start. It's fine. *I'm fine*,' she yelled over Nate's shoulder to Luca, who was coming through the door with their bags.

'Is she?' Nate demanded under his breath.

'She's fine,' Luca explained with a raised eyebrow, warning Nate not to question it.

'Look, it's great to see you, but now's really not a good time,' he said, wondering how quickly he could get them back out of the hotel as he eyed several suitcases beside Luca, who was looking around the chaos of the suite.

'Nice place you have here,' he observed wryly.

Nate closed his eyes and put his fingers to his temples in an attempt to ward off the tension headache—that he now knew was *just* a tension headache.

'It's stress,' Dr Brunner had explained. *'You've experienced a huge amount of life-altering information in—what? Two months? Less? And before that, Nate, you nearly died. These things are as serious as it gets. And if you want to live—if you truly want to live—then you're going to have to deal with the things that are holding you back.'*

'Are you even listening to me?' Hope demanded.

'No, Hope, I wasn't,' he admitted with fraying patience. He knew his sister meant well, but he hadn't intended for her to fly out to Spain when she'd caught him at a bad moment the day before and he'd admitted half of what had happened. Only half, because he couldn't even really admit it to himself just how badly he'd messed everything up.

'Come on,' Luca said, clapping him on the shoulder and walking him into the living area, casting a disdainful glance at the mess that Nate had created in just a few days. Nate tried to ignore the look Luca shared with his wife, before gesturing to the large balcony.

Hope opened the balcony door, letting both fresh air and the gentle sounds of the night into the room and, despite himself, Nate took the deepest breath he had since he'd left his home.

Gabi's home, he thought as the knife slashed his heart in two all over again.

Luca half pressed Nate into a chair and Hope sat opposite him, holding her hand out for him to take. Nate stared at it for a moment. The affection between them as siblings had always been fierce but not demonstrative. She waited and finally Nate put his hand in hers.

'Tell me. From the beginning. Tell me everything,' she demanded.

And, for the first time in Nate's entire life, he did.

Three hours later, Hope scrunched a tissue in her hands, her lip pinned beneath her teeth as if trying to stop herself from saying something Nate should probably already know himself. Coffee cups and water glasses had piled up on the table as Hope and the husband who adored her had listened to every word he'd said. Nate could see so clearly now how Luca focused on Hope and her needs, how he filled the gaping hole caused by the loss of their parents and by the emotionally stunted childhood they'd had afterwards.

Just like Gabi had for him. Just from her presence, her laughter, her awareness of him, slowly, layer upon layer, that same hole in Nate had begun to fill. The small things she had done for him to bring him into their lives, the trust she had placed in him by sharing her children with him.

The trust he had broken.

'Nate, I know that you were scared,' Hope said, holding his hand again, 'But you can't just shut down because you're scared of losing them. It's the one way to guarantee it.'

Nate frowned, disconcerted that she had so misunderstood what he'd been feeling. 'I'm not scared of losing *them*,' he said. 'Because *they* would be okay.' He shrugged. 'And that's all that matters,' he said simply. 'I'm scared of *them* losing *me*, Hope. Of them losing me and Gabi. I'm scared, terrified, absolutely bloody demented at the thought that Ana and Antonio will go through anything remotely like what happened to *us*,' he confessed helplessly, turning away from the realisation dawning in his sister's eyes.

Realisation that morphed immediately into sympathy.

Grief as fresh and raw as it had been all those years ago punched a hole in his chest. A grief for what had been, for what could be, for his children…it was too much. His hands fisted, white knuckles revealing far too much about how close he was to breaking.

'When the migraines started and I thought it was another aneurism, all I could see was us, each standing behind a coffin. I didn't even know if it was Mum or Dad,' he said, the sadness, the anger, the fear choking him. 'I can't… What if I did that to them? To Ana and Antonio. What if they—'

He couldn't finish. His words got stuck around grief and pain and loss and he couldn't speak for trying to keep back the tears he'd never been allowed to cry.

Hope's tears were falling and he was almost envious of her ability to shed them so freely.

'Okay,' she said, slowly gathering herself. 'Okay. If

something happened—*if*, then they have something we didn't, Nate.'

He looked up, wondering what on earth she was talking about.

'They have a family who love them and would do anything for them. They have me and Luca. And they have Javier and Emily. They have cousins, and while they might not have grandparents—or a reasonable version of one—there is an army of love around them and people willing to care and protect them for the rest of their lives. You and Gabi, you have given that to them. They will never be alone. They will never be cold. They will never be afraid of expressing their feelings. They will never be afraid to experiment, to learn, and they will never be afraid to love. Because *that* is the family you and Gabi are creating for them.'

'Not that they're going to lose you for a very, *very* long time,' she was quick to go on. 'Did you say any of this to Gabi?' Hope asked gently.

'I couldn't. She wouldn't let me. I know I messed up. I know I should have told her about going to Switzerland, about what I was feeling, *fearing*, but I needed to know first. I needed to know so I could manage it.'

'You can't keep that to yourself, Nate, not after everything she's been through with her parents.'

'I know that…now,' he confessed, hating that his own fear had damaged so much, not only his past but his present and maybe even his future.

'So, what are you going to do about it?' Hope half demanded, as if it were a call to arms.

Nate clenched his jaw. He knew what he wanted to do and knew what he *needed* to do. He had given her space, hoping that they might find their way back to each other.

But throughout Gabi's life she had been let down, time and time again. No one had fought for her in the way that she deserved, no one had sacrificed anything for her.

So now it was time to prove just how much he loved her. In front of the world, if he had to.

'Now, I'm going to get her back.'

Gabi gently rocked Ana in her arms, trying to get her to sleep. Antonio was inconsolable, he wore his heart on his sleeve, in his tears, and in his words. But it was Ana she worried about. She'd been much quieter since Nate had left and Gabi would catch her looking for him when she thought Gabi wasn't watching.

It broke her heart every time.

For the hundredth time that day, Gabi wiped at her own tears. She honestly didn't remember crying this much before and for some reason she couldn't stop. She'd thought she'd been doing the right thing when she'd forced Nate away. She'd thought she'd been protecting herself and safeguarding her children against a parent who lied, shut down, who refused to share himself emotionally or truthfully...but it didn't feel right.

And it hurt so, so much.

She and her daughter exhaled a slow breath of air at the same time and Gabi slowly walked over to the French windows, looking out, not at the starry night sky but with memories of their last argument.

'I was never going to be good enough, was I? You were just waiting for me to fail.'

As dusk fell over the mountain range in the distance, Gabi forced herself to feel through the fear and hurt she'd experienced that day. Because the one thing Nate *had* been right about was that it should be hard. It should be difficult to break their family up. Because that was what they had become, even in such a short time. So, after gently and quietly putting her daughter to bed, she went to the kitchen, poured herself a glass of white Rioja and went outside with the baby monitor and asked herself that same question.

Had she been waiting for him to fail?

Guilt and shame unfurled slowly in her breast, enough for her to know that what she'd done wasn't sitting right with her. It wasn't that she'd been waiting for him to fail, she thought, looking into the deepest part of her soul, but that she'd been waiting for him to leave. And she'd maybe thought, somewhere irrational and hurt and craven, that if she pushed him before he left himself it wouldn't hurt so much. Her throat was thick and ached with painful emotions and she reached for the glass to wash it down with a wine she couldn't taste and didn't want.

The sound of the front door opening yanked on her heart as she thought for just a second that Nate had come back. She turned, and nearly burst into tears to see Javier and Emily with her child wrapped tightly against her chest.

'Oh, sweetheart,' Emily said, coming straight out to the patio and bending awkwardly to wrap her arms around Gabi's neck. 'It will be okay.' Emily hushed and shushed, like she would have done for her own sleeping child, who was utterly oblivious to her aunt's turmoil.

Giving up the fight, Gabi let the tears fall again, her eyes hot and heavy. 'I'm so sorry,' she said, and couldn't help saying it over and over again.

'You don't have anything to apologise for, Gabi,' her brother insisted, and even through her own misery she could hear the clear upset in his own voice.

'What is it that you think you have done that is so terrible?' Emily asked gently, sitting down slowly in the chair beside her, mindful of her sleeping child.

Gabi searched for the words. 'I kicked him out.'

'Ha,' Javier barked a quiet laugh. 'I'd like to have seen that.'

Emily slapped her husband on the arm.

'No, seriously,' Javier replied, dismissing her concern with a wave of his hand. 'I'm sure his ego could do with a little stepping on every now and then.'

'No,' Gabi insisted, shaking her head. 'I said terrible things.'

'Did he deserve them?' Emily asked.

'Well, yes…maybe?' Gabi said.

'What did he do?' Javier growled.

'He lied to me. He…he thought he might be sick and he didn't tell me.'

'He was secretive?' Emily asked, while her husband was surprisingly quiet and shamefaced.

'*Sí.*'

'And it hurt you?'

'*Sí,*' Gabi replied.

'Well, then he deserved it,' Emily proclaimed. 'Did he say *why* he kept it from you?' she asked.

Gabi looked down at her hands, twisting in her lap. 'I didn't give him a chance.'

'Because?' her brother asked, even though she could see that he already knew the answer.

'Because I was afraid that he'd talk his way out of it.'

'Like Renata,' he concluded, looking down at the table, the muscle at his jaw pulsing as he clenched his teeth.

Gabi nodded, biting her lip. Her head hurt, her eyes were sore and her heart ached as if it would never not ache again, and she just couldn't understand what her sister-in-law was talking about.

'Our mother,' Javier started slowly, 'was no mother at all,' he said, the anger burning in his eyes strong enough to last for years. 'I know how much it means for you to have the truth, to know what is going on around you, to understand the reality of it,' he said, his words working into Gabi's heart. 'But Renata's lies were ones of pure selfishness. Might it have been that Nathanial was trying to protect you?'

'You're defending him?' Gabi asked, surprised.

Javier shook his head. 'But…sometimes lies are accidental,' he said, sharing a look with his wife that Gabi couldn't quite decipher. 'It will be okay,' her brother reassured her, returning his attention to Gabi.

'How can you say that?' Gabi asked hopelessly.

'Because he loves you,' he said simply. 'Emily knows it, *his* sister knows it…*mierda*, even *I* know it. We're just all waiting for you to know it.'

Hope unfurled deep within her heart. 'But he lied,' her fears made her protest for the last time.

'Do you think he'd do it again?' Emily asked.

'I…'

Gabi realised she hadn't even considered that. She'd drawn a line right through the mistake he'd made, not even stopping to question whether he'd learn from it. Because she had been so determined to be perfect. She'd needed to be different to her mother. She'd needed her children to have a parent, *parents*, who would be… Perfect.

'We're not perfect. We're going to make mistakes…'

Her hand shook as she pressed her fingers against her lips. 'I think I've made a terrible mistake.'

'Nothing that can't be fixed in time, *mi amor*,' her brother insisted.

Buenas tardes. I'm leaving a message for Ms Gabriella Casas. Your mother's trial has resumed and we request your presence to give witness testimony on 20th September. Please call Señor Torres to confirm.

Gabi made her way up the steps of the courthouse, with Emily and Javier by her side. They'd argued about it, but Javier had finally won when he'd told her that he'd not let her face Renata alone ever again. She'd also lost the argument about bringing the children, as Jorge was visiting his mother after a particularly bad fall and Emily and Javier had insisted they would be fine.

She had wanted to call Nate for days now, but Emily had told her to leave it a bit longer. Uncomfortable with the idea of 'letting him sweat', as Emily had said, Gabi had decided that once her mother's trial was done, she would find Nate and ask him to come home.

That thought was the only thing keeping her going as she entered the courtroom with her family behind her and they were ushered into seats at the back. But when she looked up she thought she was imagining things, because there, back on the witness stand, was Nate, looking just about as handsome as she'd ever seen him.

He looked towards her, his eyes blazing with so much emotion she felt indelibly marked by it, his gaze flickering between her and the children, and her heart nearly burst from wanting to go to him.

Then he turned to look at her brother and they seemed to exchange a brief nod, and Nate turned back to the court. Gabi glared at her brother, suspicions of their collusion forming amidst her confusion, but nothing that soothed the racing of her pulse.

Nate ignored Renata Casas and now that Gabi and his family were all here he turned his attention back to the lawyer. His pulse was pounding in his chest and for the first time in ages he wasn't scared that it was some kind of medical emergency. He simply recognised it for what it was.

The love he felt for his wife and children.

'You've requested to add to your original statement, Mr Harcourt. Is that correct?'

'Yes.' He nodded.

'And why is that?'

'Since I was last here, certain things have changed and I'm aware of the plaintiff's ability to distort facts to suit her needs, so I would like the chance to set the record straight.'

The translator beside him started speaking midway through the lawyer's objection.

'This is highly unusual, your honour.'

'As is the plaintiff's miraculous recovery,' the judge sighed, deciding to overrule the objection. 'Proceed.'

'Two months ago, I was lucky enough to have Gabriella Casas agree to be my wife. She is the mother of my children and the love of my life,' he said, staring right at Gabriella. 'And I know that Renata will try to use this to make it seem that my wife and I are trying to get rid of her and steal her business. We are not. But to make sure that she cannot use any more lies against us, I want to let the court know that I have returned my shares in

Casas Textiles to Gael Casas, Renata's brother. For the price of one euro.'

A gasp of shock went through the courtroom, none so loud as the cry of outrage from Renata herself, but he only had eyes for Gabi.

'In fact, it is not the only business I have shed recently. I have resigned from my position at Harcourts and sold two of the three remaining businesses that I own,' Nate explained into the small microphone on the desk.

'Is there a reason for this?' the lawyer asked.

'Yes. Two and a half years ago, I had a cerebral aneurism that ruptured, leading me to require surgery and intense rehabilitation.'

Another gasp went through the spectators and he saw the shock and surprise streak across Gabi's expressive features and he willed her to understand.

'Why are you telling us this?'

'Because Renata Casas uses lies and secrets against people and I no longer want to live with such things in my life. My wife showed me that I don't *need* to. She is the strongest, truest person I know and I don't deserve her,' he admitted, throwing himself wide open. 'Despite the damage done by Renata Casas, she is the most loving, caring mother, fiercer than any lioness, and the most incredible wife any man could ever ask for,' he said, hoping that she was hearing him, truly hearing him. 'And she will not be giving evidence here today, will she, Ms Casas?'

Nate glared at a furious Renata. Red-cheeked, bitter-eyed, teeth gritted, she slowly nodded.

'For the record, Ms Casas?' the judge demanded.

'No. She does not. I am changing my plea to guilty and…throwing myself on the court's mercy.'

Each word seemed to get stuck in her throat, but Nate didn't care. Their agreement had stipulated the specific wording she would use in court, and Nate knew without a doubt that this would hurt her more than any incarceration or financial punishment.

Yes, he had paid Renata a considerable amount of money, but his lawyers had drawn up an airtight agreement that would ensure Renata never darkened her daughter's door, or those of her grandchildren, ever again, for any reason.

By this point the courtroom was in uproar. Journalists' cameras were flashing away, the judge was yelling, Renata was staring daggers at him and he didn't care. He swept down from the stand, his eyes, his entire focus and being were only on Gabi.

He found her despite the chaos, cutting through the throng of people who had risen up to try to catch a glimpse of a cowed Renata Casas. He reached for Gabi as she came to him and the sense of relief poured over the wounds from the past weeks and years.

'I'm sorry,' he said the moment his hands were on hers. 'I didn't say that before. And it should have been the first thing out of my mouth. I am so truly sorry,' he repeated, feeling the rent in his heart that had opened not just that day, but many, many years before. His heart broke anew when he saw a tear fall down her cheek. 'I was scared,' he admitted. 'Terrified. The migraines to me meant that my aneurism was back and I couldn't see past the future I was giving Ana and Antonio. A future full of grief and devastation.'

Gabi's eyes became full of pity and sorrow and she opened her mouth as if to say something, but couldn't, and he was thankful. Because he wasn't finished.

'I was so damaged by the loss of my parents and the years that followed, I couldn't see past my own pain. I couldn't see what withholding that from you would do to you,' he said as he came to within barely a foot from where she stood, her body heat reaching him. 'This is not an excuse,' he said, wanting so much to reach for her. 'But I want you to know that I understand that my pain made me selfish and I will never forgive myself for hurting you the way that I did.'

Her gaze became one of longing, sadness, but also something that gave him the hope he desperately needed at that point.

'You should *never* have had to question either yourself or my feelings for you, my *love* for you. And if you give me a chance, you never will again. I know I will make mistakes. This is new and strange and talking about my feelings is awkward and deeply uncomfortable, but I want to do it for you. I want to do it for us. I want to do it for our children. Because I don't want them to become what I was... What I was before I met you.'

He broke off, searching her gaze.

'I love you,' he said. 'And I want to say it again already. I want to tell you over and over and over again. I want to say those words for the rest of my life,' he admitted, feeling the sheen of tears that he'd never had the courage to shed...until now.

Gabi startled, realising the strength of his feelings, reaching up to wipe the single tear that had escaped from Nate's eye.

'Oh, Nate, it's me that's sorry. From the moment you left, I knew I was wrong.'

'You weren't,' Nate insisted, and she smiled, wondering at the two of them arguing over such a thing.

Love swelled so much in her heart she thought it would burst but, to her astonishment, it simply grew, the muscles around it becoming bigger, stretching further to make space for all the love that she felt for Nate, for her family.

'I should have let you explain. But I was scared too. I was scared to trust in the love I felt for you and the love I felt from you,' she admitted. 'And I thought that it was easier to push you away than take the risk you might leave like my father, or not even love me, like my mother.'

'I will never let you question such a thing ever again,' he vowed, and she believed him.

'But you told them, you told the *world*, about your aneurism,' she said, shocked.

'I have no need for secrets any more,' he insisted. 'My only weakness, my only vulnerability, is you and our children,' he swore.

'And your businesses?' she asked, as if he were utterly out of his mind. 'Are you sure?'

'Absolutely. Because I know what I want from life. And that's you and Ana and Antonio. If that's as your husband, then…' He clenched his jaw before releasing it. 'Oh, God, I would love that more than the world. But if not, then I will be here as their father.'

Gabi suddenly realised that she'd not told him, not said the words that were tattooed on her heart from the very first moment she'd seen him.

'I love you,' she said, reaching up to pull him in to a hungry kiss. 'I love you so much,' she said against his lips.

For just a moment they were lost in the passion that always simmered just beneath the surface between them, until someone jostled them hard and they remembered where they were. Gabi felt a pull on her dress and found Ana careening into her arms from a slightly harassed and apologetic-looking Emily.

Glancing back to see that Javier had a firm hold on Antonio, she raised her child in her arms, but Ana only had eyes for Nate.

'Papá?' she said in such a hopeful voice that Gabi nearly burst into tears all over again.

Nate reached for her, and she went to him immediately.

'Papá!' Ana cried again, her eyes beginning to fill with tears. 'Papa here,' she said to Gabi, and this time she let the tears fall down her cheeks as her daughter looked between both of her parents and clapped, happy for the first time since Nate had left.

Nate gazed at Gabi, all the love shining in his eyes for her, for their children, and she knew that they would be okay, finally beginning to understand that marriage, love, wasn't about being perfect and achieving excellence. It was about messing up and learning about each other and about themselves, and it was about loving and accepting all the parts that came in between. That there would be arguments to come and disagreements and maybe even battles, but they would survive them all if they loved each other and relied on all the support they could get.

'Papá no go,' Ana ordered. 'No go,' she said again.

'I'm not leaving,' Nate swore, there and then. 'I'm never going anywhere without you again. Without *any* of you,' he said, staring into his wife's eyes, knowing that this time when he saw the future for his family it was filled with nothing but love.

EPILOGUE

'I DON'T LIKE IT. We're completely outnumbered,' Javier complained.

'The odds are not in our favour,' Luca agreed gravely.

'But they're just girls,' Antonio replied, before the men turned on him with a 'Woah,' a 'Hold on a minute', and a 'Don't let your mother hear you talking like that!'

Nate pulled his nearly teenage son into his side by his shoulders. 'Come here, I want to show you something.' He led his son out onto the balcony of the house located just outside of Málaga.

Four years ago, the three families had come together to buy a house big enough for all of them to get together in the summertime, or over the winter school breaks. It had become Nate's second favourite place in the world, after the home he shared with his wife and children.

Beyond the balcony, Nate and Antonio could see down into the garden, to the table where the women had gathered together to form their own plan of attack.

'What do you see?' he asked his son, pride beating fiercely in his chest, not only for his wife and daughter, but his sisters—by blood and marriage—and his nieces. *Family.* That was what *he* saw, but what he wanted Antonio to see was something different.

'They have a map.'

'Yes, they do. Which means that...'

'They have a plan.'

'Yes, they do,' Nate agreed.

'They're clever,' Antonio concluded. 'Sneaky. Ana will probably be the worst.'

'Or the best,' Nate countered.

'So, I should take her out first?' Antonio looked up at his father for approval.

'So you should not, ever, underestimate the women of this family, or any other woman, for that matter,' Nate chided. 'But yes, you should probably try and get Ana out of the game first,' he agreed.

Luca threw his head back and laughed.

'I don't know what you think is so funny. You probably have the most expertise here and you're being the least help!' Javier growled harmlessly.

'We all decided that it was only fair if I do what I'm told, rather than take any tactical role.'

'But Papá, if we're not supposed to underestimate women, then why can't we have Uncle Luca's help?' asked Antonio.

'He's got a point,' Nate admitted.

'No time,' Javier called as the large clock on the games room wall ticked down. 'We're a go!'

Everyone grabbed their water pistols and fanned out and for the next hour and a half the annual water fight consumed everyone's thoughts.

Well, mostly everyone's. The second Nate had seen his wife trying to sneak past the pergola, he'd swept her up in his arms and drew her back around the side of the house. He moved the hand he'd placed over her mouth and covered her lips with his. What he'd intended to be a fun, momentary distraction turned carnal almost instantly—as it always did, the feel of his wife beneath his hands and mouth intoxicating and addictive. His feelings for her hadn't lessened over the years but increased. There were a few grey streaks in her hair, as there were in his, but it only made her look more beautiful to him.

'Nate,' she managed, slapping him on the arm as he abandoned her mouth to kiss his way down her neck, his hands wandering to her skirts, even as she slapped them away. 'PG Thirteen,' she warned, as conscious of the family that surrounded them as he was.

'Okay,' Nate grumbled in agreement. 'Above the neckline,' he groused, returning his lips to hers.

They smiled as they heard shrieks and cries coming from the kids—and even some of the adults, everyone enjoying the yearly competition that had grown innocently enough from a disagreement between Emily and Javier that had ended in a water fight much smaller than the one currently being waged.

Gabi moaned into Nate's mouth and he'd never tire of hearing the sound, the effect on him instantaneous.

'Let's go back to our room,' he said, trying to entice her away from the fun.

'Mmm… So tempting,' she said, and he knew she meant it. He could see it in her eyes. 'But you'll have to wait—we have a war to win,' she said, just before she brought up the water pistol and sprayed him in the chest.

Laughing, she spun out of his hold and ran back out into the garden with an impressive war cry, and he thought he'd never loved her more than in that moment. He'd never not be grateful for her capacity for forgiveness, knowing that he'd come so close to not having this in his life, not only once but twice, and he had absolutely no intention of pushing it to a third time.

He hung back at the corner of the estate, watching arcs of water jet through the air, creating rainbows nearly everywhere he looked. Hope and Luca had joined forces against their two children, Felicity and Bella, and on the other side of the garden Emily had just pushed Javier into the pool, much to the delight of Lily, their one and only daughter but the light and love of their lives.

But it was Gabi on whom his gaze anchored, taking on both of their children at once. Ana and Antonio combining their forces was a sight that would always bring joy and peace to their parents' hearts.

At night they would all come together around the table and share meals, drinks, stories and even sometimes songs. Javier, always with his arm around Emily's shoulders and a smile for his daughter. Luca, his girls in his arms and his heart in his eyes for Hope. This was what Gabi had brought to him. A family, full of joy and love, in ways he never would have imagined years before.

He'd never, not even once, regretted scaling back his businesses and instead, as the children had got older and gone to school and his time had become more free, he'd focused instead on the charity work he'd begun with Luca and Javier.

He'd watched in awe as Gabi had embraced her creativity and, rather than selling her designs to Harcourts, had joined with Hope and another woman, Sofia Obeid, to start a small but immensely successful fashion brand. Seeing her negotiate herself as a designer, a business owner, a mother, a sister, a friend…it had been a pleasure for him, and an important lesson for their children. One that he was watching have a direct impact on them as they grew into the young teenagers they were becoming.

And in his later years he'd be able to look back and

know that he'd lived up to his promise—that his children hadn't had the same cold, isolated childhood that he and his sister had. That the love that Gabi had drawn from him had bloomed and grown into a garden that many future generations would benefit from. But nothing meant more to him than the love of his wife, his heart, his other half: Gabriella Harcourt.

* * * * *

THE SECRET OF THEIR BILLION-DOLLAR BABY

DANI COLLINS

MILLS & BOON

For my wonderful editor Laurie Johnson,
who surrogates my manuscript into a finished book.
Thank you for all you do.

PROLOGUE

HER HAND FELT as though her bones were being crushed against themselves. The pain was acute enough to drag Alexandra Zamos toward consciousness, but she didn't want to come back through the door into reality. That's all reality was: pain.

She fluttered her eyes open and saw her stepfather. He was the one crushing her hand. Typical. One way or another, he was always trying to maintain a cruel hold on her.

A sob of repulsion rose weakly in her throat as she tried to pull away from his grip.

"She's awake! Nurse!" Her mother's voice grew distant as her heels clicked away.

That was also typical. Winnifred Humbolt always turned her back when Sasha was at her most vulnerable. She hated her for that.

She hated both of them and had gone so far as to sell herself into a new life to escape them, but had found herself imprisoned in a different type of torture.

Where was Rafael? Why wasn't he here to shield her from them?

Her heart lurched as she realized she was in a hospital. Stark fear of what she might face had her longing to sink back into oblivion, where nothing could hurt her ever again, but she heard his voice.

"Let me see her." The grit in his tone, carrying from a nearby room, made her heart swerve again.

Relief washed over her, especially because Humbolt finally released her hand. She never, ever called her stepfather by his first name, Anson. Why would she when it annoyed him so intensely to be referred to like a butler?

But now she was forced to gather up her defenses against her husband. Rafael was a formidable man. She didn't dread seeing him the way she loathed her stepfather, but she feared how easily Rafael could destroy her in other ways. He already had.

"Do you love me?"

"That was never part of our agreement."

It wasn't. For a long time, she had been able to keep her guard up around him, but over time her defenses had eroded. He'd crept under her skin like a splinter. Every tiny remark, no matter how gently delivered or kindly meant, became a stiletto to the heart.

Then she had gone and revealed how vulnerable she was to him. What a mistake! Her husband drank power like a protein shake every morning. He loved it more than he could ever love her. She should have realized that before she bared her heart to him.

She couldn't live this way anymore. She really couldn't.

"Signora Zamos?" A nurse smiled and leaned over her. "I'm going to shine this light in your eye— Sorry."

Signora? Were they still in Rome? She had assumed America, since her parents were here. How had they arrived so quickly?

Confused, Sasha tried to flinch away, but the nurse was relentless, forcing a peek into her other eye.

"What happened?" Her voice was as scuffed as a flake of skin.

"A car crash, I'm afraid. You have a concussion. Can you tell me your birthday?"

A car crash? *When?* After the gala?

"I don't remember it." She meant the crash. The last thing she remembered was taking that tiny chance at being honest, really honest, with her husband. She had thought that maybe, if he loved her, he might accept all she'd done.

Love had never been part of their agreement, though. And learning he didn't even love her like this, when she worked so hard to be the wife he wanted, destroyed her. She hadn't dared reveal the rest.

"You don't remember your birthday?" her mother was asking with alarm, looming on the other side of the bed so suddenly that Sasha recoiled.

"Please." The nurse motioned for Sasha's mother to give her space.

Winnie refused to budge, leaning closer to urge loudly, "You remember *me*, don't you? I'm your mother, Alexandra."

All Sasha could think was, *No, you're not.* Not in the ways that counted. She knew how a real mother behaved and she had been robbed on that front.

"Can you tell me your mother's name, Signora Zamos?" the nurse asked gently. "Do you know where you are?"

The nurse's English held an accent that was a mix of Italian and Tagalog, if Sasha wasn't mistaken. She presumed they were still in Rome, but the path to escape her parents for good unrolled like a red carpet in her mind. If she didn't acknowledge their place in her life, they wouldn't have one, would they?

"No." Driven by years of mistrust and manipulation, she claimed, "No. I don't know who they are."

"What about me?" The tense, masculine voice prompted the nurse to step aside, revealing Rafael.

He sat in a wheelchair. The side of his swarthy, gorgeous face was bruised. His eye was swollen and his lip cut. His arm was bandaged from elbow to wrist, his leg was in a cast, sticking straight out.

Sasha was struck dumb by horror. Hot tears pressed against the backs of her eyes. She was furious with him. She was so hurt she kind of hated him. But she also loved him, which meant that his injuries devastated her. She had nearly lost him!

But love was never part of their agreement.

He needed an heiress and an heir. He was obsessed with securing his empire. He didn't need *her*. He had her money and his successor was on its way, hopefully still safe in the belly of their surrogate.

Molly hadn't been with them, had she?

Sasha looked around with anxious confusion, panicked that she couldn't remember when or where the crash had happened.

"What day is it?" She had texted Molly yesterday that she would call her in the morning. Was this the morning after the gala?

Oh, God. If something had happened to the baby—

She couldn't take that thought. It was a last straw of anguish. She draped her forearm over her eyes, hiding from all of this, unwilling to hear what might come next.

"Alexandra," Rafael growled. "Look at me."

Someone must have pushed him closer to the bed. He took her limp hand. Her fingers felt bruised and sensitive after withstanding Humbolt's clammy crush, but Rafael's warm grip was careful if not actually tender. He guided her arm to rest their linked hands in the middle of her chest.

She couldn't help looking at him and grew worried when she realized the way he was angled to reach her hand was causing him to grimace in pain.

She withdrew her hand so he wouldn't have to extend himself.

His irises were such a dark brown they often seemed black, but they flashed with fire as he sat back and brought his hand into his lap. His mouth tightened in dismay.

His lashes were too long and thick and pretty for a man. That had always annoyed her, that he possessed such natural beauty while she had to visit salons for extensions. But she noted with distress that his jaw was stubbled with what had to be two or three days' worth of beard. His cheeks were gaunt beneath his bladelike cheekbones. His face was lined with strain, his eyes sunken from lack of sleep.

And those compelling dark eyes were trying to consume her soul.

"Do you know who I am?" he asked.

Was that a real question?

No. She gave a small shake of her head. She had never really known who he was. They were honest with each other, mostly, but never open. Never revealing.

Something tortured flashed across his expression. He reached again for her hand and rubbed his thumb restlessly into the V between her thumb and finger.

They were both battered and in pain, but there was still that tingle of energy between them. Of *life*.

"I'm your husband. Rafael." He waited a beat, watching for recognition to dawn.

Her feeble desire to protect herself from him grasped onto the charade of lost memory. It was a strong, serviceable shield that would brace her against everyone who was asking too much of her right now. She mustered a deliberately blank look.

Maybe there was wary curiosity behind it, though, because for the first time in the longest time, she felt she had stolen back a little power for herself. She had drawn a wild card, one that she could hold against her chest until it was the right time to play it.

She hadn't held a card this explosive since—

She veered from touching that raw, exposed nerve.

Take your hand from his, she told herself, but she loved his hands on her.

That had always been her downfall. From their earliest days, she had thought their physical connection would be enough to sustain her, but it wasn't. Not when her past and present were being stretched and wrapped like an elastic band around her, coiling and coiling upon itself, growing tight enough to cut off her breathing while threatening to snap altogether.

"I'm glad you're awake. I was worried." Rafael sounded sincere, but she didn't put much store into that. *Let's give the people the show they came to see*, he often said. "When can we go home?" he asked the nurse.

Sasha pulled her hand from his, earning another sharp glace from Rafael.

"She'll come home with us," her mother said. "Won't she, Daddy?"

Sasha nearly threw up.

"Yes. She's confused and needs her mother," Humbolt said firmly.

Sasha locked eyes with the nurse. "Surely there's a—"

Clinic, she was going to say, but Rafael was talking over her, staring down Humbolt.

"Alexandra is my wife. She'll come back to our home in Athens. With *me*."

"You can't look after her like that." Humbolt sent a condescending wave at Rafael's condition.

"It will be a day or two before either of them are well enough to travel," the nurse hurried to interject, trying to defuse the confrontation. "Decisions don't have to be made right this moment. The doctor will want to assess both patients and run more tests. Let's let them rest." She ushered Sasha's parents from the room.

Rafael hovered beside her, but Sasha closed her eyes and turned her face away.

He swore under his breath and she heard the orderly wheel him away.

CHAPTER ONE

Three years ago...

RAFAEL ZAMOS HAD become a chameleon capable of blending into whichever surrounding would provide him the best chance of survival.

Tonight, he'd put on his bespoke tuxedo and walked into a New York ballroom where old money elites were gathered. A young woman in a short black dress tried to check his name off a list on her tablet, but he gave her his most dispassionate, reptilian stare.

"Have a nice evening, sir," she stammered and allowed him to pass without having to say a word.

That was the funny thing about power. A lot of the time, it was something other people gave you, especially if you created the impression that you already had an abundance of it.

He didn't have as much as he wanted. He doubted he ever would. He'd been on the wrong side of power often enough in his childhood that he had an insatiable thirst for it now, to ensure he was never at anyone's mercy ever again.

That resistance and thirst had drawn him here tonight. Competitors back in Greece were beginning to see him as a threat and were flexing their muscles against him. Yet again, he was being pressured to quit rising above his station.

Rafael was beyond literal fights that left him bleeding on the ground. No, he understood that tailored suits were a type of armor and the right connections could be an impermeable shield. He hated being beholden to anyone, but strategic partnerships would reinforce the place he was carving for himself as a global player in international trade. No one closer to home was willing to align with him, but an American pillar would do nicely for now.

These snobbish circles were notoriously hard to penetrate, though. They could smell an imposter a mile off. He was already receiving the side-eye as he accepted champagne and scoped out the roomful of balding, heavyset men with bejeweled, middle-aged wives. The few youthful women were likely trophies. This wasn't an event for mistresses. It was a political fundraiser of some kind. The power behind the power.

But who the hell was *she*?

Rafael's abdomen tightened as though taking a punch while his gaze fixated on a blonde woman of midtwenties who floated to the center of the ballroom in a risqué gown of diaphanous purple. The fabric twisted from one shoulder across her breasts and around her torso before it fell in mostly see-through panels around her naked legs. Well-placed spangles on the underlay covered her nipples and mound, but it was barely decent. He could see her ass.

Which was a joy to behold. All of her was mouthwatering.

He was not the only person who noticed. Everyone turned their heads and goggled their eyes. Even the music faltered briefly, just long enough for a curse to be heard from some distant corner of the room.

A fiftyish woman in a blue gown with a skirt like a church bell bore down on the newcomer. She had to press her skirt down to lean close enough to scorch the blonde's ear.

The blonde, much to his everlasting respect, maintained a bland smile of disinterest, barely acknowledging whatever was being said as she scanned the room and landed on making eye contact with *him*.

Another blow struck his midsection, radiating heat into his chest and low into his groin.

Mine, he thought. It wasn't a conscious thought. It was far more primitive than that. It was a basic claiming that resounded in the most atavistic parts of him. Lizard brain, gut, testes.

While everyone was exchanging looks and straining to hear whatever was passing between the women, Rafael strolled over to them, eating up all those well-displayed curves and the way her aloof expression narrowed to interest in him.

"Hello, darling. I was waiting for you." He loved using phrases like that. They suggested he'd been invited and caused people like the older woman to trip into courtesy as they tried to welcome him while also trying to place him.

His accent always threw them, too. His mother had been Romanian and he had spoken Greek since childhood, then was taught English by an Australian-Indian, so there were subtle undertones that always had people blinking in confusion.

"You look beautiful. Shall we dance?" he asked his new obsession.

The blonde used her thick lashes to screen, then reveal aquamarine eyes that were likely contacts, but he found her whole package of unapologetic sexuality irresistible.

"The dancing starts after dinner, sir," the older woman said in a corrective tone.

Rafael immediately despised her for it. He would not be thwarted.

Fortunately, the blonde seemed to feel the same. She offered him fingers that were taloned with long, dark purple nails. "I thought you'd never ask."

If Rafael had been a man who believed in such things, he would have called this love at first sight. In reality, it was animal attraction and like finding like, but it was heady. This woman not only knew how to command attention, she wielded her influence with fascinating ruthlessness.

He steered her through the formally set tables and the murmuring crowd until they reached the dance floor. It was occupied by a raised dais and a podium that would presumably be removed after the speeches. Behind it, the orchestra was working through a mix-and-mingle set with a subdued, lazy tempo that didn't require proper steps.

Rafael slid his hand from the woman's hip to her lower back, liking that she wore such tall heels because it put her nearly at eye level with him. She pressed closer and twined her arms around his neck, allowing him to fold his arms all the way around her narrow waist, securing her pelvis to his. She offered an amused smile at the stir they provoked.

"Your gown is making an impression."

"On you?" She arched a hairbreadth closer, well aware she was causing a specific stir in him.

"On everyone," he clarified. But yes. Absolutely on him. She was pure nitroglycerin. He would have to be very careful, but he wanted to bottle her and keep her forever.

"It's not just the gown. It's who's wearing it." Her fingertips traced a line along the back of his collar. Her tickling touch caused his scalp to tighten along with every muscle in his body.

"Are you not supposed to be here?" he asked idly. "Welcome to the club, angel."

"Did you crash this party?" she asked, pretending to be scandalized. "I think I just fell in love." She knew how to use her lashes to best effect, sweeping them down so her gaze traversed his shoulders and chest in a way that felt like a caress. A claiming.

He firmed his hold on her, enjoying the small hitch in her breath and the way her gaze flashed back to his, filled with startled heat.

She didn't know what to do with the fact that he was having the same effect on her that she was having on him. He liked that. He liked it very much.

"You don't know who I am?" She seemed skeptical of that.

"A goddess, I presume."

"A demon, more like. But I was not only invited, I was given strict orders to wear something appropriate, since I'm expected to stand with my mother behind my stepfather as he accepts his participation ribbon for being a good political donor." The corners of her mouth curled with bitter satisfaction at how mercilessly she'd clapped back.

Her rebellious spirit was both a draw and a warning, one he didn't let deter him.

"And who is the man looking like he wishes he was holding dueling pistols instead of champagne glasses?" Rafael had been a target from his earliest years. He clocked any threat, even lightweights like that privileged crash test dummy glaring daggers at them. The man was roughly Rafael's age, approaching thirty, well-dressed. Rafael was certain the man was richer and better connected, but Rafael could take him if it came to it.

"Do we call him a man if he agrees to marry the woman his father picks out for him?" She tilted her head in mock curiosity. "His mother still buys his underwear."

"You're his fiancée?" That was news he didn't care for. His hands unconsciously tightened on her.

"Not yet." Her fingertips moved to the hollow at the base

of his skull. She caressed and explored. Pressed with invitation. "You should kiss me now, while I'm still unattached."

She was toying with him for her own purpose—he knew that, but he was willing to take the kiss she offered purely for the thrill of it.

It was more than thrilling. As he met her parted lips with his own, electric heat shot through him. He would typically be a gentleman and allow her to set the pace, but with her, he tilted his head to capture her soft lips more thoroughly. He stopped dancing and cupped her head and *took*. He learned the shape of her pouted lips and the texture of her tongue and the erotic taste of her mouth.

He did everything he could to imprint himself on her.

Take me. Have all of me. Everything.

That willingness to give up all of himself rang bells of alarm within him, but the receptive tag of her tongue sent pure lightning into his groin, emptying his brain. He reacted in a borderline barbarian way, excited by how eager she was.

Yes, she was a potent and dangerous woman. She could strip him of all his hard gains, but in this moment of carnal greed, he didn't care. Her nails curled into his jacket as she dragged him closer, demanding more of him. He was beyond willing to let her drain him dry.

Hell, he was ready to have sex with her right here in the middle of the dance floor with her parents and the rest of the world watching.

Was that all this was for her, though? A show?

He dragged his head up, mouth burning, gaze on the lipstick smudged across her mouth.

"You're using me." It wasn't an accusation. It was a statement of fact, but he kept her hips pinned to his, both to hide and soothe his raging erection.

"Not entirely," she breathed against his chin. Her curves pressed willingly against him. She blinked in a way that suggested she was as blown away by their kiss as he was. "I wanted to know how that would feel. Making a scene while we did it was icing on the cake."

He wasn't sure he believed her, but his focus had narrowed to a very basic, libidinous desire to mate with her. Right now.

"Come with me." It was a command, but it was also a question. A test. Was she really as carried away as he was? Would she quit showboating for these pearl-clutchers and take this to its next steps?

"I thought you'd never ask." She slid her hand down his sleeve to clasp his hand, then led him from the ballroom, ignoring the gasps they left in their wake.

He was likely nuking any chance he had at finding a business partner among them, but he didn't care, not when she had become his entire reason for existing.

Thankfully, he was staying in the hotel's penthouse. It was an extravagant move, given how overleveraged he was, but it had been another means of reducing friction when he entered the ballroom. He tapped his card to the elevator mechanism and they shot upward.

"Who are you?" he asked her.

"Do you really want to talk?" She slid into his arms.

He did not. He had never had a blind hookup in his life, always careful he wasn't leaving a flank unprotected, but as he succumbed to the urge to kiss her, he understood how Troy had fallen. Power and lust were two sides of the same coin. Spend one, lose the other.

He fought allowing lust to win, but she was taut against him again, and this barely there dress of hers was almost like stroking her naked skin. Everything in him wanted to claim her. If he'd had a condom on him, he would have had her in the elevator.

The doors slid open with a ping and he dragged her down

the hall and into his suite, prepared to shout, "Get out!" if he saw a single maid, but it was empty.

He pressed her to the wall and discovered exactly how well matched they were as they both gave in to this devastating passion. His body ignited, prompting him to yank at the buttons of his new jacket, possibly tearing them as he fought to free himself.

She pushed the jacket off his shoulders, then began searching for the buttons between the pleats of his shirt.

Her skin was much easier to access. He dragged up the cobweb of her skirt. There were yards and yards of the stuff, but it was deliciously cool and soft. Almost as delicious as the smooth thigh he eventually found.

She broke away from their kiss to gasp for breath.

"No?" He would *die*.

"No. I mean, yes. Touch me," she said in a voice that shuddered with want.

He couldn't help the rumble of an animalistic growl that resounded in his chest. She was so soft, so smooth, warm and undeniably feminine. He found the thin line of a flesh-toned thong at her hip and watched his hand as he followed it.

The sheer purple of her skirt bunched against his wrist as he arrived at the crease next to her mound, so warm and smooth. So sensitive and responsive her breath shook as he drew light patterns there. She bit her bottom lip, eyes heavy lidded.

"You want this?" His voice was lost in the well of his chest.

"I want everything," she whispered. "Except talking."

He snorted. "Tell me if you need me to stop, then. Otherwise, I'm taking us all the way."

He barely gave her the chance to exhale a potent, "Yes," before he swooped to capture her mouth again. At the same time, he broke the band on the miniscule triangle of silk and claimed what he found behind it.

She jolted and moaned into his mouth, whimpering as he pressed his palm over her mound, waiting for her to press back before he began to explore. The abundant moisture he discovered nearly blinded him with excitement. The way she trembled and moaned nearly undid him.

He was so aroused, he could have taken her to the floor and lost himself in her right here, but he was determined to keep hold of some trace of control. If she wanted all the lust in him, she could have it. She would not steal his power over himself, though. No, he would have the upper hand here, not her.

To that end, he deepened his caress, sliding his finger-tip around and across the swollen knot that made delicious sounds pang in her throat. Around and around and around until she was arched and bunching his shirt in her fists and moaning with abandon into his mouth.

Oh, that was lovely. He pressed his wide palm over the soaked heat of her again, holding it steady for the rock of her hips as she rode out a shuddering climax. Her pulses and throbs were so intense, he felt them like a hammer strike in the tip of his erection, but he didn't allow himself to fall over the edge. Not yet.

"*You're using me*," this stranger had accused her and, yes, Alexandra had been using him to scandalize her mother.

But once he had kissed her? Now?

She was using him all right, but it was purely for a type of pleasure she hadn't known was possible for her. She had gone into that ballroom feeling so trapped, she might as well have been a genie compressed into a bottle. She'd barely been able to breathe, but now she was panting and flying. Soaring.

She was free in a way she hadn't expected to ever feel. Not with all the hang-ups she had around sex. Her beauty and sexuality were weapons she had learned to use to disconcert and humiliate, so they couldn't be turned on her. They had never been sources of *pleasure*.

Until now.

Until this stranger showed her what her body was capable of.

With charged kisses and languid caresses, he was teaching her to not only embrace her sensuality, but express it with abandon. She stroked her hands over his bared chest and delicately sucked his tongue.

In some ways, it was terrifying to let him take these liberties and pull forth such a wild response, but it was a step forward that she grasped with both hands. This was only for the one night anyway. It's not like he would toy with her this way forever.

He took her at her word about not talking. As her body wilted in the aftermath of a life-altering orgasm, he scooped her up and carried her to the bedroom. He stood her beside the bed, then stepped into the bathroom to retrieve a box of condoms that he threw onto the mattress.

In a kind of haze, she turned to offer her zip, lifting her hair out of the way.

He obliged by lowering it, slowly, setting kisses along her spine and leaving a hot pool of breath against her skin, all the way to her lower back.

Shivering, she dropped the gown and stepped out of her shoes. Her thong was already gone. She slipped onto the bed and turned to face him.

He was stripping without taking his eyes off her, skimming away trousers and boxers in one move, revealing he was very aroused. His erection was steely and dark, his expression barely civilized.

As he set a hand and a knee on the mattress, starting to loom over her, she retreated slightly, daunted. Her hand instinctually pressed at his chest.

He froze. "Changing your mind?"

"I'm not sure." She wanted this. She did. But she had forgotten how physical sex was. How overwhelming. How vulnerable it made her feel.

"That's fine." His expression grew shuttered. "I'm disappointed, but not angry." He shifted to the side so she could rise off the bed if she wanted to.

Ironically, the fact that he was so willing to stop this late in the game made her trust him more than she had a split second ago.

What was she supposed to do? Go the rest of her life without ever having sex again? It had already been eight years. Here was a man who was not only respectful enough to stop but who turned her on like no one else ever had.

"Will you—" she cleared her throat "—let me be on top?"

He dropped onto his back and folded his arms behind his head. "Help yourself."

"I might stop again if I get nervous," she warned, eyeing the banquet of tanned skin stretched firmly across the sort of muscles that belonged on an athlete. A swimmer, maybe. He had wide shoulders and well-defined abs. A light pattern of hair lay flat against his skin, thicker against his breastbone and thinning as it extended to his navel.

His thighs were equally tanned and well-built, but she only noticed that in the periphery. She was studying his erection, hesitantly reaching out to draw a shy line down the length with her fingertip, both amused and intimidated by the way the thick muscle twitched under her touch.

"Are you a virgin?" he asked with puzzlement.

"No." She choked on a harsh laugh. If he only knew her

history, he'd swallow his tongue before suggesting that. "No, it's just been a long time for me."

She slid closer and he gathered her atop him. He was a hot beach that felt like pure decadence to lie upon. Shifting against him produced sensations that were as erotic as the caress of a tropical surf. The satin-covered muscles beneath her called to the most primitive woman in her, teasing her to braid her legs with his so the damp tip of his erection sat in the crease of her mound. Her loins throbbed with awareness as she lowered her head to kiss him.

She knew she wouldn't hesitate again. This was too good. She rocked her mouth against his in deep, unhurried kisses.

She might have made a mistake, however, in allowing him to have both hands free. He took full advantage, skimming his fingertips over her back and buttocks, sensitizing her to his touch before he erased all those tickles with a firmer stroke that ironed her onto his front.

Then he became even more deliberate, palming her backside in a way designed to reignite her passion. When one hand cruised up her waist and sought her breast, she angled so he could cup the swell and toy with her nipple.

She moaned, subtly writhing with a need for *more*. More friction. More of those wicked caresses of his thumb against her nipple. More intimacy and intention and sinful attention where she longed to feel it most.

She brought her knees up so she straddled his thighs, rising to reach for the box of condoms. She offered one to him.

"Sure?"

She nodded.

He held her gaze as he took it, bit the corner, and ripped it open. As he rolled it on, old ghosts swirled through her psyche, but he moved his hand to the seam of her sex and all other thoughts disappeared. Her eyes fluttered closed and the only thing she was aware of was the way his thumb lightly traced a tantalizing line of sensations that made her feel like a flower blossoming open.

As need coiled through her, her hips rocked, seeking a deeper touch and the fulfillment she knew he could offer.

"Take me when you're ready." His smoky command was so husky and mesmerizing, she couldn't do anything but obey.

He held himself for her and she guided herself onto his length, letting out a soft cry of ecstasy as she sank down, stretched and caressed and connected to him in a way that left her wordless. Dazzled.

She braced her hands on his chest and stared into his eyes. They'd been all pupils a moment ago and were now glittering slits behind the tangle of his thick lashes. He was inordinately handsome, with clean-shaven cheeks beneath high cheekbones, a hawkish nose, and a mouth that could spawn a thousand fantasies. His brows were heavy, his jaw strong, his rakish hair rumpled by her fingers.

She could look at this face for the rest of her life, she thought whimsically.

His hands were drawing absent patterns on her thighs, but climbed to her hips, skimmed along her waist, then cupped her breasts. He circled her nipples with the pads of his thumbs.

Her body reacted by shivering and tightening around him. She leaned into his touch, then bent the rest of the way down to seal her mouth to his.

That seemed to be his undoing. He rolled her beneath him and began to thrust, pausing when she gasped in awe at the joyous pleasure that crashed through her.

"Don't stop!" she cried with anguish.

That was it. His body gathered and he became her whole world, seeming determined to create a memory she would never forget. Determined to claim her in every way—with his mouth, with his touch, with his sex. With the sound of his voice and the smell of his skin.

She couldn't track all the sensations or all the ways she was losing herself to him in those heated moments. She only knew later that that's what had happened to her. He destroyed her in the most sensual way possible. She welcomed it. By the end, when he dared to slow his strokes, holding her on the precipice of culmination, she was utterly at his mercy.

"Please," she whispered.

His fingers tangled in her hair. He held her for a long, drugging kiss, holding them both in this magical place of pure sensation. She felt like a single, exposed nerve, the very air almost too much on her hot, damp skin.

He withdrew and returned with a powerful flex of his hips, propelling her into such a powerful orgasm, she screamed.

His hips crashed into hers again and again, increasing the power of her release. He was off the leash and it was glorious.

Ecstasy was her new home. It gripped her and imbued her and emanated from her as he lost his rhythm and melded their flesh. He shouted with triumph and the pulses within her echoed the slam of her heart.

CHAPTER TWO

AFTER HIS ORGASM turned him inside out, and Rafael was exhausted on the bed beside her, he had a disturbing moment of feeling vanquished. *Beaten.*

But when he turned his head on the pillow, she was looking at the ceiling with an expression that reflected what he was feeling. Awe?

She slid him a look from the corner of her eye and immediately rearranged her features into smug amusement.

"Well, that was something, wasn't it?" She pulled the edge of the bedspread across her middle and curled toward him. "Thank you."

"It was very much my pleasure." He discarded the condom into the wastebasket and fell back onto the bed beside her, too sated to move more than that.

"I should leave." She sat up and her hair fell forward to hide most of her profile.

He studied her curved spine and couldn't resist setting his thumb and middle fingertip against the dimples at the top of her backside.

"You don't have to," he heard himself say. "Unless you need to get back to your party?"

"Can you imagine?" She kept the bedspread secured to her breasts, but braced a hand behind herself so she twisted to face him. "What do I look like right now? A ghoul from the crypt? A drunken clown?"

He likely wore more of her lipstick than she did. Her eyes were smudged and smoky and heavy lidded.

"You're sexy as hell." It was only the truth, but saying it caused a strange tremor in his chest. "I'm sure you know that."

"It's still nice to hear it. When it's sincere." Her pensive gaze lifted to the closed drapes.

He was equally disturbed. This had been the best sex of his life, which made it a purgatory of sorts. It was a memory that could imprison him for eternity.

He dismissed that melodramatic thought, attributing the heightened eroticism to their being strangers, and reminded himself she had only slept with him to irritate her parents.

Which didn't bother him, but didn't *not* bother him.

"I'll stay long enough for a shower, if you don't mind." Whatever blue mood had started to take hold in her was discarded with a careless smile. She threw off the bedspread and rose to walk into the bathroom.

He heard the toilet and the tap and imagined she was using the complementary makeup remover pads. When the shower started, he quit pretending he wasn't going to join her.

"Oh, hello," she said when he opened the glass door and joined her inside the marble-tiled enclosure. It was more than big enough for both of them with nozzles and sprays from all directions.

"Hello to you. Blue eyes." He cupped her face, looking into irises that were now the color of a clear sky over a mountain lake.

She reacted to his touch with a grasp of his wrists and a dazzling sparkle inside those pretty eyes. Her lips parted in invitation.

"I'm Rafael," he told her.

"Alexandra." The minx guided one of his hands down to shake hers. "It's a pleasure to meet you."

"Isn't it?"

It really was. For the next seventy-two hours, they barely left each other's sight. They shared the bed and the robes, the shower and meals and bottles of wine.

The concierge delivered more condoms and a handful of other necessities, but housekeeping was turned away and all calls ignored. Occasionally, Alexandra shrugged on one of his shirts, but more often than not, they were naked on the wrecked bed, dozing, talking about innocuous topics— movies and travel and whether horoscopes had any basis in reality, but mostly, they made love.

He learned that her feet were ticklish and she was not only the stepdaughter of a Very Rich Man, she was rich in her own right. Her father's family had amassed a fortune in publishing over several generations. Her mother's family were also Old Money with ties to industrial age railway tycoons.

"My father died when I was young. I don't remember him," she said with a philosophical shrug. "Humbolt pounced on Mother like a hyena on a wounded wildebeest and took control of her, her fortune, *and* my trust. That money he was being lauded for donating? *Mine.* What a paragon." Her lip curled in contempt.

"But he doesn't control you."

"Not for lack of trying, believe me." She quit tracing the pattern in the headboard and rolled onto her stomach so the sheet twisted around her. "What about you? What will I learn when I stalk you online after this?"

"I was born in Romania. My mother brought me to Greece to find my father who was Greek. We never found him. She passed away when I was five. I went into foster care, bounced through some group homes, then landed with a Greek couple who chose to adopt me. I grew up on the outskirts of Athens."

"Were they nice? Your adoptive parents?" She was giving him doe eyes, which made him uncomfortable.

"Yes." They'd tried to be, not that he'd known what to do with it. He'd had many a hard knock by then. His mother had barely scraped by, then died overnight. He'd been teased at school and scrapped his way through it. His adoptive parents had been withdrawn for their own reasons so Rafael had never fully seen himself as their son.

"My father died when I was seventeen. Heart attack." Rafael couldn't help the bitterness that invaded his voice and quickly averted his thoughts from that day. "I took over the family business, but there were vultures who wanted it for themselves. They tried to use the fact I was adopted against me, saying I wasn't legitimately my father's son, that I wasn't Greek, or not Greek enough. So I keep that information in my bio online, next to my brief arrest for breaking and entering."

"Oh." Her brows went up. "You are colorful."

"It was a misunderstanding. Or, I should say, another attempt to keep me from taking over the business. It was soon cleared up."

"What kind of business?" She cocked her head.

"At that time, a marine service operation for small and midrange vessels. There was always potential for more, but my father was never able to maximize it. There was a cartel who kept him in his place. When he died, they thought they wanted the company more than I did. They were wrong."

Her eyes widened. "What did you do?"

Whatever he had to. He deliberately sidestepped that question, trotting out the patter he gave any reporter who asked a similar question.

"Thankfully, like any adolescent, I was into gaming. When I wasn't working at the shop under my father, or going to school, I made videos. I'd become an influencer of sorts. I was making decent money, enough to help with my parents' mortgage. My father didn't know that. My mother handled all the books at the business and at home. She also knew that if these enforcers realized we were getting ahead, they'd put more pressure on us so she kept it under her hat. My father didn't live to see it, but having the house paid for gave me something to leverage when I took over the business. I was able to hire security and modernize. That set us up for growth."

He didn't mention the particularly ugly knife fight that had served as a warning that he was not the pushover his father had been.

"Recently, we expanded into larger ships and shipping beyond the Med. Zamos International? Heard of it?"

She wrinkled her nose in apology. "I have now."

"I'm still seen as an upstart," he admitted. "I've ceased to be a minnow that can easily be swallowed, but that makes me a genuine rival to the bigger players. I crashed your stepfather's party looking for American connections into the Eastern Seaboard, to shore up my position."

"Oh, dear. I have to be honest, Rafael. Stealing me away like this?" She drew a circle to indicate their love palace. "It has screwed your chances with everyone in that room. Pun intended. Humbolt can't disown me for misbehaving, but he can punish my friends by blacklisting them."

"I knew what I was risking when I approached you." Did he, though? He wasn't angry at her, per se, but he was angry he had allowed his libido to rule him. The longer he stayed here with her, the more opportunities he was allowing to slip away.

"Let me make it up to you," she purred and sprawled across him while she began kissing her way south.

Carnal hunger dug its claws into him, dimming his ability to think.

Last time, he promised himself, and crooked his legs open so she could kneel between his thighs.

"For you," Rafael said while she was dozing off their morning lovemaking.

Sasha thought he had risen to let in their breakfast, but he set a gorgeous bouquet of orchids and bird-of-paradise onto the night table.

She sat up, stomach lurching sickly, but hid her humiliation behind a bland smile. "I've overstayed my welcome. You should have said."

"Not at all. They're not from me." When his flinty gaze met hers, her heart stalled. Was he jealous? Suspicious?

He plucked the card with two fingers and offered it to her.

Her nerveless fingers didn't want to work. She wound up tearing the tiny envelope to withdraw the card that read, *Call your mother.*

"Mother." She flicked the card off the bed. "Took her long enough to find me. You weren't on the guest list, though. Were you?" She dragged the sheet across her breasts and bunched the pillows behind her so she could slouch into them with a sigh and a wry smile. "That must have annoyed her, having to ask around to find out who you were. Now everyone knows you were an interloper. She'll use that against you. Sorry." She wrinkled her nose at him.

He made a noise of acknowledgment that also rang with discontent. "Coffee?"

"There you go seducing me again." She was trying to return to their easy banter, but seriously, everything about him seduced her. The belt of his robe was negligently tied at his waist, leaving the lapels gaping to reveal his tanned chest.

He countered with, "I can't seem to help myself," but his tone wasn't as light as it had been. Reality was permeating the air like the perfume of the orchids.

She watched him amble from the room and even his silhouette of wide shoulders and the laconic slap of his bare feet made her ache with longing. She knew she ought to leave, but couldn't seem to make herself.

"It's hot," he said when he returned and set the two cups of coffee beside the bouquet.

Sasha wanted to knock the flowers to the floor, but they were only a symbol of the thing she really didn't want—to speak to her mother. She didn't want to leave this bubble of intimacy and pleasure. To leave *him*.

He didn't walk around and climb into the bed beside her, the way he'd done most other times he returned to this bed. He sat on the edge of the mattress facing her.

"Exactly how will your mother try to make me uncomfortable?" he asked.

Oh. They were facing reality, were they? How disappointing.

"Socially," she replied. "She'll have you cut from invite lists to galas and events."

"I'll go anyway." He dismissed her reply with a shrug.

A sunny ball of hope broke open in her chest, then a shadow moved across it.

"Humbolt is the greater threat. He's spent twenty years using my father's money to curry business connections and political favors. He has a lot of sway when he wants to use it. God, I hate him." She shoved her legs out straight as though she could kick that man out of her life once and for all. And now he was trying to marry her off to that insipid—

She sucked in a breath of realization and sat up, curling

her legs beneath her so she knelt as she faced Rafael. She set her hand on the white velvet of the robe that coated his strong shoulder.

His cheek ticked in awareness that she had let the sheet drop and was naked before him, but his gaze remained locked with hers.

"Yes?"

"You and I should marry." She was shocked that such words spilled from her lips, but they felt right.

"Oh?" He used the excuse of leaning to pick up his mug to force her hand to fall away. "I was planning to wait until after I turned thirty-five."

"How old are you now?"

"Twenty-nine. But I have hundreds of goals ahead of me before I settle down. Thousands. *Billions* to acquire," he added with dry significance.

"I don't want to marry, either." She dragged the sheet in front of her, but stayed kneeling on the bed, gaze turned inward while she spoke her thoughts aloud. "When Humbolt realized I was coming up to twenty-four, he also realized that puts me a year away from taking control of my trust. I could have taken the reins sooner by marrying anytime, but I couldn't stand the idea of a husband. I still don't want one, but Humbolt has handpicked this son of his crony. He thinks this dolt will keep me in line and allow him continued access to my fortune. Mother wants everything done properly, of course. A year-long engagement and all that nonsense."

"This isn't the Dark Ages. Tell them no and wait it out," Rafael suggested as though it was just that easy.

"I was planning to, but Humbolt holds the purse strings and uses them to bring me to heel. I've put aside a nest egg," she confided, proud of the way she'd embezzled from her own funds. "It's a hoard of jewelry in a safe-deposit box.

I'm like a *dragon*," she said on a chuckle, then sobered. "It's enough to keep me going for a while, but it's insurance for something else." She veered from letting herself worry about publicity and legal fees. It wouldn't happen. She was always really careful to keep her secret very much a secret. "Mostly I *hate* the idea of walking away and allowing him to keep my money. So I have to fight for it. But the last time I outright defied him, he had me placed on a psych hold so—"

Rafael swore. "Are you serious?"

"Yes. I was still a teenager. I was supposed to go back to boarding school in Switzerland, but instead I went to Ibiza for six months." That was the cover story she always told when referring to that time of her life. "I don't think he would go to such an extreme length now, given he's trying to marry me off, but he'll find some other way to make my life miserable. I refuse to let him *win*, though. It's *my* money. And he's been using it—and me—for his own gain for almost twenty years. I don't *want* to put up with another year of him and Mother holding me at gunpoint."

"How much money?" he asked curiously.

"A hundred and fifty million. I get the balance when I have a baby or turn thirty. Five hundred million, give or take. I imagine that sort of asset would be helpful to you, if you had access to it?" She fluttered her lashes at him, knowing it damned well would.

He was impervious to her flirting, though. Her lover was gone. Rafael might as well be wearing a three-piece suit and a fresh shave. He was all business.

"It would," he acknowledged with an unreadable expression.

"My sense is that you'd like to continue having sex with me? At least for a while? Am I wrong about that?"

"I was going to suggest we continue this affair." His cheek ticked again.

"Then here's what I propose. I'll tell Mother this was a final fling and I'm ready to play ball. That will distract them long enough for you and I to negotiate our prenup."

His brows went up, but she wasn't an idiot. She'd had to look after herself once before and knew how to do it.

"We'll marry in secret then, *bam*!" She punched into her own palm. "We'll hit them with it in a few weeks." She was already laughing at the shock on their faces.

"That seems like a lot of unnecessary drama and subterfuge."

"Would you rather announce our engagement and watch Humbolt use my money to try to destroy you?"

"Is that a threat?"

"*No*. I'm telling you what kind of man I'm dealing with. But if you don't want to marry me, that's fine." His rebuff stung, though. It really did. "I'll find another way," she decided. "Another man. I had made up my mind not to marry so I didn't even consider this avenue, but now that I have, I'll shop for my own docile but useful idiot…" She threw off the sheet and scooted to the edge of the mattress.

Rafael stuck out his arm to stop her, then leaned across to set his coffee back on the night table. "I didn't say I don't want to. Tell me why you're so averse to marriage."

"Because I don't want to be controlled by anyone." She looked pointedly at the arm barring her exit from the bed. "Least of all a husband."

"I'm capable of reason. And I'll need an heir eventually. It sounds as though you will, too."

Her heart contracted along with her pupils, turning the room blurry at the edges. Pure adrenaline stung her veins, the kind that urged flight. She fought revealing the panic that quickened her breath and jerked her gaze free of his.

She plucked at the sleeve of his robe, silently requesting he remove his arm.

He drew back and she rose to pick up the shirt he had discarded across the back of a chair. She shrugged herself into it, frantically thinking while she buttoned it.

"Having a baby purely to take control of my fortune is wrong. Let's see how we get on," she suggested, noticing the tremble in her hands as she rolled the cuffs up to expose her wrists. "If we're still married in a few years, we'll discuss children. There's every chance we won't be. I'm a rebellious spirit. Some would call me a hellion."

"I noticed," he assured her with a brief glint of amusement. "But I appreciate your candor. In fact—" he narrowed his eyes "—this would only work if we are completely honest with each other. You can't play any of these bait and switch games with me. We need to be able to trust each other. You understand that, don't you?" His tone was still light, but she heard the warning in it.

A shiver of premonition chased down her spine.

She trusted him. Physically. She would do some digging to be sure she could trust him with her money. With her heart, though? With her *secrets*? She doubted she would ever fully trust a man again.

"There's a difference between being honest and being transparent," she said. "I can promise to be honest with you. Faithful, definitely." She had a bleak sense that she would never feel this same desire for any other man, so that was an easy promise to make. "But I will choose how much of myself and my past I want to share with you. By the same token, it will be your choice how much of yourself you share with me."

"You're starting to sound too good to be true, Alexandra." He was still sitting on the bed and leaned back on his hands, robe gaping to expose his inner thighs. He was barely decent and so sexy, her mouth dried.

"'Good' is the last word people would use to describe me," she assured him.

"I happen to know you're *very* good. Come here and show me how good. Seal the deal," he coaxed.

"I *just* got dressed."

In his shirt and nothing else.

Get used to it, she thought. She was about to use him and his trappings as a shield, but she would have little protection against *him*.

Nevertheless, even though her heart was pounding in apprehension, her feet took her to the bed.

"You really want to do this? Marry?" She set her hands on his shoulders and her knees on the mattress, straddling his lap.

"I do." His wide palms immediately climbed beneath the crisp cotton of the shirt, claiming her naked skin.

It's worth it, she told herself. *Whatever happens, it will be worth it for this.*

Two weeks later, Rafael walked with his new bride into a Manhattan mansion.

Had he had reservations about marrying her? Probably not as many as he ought to. When they had parted after their three-day sex fest, he had promised to call her, but had thought about getting on a plane straight back to Greece. He had a lot to protect and could have made any excuse to go home and guard it.

The minute she was out of his sight, however, he wanted her back. That was the uncomfortable truth that he kept to himself as he lingered in New York.

They'd seen each other intermittently as they met with lawyers and stole a few passionate interludes. Each time, he had grown more fascinated with her. More eager to have her with him all day, every day. Every *night*.

There were crude expressions for this level of desire-related impulsiveness. A distant part of himself understood he was operating on pheromones and ego. She was rich and beautiful and alluring. Any man would want her, but she was clearly capable of acting in a calculated fashion to get what she wanted.

That side of her was equally fascinating to him, though. She knew how to direct her lawyers so they were very thorough in how well they protected her, ensuring she had several avenues out of this marriage that wouldn't break her financially. This wasn't her first rodeo, as the Americans said, which prompted him to say, "You seem to know what you're doing in a boardroom. Why have you never put your lawyers onto your stepfather?"

"So he could spend my money fighting me? And use it to run a smear campaign against me?" She combed square nails, which were now a bubblegum pink, through her loose blond hair.

Rafael wasn't oblivious to the sort of things men said about women, especially when they were trying to crush them in court, but she seemed to embrace the reputation of a scarlet woman, so what else could intimidate her badly enough that she would rather avoid it?

"Putting you on him will be much more effective," she said, smoothing his lapel. "I've done my homework, you know. Once Humbolt realizes who he's dealing with, he'll start to mind his manners. Did you really steal a boat from a mafia don?"

"That is a colorful way for the press to spin my exercising a contract clause. I took possession of a ship when the repairs went unpaid." Had he also set the man up for arrest, thereby making it impossible for him to make his payments? Perhaps. But that was between him and his very unbothered conscience.

"Hmm, well, I can't wait to see how Humbolt reacts when he realizes this particular ship has been commandeered by a pirate." Her mauve-colored lips tilted into a smirk.

Oddly, the fact she made no bones about using him against her stepfather reassured him. He knew exactly where they both stood.

He had also done his homework and was pleased to learn that, along with the financial advantage of leveraging against her trust fund, he was marrying a woman who had connections to aristocracy, heiresses, and socialites around the globe. Alexandra might be named in more than one celebrity clickbait story, or wear scanty outfits to upper-crust galas, but her scandals were deliberate. She knew exactly what was expected in every setting and would help him blend seamlessly into those places himself.

He was quite satisfied with this arrangement of theirs, even when she said at the courthouse before they spoke their vows, "I will promise to honor you, but I can't promise to obey. Also, I'm growing fond of you, but I will probably never love you."

Perhaps he should have asked her why not, but that would risk her telling him that she could see through his tailored morning suit to the gutter rat he'd once been.

"Good," he said instead, meaning it. Love was a liability. People you loved could be used against you. Love made you helpless. "I need someone who is self-sufficient and won't ask me for things I'm incapable of offering. You are the yin to my yang, Alexandra."

Their vows had seemed moot at that point. They understood each other perfectly, right down to their mutual enjoyment of the commotion they created as they arrived in the sitting room of the mansion, where well-dressed couples were gathered for what was supposed to be Alexandra's engagement brunch.

Along with Alexandra's parents, her pseudo fiancé was there along with a handful of other middle-aged and older couples.

Alexandra's hand tightened in his, sending a frisson of warning through Rafael. He followed her startled glance to a man in his late forties, but she was already looking elsewhere, smiling with vicious joy at the way everyone had frozen in shock.

Their audience was taking in their joined hands and the swallowtail jacket that Rafael wore with an ivory vest and striped trousers. Alexandra wore a demure, figure-hugging dress in oyster white that ended below her knees. A short cape topped it, falling from her shoulders to her elbows.

She was classy and willowy and unabashedly smug as she stated, "There's been a misunderstanding. When I said I was ready to marry, I meant that I had found the husband I want." She smoothed her free hand along the sleeve of his jacket.

"No," Winnie Humbolt said in a gust of appalled disbelief. "I won't allow it."

"It's done." Rafael looked with suitable adoration at his entrancing bride. He could see she was having the time of her life dropping this bomb, and he couldn't help the rush of pride that he could give her this. "We've come from the courthouse."

Her mother raked in a gasp and looked as though she wanted to faint like a Victorian dowager onto the nearest couch. Humbolt was turning crimson, flapping his lips, nearly apoplectic.

"We'll have it annulled," Humbolt stammered. He shook with rage as he waggled his finger. "You're not in your right mind. You have a history."

"Try it." Rafael snapped his head around to skewer the man with his most lethal glower. "Try to take my wife from me. Try to harm her. See what happens." He had never been so sincere in his readiness to kill a man.

Humbolt's color drained. "Don't come into my home and threaten me."

"But it's not yours, is it?" Alexandra said in mock apology for having to correct him. "My name is on every piece of real estate that you live in. Now that I'm married, I've sent the paperwork to the various institutions, letting them know that I will control my assets from now on."

"You can't—" Humbolt started to bluster, but Rafael overrode him.

"I've put my own team onto performing a full audit," Rafael warned. "Don't bother trying to squirrel anything away. If Alexandra wishes to let you continue living here, that is her choice, but do be careful how you treat her going forward. I protect what's mine." He switched to a much sweeter tone when he asked her, "Do you need to pack anything for our honeymoon, darling?"

"I don't need anything but you from now on." She was gushing for their audience's sake, but he lapped it up all the same. "We'll be in the Maldives, but we won't be taking calls. Newlyweds." She sent a squinched smile at the group of slack-jawed faces.

"Alexandra!" her mother cried as they started to turn away. "Are you pregnant? Is that why you've married him?"

Alexandra jolted as though a spear had landed in her back.

"No," she choked out as she turned. "I married him to get away from you, Mother. I thought that was obvious. Also, because he's good in bed." She put on a moue of affection as she gazed up at Rafael. "That's more than she can say about *her* husband."

"I'll fight this," Humbolt warned. "You'll be sorry."

"I'm sure you can make all of us very sorry if you start muckraking." Alexandra shot that at him with a blast of ice from her eyes. "I suggest you cool off and think about whether it's worth it before you do anything rash."

Did she flash a look toward that fortyish man? Or was that Rafael's imagination?

He would never know. Alexandra tugged on his hand, saying facetiously over her shoulder, "Thank you for your warm and sincere congratulations. Goodbye!"

CHAPTER THREE

THEIR HONEYMOON LASTED a year, until the following May.

Oh, they had their spats. Rafael had not risen from being picked up off the street and stuck in an orphanage, to middle class, to obscenely wealthy without possessing self-serving, driven, and occasionally ruthless attributes. He didn't apologize for that, but he learned to restrain his worst impulses for the sake of a peaceful marriage.

Alexandra *was* difficult at times, but it came from being a passionate person who had been materially spoiled all her life. She had a strong grasp of her own worth and wasn't afraid to hold her ground when she decided she wanted something.

For the most part, however, they were aligned in their goal, which was to become a force to be reckoned with. While he accumulated the power of money, she nurtured their connections and influence.

Rafael knew why he needed the security of being dominant and untouchable. He never again wanted to be as vulnerable as he had been in his early years. Alexandra hadn't ever been cold and hungry, sleeping behind dumpsters, though. She hadn't been knocked around for being unable to read and write, then for doing it better than anyone else. She had never been surrounded by four grown men determined to punish a young man who was growing too big for his britches.

Which wasn't to say he didn't see the small abuses her stepfather attempted to visit upon her. Every few months, a rumor would surface that Rafael had brainwashed his wife or that she was heavily medicated or otherwise incapable of making her own decisions. Humbolt sold her favorite car "because it had become a liability" and forced her to fly in for meetings that were canceled at the last minute.

Rafael always retaliated. He paid for renovations at her summerhouse in Martha's Vineyard, closing it the week before her parents were scheduled to use it. He insisted they ship a number of rare paintings to their home in Athens and had his accounting team continually put pressure on Humbolt for financial reports that Alexandra didn't need.

It was tit-for-tat nonsense that didn't seem serious enough to get under Alexandra's skin as far as it did, but he didn't complain since her hatred of her parents made her as determined as he was to conquer and rule all corners of the world.

For the most part she managed her own money, but she frequently invested large chunks with him that he used for acquisitions and expansions, typically doubling her money before he rolled it back to her.

Meanwhile, she protected and assisted him in his endeavors by keeping her ears open. She would caution, "I've heard there's bad blood there. Cover yourself if you get into bed with them." Or, "Her father is in oil, if that interests you. We could invite her family onto the yacht."

The *Alexandra* was a forty-meter superyacht that he purchased when Alexandra had heard a rumor that a lesser royal was in trouble and needed a quiet bailing out. Rafael bought it for a third of its true value and regularly leased it out so it paid for itself. It had become not only a jewel in his corporate crown, but an excellent means of conducting business in a relaxed setting.

They had it to themselves on their first anniversary—with a full crew, obviously. Neither of them could be bothered to do more than carry a used cup to a sideboard for a refill, but they had no guests and thus were entertaining each other in their very favorite way.

Tonight, Alexandra was on her knees between his feet where he sat on the bed. She was curling his toes as she drew out his pleasure with tantalizing slowness, lavishing attention on his throbbing erection, humming with pleasure as she anointed him.

He watched as long as he could, fighting to hold on to his control. As much as he adored this act, however, he far preferred to hold back and prove to both of them that he was his own master, not her.

"Stop," he commanded in a voice that was so thick, it barely emerged from his throat.

She lifted her head, eyelids swollen, lips lax, the picture of eroticism.

"Are you not enjoying this, darling?" She blew softly on his wet flesh, causing his balls to tighten. The root of his shaft pulsed in her fist and he nearly finished from that alone.

"I want to be inside you." He lay back in a silent command for her to straddle him.

"Are you sure?" She pressed her fist down, drawing his skin taut as she painted a flagrant pattern with her tongue, tracing the shape of his tip. The dance of her tongue in the most exquisite place was his defeat.

With a guttural shout, he caught the worst of it in his palm, spilling the rest onto his belly, but as delicious as that orgasm was, he was irritated that she'd got the better of him.

She kissed the back of his hand and purred, "Such a gentleman."

She rose and walked away, still wearing the bra and garters and hose and five-inch heels that had brought him to attention before she'd tantalized him past his point of no return.

She returned with a warm damp cloth and cleaned him up with tender care.

His heart was still unsteady, his blood sizzling. He was so sexually gratified, he shouldn't be taking issue with the smug curl at the corners of her mouth, but he did. He felt... not weak, exactly, but not as superior as he liked to be.

Not that he wanted to lord over her. It wasn't like that between them. He had a lot of regard for this woman who wore tantalizing lingerie purely for his pleasure. The demicups of her bra were low enough to reveal her areoles, and the front of the thong barely covered her landing strip. Eyeing that peek and tease outfit was already causing him to twitch back to life.

She slipped out of her shoes and sprawled alongside him, warm and soft. Her hair fell around his face as she kissed him with the sort of passion most men dreamed of experiencing just once. He steeped himself in her constantly, basking in the fact that she was all his.

Yet she wasn't. *That* was the piece that was unsettling him. In this year of marriage, he had become deeply invested in their partnership. Sometimes he wondered if he was more invested than she was. He wasn't sure why he had that impression, but it had something to do with the way she drew firm boundaries around parts of herself and her past.

He wanted to know this was more than what it had been when they started, which was a combination of a very delicious affair and a very advantageous business arrangement. It should be a relief to him that their hearts weren't inextricably entangled, but he wanted a deeper commitment from her, something that cemented her place in his life.

"We should talk about children," he said when her lips slid to nibble at his jaw.

"Whose?" she asked, playing obtuse.

"Ours," he clarified.

"Right now?" Her tone lilted with disbelief.

"Soon," he deferred, recognizing he'd blindsided her and was losing more than the mood. Shadows of withdrawal had cooled the heat in her blue eyes. That was the exact opposite of what he was after.

He rolled so she was beneath him and set about returning the pleasure she'd given him tenfold. It took a few drawn out kisses for her to catch up, but then her desire reignited and she surpassed him, becoming frantic. When he ran his tongue beneath that thin strip of lace between her thighs, her hand fisted in his hair.

He loved when she was like this, clawing at him as though she couldn't get enough of him. He was both cruel and generous, insisting on taking her over the edge more than once before he finally entered her. By then, her lingerie was nothing but torn wrapping paper off an elegant gift, discarded on the floor, while she was naked and arching with abandon, welcoming his every thrust.

It was raw and rough and maybe imbued with his own desperation to bind them indelibly. It was also powerful, culminating in the sort of supernova climax that had her screaming and him shuddering in a paroxysm of ecstasy that damned near destroyed him.

In the aftermath, they were puddles of quivering flesh, exhausted. He barely had the energy to touch the button that doused the lights or drape his arm across her waist to spoon her into him.

He was roused some indeterminate time later, aware she was trying to leave the bed.

"Where are you going?" he asked through his desire to remain asleep.

"Nowhere," she murmured.

He thought he heard her sniff. It yanked him to a higher level of consciousness.

"Are you crying?"

"No. I have an eyelash in my eye. It's gone now. Go back to sleep."

He had a fleeting thought to turn on the light, but she snuggled her bottom into him and sighed, relaxing. He closed his eyes and drifted off again.

I can't lose him, Sasha thought as she stared into the dark.

Rafael's arm was heavy on her waist, but no matter how deeply asleep he was, he always noticed when she left the bed.

She had been weeping silently, afraid she would wake him, but putting physical space between them was next to impossible when lying against him was exactly where she wanted to be for the rest of her life.

Because she loved him? She was trying not to label it. That would give him even more influence over her than he already had. She was very careful to keep parts of herself back, pushing a persona of a spoiled heiress, an extrovert who loved to hostess, and a devoted if emotionally aloof wife.

She *was* devoted. She loved those moments when she made an introduction that clicked for him, or when her ability to charm a tycoon's wife smoothed the way for their husbands to strike a deal.

She loved being everything he needed because he was pretty much all she needed. She could survive without him; she knew she could. She had done it for years, but that's all she'd been doing: surviving. They had been long, lonely years filled with empty conversations at boring events with people who failed to interest her.

With Rafael, she thrived. They challenged each other and made each other laugh. He tapped into her stores of creativity, whether it was formulating a social strategy or designing their dream home. He gave her sensual pleasure that was like a drug, it was so intense and addictive.

Now he wanted a baby. She didn't ask why. It didn't matter why. If he wanted one, she had to decide whether to give him one or leave, because he had made clear from the beginning that this day would come.

She wanted to give him a baby. She wanted one for herself, but here came the tears again, welling up like blood from a wound.

She clenched her eyes shut, fighting the sobs that wanted to rack her body. Her lashes grew wet anyway and pressure built in her throat.

Her longing for a baby was so intense, it nearly stopped her heart, but it came with old and new yearnings. Hope and grief. Conflict.

Should she tell him?

No. Everything in her clenched up at the thought. There was too much shame in her, not for having a baby as a teenager and not even for placing her daughter with a loving family. On the contrary, she believed she had done the best thing for her daughter. At sixteen, she hadn't been ready to become a mother. Raising that baby with her mother and Humbolt would have been abuse, plain and simple.

Instead, she had done everything she could to provide a good life for her child, leaving her with a mother and a girl she had regarded as a sister. She was envious of the life she'd given her daughter.

No, her shame stemmed from how her baby had been conceived. Logically, Sasha knew that a married man of thirty who seduced a teenager was a predator, but it hadn't seemed like assault at the time. She'd been certain she knew what she was doing. It had been mischief. Something she had imagined throwing in Humbolt's face at some point.

As with all teenage rebellion, she'd been hideously naive to the consequences. She'd been four months pregnant before she had even begun to suspect it. By then, Humbolt had figured out who she was seeing. He blamed the affair on her. He knew which side his bread was buttered on and had been determined to protect his associate. *She* had tempted a married man, he said, calling her all sorts of horrific things. Did she want to destroy innocent lives? What of the man's wife and children? Had she thought about anyone but herself?

She hadn't, of course.

"Never tell your mother," Humbolt had warned. At first, she'd been too upset to even think of doing so. Later, she'd been under a legal obligation to bite her tongue, but her mother had suspected the affair. That's why she had begun suggesting Sasha go back to school early.

By the time Sasha was sitting in a teen clinic in a rural part of New Jersey, having come as far away from Manhattan as she could get in hopes she wouldn't be recognized, she had known she was very much on her own.

Patricia Brooks, a midwife and reproductive counselor, had become her angel. She was the first person in Sasha's life to treat her as a person. Not an heiress who deserved a deferential attitude. Not a daughter, or stepdaughter, to be criticized and controlled. Not a sexualized body to be objectified, but a human being who could make decisions for herself.

Patty had laid out all of Sasha's choices, none of them without drawbacks.

"I have a duty to report if there's abuse," Patty had also said. "If the father is that much older than you..."

"If you tell anyone, I'll run away. I swear I will. My parents can't know I'm pregnant."

If she'd been an adult and having a baby, Sasha could have used the circumstance to take control of her trust, but having the baby while she was still a minor only created two people Humbolt would use for his own ends. Her baby would become another point of leverage Humbolt could use against her.

Termination was still on the table, barely, but Sasha had wanted to have the baby. In some ways, it had been the ultimate act of autonomy, exercising that monumental decision all by herself, but it was also love—not that she fully understood that emotion. Given her upbringing, it had been more of an attachment to the idea of love, but she'd felt something toward the baby that was bigger than anything she'd ever felt before.

On her third visit with Patty, when she told her that she wanted to have the baby, but couldn't raise it and didn't have anywhere to stay while she waited out her pregnancy, Patty invited her to live with her. She had a daughter at home of a similar age. She couldn't imagine Molly being in dire straits like this without anyone trustworthy to turn to.

Patty was risking her midwife practice by sheltering Sasha, but she was the calm, sensible counsel Sasha needed at the time. She helped her find a lawyer who handled asking the father to relinquish paternity. That was necessary for adoption, but Sasha refused to let him off without consequences of his own. She demanded an enormous trust be set up for her baby and didn't give a damn how he explained it to his wife.

He had gone along with it to "make the problem go away." His only stipulation was that Sasha couldn't tell anyone that he was the father, not even their child. Sasha was fine with that. She didn't need him. She had Patty.

And Molly.

At first, Patty's teenage daughter had been a bit of a pill, not sure what to think of this pregnant stranger who had moved into their spare bedroom, but over the ensuing months, they became as close as sisters. Or at least, the kind of sister Sasha had always wished she'd had.

In those days of homeschooling online and learning to cook and never caring about makeup or hair color or what she was wearing, Alexandra became herself. Sasha. She laughed at silly things and took nature walks like a country bumpkin and she grew a baby she loved in the way Patty loved Molly. In the way the two of them loved her.

Sasha could genuinely say it was the happiest time of her life—until she went into labor. That had been horrible, but thankfully quick and uncomplicated.

Then she was holding a tiny girl who looked too small for a long name like Elizabeth, which was the name she'd chosen.

Molly said, "You could call her Libby," and that's who she became.

If she could, Sasha would have lived with them forever and raised her daughter there, but her mother was finally suspecting she wasn't in Ibiza. Staying here would risk all the careful precautions she'd taken to hide that she'd had a baby at all.

"I have to leave, but I can't bring her with me," she told Patty when her daughter was a week old. "I *can't*."

"But—" Molly protested.

They were close enough by then that Sasha knew what was bothering her friend. Molly had said it once before.

"How will you leave your baby with strangers?"

"If you're absolutely certain this is what you want," Patty said carefully, "then I wonder if you'll consider letting me adopt her? It could be an open adoption," Patty rushed on. "That way you could check up on her and see her anytime."

Such profound relief washed through her, Sasha barely heard Molly say a quietly ecstatic, "Really, Mom?"

"You can never tell anyone, Moll," Sasha warned her. "Ever. I mean that."

"I know," Molly said solemnly. "I swear I never will."

Three days later, Sasha signed the papers and walked away from her baby, confident she was leaving Libby with people who would give her a far better life and infinitely more love than she could.

It broke her heart. It left her numb for a year or more, uncaring that Humbolt had her assessed by a counselor who diagnosed her as having used toxic drugs. She'd gone to rehab meetings for months, never telling the counselor the real reason she was disassociated and depressed.

Eventually, she rallied enough to go back to school. She returned to ski holidays and attending film premiers and, pretty soon, she had almost convinced herself that it had simply been a very weird dream. It hadn't really happened.

It had, though. She was already a mother.

And she couldn't bring herself to tell Rafael. Keeping Libby hidden was as much for her daughter's protection as her own. Even if he were to find out at this late stage, Humbolt could cause a lot of damage to Libby's life. To Patty's. He would do his best to ruin Patty's career, possibly try to have her arrested.

What would that do to Libby? To all of them?

No. Sasha couldn't expose them to any of that. She would hold on to her secret until she was in her grave or Humbolt was in his.

In the meantime, she would have a baby with Rafael. This time she would keep her baby and everything would be perfect and wonderful.

She finally fell asleep, waking late and finding Rafael on deck, already finished with his breakfast and nursing his second cup of coffee.

"I left you sleeping, thinking you needed it. You were restless last night." He searched her gaze.

"Too much champagne," she said with a breezy shrug. "Good thing I got that out of my system since I won't be allowed alcohol if we're trying for a baby."

"Really?" A light came into his gaze that made her heart flip over. "You want to?"

"I do." Her insides were vibrating as she let him draw her from her chair into his lap, never dreaming in that moment that *try* would become such a loaded, painful word.

CHAPTER FOUR

Fourteen months later...

AFTER MONTHS OF CAJOLING, Rafael had finally got Gio Casella onto his yacht.

Gio was his contemporary in age, but old, old money from Genoa, Italy. He ran a sprawling, well-established global conglomerate, Casella Corp. Hammering out a deal with him would go a long way to finally proving Rafael had as much right to ply international shipping waters as anyone else.

Gio was not, however, interested in the female company Alexandra had arranged for him.

Jacinda was the niece of someone moderately important from somewhere vaguely notable. Alexandra knew her from her boarding school days. Jacinda was beautiful and well-mannered, but a little too blatant in her attempt to earn Gio's favor. She had taken off her top as she entered the pool, and her breasts were definitely lovely, but she was practically rubbing them all over Gio, which Rafael suspected from Gio's indifference was actually more irritating than tantalizing.

Perhaps a swim after lunch had been a bad idea. Rafael should have suggested they get back to business, but Alexandra had been tasked with entertaining the rest of their guests all morning. He'd brought Gio out to the lido deck hoping a relaxing drink would keep everyone sociable and happy.

Alexandra had her own top off, all the women did, but even though she was lying on a lounger, she didn't seem to be relaxed. She'd been off her game when she assembled this particular crowd, misjudging Gio's bachelor status as a man looking for a good time. Rafael couldn't take her to task for it. She had been going through a lot. It was distracting her and causing fissures in their relationship.

A week ago, as they'd been preparing for this trip, she'd got her period. Again.

"Perhaps we should consider other options," he'd said when she had announced that with her usual *discussion over* tone.

"We're running out of options, aren't we?" she'd snapped.

That had been the third round of IVF so she wasn't wrong.

"Look, I know you're disappointed, but—" he began.

"Don't tell me what I feel." Her mood went from ice to explosive in a millisecond, leaving her shaking and teary as she glared at him. "Don't tell me this is okay. This is something my body should be able to *do*, Rafael."

"*I* want to quit trying while we reassess," he said firmly, making that decision for both of them. "We could both use a break from the pressure."

"Oh, could you? Do you need a break from filling a cup once in a while?" she asked, voice pitched to the height of resentment.

He clenched his teeth against engaging. Whatever frustration he was suffering, she was going through worse. He knew that. Injections and procedures and waiting, only to find it hadn't worked.

But he stuck by his decision. When they came aboard,

he brought her a glass of wine, which she accepted with an air of resignation.

Since then, she had been drinking freely, not getting sloppy, but acting more the life of the party, the way she had in their early days. She trotted out salacious stories from "before my husband tamed me," and flirted outrageously with him, leaning to show him her cleavage and gripping the inside of his thigh over dinner.

Rafael didn't mind. Whenever she teased him in front of an audience, she always came through behind doors. He dismissed it as her blowing off steam from their latest disappointment, but he realized her infertility was affecting her far more deeply than she was letting on.

He *hated* that she took her body's inability to get pregnant as a personal failure. It was bad luck and he was genuinely saddened by it, but he couldn't say so. Anytime he tried to talk about it, she shut things down with the swiftness of a guillotine blade.

He was also off his game, he admitted to himself as he stepped behind the bar to make martinis. He was hoping another round of drinks would relax his wife and loosen up Gio, but he was probably better off asking the man to head back to the negotiating table.

As the suggestion formed on his lips, his purser arrived with an unfamiliar young woman. She wasn't part of the crew and reminded him vaguely of someone who might show him to a table at a streetside bistro. She wore a simple cotton blouse over wide-legged pants and mass-made sandals. She held a leather portfolio and her skimming glance locked on Gio where he lounged in the pool.

Gio had mentioned something about bringing two assistants aboard so unrelated work could continue while he negotiated with Rafael. Rafael had assented and forgotten about it.

He would have dismissed the interruption as completely unimportant but his wife hissed with unmistakable enmity, "What are you doing here?"

The poor woman was taken aback and looked like a shop-girl getting a dressing down over not having a requested size in stock.

It wasn't like Alexandra to be openly rude to anyone except her parents. She typically used honey, not vinegar, especially with staff. Was she still angry that he'd suggested they take a break from trying for a baby, and taking it out on this stranger?

"What's wrong, Alexandra?" Jacinda said from her position beside Gio in the pool. "Is the help supposed to stay belowstairs? You're such a snob."

"Molly is my assistant's assistant," Gio said crisply. "What do you need, Molly?"

"Valentina...um..." She waved the portfolio, looking pale at having been put on the spot. "She said you wanted to sign this as soon as it was ready."

"Your executive assistant has an assistant?" Rafael drawled, trying to defuse the tension that charged the air like electricity. "No wonder it was so difficult to get hold of you to extend this invitation."

He shot a look at Alexandra. She knew how important Gio was to solidifying the trade and cargo arm of the Zamos Corp.

Alexandra was shoving her arms into her cover-up, pushing her sunglasses onto her nose, and dropping a sun hat over her hair, but her mouth was tight with dismay.

Gio said something and left the pool so Molly could bring the portfolio to him.

Rafael wasn't really tracking the pair, too busy watching his wife as he finished shaking the martinis, then poured them out. When he took one to Alexandra, she said, "Thank you, my love," and took a big gulp. A *big* one.

What the hell was going on?

He glanced toward Molly. She was handing a pen to Gio, her back stiff as a board.

Rafael felt some compassion for her. He'd been on the receiving end of a "you don't belong here" fugue many times himself.

Gio signed the document and looked to Rafael. "I'd like this in London by morning."

"Of course." Rafael nodded at the purser to make it happen.

"I'm very sorry," Molly murmured, seeming cowed. "I'll stay below from now on."

"I was just surprised." Alexandra was on the defensive, finally catching up to how poorly she was behaving. "I'm usually informed when guests bring staff aboard."

"You thought we had a stowaway?" Rafael sipped his glass of icy gin, still thinking she was acting grossly out of character.

"What exactly do you do for Gio?" Alexandra asked Molly, finally dredging up the charming woman he was more familiar with, the one who showed everyone polite interest and effortlessly smoothed over social hiccups. She asked about Molly's duties, then wound up overcompensating by inviting the woman to breakfast. *What the hell?*

Molly agreed and left. A short while later, Rafael and Gio dressed and retreated to the office, where they continued discussing their potential partnership.

Rafael was still distracted, though. With his business thriving and this deal looking as though it would go through, he should be feeling more confident than ever, but he kept thinking about how the desire for children was eroding his marriage. Alexandra was suffering. He couldn't ignore that, nor did he know how to fix it. The whole thing filled him with a painful, nagging helplessness—which was the worst feeling in the world for him.

What the hell was he going to do?

Her past was catching up to her. Sasha could hear it like hounds in the distance, yelping and howling as they pursued her.

She hugged her silk kimono against the breeze coming through the open doors to the deck off their stateroom. It wasn't a cold wind. After growing up in New York and schooling in Switzerland, she rarely allowed herself to suffer anything below a balmy seventy degrees. That's why she had married a Greek and settled with him in Athens.

That's why she had persuaded him to sail them south, so she could feel these hot, dry winds off Africa, hoping they would dispel the chill of harsh reality that seemed determined to take residence in her bones.

"I was plan—"

Sasha jolted when Rafael's hand touched her shoulder and his voice resounded behind her ear.

"Did you not hear me in the shower?" he asked in an amused rumble. He folded his arms around her as an apology for startling her, drawing her back into his naked chest.

In moments like this, when his hard arms were around her, she felt safe and cherished and almost believed they would be okay.

"I was just thinking," she murmured, letting herself melt into his humid, near-naked frame.

"About?" His prompt was a warm vibration against her back.

About how angry she was with her body. How she felt as though these fertility problems were her fault. That this was some sort of karmic punishment.

It wasn't. Not exactly. Endometriosis happened to women who hadn't already carried a baby. There was no known cause. They only knew that it got worse with time. Perhaps if she'd tried to become pregnant sooner, she would have had a better outcome, but she hadn't. How could she have known? Her symptoms hadn't been bad enough for her to know a fertility problem was developing.

When she didn't answer him, Rafael rubbed her upper arms and said, "I'll call off your meeting."

"What? Why?" She stepped out of his arms and turned to confront him. He could be so overbearing sometimes!

And damn him for being built like a god. He wore only the fluffy white towel that barely clung to his hips. She was accosted by his naked chest, each muscle delineated to perfection. Her very favorite thing was to kiss the planes and subtle dips of his shoulders and chest and biceps and throat, where she could make him swallow simply by looking there.

"You got a little loose last night." His wide hand cupped the side of her neck. "I'm not complaining. *At all*. But you should sleep in."

Her cheeks stung and she couldn't bring herself to lift her gaze to his smug smile or the gratification in his gaze. She'd been all over him last night. She had played it off as being tipsy, but it had been more than that. Desperation had driven her to rub and writhe and take him in her mouth. To sob and encourage him to take her deeper. Faster. *Harder*.

So much of their lovemaking seemed to be driven by desperation these days, as though they both sensed how close they were to being rent apart.

Maybe it was just her that felt that way, though.

"What's going on?" His thumb tilted her jaw upward, gently insisting she look at him. His expression had turned grave. "Regret?"

"For last night? Of course not." That was true, but other

things? Oh, yes. She had so many regrets, she was drowning in them.

It was causing the veil between Sasha and Alexandra to slip, which terrified her. Alexandra was the strong woman she wanted to be. The one who didn't suffer fools or heartaches and was impervious to the cruel impacts of life.

Sasha was tortured and needy and yearned for love. She *hurt*. All the time.

She did what always worked when she was agitated and feeling defenseless around him. She reached for *his* veil, the edge of the towel he wore, plucking it loose while boldly holding his gaze.

"Did I sound like I was suffering regrets last night?" she challenged.

His lips parted to say something, but his breath turned to a hiss as she dropped the towel and caressed his hardening flesh. Something flashed behind his eyes. Suspicion? He knew she was trying to distract him.

She licked her lips suggestively and started to sink to her knees.

"No." His voice was gruff. He took hold of her arms, stopping her. "I was rough with you last night. Let me kiss it and make it better." He dragged her against him and the heat of his body penetrated the thin silk of the kimono, stealing her ability to speak. His hand fisted in her loose hair and tugged her head back so he could capture her mouth with his own, kissing her long and deep.

She splayed her hands on his naked skin, instantly overwhelmed. Distantly, she knew she ought to catch herself back from the rush of desire, from the way she so easily capitulated to him, but her hands roamed all over his back and buttocks, trying to touch all of him. Trying to incite him. Trying to be the one in charge.

He did the same, but with greater effect. His slow hand

rubbed silk against her skin, conveying that she could become as frantic as she wanted, but he was in no hurry. Not today.

"D-don't you have people waiting for you?" she asked breathlessly, when he slid his lazy kisses into the crook of her neck.

"They can wait."

This, too, was her downfall. He made her feel special. He made her feel as though she was his priority. The only thing that was important to him.

She desperately needed that right now.

She lifted her arms to curl around his neck, but he stopped her so he could tug open her kimono. His gaze dropped to admire and caress her breasts.

"Are your nipples sore? I'll be gentle." He bent to lick one, leaving it wet and tightening as the breeze from the open door washed across it. "I thought we had both used up our capacity for sexual hunger last night." He cupped and weighed her breast in his hot palm. "But I'm suddenly starving. Are you sure you want this?"

"Always," she admitted on a pang of distress, then rallied, trying to save face. "Why? Afraid you can't keep up with me?"

She tightened her arms around his neck, trying to mash herself against him. She felt him stiffen before he made a noise that was a scoff and a scold.

"*Glikia mou*, you know your pleasure is my pleasure. I'll always deliver as much as I possibly can." He scooped her up, so her legs instinctually wrapped his waist. "Until you beg me to stop."

As he took a few steps, his erection shifted against the naked flesh that was still tender from their energetic lovemaking last night.

Then she was falling, clasping in panic, but he was catching her before setting her on the settee that ran beneath the windows.

One lingering kiss on her lips was all he gave her before he knelt and arranged her so he could bend and anoint her most intimate flesh. He rubbed his freshly shaved cheeks against her inner thighs and blew softly on her sensitized mound and tasted her in a lazy and oh, so tender fashion.

"Rafael," she moaned.

"What do you need, *louloudi mou*? Stop?"

"No," she moaned, feeling as though she would burst. "Please don't stop."

He growled out a noise of satisfaction and set to pleasuring her, refusing to rush, making her arch and sob and dig her heel into his back.

It was infuriating to be this helpless to him, but it was such a wondrous trap to be held in. When they were like this, all her anguish and regret fell away. She was nothing but a single point of pleasure, needing nothing beyond the continuation of these incredible ripples of sensation.

There was something lonely and solitary in this particular moment, though. She wanted him to be as caught up as she was, thrusting into her with abandon. The longer he pleasured her, the more she felt herself slipping away. He was stealing pieces of her soul, one by one.

"I want you inside me." She caught a handful of his hair, but he only hugged her thighs in his strong arms and pressed his tongue to that bundle of nerves, so swollen and throbbing.

Climax twisted through her abdomen. A ball of joy detonated within her, sending shock waves of ecstasy through her limbs.

He lightened up, but didn't let up, continuing to pleasure her through the peak and into the trembling aftermath.

Her belly was still quivering and her heart rate still uneven when he rose to stand over her, fully hard with arousal, gaze taking in her helpless sprawl.

She didn't even have the strength to reach out and grip him in her fist, but he didn't seem to expect it. He trailed his fingers from her navel to run a caressing knuckle along the underside of her breast, then brushed a tendril of hair from her cheek.

"Thank you. I enjoyed that." He bent to retrieve his towel.

A sob of disbelief hit her throat. "Don't you want to…?" *Take me*.

"Later. Gio is expecting me." He slid a glance to the clock on the night table as he rewrapped the towel around his hips. "I'll cancel your breakfast meeting so you can sleep."

"*No.*" She sat up, mind still scattered.

"Why not? It's not important."

He said it very casually, but the full weight of his attention zeroed in on her.

Oh, you bastard, she thought.

This whole thing was a deliberate attempt to disconcert her. Which she would have found contemptible if she hadn't tried it first and *failed*.

"I need something to think about beyond my own inadequacy." She stood to retie her kimono.

"Stop that," he ordered. "It's not helpful to blame yourself. *I* don't blame you."

"Goodness, if *you* don't blame me, then I shouldn't dare, should I?" She knew that would get a rise out of him. That's why she'd said it.

They glared at one another, turning into the worst pair of bickering fools. If she had seen anyone else behaving this way, she would have said, *Get a divorce, already*.

The thought sent ice tumbling through her, chilling her bones.

"No," he said grimly. "You shouldn't." He walked into the bathroom where she heard water begin to run.

So arrogant. And yet he was trying to be supportive in his way. He didn't know, though. He didn't know why she was so angry with herself.

Tell him.

Then what? What if he looked at her with the same contempt Humbolt had shown? With the same contempt she felt for herself? She couldn't take that. She really couldn't.

He walked into the closet so she went into the bathroom where she hung her kimono and stepped into the shower.

By the time she came out, he was gone.

CHAPTER FIVE

"Molly. Thank you for coming." Sasha used the lofty tone her mother would use when welcoming a decorator or some other contracted person into her home. She let her into the stateroom, then glanced up and down the empty corridor before closing the door.

When she faced Molly, she found her old friend turning a slow circle in the middle of the lounge. The suite was enormous, with a bookshelf as a partition between the parlor and the bedroom, then a private deck in the bow.

Molly's brunette hair was in a tidy bun, her pantsuit off-the-rack. She was still a bit of a country girl with her eyes agog and her jaw slack, but she was also Molly, so her heart was on full display.

"I am *so sorry.*" Her expression crumpled into anxiety as she faced Sasha. "I had no idea you were Alexandra Zamos. I wouldn't have come. I certainly wouldn't have shown up on the lido deck! I won't say a word, Sash." Her voice was barely above a whisper. *"I swear."*

Sit down. Let's eat. That's what Sasha had planned to say to her, before she asked Molly how much money she wanted to keep her trap shut.

Instead, she found herself rushing forward and throwing her arms around her.

Molly released a small "eep" of surprise before she hugged

her back. They were no longer adolescent girls. It made their hug unfamiliar yet still a homecoming. The acceptance in it was water on Sasha's parched soul.

"It's so good to see you," Molly said.

It's good to see you, too.

That's what Sasha wanted to say, but she was starting to cry.

How embarrassing. She hadn't fallen apart like that in years. Maybe ever.

Oh, she cried every time she got her period, but with anger, cutting short her pity party as quickly as she could, then swiping away her tears with resentment.

This had been a release of emotions she had bottled the day she'd walked away from Molly's home in New Jersey. From her baby and the only other two people in this world she loved with all her heart.

Sasha washed her face and came out with a cold face-cloth that she continued to dab against her eyes, hoping to reduce the swelling and redness before Rafael returned.

"Sit. Eat. Please," she said with an impatient wave toward the table when she saw Molly was still hovering. "How's your mom?"

"Good. We're all good." Molly sat, but her eyes were red from shared tears and she pressed a tissue beneath her nose before looking at Sasha with an earnest expression that searched hers while shining with expectation of some kind. "Libby is wonderful, Sash. She's so smart and funny. Sometimes she asks about y—"

"Don't," she choked, feeling as though she'd been stabbed in the chest. "I can't hear about her, Molly. I can't." Especially now, when she knew Libby was the only baby she was likely to ever carry.

Such longing gripped her, she could barely breathe. Tears rose hotly in her eyes again.

In an attempt to regain her composure, she sat to pour their coffee, thinking her mother was good for something, having taught her to ignore difficult displays of emotion and pretend all was well.

She had to explain, though. "Rafael doesn't know. I've never told anyone. It has to stay that way."

Molly's silence was thick with hurt. When she spoke, however, her voice was stiff with indignation. "I understand and respect that, but I won't pretend my sister doesn't exist."

And that right there, that mixture of compassion for her, with fierce pride and defense of the child she called her sister, told Sasha she had made the right decision leaving her baby with Patty and Molly.

"Can I ask how you met Rafael?"

Sasha leaped on telling that story, painting a full picture of how gorgeous he'd been in his tuxedo, how he'd asked her to dance and she'd felt as though she was in a dream.

"All under the nose of some knob my parents wanted me to marry."

Molly lifted an amused look from her poached egg and smoked salmon on a toasted crostini. She was so refreshing. Molly didn't fuss around with diets or hair color or push-up bras. *Her* mother had taught her that if a man didn't love you as you were, then he didn't love *you*.

Sasha had always envied her that confidence in her own self-worth.

She finished out the story with the secret elopement and dramatic announcement over brunch. She almost added, *Libby's father was there*, but she shied away from that part of it. It had been enough to throw her new husband in his face.

"It sounds like love at first sight," Molly said with a wistful smile.

Sasha's cup hit her saucer with a loud clank.

"We agreed from the beginning that we were using each other to some extent. In a practical way, I mean. Not cold-hearted. Our feelings have grown over time." It wasn't dishonest to say that, but she didn't want to admit to anyone, including herself, how uneven the emotional investment was between herself and her husband. "Rafael indulges me, which I can't say I hate." Even if she wished his "darlings" and other endearments were more sincere. "He's caring and supportive." In his way.

It's not helpful to blame yourself.

"We have each other's respect, which is more than I expected to have with any man." Mostly. She recalled his assertion of control this morning and grew pensive, then insisted brightly, "The sex is fantastic." She offered a wicked grin, ignoring the ache of loneliness that had been sitting like a block of ice in her middle for the longest time.

"I'm happy for you, Sash." Molly wasn't exactly gushing, though. She was trying to peer past the veneer of nonchalance that Sasha wore.

"What about you?" Sasha turned the tables. "Anyone special in your life?"

"No." Molly's cheeks went pink as she reached for her coffee. "I'm focused on my career."

"You mean your boss?" Sasha teased.

"Oh, my God. *Please* tell me it's not obvious?" she begged with mortification.

"I was almost catatonic with shock yesterday, but I could still tell there was something between you. Are you seeing him?"

"God no! He doesn't even know I'm alive."

Sasha's radar had picked up something else, but she kept it to herself. She knew how people at Gio's level operated. A few short years ago, he had nearly married a woman who had noble roots, a vineyard in Tuscany, and a château in the south of France. Molly was far more special than any of those things, but a rich prat like Gio might be oblivious to it and see only a pretty woman with a crush that he could use for his own ends.

"I can't help being attracted to him," Molly confided with a cringe of helplessness. "You saw him."

"I only have eyes for my husband," Sasha insisted, but she wasn't dead. Gio Casella was definitely a looker. "Promise me you won't let him play you like a flute."

"Don't worry. It's never going to happen. I wouldn't know what to do if it did. I can't imagine being involved with someone who lives like this." Molly glanced around. "I'm glad you're happy, though."

Me, too, Sasha tried to say, but had to bite her lip because it was starting to quiver. The raw, septic wound in her heart burst open and the words flowed out.

"I can't get pregnant."

"What?" Molly sat up straighter, then reached across to squeeze her hand. "It can take a long time for some people, Sash. Don't lose hope. Do you want to call Mom? She might be able to help." She looked for her phone.

"It's been a year and a half." Which was nothing. She knew there were people who tried for a decade before they saw results, but Rafael had insisted they take a break and that terrified her. If she couldn't give him a baby, would he still want *her*?

"I'm seeing specialists and we've tried IVF *three* times." Sasha picked up the damp cloth to press it against the salty tears beginning to burn the edges of her eyelids again. "We both want a baby, but my body won't work and it's so unfair, Moll. I did this once before. I should be able to do it again." The resentment was rising like a tide, pushing the tears into her eyes and nose and throat. "And I keep thinking it's my fault that—"

"No. Sasha, *no*." Molly reached to crush her hand in her two warm ones. "Talk to Mom. She'll tell you there are a thousand reasons a woman might have trouble conceiving. None of them are your fault. But you also know that if you want to be in Libby's life, we would love for you—"

"No. Molly." She snatched her hand away and shifted sideways in her chair, clutching where her chest was still cleaved in half by that long-ago loss. "Rafael wants an heir of his own. Not... I mean, we've talked a little about adoption, but he's adopted. I can tell there's a part of him that wants a blood connection, you know? I want that, too. I want *our* baby and I'm so angry with myself that I can't give him this."

"Is *he* angry?" Molly's voice hardened. "Is he putting pressure on you?"

"No." She dashed at the tears that were overflowing her lashes. "He said we should take a break from trying, which makes me feel like even more of a failure."

"Oh, Sasha." Molly started to come around to hug her, but Sasha brushed her off.

"You'll make me cry again." She picked up the soggy cloth and pressed it to her eyes.

"Take that down and look at me."

She didn't want to, but Molly sounded so much like Patty with that firm tone of tough love, she dropped the cloth into her lap.

Molly was crouched in front of her, somber. "A man twice your age took advantage of you. You didn't do anything wrong—"

"He was married, Molly. I knew it was wrong."

"You were *sixteen*. He was an adult. He said he loved you. He manipulated you and left you to deal with a pregnancy *alone.* Do not pretend your crime is equal to his. That's something Humbolt would do, and you know what a piece of garbage he is."

Sasha pushed the wet cloth against her eyes again, pressing back emotive tears. She was touched by the way Molly was still willing to be her champion.

It was true, though. She could still hear Humbolt calling her a slut and a homewrecker and some dark part of her continued to believe it.

"Have you ever talked to anyone? A counselor?" Molly was smoothing her hair the way her mother had done when Sasha had been so troubled, living with strangers, contemplating the biggest decision of her life.

"About him? Never. My fertility specialist recommended someone for the pregnancy troubles, but I'd have to tell them about all of that and..." She looked helplessly to Molly and her heart constricted with agony. "I can't. I can't talk to anyone about any of this. There's no one I trust. Rafael tries to understand, but he doesn't." And she didn't trust him—them—enough to reveal it to him.

"Talk to me, then. Get it off your chest." Molly moved back into her chair.

Sasha took a deep breath and breathed out all her hopelessness.

"It's endometriosis. Severe. I can keep trying until the cows come home, but I'll probably never get pregnant. I don't want to accept that, but I can't keep doing this with the shots and the exams and the procedures that fail. It's like having a miscarriage every time because I convince myself that I'm pregnant, then I'm not. And it makes me such a moody bitch I don't know how Rafael stays married to me." Her voice turned into a choke as the fear of her marriage ending ran through her like an electric current, hot and painful. "Why did I get pregnant by a man I hate, but I can't get pregnant by a man I love? It's so *unfair*, Moll."

"Oh, Sash. I'm so sorry." Molly's expression was agonized on her behalf.

For once, the weight of her sadness shifted slightly. It was no longer suffocating her. Molly was holding some of it for her and that made her want to hug her. How could she keep her in her life, she wondered? Yesterday, she had told Gio she wouldn't try to poach his assistant, but she would gladly pay Molly to be her friend again, just for this little bit of emotional support she offered her.

"Have you considered a surrogate?" Molly asked gently.

"Not seriously." Sasha sighed again. "I would have to tell people why I need one." Failure was inching back into her tight throat.

"You don't have to tell anyone anything. It's your business how you make a baby," Molly said with affront.

"We'd still have to interview people. Whoever we chose would be a stranger. It feels too invasive to let someone I don't know into our lives like that." She was greedy. Insecure, maybe, because she didn't want to share Rafael with someone she didn't know and trust. "That's why I want to do it myself, but I *can't*. And I'm so tired of being miserable and useless and *alone*, Moll." Her eyes welled afresh, which just made her mad because tears were useless, too.

"Oh, Sasha, stop punishing yourself. I wish you'd let me tell you how happy you made us. I know that doesn't fix anything for you, but I wish you could be proud of what you gave us. If I could—" Molly bit her lips, apprehension coming into her face.

"What?" Sasha looked behind her, terrified that Rafael had walked in and overheard them, but the room was empty. "What?" she insisted to Molly.

"I needed to double-think what I was going to say,"

Molly said with a twitch of bemusement around her lips. Her brows gathered into a frown of gravity. "Because I don't want to say it unless I mean it, and I do. If I could give you the same happiness you gave us, I would, Sasha. What if I tried? What if I was your surrogate?"

Sasha's heart took a hard bounce.

"Moll." She made herself dismiss the offer because Molly was just being her kind and loyal and heart-forward self. Sasha hadn't known how to maintain their friendship without risking Libby, but she was sorry she had let so many years go by without speaking to her friend.

"I'm being serious." Molly leaned forward with the earnest, open warmth that filled Sasha with optimism that, somehow, things would work out. "I would need tests to see if it's feasible, but you know how badly I had always wanted a sister. You gave me one. I would argue that you gave me two, because I've never forgotten you." Her mouth widened with a sentimental smile. "And Libby has been such a gift, Sash. I can't even describe how much Mom and I love her. If I could give you someone to love that hard, then I want to."

"Molly, stop. How would I even explain it to Rafael? How—"

"'How' is a yes," Molly noted with her mother's clear logic. "You're saying you'll let me try. Aren't you?"

She shouldn't, but hope was making her latch on to the logistics, skipping right over whether allowing Molly to do this was wise.

But it would bring her friend back into her life. It would mean she didn't have to tell anyone—including Rafael—about her past because Molly already knew.

"It's too much for me to ask of you, Moll," Sasha protested weakly.

"You're not asking. I'm offering." A huge smile was

breaking across her face. "Please let me try. I want to do this for you if I can, Sasha. I really do."

Sasha was speechless, unable to imagine how they would manage it or how she would repay her, but she jerkily nodded. "If you're sure, then yes. Please. Let's try."

"Do you have business in London soon?" Alexandra asked when they arrived at their villa in Attica, overlooking Dikastika Bay, about an hour from Athens.

Built to his wife's specifications, the house had more stairs than Rafael would have liked, given its five floors, but it was not only tasteful and the envy of any guest for its panoramic views, river stone pool, and xeriscape grounds, but it felt like a home. They casually shed their travel clothes and dipped naked into the water, confident their staff would busy themselves with unpacking and allow them their privacy.

"Nothing pressing, why?" He'd been away from the office for nearly two weeks and, while he was productive aboard the *Alexandra*, he had a lot to attend to at headquarters now that he was back, not least of which was following up on the fine points of the deal he'd negotiated with Gio Casella. Gio had a London office, though. Perhaps it would be useful to meet with him there.

"I think I've found us a surrogate."

"What?" He ducked and arrowed closer to her in a wide sweep of his arms, surfacing where she was treading water, but he could stand on the bottom of the pool. "How? *Who*?"

"You don't sound pleased." The blur of her naked body shifted as she also reached her foot toward the shallow end and stood on the bottom.

"You've never wanted to talk about a surrogate." Granted, that had been as they were going into the third IVF, but...

"This seems like something we ought to discuss and decide together."

"We're discussing it now." She was being her loftiest, most irritatingly snooty self, barely looking at him as she turned her back and waded to the stairs.

She continued to be the most alluring woman he'd ever seen as she stepped naked under the outdoor shower, keeping her hair out of the water as she'd done in the pool. She rinsed, then turned off the spray before shaking out a bath sheet from the cupboard.

"Or not," she added as she wrapped the towel around herself, referring to his dumbfounded silence.

"Tell me, then." He came out behind her and snapped the shower on, blasting the water against his face and chest, turned to rinse his hair, then snapped it off and accepted the towel she handed him.

The evening was cool, but he didn't dry off. He wrapped the towel around his hips and followed her up the outer stairs to their bedroom.

The maid quickly excused herself and hurried from the room, leaving them to the long shadows of sunset while they dressed.

"You remember I had breakfast with Gio's assistant?" There was something in her voice that made his ears strain, certain there was more to hear in her tone than its deliberate casualness.

"Molly," he recollected.

"You remember her name?" Her head turned so she could sear him with her gaze.

"No need to be possessive, darling. Banking names is a useful skill."

"Hmph. Well, we got to talking about my issues."

"How?" It came out with unvarnished astonishment. "You never talk about it with anyone." She barely talked

to him about it and had flatly refused to see a professional counselor, no matter how much he and their fertility specialist suggested it might be helpful.

"She mentioned her mother is a midwife." She shrugged. "It came out and, long story short, she offered to be our surrogate."

He choked on disbelief. *"Why?"* As if he didn't know.

"Are you really going to look down on someone who is willing to carry a pregnancy for money? You married me for mine," she reminded him.

"Touché." His reaction had been a reflex of his well-honed cynicism. He stepped into his trousers. "You're right. It's labor." Literally. He'd never thought of it that way, but, "It deserves compensation."

"Is that what you think being my husband is? *Work*?" she asked with affront, head poking from the knitted top she pulled over it.

Damn, she was prickly these days.

"More of a calling, darling," he assured her, approaching to skim his hands alongside her neck, freeing her hair from the collar. "But I deserve danger pay sometimes."

He started to drop a kiss on her mouth, but she turned her face away, brows elevated to a piqued angle.

He kissed her cheekbone and testily turned away to search out his own shirt.

"What makes you think she's the right sort of person?" he asked as he threaded his arms into his sleeves. "Has she done it before?"

"No." She pulled on snug yoga pants. "She warned me that could be a roadblock. Doctors don't usually work with a surrogate who hasn't had a successful pregnancy of their own."

Rafael dismissed that. Nearly any roadblock could be overcome for a price.

"What makes you think she's right for the job?" For *us*?

"She's discreet."

"How do you know?"

"She wouldn't be working for Gio if she wasn't."

True.

"She seems conscientious and capable of restraint. I offered her a mimosa, but she refused. Said she was on the clock."

"High praise."

"Look, you know I don't trust easily. She seems honest and responsible, plus she's stationed in London. Dr. Narula started her practice there. I imagine she still has good contacts to recommend. This saves me advertising my infertility to find someone else. I think it's worth exploring. At the very least, we should let her get tested to see if she's suitable. I won't get my hopes up until I know whether it's even possible."

Rafael's instincts were still prickling, telling him there was more going on here than she was revealing, but he was so damned relieved that she sounded optimistic for a change, he didn't want to ruin it by voicing misgivings. She was right. There was little harm in running the tests.

"If this is what you want, then fine. Find out if she's suitable."

"Really?" Finally, she turned to face him.

Alexandra was a sophisticated woman with a razor-sharp intelligence and a jaded sense of humor. She was so beautiful, she knocked the breath out of him and had from the first time he'd spied her across a room, but occasionally, like now, when her face was clean of makeup and her poise slipped to reveal how badly she wanted something, she looked very young and vulnerable.

It caused a dip and roll inside his chest, one that had always disturbed him, because that's not who they were. He relied on her to be as guarded and battle-ready as he was. Armed to the teeth.

Most of the time she was. The last thing he would call her was "maternal," but in this moment, he couldn't ignore how badly she wanted a baby. He wanted to give her a family in any way he could. If that meant hiring a surrogate, so be it.

"Yes," he said firmly, cupping her cheek and pressing his mouth to hers, heartened when her cool hands arrived on his neck and her lips clung to his. "I want you to be happy, Alexandra. I've always wanted that." He had thought that was an easy assignment until the baby troubles arose. "If you think this will work, then proceed."

She curled her arms tighter around his neck, so her whole body was stretched against his and breathed a heartfelt, "Thank you," against his ear.

CHAPTER SIX

BETWEEN CHRISTMAS AND travel and various tests, then the harvesting and fertilization of fresh eggs and mandatory counseling, it was April before implantation occurred.

Sasha had offered to stay in London with Molly while she waited out the result, but Molly was working. They were both aware that it might take several rounds before there was a successful implant. Molly had agreed to try three times, which Sasha thought was more than generous, considering how invasive and time consuming the procedure was.

So Sasha was with Rafael in Rio de Janeiro, eating breakfast on the terrace of their hotel room overlooking Copacabana Beach, when "Dr. Kala Narula" came up on her phone.

She stabbed to accept the call. Kala's assistant brought Molly onto the screen in a separate box, then Kala appeared.

"Good morning, Alexandra. Hello, Molly. Is Rafael here, too?" Kala asked.

"Yes." Sasha flashed a look to him and tightened her hand on the phone.

He set down his coffee, listening intently.

"Congratulations—"

Sasha's ears filled with water. She didn't hear the rest. Stinging waves of emotion rolled through her. Were they positive feelings? Negative? She didn't know. She only knew they made her heart race and her lungs search for oxygen. She couldn't see anything but a blur.

Rafael said something and took the phone from her limp fingers. She heard Molly sounding breathless and excited.

Why don't I feel that way? Why am I not happy?

"I think she's in shock. I'll have her call you later, Molly. Thank you." Rafael sounded warm and sincere and almost as though he was speaking through laughter.

He was happy. She could hear it.

"Agápi mou?" He clicked off her phone and set it aside, then drew her from her chair. "There it is. We've done it."

No, they hadn't. *She* hadn't.

"You're shaking." He hugged her, still sounding as though he was chuckling over her reaction.

"Anything could still go wrong," she blurted, wedging her arms between them.

Not that she wanted anything to go wrong. No. Absolutely not. She wouldn't wish Molly to go through a miscarriage or any sort of trauma.

The magnitude was hitting her, though, of exactly what she was asking from her friend. Why would Molly agree to this?

I don't deserve it.

Rafael kept his arms around her as he studied her through hooded eyes.

She swallowed, realizing she was displaying all the wrong reactions.

"Everyone knows you're not supposed to tell people until three months have gone past. I don't want to b—" *Become attached.* "Believe it until I know it's really going to happen."

She brushed free of his arms and moved to the rail.

"I don't want my parents to know. They *can't* know," she added, turning her head to impress that on him. "Humbolt will definitely start shoring up his position." He still had control of the bulk of the estate. Portions were designated for her mother's use for her lifetime, which was the excuse Humbolt used to muck with everything. "I wouldn't put it past him to find Molly and harass her..." Expose everything. Endanger the baby.

"Once the b-baby arrives, the whole arrangement shifts," she continued. "I'll finally be able to oust him. I can't risk him being forewarned."

"Is that the only reason you've wanted a baby?" Rafael's voice chilled with cynicism.

"No." She flung around to face him, still dizzy.

If that was all she wanted, she could have revealed Libby years ago. She had thought about doing it thousands of times, but that baby—Molly's little sister—was not a weapon. Sasha had always believed that the most loving, selfless, maternal thing she could do for Libby was to allow her to live outside the nest of deadly spiders she'd grown up in, but it was hitting her that she was about to bring a new baby into that.

What had she done?

And there was Rafael looking at her as though he didn't recognize her.

"No." Her voice was still strained, but she forced herself to pull it together. "But it *is* my money. My father intended it for me and my children. I refuse to let Humbolt keep his foot on my neck. You wouldn't, in my shoes. Would you? You'd fight as dirty as you had to."

"True." His mouth was stern as he watched her through the screen of his lashes, looking impossibly handsome when he was like this—still and severe, freshly showered and his shirt open at the throat. "But financial gain wasn't the first thing that leapt to mind when I heard we have a baby on the way."

"I guess that makes you a better person than me, doesn't it?" she said scathingly, before turning back to the rail and the view. She didn't see anything but a blur, though. She only saw that the baby wasn't fixing anything between them at all. How had she thought it could? How was she still making wrong decisions this late in the game?

No. It wasn't a wrong decision. She wanted her baby. Rafael's baby.

Oh, God. She buried her face in her hands, not sure she could handle how badly she wanted the baby Molly carried. If it failed to arrive...

"Alexandra." His hands closed over her upper arms and his voice was gentler as he spoke behind her ear. "I refuse to have a fight when we've just received such happy news. You *are* happy, aren't you? Because you've left it late to change your mind."

"I *am* happy," she insisted. She turned to face him, eyes hot with tears she was fighting not to allow to fall. "But I'm scared." She was rarely this honest with him about her feelings, but they bubbled up out of her. "I'm scared it won't work and we'll be back to square one. I'm scared—" To be a mother.

Her voice hiccuped into a painful bubble that was caught in her throat.

This time she would keep her baby. She would have to learn how to guide it through all the trials of life. What the hell did she know about loving and caring for someone? Teaching them how to be good and kind?

"What happens if I'm a terrible mother?" she asked in a choke. "What if I ruin our child?"

"Ruin? Or spoil?" He brushed a stray tendril of hair from where it tickled her cheek and tucked it behind her ear. "I'm sure we'll both be overindulgent, but even if we make mistakes, I'm not worried. Your mother is incompetent at best and you turned out beautifully."

"Ha!" she barked and fresh tears pushed against the backs of her eyes. Her chest hurt. Really hurt. She kept her arms wedged between them, resisting him and what he'd just said because he was *wrong.*

"So you were an unruly party girl for a few years." He laced his fingers behind her lower back. "That's what makes you interesting."

Most of her stories on that front were exaggerated or appropriated from her friends' exploits. It had always served her to be seen as wild. It drove her parents up a wall and threw them off the scent of what she'd really been up to at sixteen.

"Alexandra." His hand burrowed under her hair and cupped the side of her neck. "Every parent has moments of self-doubt. I'm sure we'll have many, but we're a good team. We've proven that."

A good team. Her heart panged. Was that all she was to him? Someone who wore the same jersey?

"We'll get through whatever we face so long as we do what we've always done—be honest with each other."

She swallowed back another scoffing, *Ha!* Her eyes refused to lift higher than the buttons on his shirt, fearing he would see how much she was hiding.

"You are always honest with me, aren't you?" he pressed.

Her pulse seemed to beat harder against the palm that still rested against her throat.

"Yes." Her voice rasped over what felt like a lie. She *was* honest with him.

But not transparent.

"Let's not borrow trouble, then. If something happens, we'll deal with it together." He drew her into his embrace once more, urging her to melt against him. His mouth pressed to her temple and his voice held a note of awe. "Let's take a moment to celebrate our first baby being on the way."

His first.

Her whole body checked, but she made herself override her stiffness and hugged him while hiding her face in the hard plane of his chest.

They were back in Athens when Rafael realized he had expected the baby news would restore their marriage to the way things had been before they had embarked on trying to start a family.

It wasn't like him to delude himself. He was an unapologetic realist, but it struck him rather hard when he realized the distance between him and his wife was growing, not shrinking.

She still had conflicted feelings around her own fertility, he supposed.

They'd had to take mandatory counseling sessions before Dr. Narula was willing to allow Molly to surrogate so he had as good an understanding as a man could have of how Alexandra might be struggling with a sense of failure or inadequacy, especially now that they were relying on someone else to carry their baby.

He had mixed feelings about the process himself. As Alexandra had said the first time they'd considered "other options," using a surrogate felt as though they were allowing a stranger to infiltrate their marriage.

Not that he had any quarrel with Molly. He found her to be pleasant and eager in the way of an A-student who wished to earn top marks for baby-building. She might be doing this for financial gain, but she wasn't greedy about it.

On the contrary, she had brought a sensible figure to the table based on the going rates in the U.S. and other countries that allowed compensation for this particular service. She had asked him to cover expenses like health care, maternity clothes, and putting her career on hold, but it was all very reasonable.

She'd been appalled when Rafael added a zero to the end of her opening ask, then tried to talk him down, which had been amusing. He related to her, though. She wasn't an orphan, but she came from humble, middle-class roots and brought those practical sensibilities with her along with a streak of ambition. Hers wasn't nearly as cutthroat as his own, but he respected her for having one.

She had also brought up a number of considerations he hadn't thought of himself, proving she took this task very seriously.

From the beginning, she had been accommodating and discreet, happily signing a nondisclosure agreement while she went through the early tests. Once she was determined to be a healthy and suitable candidate, and they decided to proceed, they had sat down to negotiate the actual surrogacy agreement. Molly had raised intelligent questions around what would happen if they were unable to take custody or some other misfortune befell any of them. She had been all business and very flexible on every point except two.

"With regards to the nondisclosure agreement, I would like to include my mother in this process moving forward. She's a midwife and very well versed in patient confidentiality. You won't have any concerns around that side of it and she will be an enormous emotional support and resource for me."

"We can agree to that," Alexandra had said promptly, despite the fact that she was the one who always insisted on profound secrecy.

Rafael found it odd that she was so willing to trust someone she'd never met, given she was such an alarmist where her parents were concerned. He understood her concerns around them, but often wondered what she thought they could do to her at this stage. She was an adult, married, living away from them. Given his growing assets, she didn't need the fortune that was supposed to come to her. He understood and respected her desire to take possession of what belonged to her, but he wasn't afraid to put her stepfather through the wash and hang him out to dry in the courts—or physically, if necessary—should Humbolt truly misbehave, yet she seemed to feel her stepfather held something over her.

There were times he wanted to prod her on that, but one of the strengths of their relationships was the boundaries they drew around their pasts. They accepted each other as they were right now, which was exactly the way he wanted it.

But given how carefully she managed what her parents knew about her life, he was surprised that she was willing to air their private business to some unknown woman in America who lived only one state over from them.

His wife and their surrogate seemed to have forged an immediate connection, however. As soon as Alexandra agreed that Molly could tell her mother, Molly smiled with relief. Her "Thank you" almost seemed to transmit more than gratitude. A silent message?

The hairs on the back of his neck stood up. What—

"I understand you'll want a thorough background check on me and my mother." Molly addressed that to Rafael. "I will consent to that and I'm confident my mother will, but within that agreement, I want your promise that you will not delve into my sister's birth history. She knows she's adopted, but it's for her to pursue the identity of her birth parents if or when that becomes something she wants. It's not your place to reveal that and that information has no relevance here."

Her gaze slid to Alexandra and she quickly spoke for both of them *again*.

"Rafael understands that sort of intrusion very well. It's public knowledge that he's adopted, but there have been times that's been used against him. He wouldn't do that to a helpless child." The look she sent him was both challenge and wariness, like the point of a knife under his chin, daring him to contradict her.

He didn't know which shocked him more, that she was putting words in his mouth or that she would doubt his ethics on this front. That *hurt*, which wasn't something that happened often. He and Alexandra had a perfect relationship—one that was affectionate enough to let down his guard with her more than he did with anyone else, but superficial enough that he was rarely stung more deeply than ego level when they argued.

"It's true," he said briskly, steeling himself against those harsh memories of being kicked to the ground and called every sort of name. Bastard. Imposter. *Garbage*. "I don't see any reason to find her birth parents since they're firmly out of her life and won't impact ours. I agree to leave her out of the screening."

Was it his imagination or did Alexandra exhale when he agreed to that?

He glanced at her, but she was adjusting herself in her seat and flicking her hair behind her shoulder, smiling blandly at Molly.

"Let's move on to how we'll keep your pregnancy under wraps once it becomes obvious," Alexandra said.

"I can take a medical leave from work. I've looked into it and they don't need to know what it's for," Molly said. "As much as I would love my mother to attend the birth, that would require my going back to America. I don't think that's ideal for the level of privacy you're seeking. As long as I'm given consistent care, I'm open to delivering wherever it suits you best. Athens, perhaps?"

"She could stay at the island villa once she's showing." Alexandra glanced at him. "It's private, but only a short helicopter flight to Athens when she goes into labor."

"Would you stay there with me?" Molly brightened as she looked to Alexandra.

"Why?" Rafael interjected flatly, instantly feeling threatened for no reason that he could fathom.

"To bond with the baby." Molly blinked in surprise, as though that should be obvious.

"Oh." He looked at his wife.

Alexandra did that thing where she dropped her lashes and painted a bored expression across her face, completely masking her thoughts.

"Let's see how things go," she murmured, not committing.

The legal side of things wrapped up very neatly after that. Before he knew it, they were getting the call on the terrace in Rio. The pregnancy was confirmed. Their baby was only the size of a kidney bean, but was already taking up all his thoughts, filling him with more anticipation than he had expected to feel.

He would swear he wasn't a sentimental man, but there was something very elating in knowing he had a baby on the way, one who was a mix of him and Alexandra. A link that could never be undone.

Why? He was enlightened enough to know that masculinity was a construct, not something that was proven by procreation. He had taken on his adoptive father's name and business, making them his own. There was no reason to feel he couldn't have done the same with a baby who did not share his bloodline.

Others placed importance on those things, however, which definitely played a part in his sense of satisfaction. A dynasty was not built on one man clawing his way to the top. An heir represented continuity. For that reason, he wanted to tell the world that he did, indeed, have a baby on the way. It was a final checkmate in the external chess game he'd been playing since he'd taken over his father's business.

His mother hadn't had the capacity to fend off the sharks that had come circling back then, the ones who'd been frenzied by the scent of blood in the water. Those predators hadn't taken him seriously and even the employees had smirked at a teenager ordering fully grown men back to work. The only authority he'd had at the time was his status as "heir" and many had tried to dismiss it as an illegitimate title.

So yes, having a baby with his DNA mattered, but that wasn't the source of this simmering satisfaction. This was a sensation of being pulled toward something bright and solid. It was an indelible connection to his wife.

That was it. That was the reason for his sense of triumph. It wasn't the achievement of making a baby. It was the unbreakable bond their baby represented.

Why was it so important, he wondered with a twinge of unease? It smacked of a sop against uncertainty, something he refused to let himself feel.

But his wife seemed so damned elusive and unpredictable these days! He couldn't help feeling he needed all the hooks and grapples he could get to hold on to her. The baby was due around Christmas, but he wanted to hurry the time away. He wanted to begin planning for this addition to their family, accumulating more evidence of their baby's impending arrival.

Instead of sharing his enthusiasm, however, Alexandra grew tetchy and obstructive. She constantly reminded him that, "Anything could happen."

At the same time, she became scrupulous about protecting Molly's interests, chasing down every promised chunk of money to ensure it was sent on time. Molly's compensation was tiered so that she received funds every week of pregnancy, but those payments were automatic.

"Did she say there was a problem with the transfer?" Rafael asked Alexandra.

"No, but I want to be sure she's being looked after. She has morning sickness. I think we should give her a bonus for putting up with that."

"That's covered under the contract. If she's too unwell to work, she can go on leave early and we'll replace her salary." Once she stopped working, she would move into the island villa, where they would provide everything she needed until the baby arrived. On delivery, Molly would receive her final payment and go back to her career.

"For God's sake, Rafael. Quit being such a hard-ass," Alexandra snapped. "You have no idea what she's going through."

"No," he agreed. "I don't. Ask her to include me in your text chain."

"It's girl stuff," she argued. "She doesn't want to share those sorts of details with you."

"Nevertheless." Rafael kept a firm grip on his patience. "I want updates. I can't help wondering if she's manipulating you—"

"Do *not*." She clasped her phone to her chest as though he were physically trying to take it from her. "I know what being manipulated feels like. That is *not* what she's doing. She mentioned it was a rough week and Dr. Narula said her checkup was fine, that she can keep working if she wants to, but *I* want to be sure we're doing everything we can to make this as easy as possible for her."

In moments like this, he was both heartened and suspicious.

"Are you worried about the baby or Molly?"

A stunned pause, then, "*Both*. Obviously."

She rose to stalk away.

"Alexandra." He took a long step to catch her wrist, keeping her beside him. "This is guilt, then?"

For one second, there was such a look of naked culpability on her face, his heart bounced in reaction. Then she pulled free.

"This isn't like asking the maid to pick up the dry cleaning. We're not putting her out for five minutes. Her entire life will be going on hold."

"Yes, but she understood that was the nature of the assignment. Didn't she? Ask her to call us when she has a moment." He nodded at her phone. "I'd like to speak with her."

"Why?" Her hand tightened on her phone again and her jaw set. He could see all sorts of angry thoughts brewing behind her expression.

"Because I want to know how she's feeling." Mentally and physically.

"*Fine*," she said through her teeth.

What the hell?

That was the moment he realized that he had thought they would return to the more relaxed, comfortable dynamic of their early marriage. Instead, there seemed to be yet another layer of tension.

Perhaps Alexandra was simply worried about the baby. If Molly wasn't feeling well, that would trigger her concern for the baby. That made sense, he supposed.

Molly called the next day to reassure them that everything was going well, mentioning the morning sickness was an inconvenience, not severe. She urged them not to worry.

They saw her in person a few weeks later, when they flew to London for her twelve-week scan. She seemed to be her bright, happy self, smiling in greeting when they entered the clinic to find her already there.

The women embraced like long-lost friends, which didn't really surprise Rafael. They texted often and seemed to be growing closer by the day. It did strike Rafael as strange, though. Alexandra was usually aloof with everyone, even women she'd known since her school days.

"Ugh, Sash. Don't hug me so hard," Molly protested with pained humor. "I drank half the Thames to get ready for this."

"Oh. Sorry." Alexandra chuckled.

Molly left with a nurse a moment later to change into a gown.

"Did she call you Sash?" Rafael asked.

"Hmm? Oh. Yes. Short for Sasha." Alexandra began rummaging in her purse. "She told me she had a child-hood friend who had my name and went by Sasha. It's cute, right? I said she could call me that." She ran some balm across her lips and dropped the tube back into her purse, not meeting his eyes.

"Sasha is already short," he pointed out, puzzled by exactly how close they seemed to have become. Exactly how often did they talk?

"Mr. and Mrs. Zamos?" A nurse escorted them down a short hallway into a darkened room. Molly was on a table. A sheet was draped across her upper thighs and tucked into the waistband of, presumably, her underwear. Her hospital gown was bunched up to her rib cage, exposing a belly that was still very flat.

The doctor had said this was an external scan and would

only proceed to internal if that was deemed necessary, but Rafael still hesitated, feeling as though he was walking into something too personal.

Alexandra hurried toward the bed, though, and clasped Molly's hand. "Okay?"

"Mmm-hmm," Molly said. "Excited."

Rafael stood behind Alexandra and clasped her upper arms as they all looked at the screen.

The technician started with gray scale, two-dimensional imaging, pointing out the baby's heartbeat.

Both women caught their breath. Rafael let out a surreptitious breath of relief.

But as the tech took various measurements, changing the view, reality began to sink in. That was their *child*. Not just his progeny, not just an extension of Alexandra, but it would look like her and show pieces of her remarkable personality. A high-pitched voice would ask impossible questions and small legs would jump off too-high ledges and someday get behind the wheel of a car.

His heart began to thud harder. Energy gathered in him, a force that wanted to close his hands protectively around that small form and guard that life with his own.

The technician switched to a three-dimensional image. A fully formed fetus appeared on the high-def screen in shades of peach-yellow. The baby crooked one knee to block identifying its sex, then, much like a tourist in a hammock, yawned and stretched.

They all chuckled. Except Alexandra. She released a choked noise and her shoulders convulsed in his grip. She suddenly ripped herself away from him and headed out the door.

"Sasha!" Molly cried.

"Alexandra!" he said at the same time and hurried after her. She was already pushing into the powder room across the hall and locked him out as he arrived at the door. He bit back a curse.

Molly came out of the exam room a moment later, still wearing the hospital gown.

"Seriously?" she asked as she realized the door was locked. She rapped on it. "Sasha. Don't make me pee on the floor."

The lock clicked and Molly slipped inside, but Alexandra didn't come out. The lock clicked again.

CHAPTER SEVEN

"WHAT THE HELL was that about?" Rafael asked when they entered the hotel suite they were using here in London.

"I had a wobble," Sasha said, playing off her breakdown as though it was nothing.

"A *wobble*?"

"I got emotional. You're constantly worrying that I don't really want this baby. Surely it makes you happy that I—" Her throat closed.

Don't cry. Not again.

She had already soaked Molly's shoulder.

Her phone pinged. It was the clinic sending photos of the scans along with a confirmation that the pregnancy appeared to be progressing without issue.

She couldn't look at that image again. It flashed her back to her own scan twelve years ago. The intense longing that followed was too painful to bear.

I want my baby.

That's what she'd been thinking as she saw the tiny image that Molly carried. She wanted that baby and she wanted her first one. She wanted her bab*ies*.

And she felt set apart from both of them. Some of that was her own doing. She was deliberately keeping herself from Libby's life. She told herself it was for the girl's well-being, but it was also because she wasn't ready to untangle her feelings over giving birth and relinquishing Libby to adoption. She sure as heck wasn't ready to articulate any of that to Rafael.

"Maybe you should check in with the counselor once we're home," Rafael suggested.

"I'm sure she'll say this is normal," she dismissed.

He snorted.

"Normal for people in our situation." Was it, though? She felt as though she was walking farther and farther onto ice that was beginning to crack. The shards would shred her on the way through before frigid waters closed over her, suffocating her completely.

She stood at the window looking out, not wanting Rafael to see how fragile she was. How close to her breaking point.

"Now that the scan had confirmed everything is fine, Molly said she'll put in her request for leave. She's not showing yet so she thinks she'll stick it out another four to six weeks."

"Is that what you talked about when you were locked in the toilet with her for thirty minutes?"

"Oh, my God, Rafael! Do you really want to know what I said?" She flung around to face him, feeling persecuted. "I told her that as grateful as I am, I resent her, too, because this has come so easily to her. I'm the one who should be carrying our baby." She stabbed at her own chest.

He sucked in a breath and his head went back.

Molly hadn't been shocked by her words, probably because the counselor had warned them both that Sasha might feel this way. Sasha had apologized even as she said it and Molly hadn't taken any of it to heart. They had hugged it out while Sasha spilled out all her worries about becoming a mother. Her fear of being a bad one.

"When we married, you said you would need an heir. I'm

trying to give you one." Jagged sensation tore up her voice. "I can't help that this has been hard for me."

"I know it has." His expression flexed with torture. He lifted his hand to rub the anguish off his face. "If I had known—"

"Don't," she warned coldly. "Don't say you wouldn't have come this far because I want that baby. But I don't know what you want from *me*."

"I want my wife back," he said with blistering frustration. "This…" He waved at her from eyebrows to open-toed pumps. "I don't know who this is. You're becoming a stranger."

She choked on a humorless laugh, turning her face to the window again because this person was closer to the real her than the woman he'd been living with for the last three years. Sasha was broken and messy and tired of making the best of the choices she'd made, but she didn't know how to make new ones. Not without losing the pieces of this life that she valued. Like him.

She couldn't tell him that, though, could she? Not if he was already frustrated that she wasn't the superficial socialite he'd married. Did he really want her to be that and only that?

Despair thickened her tone as she said wearily, "I don't know you, either, Rafael."

"How is that possible? I'm exactly the man I was when we married. Only richer," he said pithily.

"Exactly. I don't know anything more today than I did three years ago." She rounded on him again. "I know your parents' names and where the marina was located. I know you once got arrested for breaking into it, but what happened after that? Who bailed you out? Why do you have a scar under your chin that is so thin and straight that it looks like it came from a knife? Hmm?"

His expression shuttered, exactly the way it always did if she brought up something he preferred to pass off as "nothing worth talking about."

"I know the deal with Gio will put you into the Nine Zeroes club, but all you talk about is how quickly you might double it. Why isn't one billion enough? Why does it have to be two? You say you want this baby, but why? So you can task them with all this work that makes you so short-tempered?"

"I'm not short-tempered," he bit out.

"We promised never to lie to each other," she shot back.

"Fine. I'm not short-tempered about work. It's this." He pointed at her. "You fell apart in the doctor's office, but won't tell me why. Is that really all you talked about? You needed thirty minutes to tell Molly you have complicated feelings about her carrying our baby? Why the hell are you so reluctant to tell *me*?" The last came out like the dying breath of a dragon.

"Because you don't want to hear it! You sure as hell don't want to give me the same courtesy. Did you hear yourself just now? I asked you a half dozen questions and you turned it around on me, not answering a single one of them."

"My mother bailed me out," he muttered as though it was obvious. "And you want money as much as I do." He turned away to pour a drink at the sideboard.

"No. I want *my* money. I don't want to let someone take what belongs to me. That's different from wanting to collect it and hoard it and use it to take over the world. Why are you so determined to do that?"

He stood very still. She could only see his profile, but she saw his cheek tick. Otherwise, he was like a statue. He blinked and finished pouring.

"I'm not as mysterious as you want to believe. I've told you there were criminal elements that threatened my father's business. That left me with a distaste for being at anyone's mercy. Money is power and that's why I like having an abundance of it." He turned to face her as he sipped. "None of that means I don't want to hear about the things that worry you. I can't fix it if you don't tell me what's broken."

"*We're* broken. How can you not see that?" she cried.

"We're going through a rough patch," he dismissed as he lifted the drink to his lips. "A lot is changing very quickly. We'll adapt and be fine."

Profound disappointment rang through her. How could she show him where and how she was broken if he wasn't willing to do the same?

"I will always be here for you, Alexandra. You can trust me. I hope you believe that."

She didn't. That was the hard truth of the matter. Every time she thought about revealing her secrets and her heart, she remembered how he had praised her for her self-sufficiency the day they married. She was the isolated yin to his autonomous yang.

That was the reason she was afraid to breathe. She felt as though she stood alone on a pile of crumbling rocks that would disappear at any moment and didn't trust him to catch her.

He swallowed his drink in two gulps. "I'll get some work done before we go out tonight."

She couldn't think of anything she wanted to do less than attend a premiere, then rub elbows with famous stars, politicians, and dry-necked aristocrats.

"I'll have a nap," she claimed, doubting she'd get a single wink.

For the first time, he left without kissing her or even looking back.

For the next three weeks, they went through the motions of their marriage, but things remained off.

It was as much Rafael's fault as Alexandra's. She had asked him for basic facts about himself and he hadn't wanted to share them.

Why did he need a billion dollars? Twice? So he would always have a bed and a solid roof and he wouldn't have to hide like a rodent behind a dumpster. So he could prove that he was worthy of his wife.

In many ways, he was more similar than different from the criminals who had extorted from his father. In order to best them, he'd had to meet them at their level. He had paid protection fees and bribes and even turned to blackmail a time or two. He had run cons and double-crossed devils. He had felt the blade of a knife score the skin of his throat and had taken that knife then used it to send his opponent running, trailing red.

That the man had subsequently died was as much the fault of the illegal doctor who had treated him as the wound Rafael had inflicted. Rafael could call it self-defense, but it didn't erase the literal blood on his hands.

Eventually, he'd been deemed impossible to kill or cow. Since then, he had been able to stay this side of the law, but that only encouraged challenges from legitimate players—who all pretended their own fortunes hadn't been built on long-ago piracy and privateering and other unsavory acts.

The rise from middle-class roots to millionaire was the story he preferred to tell. No one, least of all his wife, needed to know he came from the gutter. It was too humiliating to revisit. Irrelevant. He much preferred her to see him as he was now—rich and successful. Powerful. Untouchable.

He preferred to blame their surrogate for the growing distance in their relationship, rather than this wall he kept so stubbornly around himself.

At least Molly didn't seem to intrude on their sex life. He

and Alexandra made love with frequent and devastating passion, which was the reason it didn't bother him that Molly hadn't yet left her employment. Alexandra was talking about joining her on the island when she moved to their villa and that thought caused an itch of possessiveness inside his chest.

They were in Rome, getting ready for a gala, when Alexandra frowned at her phone "Hmph."

"What's wrong?"

"I'm not sure. Molly says, 'Everything is fine, but I've hit a snag with putting in my notice. Call when you have a minute so I can explain.'" Alexandra's attention skimmed past him to where her team of stylists were arriving, wheeling in a rack of gowns and carrying their cases of implements into the spare bedroom of their hotel suite. Her shoulders fell. "I'll call her tomorrow. After we get tonight out of the way."

Tonight's gala was an important one. Ostensibly, it was an art auction to raise funds for orphaned children, something Rafael was more than happy to support, but the attendees were tycoons from across Europe. He and Alexandra had been given a seat at Table One. It was the equivalent of being given the secret handshake and a decoder ring. Rafael was taking his place as One Of Them.

Whether Gio Casella would be at that table remained to be seen. Rafael's almost inked deal with him was definitely the reason Rafael was being seated there. The rumor of their budding partnership was giving the impression Rafael was a direct vector to the Casella Corporation, exactly as Rafael had hoped. Accepting the royal treatment for that was a tiny bit premature, but only by a few days. He and Gio were scheduled to meet in Athens for a photo op next week.

Perhaps he *had* been testy about work, Rafael acknowledged with an inward sigh. This partnership and the benefits it would bring were looming large in his mind, but maybe he should let that be enough for a while.

He mentally scoffed at himself. Him? Take his foot off the accelerator? That wasn't in his nature. But he definitely needed to give more attention to his marriage, especially with the baby coming.

He left the suite for a few hours. He had meetings, but he picked up a peace offering for Alexandra and returned to dress in his tuxedo.

Her stylist had sent him a snapshot of the strapless corset gown she'd chosen, so he knew the collar of five strings of diamonds would suit it. A radiant-cut pink diamond would sit in the hollow of her throat and match the watermelon pink of the silk she wore.

That should have meant he was prepared when she emerged from the bedroom, but even though he regularly saw her in glamorous regalia, she still had the power to squeeze the breath from his lungs. She wore long pink gloves and upswept hair and glossy pink lips.

In contrast, her blue eyes seemed to shimmer like a mountain lake that beckoned in the distance but couldn't be reached. Not easily.

"You look beautiful. Any further adornment is superfluous," he said with the throwaway charm he had cultivated as carefully as the rest of his image. "But this is an important night for us. I wanted to mark the occasion."

A shadow came into her eyes. Skepticism? Disappointment?

A sting of adrenaline shot through his limbs. "You don't like it?"

"It's a lovely addition to my collection. Thank you." She turned her back, inviting him to put it on her.

His fingers were unnaturally clumsy. Those words "addition to my collection" caused his pulse to pound in his ears. For some reason, he recollected her long-ago boast that she had *put aside a nest egg like a dragon.* His mind raced, trying to remember the last time he'd visited their safe-deposit box. She was the one who rotated her jewelry in and out of it, depending on the events that were coming up in their calendar.

As much from habit as desire, he pressed a kiss to her nape once the necklace was secured.

She shivered, which was heartening, but then she touched the necklace and swallowed as though she found it restrictive.

Are we all right?

He didn't ask the question because he didn't want the answer, which was pure cowardice.

"This will only work if we're honest with each other."

Those words had been his. They were as true today as they'd been three years ago.

He wasn't being *dis*honest, though. He genuinely believed they would get through this. Once the baby was here—

Damn, but this baby was carrying a lot on its very tiny shoulders.

The driver buzzed to signal their car was waiting.

Alexandra smoothed her expression into the haughty one that the paparazzi loved to capture, but she was uncharacteristically quiet at the party. Normally, she would extend herself, entertaining their table with anecdotes and cheeky wit, winning everyone over.

Tonight, she barely seemed to be in the room. When he held her on the dancefloor, she was stiff with tension, her face a cool mask he could hardly read.

"Are you not feeling well? You've been quiet."

"I can't stop thinking about Molly. She should have given notice right after the twelve-week scan. It's coming up to fifteen. I know Gio's been traveling and she wants to do it in person, but she's putting on weight. Someone is bound to guess—"

"Can we have one conversation where we don't talk about her?" he asked curtly.

She drew her head back in shock.

"She's an adult who knows her assignment," he continued stiffly. "If she's worried about discovery, she should put in a request for a medical leave and *leave*."

"She's a conscientious person—"

"Yes, I know that. That's why there's no reason for you to worry about her. She'll figure it out."

"You really don't care about her at all." Her arms dropped away from him.

"I care about her the exact amount that is appropriate for her place in our life. *You* care about her too much. I don't understand why."

She took that like a slap. She was stunned, cheeks flushing with angry heat.

Rafael was aware of people noting that they had stopped dancing. It wasn't the type of stir he liked to create.

With his heart pinballing in his chest, he drew her off the dance floor and into a quiet corner of the room.

"What is going on?" he demanded.

Her mouth parted, closed. She shook her head helplessly, then searched his eyes.

"Are you happy, Rafael?"

"Of course," he stated promptly. "We're achieving everything we set out to achieve." He nodded toward the room at large, where he'd been welcomed warmly all evening. "Once the deal is signed with Gio, my position will be secure." He would always have room for growth, but there would be less chance of a serious backslide into losing everything. "My heir is on the way and you'll soon have the means to pry your stepfather off your fortune. This is a very good moment for us."

"But what about *us*? Babies put more pressure on a marriage, not less. We're in trouble, Rafael."

"It's nothing we can't fix." She was taking sandpaper to his organs. He looked around, but people had lost interest in them. He still felt the heat of a spotlight.

"How?" she asked with misery. "This isn't about the baby. It's about *us*. Sometimes I think that if you loved me, I could trust you enough to…" Her desolate gaze cast about the room, looking for something that had him tensing as though bracing for a blow.

This was edging into places he had closed off a long time ago, places that she occupied to some extent, but he was careful about how far inside him she infiltrated. Otherwise, he would be too exposed. Too vulnerable.

"Love is a liability." It was power. If you gave it to someone, they held that power over you. Or they could be used against you. Your own feelings could be. "We agreed on a partnership that benefits both of us," he reminded her.

She looked at him with profound disappointment. "Yes, well, you said I've changed and I have. I've fallen in love with—"

The gravel in his stomach turned to curdled milk. His ears filled with water.

"—you."

His relief was so intense, he laughed. "I thought you were going to say Molly."

"What?" She snapped her head back. "No! You. Although God knows why." Her eyes gleamed with angry tears. "I love *you*, Rafael. And you don't love me back. Do you?"

His next breath came in like powdered glass. In some ways, it glinted like magic dust, filling him with an unfamiliar type of joy, but another part put the brakes on. Hard.

Was she even telling the truth? There had been a time when he wouldn't doubt her word, when he would believe anything she told him because they were always honest with each other. They might not have married for love, but they had trust.

Or did they? He had begun to suspect there was much more he ought to know, but she was a closed book.

"Love wasn't something we expected to happen, was it?" It was a grasp of the wheel to steer them from a dangerous cliff, but he overcompensated, sounding cool and impatient when he ought to be kinder.

"You don't," she confirmed, holding his stare with betrayal clouding her eyes.

Before he could backtrack, she stalked to their table where she gathered her wrap and clutch, claimed a headache and said good-night to their tablemates.

The silence as they climbed into the car was thick enough to slice with a knife.

Rafael should have left it that way. Instead, he instructed their driver to put in his earbuds so he and Alexandra could have some privacy. He should have waited until they were back in their hotel suite. He would tell himself that again and again over the next months.

I should have waited.

But he didn't.

"I'm entitled to be surprised," he said as the car pulled into traffic "When *you* proposed to *me*—" He deliberately reminded her of that. "You told me this wouldn't happen. Our marriage is a practical one."

"And once we have what we wanted, do we stay married?"

"Don't throw out ultimatums you're not prepared to back up," he commanded.

"I'm not. Everything is in place for a clean split." She was talking about their prenuptial agreements, which had been very meticulously crafted for such an eventuality.

"We're not divorcing," he said through his teeth. "We have a baby on the way."

"I *know* that!" she cried loud enough to catch the driver's attention.

That was what Rafael would live to regret forever, that he had prodded her into that burst of emotion. It distracted the driver long enough to touch the brakes in the middle of racing through an intersection.

If he hadn't done that, the car that was jumping the light, accelerating, would have missed their rear bumper by a hairbreadth as they zoomed beneath an amber turning red.

Instead, Alexandra's expression flashed to horror in a blinding light. There was a screech of metal and an impact that rotated the car, throwing Rafael toward her.

CHAPTER EIGHT

RAFAEL WAS BEGINNING to appreciate Alexandra's hatred toward her parents. He'd always seen her mother's superficial nature and timid deference to her husband as pitiful. Humbolt was a self-important bully who occasionally needed a threat of legal action to back off, but he was a coward at heart so he didn't deserve to be feared.

Then Rafael overheard them trying to transfer his unconscious wife to New York and nearly came out of his skin.

They must have heard about the crash on the news and leaped on the first plane to Rome, but their concern was very much for themselves, not Alexandra.

"A move like that would be dangerous." That Italian-accented voice sounded like one of their doctors. "We haven't detected any bleeding on the brain, but we're presuming concussion and treating her accordingly."

"But why isn't she waking up? We can get better treatment in America," Winnie Humbolt claimed.

Better than a world-class private hospital in Rome? Rafael's driver had been conscious enough to identify them to the medics, ensuring they were given top-level care from the moment they arrived. The driver was also receiving treatment here and thankfully would make a full recovery.

Rafael wouldn't take a full breath until he heard the same thing about his wife, though.

"We're keeping her sedated as a precaution," the doctor said in a placating tone.

"Tell your chief of staff to make the arrangements." Anson Humbolt used the brisk tone of a man who was used to stepping on people to get what he wanted.

"Doctor," Rafael rasped in the strongest voice he could muster. It made his entire body throb.

A man in a white coat pushed through the cracked door, revealing Winnie and Anson Humbolt hovering in the hall, looking wrinkled and weary from travel.

"If you allow them to take my wife anywhere, you are the second person I will kill on the way to getting her back." Humbolt would be the first.

It was a laughable threat, given he was still swimming in anesthetic from the surgery he'd had last night, to pin his broken leg. He could only see out of one eye and the twenty stitches on his arm gave him only one good one for swinging a punch, but he meant every word.

"Rest, signore," the doctor urged him. "Your wife is stable and her vitals are strong. She isn't going anywhere until she wakes and we can assess her condition."

Aside from hitting her head on the window and bruises from her seat belt, she had escaped serious injury, but he wished they would wean her off the sedation so he could see that for himself. The physical pain in his body was nothing compared to the urgency to know she was all right.

It took another day. The doctor told him in the morning that they would ease up her medication, but it would take until later in the afternoon for her to come to.

Rafael was dozing off the semisolid meal they'd fed him, trying to ignore the acute pain he was in, but he was keeping his own dosage of painkillers light, wanting to be sharp enough to monitor everything that happened across the hall.

When he heard Winnie cry, "Doctor! She's awake," he urgently thumbed the call button until his nurse hurried in to see him.

"Get me to her," he ordered.

A burly orderly appeared, but moving off his bed into a wheelchair was an ordeal that almost had Rafael fainting from the pain. His need to see Alexandra was all-encompassing, though. He gritted his teeth and waved an impatient hand.

He was pushed into her room in time to hear her say, "No. I don't know who these people are."

"What about me?" he demanded.

The figures gathered around the bed parted, allowing him to see the pale, delicate face of his wife. Her expression widened in alarm at his bruised, beat-up, unshaven face.

Was that fear that flashed behind her eyes? He reached out to take her hand.

"You know who I am. Don't you?" How could she not? They were two sides of the same rare coin.

Everything is in place for a clean split.

No. Absolutely not. It wasn't possible. Besides, she loved him. She'd said so.

But she shook her head, which had him feeling as though his insides were wedged open.

"I'm your husband. Rafael." Was he missing something in his own drug-addled state? Surely, she couldn't have forgotten him. *Them.*

She only stared at him blankly.

Through his shock, he realized her parents were pressuring her to come home with them.

"No." It didn't matter whether Alexandra knew him or them or herself. *He* knew she would never forgive him if he let them take custody of her. He would never forgive himself. "Alexandra is my wife. She comes home with me."

* * *

What have I done? Sasha wondered as they left the hospital for their private jet a few days later.

Right up until she was climbing into the car, her parents had kept up their pressure for her to go back to America with them. It had only fueled her ruse that she didn't recognize them. She knew it was childish. Unethical. Cruel, even, especially to Rafael.

But she was angry with him, too. All she could think about what how truly degrading it had felt when he had laughed—*laughed*—at her declaring her love for him. Why did she have to love him at all, especially this hard? *Why*?

"Why" didn't matter. She wasn't going to let him hold it over her. If she didn't remember saying it, it hadn't happened. Not for her.

Letting go of her memory, of her history, was enormously freeing. It allowed her to put down the burden of being Alexandra and say what was really on her mind. When her mother had noticed her broken nails and suggested a manicure, Sasha had turned up her nose.

"I don't like false nails." She didn't like a lot of things, especially criticism from her mother.

"That's not a flattering style," Winnie said when Sasha gathered her hair into a half topknot.

"It's comfortable," she said blandly, then told the nurse she was done with visitors for the day, forcing them to be shooed out.

Without the guilt of her past as a pressure point, Humbolt was toothless, too.

"You're hurting your mother's feelings by refusing to come home with us," he said the next day, when her mother stepped out of the room to fetch coffee.

"Oh? Winnie said she wants me to stay with you because she's afraid Rafael will evict you if I don't remember you, and that you have nowhere else to go. Is that true, Anson?" she asked with baffled curiosity. "Do you not have money of your own?" She knew he didn't.

She took him aback using his first name. He stood taller and erased her words with a wave of his hand. "No, no. She wants to look after you because she cares about you."

"So you *do* have somewhere to go. Because I understand all the properties are actually mine."

"Listen, girlie. Don't try to play hardball with me." He came closer to the bed.

She picked up the call button.

His mouth tightened. Aside from taking a rough grip on her arm or other manhandling like that, he'd never been outwardly violent, but he loved to belittle her. Hundreds of times, he had turned her insides to stone with a contemptuous glower like the one he wore now.

For once, she truly felt impervious to it.

"There are things I could bring up that you'd rather weren't made public," he warned. "Things that would send your husband running and ruin your life."

"But I would still have my fortune," she clarified, tilting her head in thought. "And since I've already forgotten the life I had, it doesn't matter if you burn it down. I'll see how it goes with my husband. If things don't work out, I'll need my house. You should start making other arrangements."

He was *not* happy with her inability to be intimidated. He tried to sic her mother on her and Winnie brought to bear some of her best guilt-saturated manipulation, but a lack of memory served Sasha there, too.

"I know I should feel obligated, but I don't."

She refused to apologize for her lack of sympathy. The only thing she was sorry for was allowing Humbolt to bully her as long as he had. When they left Winnie and Anson on the sidewalk in Rome, Sasha was confident it would be the last time she ever spoke to them.

Leaving her parents in the dust seemed to be the impetus in Rafael's decision to head back to Athens, despite being told he would need another surgery.

Sasha should have stayed in hospital herself. She was mostly uninjured, but persistent headaches ran the gamut from dull to debilitating. The doctor said she should expect that to continue for weeks, possibly months, but hoped they would dwindle over time, provided she got plenty of rest and gave herself time to heal.

Rafael was limping short distances on crutches, but should be using a wheelchair. Too much stress on his forearm could pop his stitches, but she would love to meet the person who successfully told Rafael he wasn't allowed to do something.

As they boarded the jet, Sasha debated coming clean to him about her memory but a private nurse was traveling with them along with Rafael's assistant, Tino. The flight was less than two hours so they stayed in their seats, rather than move into the stateroom where they would have had more privacy.

Some of the shades were open so Sasha kept her sunglasses on. Rafael's breath rattled out as he settled into the seat beside her.

Pity for both of them rolled through her along with a tingling longing. She yearned for the comfort of his touch. She had nearly lost him!

She didn't care as much that her own life had been endangered. Her baby would be safe with Molly no matter what happened to her. She already knew that, since her first one was. Thank *God* the baby hadn't been at risk in that crash.

But nearly losing Rafael was terrifying. It made her realize how much she really did love him, even though she was still furiously angry with him.

Love is a liability.

It sure was. That's why she was pretending she hadn't offered hers to him.

She had come so close to telling him everything that night! The affair with a married man, Libby, her real relationship with Molly—whom she did love, but not in the way he'd suggested.

He had laughed at her for saying she loved him. Her trust and willingness to share had been shattered at that point. Even if he did care about her to some extent, it was only the exact amount that was appropriate for a wife who had helped him achieve what he wanted to achieve. She couldn't stand that she had practically begged him to feel more. She must seem utterly pathetic in his eyes.

As the plane took off, she glanced to see the nurse and assistant were ensconced at the back of the cabin, and turned her head to study the mottled bruise on the side of his face.

An urge to kiss it better nearly overwhelmed her, but he turned his own head to ask, "You really can't remember anything?"

She was glad she was wearing her sunglasses because her eyes reflexively widened in alarm as she felt pinned by his hard stare. She sidestepped by focusing on the memory she genuinely had lost.

"The driver told the investigators that we were arguing." An officer had come by her room to ask what she remembered of the crash. She had told him with complete honesty that she didn't recall anything about being in the car. "He said we distracted him. Is that true? Or is he trying to get out of taking responsibility?"

"It's true." Rafael's mouth flattened into a tight line. He looked forward again, eyes closing in a slow blink. "He was startled into hitting the brake and glanced back at us. He didn't see the other car jumping the light and stopped right in front of it."

Rafael had taken the brunt of that? She felt ill.

"What were we arguing about?" She could hardly speak around the lump in her chest.

He drew in a breath to speak, then let it out, seeming reluctant to answer.

"You told me you loved me. You don't remember saying that?" He turned his head again, sending the intensity of his narrow-eyed gaze across her face like a laser that left every inch of her skin feeling scorched.

Oh, God.

She used one hand to cover the other as it curled into a fist in her lap.

"How is that an argument?" her scattered brain managed to ask. "We're married. Don't we love each other?"

It was unkind of her to use her lie as a tool to poke at him and their marriage, but she had no defenses otherwise. They would be right back to that impossible cold war except he'd have her heart in his pocket. This was the only way to take herself back from him.

"I want to say yes," he admitted heavily, causing a pulsing sting to shoot through her veins. "But we made a deal when we married that we would always be honest with each other. I want to honor that."

Wow. Nothing had changed. They had nearly been killed, but it hadn't moved the dial on his feelings for her. She felt as though the floor had dropped out of the plane and she was plummeting to the earth at a million miles an hour.

She had known all along that he didn't love her, though. For a long time, it hadn't mattered. Not until they had tried to start a family and the weight of her first baby became too much to bear. If she couldn't trust him with her heart, how could she trust him with the innocent person inside it? That's what this came down to.

"So you don't love me. And that's why we were fighting?" It was painful to force this clarity, but it hardened her resolve to keep up this game. "Why are we even married?"

"I'm very fond of you—"

"Fond," she choked. "Fond is how you feel toward a great-aunt who offers you peppermints. Why did you even bring me with you today? Why not send me home with my parents if you don't care what happens to me?"

"I *care*," he said through his teeth. "You would never forgive me if I let them take you. And you're *my wife*, Alexandra. Even if you don't remember it. I protect what's mine."

She snorted, realizing she had always been one more asset he had collected. She wanted to cry, but only closed her eyes, claiming, "I'm tired."

It must have been the truth because the next thing she knew, they had landed in Athens. Rafael was equally groggy and sullen as they were driven to an unfamiliar villa on the outskirts of Athens. It was more modest than the places they usually stayed in, but it had a pool and a casita where the nurse went to unpack.

"There are too many stairs in our home in Attica," Rafael explained as he limped into the lounge behind her. "Also, my assistant said it was staked out by paparazzi. I bought this for my mother, not that she lived to see it. An agency manages it as a vacation rental, but it happened to be empty. You've never been here so it won't be familiar to you."

Sasha took in the open plan of the main living area with its tasteful, if generic, furnishings. An L-shaped countertop divided the kitchen from the dining area and sliding doors led out to the patio.

"When did she pass?" It was a natural question to ask under the circumstance, even though she already knew the answer.

"A few months before you and I met."

He had told her that in the early days of their marriage,

but had barely mentioned his parents since then. Sasha hadn't asked a lot of questions because she hadn't wanted him to pry into her own past.

That risk was no longer a factor, though. Was it?

"Were you close with her?"

After a hesitation, he said, "I'm adopted. Have you read anything about me online?"

"No." She was dying to check in with Molly, but… "My phone is broken. The doctor said I should stay off screens anyway, because they're likely to make my headaches worse. Is that your answer? That you weren't close to your mother because you're adopted?"

He was opening the cupboards in the bottom of the china cabinet and came up with an unopened bottle of Scotch and a heavy sigh.

"I had a closer relationship to my parents than you have with yours," he said drily. "But they adopted me at eight, almost nine." He glanced up from pouring a generous amount of Scotch into a glass. "I was about as civilized as a feral cat."

She wanted to ask if he thought alcohol was a good idea, but she had never heard him describe himself that way. "How do you mean?"

"I was skittish. Didn't want to be touched. My birth mother brought me from Romania when I was four. She was trying to find my father, who was Greek, but I have come to believe he lied to her about what kind of man he was."

"Greek?"

"Rich," he clarified pithily.

He stacked his crutches under his good arm and leaned on the cabinet, then used his injured arm to lift the glass to his lips. He took a deep gulp, as though he'd been waiting a year for that alcohol to hit his bloodstream. His breath hissed out in a mix of relief and burn.

"She wasn't trying to cash in," he continued. "Only force

him to support the child he'd made. I can remember her saying, 'He can give you a better life than I can. We just have to find him.' We had nothing when we arrived and never managed to accumulate more than a few blankets and enough food to keep us alive. I don't know what kind of work she did. Something menial. She would leave me with a woman I didn't understand and snot-nosed children who weren't afraid to knock me around for whatever I had that they wanted."

She couldn't help the pang of protest that resounded in her throat.

"I learned to knock back," he assured her with a negligent shrug. He gave his glass a dispassionate swirl before taking another sip. "One morning she didn't wake up. I didn't know what to do so I walked to the day care and told her. She turned me away, told me to go home. I realize now that she was afraid she would get in trouble for taking in too many children and helping illegal immigrants. She must have made a call, though. When I got back, police were there. I was taken to a home, but I ran away. I wanted to find my mother."

Her hand lifted to cover where her heart turned over in her chest, hurting for that lost little boy.

"I was on the street for three or four weeks, I guess. There was an older girl—a prostitute and way too young for it—it's all a blur, really, but she was nice to me. Taught me how to shoplift and how to find a place to sleep. I really liked her, but I was caught stealing and sent to a group home with bars on the windows. I couldn't run away and find her to tell her what had happened to me. That's always bothered me, that I didn't say goodbye to her."

He shook off the memory and gulped again from the Scotch.

"How old were you?"

"By then? Six. I overheard people talking about sending me back to Romania. I kept telling them my father was Greek, that they had to find my father. They never did. I have no idea if they tried, but I was put in a school for troubled boys. Between the strict teachers and my fellow students and the toughs in the group home, I got plenty of lessons on how to ignore pain." He nodded at his broken leg.

As it turned out, she was glad she hadn't known this about him. It was far too painful to hear, but she stayed silent, letting him continue.

"By the time I was adopted, I was a rough piece of work, but I had come to appreciate a dry bed and regular meals. I knew how to mind my manners to get those things. I was competitive as hell and had realized there were many ways to beat someone, so my grades were top of the class. I guess that's what my parents saw in me, a boy who was intelligent enough to take over the business and hardened enough not to collapse under the pressure the local thugs put on them."

"That's a lot to ask of anyone, let alone a boy."

And why had he never told her any of this? It was taking all her control not to ask that.

"They lost their son in a drowning accident or they would have put it on him." He shrugged. "They were adamant that I wasn't a replacement for him, but what else was I?" He topped up his Scotch. "They were close to fifty when they adopted me. My mother was the driver in that, wanting someone to look after them and the business once they retired. My father and I got along well enough, but we were very different. I was ambitious and driven. He was…tired. Grief-stricken and worn down by life. We didn't talk much unless it was about the business. He didn't take care of himself. He had high blood pressure. His heart attack wasn't a shock."

"I'm so sorry," she murmured.

"When he passed, my mother was convinced the business would be stolen from her. She didn't realize what a punk I really was. That was probably my greatest con, hiding that from her," he said with a smirk. "And you, of course."

"W-what?" She was so dumbfounded by his revelations, by the fact he was sharing so much, she set a hand on the wall to keep herself from falling over.

"Will you put this on the table for me?" He held out his refilled glass.

"Yes." She reflexively hurried forward to take it, but he didn't let it go.

"You were angry with me for a lot of things," he said gravely, staring through her sunglass lenses in a way that seemed to peer all the way into her soul. "You said that in three years, I hadn't told you anything more about my-self than what you knew the day we married. You weren't wrong. I *hate* talking about my childhood." He scowled with distaste. "I've always wanted you to see me as I am now, not the way I was then, but I want you to stay in this marriage. That means you need to know me enough to trust me."

"Why is it so important I stay?" If he didn't love her, if he was only "fond" of her, what did it matter what she thought of him or whether they shared a house or a bed?

Wait, was that what he wanted? Sex? She kind of did, too, but it had become really hard to engage in physical in-timacy while knowing she was investing so much more of her heart than he was.

On the other hand, if he had lost his mother so tragically, then regarded himself as a replacement for a couple's "real" child, she had to wonder if he knew how to attach himself to anyone. She hadn't, not until she had been given love in its purest form. Even then, she had resisted allowing love into her life. She was resisting it again, too conscious of how vulnerable it made her.

"Let's sit down," he said, glancing toward the sofa. "There's something else you need to know. I'm not sure how you'll react."

She nervously carried his drink to a coaster on the coffee table, suspecting what was coming as she settled into the opposite corner and tried to appear appropriately curious.

He winced as he sat. His casted leg stuck out at an angle against the table legs.

"We're expecting a baby."

It took everything in her to let her lips part in shock.

Seriously, why was she continuing this stupid charade? *I know.* That's all she had to say. *I know.*

But she didn't want to go back to where they'd been at the gala. She wanted this, where he confided in her even though it was difficult for him. Would he do that if he knew she remembered everything? No. He would expect her to be Alexandra and would return to being closed-off Rafael, leaving her wondering what was going on behind his remote expression.

"How?" she asked. "The hospital didn't tell me—"

"We're using a surrogate. Molly."

She blew out a breath and covered her face with her hands, dislodging her sunglasses as she leaned her elbows onto her knees. She was mostly trying to hide the fact that this news wasn't as big a shock to her as he thought it was, but she was worried about Molly and had to press back on her instinct to ask about her.

"We were having trouble conceiving," he continued.

No, *they* weren't. His sperm had no trouble seducing her eggs into becoming embryos. She was the one who couldn't hang on to them.

"Molly is about sixteen weeks along by now? She heard about the crash on the news and has been reaching out, but—" he cursed "—she's engaged to her boss."

"What?" Astonishment had her lifting her face from her hands.

It was a huge mistake. She had leaned forward on the sofa at just the right angle for the sunlight to glance off the pool, sifting between the furniture legs in the dining room and straight into her eyes.

She clenched her eyes shut, but the damage was done. Stars were exploding behind her eyelids.

"I know," Rafael was grumbling. "It's completely inappropriate. She signed a binding NDA to keep the pregnancy strictly confidential. I don't think she would tell him she's carrying our baby, but maybe this explains why she hasn't given her notice yet? The whole thing is suspicious. It's made worse by the fact that Gio Casella is a business partner of mine. We were about to sign off on a partnership deal a few days ago, but he put that on hold because of our crash. Now I'm afraid to talk to her in case she tells him—"

"Rafael." She weakly fluttered her hand in his direction, using the other to shield her closed eyes. A halo of pain was forming inside her skull, pressing outward. Dread and nausea combined in her middle.

He cursed and caught her hand. "Migraine?"

"Yes. I need to lie down."

"Your glasses." She heard one of his crutches tumble to the floor and winced at the noise. The cushion dipped beside her, then the sunglasses pressed into her hand. "I'll text the nurse to take you to the bedroom. I'd take you myself, but—" He cursed his crutches. "She's coming with a pain pill and ice," he said a moment later.

"Thank you," she said meekly, aware they had so much more to talk about, but right now, she needed a dark room and silence.

CHAPTER NINE

RAFAEL LOST A few more days to another surgery to adjust a pin. It was relatively minor in the grand scheme of things, but it left him bedridden and dopey, which made him grumpy.

Alexandra was marginally better. She joked that she had become a vampire, afraid to leave her room during daylight hours, but it wasn't funny. She had little color in her cheeks and her lips were often white. She didn't eat much, didn't move much, and couldn't watch television or look at a screen for more than a minute or two. Any loud noise or bright light sent her straight back to bed and a cooling eye mask.

They were sleeping apart and that bothered him most of all. He didn't expect her to run away, but he wasn't convinced she wouldn't.

He loathed any type of uncertainty and kept remembering her saying, *"Everything is in place for a clean split."*

"Are you awake?" he asked in a whisper when he finished a long day of trying to catch up on work and found her lying on the sofa in the dark, wearing pajamas and her sleep mask. A dated romcom was playing on a very low volume on the television.

"Yes." She bent her knees as an invitation for him to sit on the cushion. "Who were you yelling at?"

"I wasn't yelling, was I?" He lowered into the corner of

the sofa with a hiss of weary pain, trying to recollect who he'd been speaking to.

It could have been anyone. Much was on the line if he didn't put out this dumpster fire that his life had become. He wouldn't be ruined if Gio failed to sign that deal, he kept reassuring himself. He would merely be humiliated and set back. Significantly.

Alexandra would be fine. She had always managed her own portfolio, investing with him at different times, but mostly keeping her money in relatively stable assets like real estate. He was currently leveraging against some of her assets, but there were firm firewalls in place. He'd lose everything while her fortune would barely be dented. That was both reassuring, but also galling to his ego. It probably wouldn't have bothered him so much if they were in a stronger place, but everything felt very tentative right now.

He looked to where her ankles peeked from beneath the hem of her lime green pajama pants. Her bare toes were curled. Wariness? Or sexual tension?

"Did I start one of your headaches?"

"No. You weren't loud enough for me to hear what you were saying, but I could tell you were swearing."

He had a lot to swear about these days, not least of which the fact that she was suffering. "Have you had one today?" He deliberately kept his voice quiet.

"No. But, I don't want to jinx it by bragging about it."

He smiled faintly. Sometimes she sounded exactly like the woman he knew. Other times, she was a reticent stranger. He wanted to push and prod and establish exactly where they stood, but she was so fragile he had to handle her with great care.

He guided her feet into his lap.

She resisted. "What are you doing?"

"I'll rub your feet."

"You don't have to."

"I want to."

"Why?"

Because it had been a lifetime since he'd touched her.

"To help you relax," he claimed.

A strangled noise resounded in her throat.

He smiled with amused gratification and gently crushed her feet in his closed hands before focusing on the left one.

"Isn't there some sort of therapy that uses pressure points on the foot? Perhaps I can cure your headaches for good."

"I'm ready to try anything," she said with a sigh, allowing her legs to relax. "How do you feel?"

"Fine."

"I thought we don't lie to each other." Her voice wavered between facetious and challenging.

"My leg is killing me," he admitted. "I'm tired and frustrated that I tire so easily. I'm furious that Gio is dragging his feet. It puts me in a bind."

"I keep thinking I should call her." Tension returned to her foot. "The surrogate. Molly, was it?"

"And tell her that you've forgotten she's carrying our baby?" He carefully worked his thumb against the stiffness in her arch. "I'm concerned about how close she's become to Gio."

Last he'd checked, they'd been in London, but Gio was due to come to Athens this weekend. Rafael had deliberately not spoken to him, letting their teams reschedule everything as though the crash had been a minor inconvenience and there was nothing to worry about.

"What would you say to her?" he asked. "How do you feel about becoming a mother?"

She seemed to go very still. He had the strange impression that her foot went cold in his hands.

"How do you feel about becoming a father?" she asked in a strained voice.

"We both want this baby very much," he assured her.

"You're very good at avoiding direct answers."

He would bet her brow was wrinkled in consternation behind that mask.

He sighed.

"I don't like revealing what I want," he admitted. "It allows people to use it against me. It gives them the opportunity to take my toy or hold my company hostage or threaten my parents."

"Did people do that to you?"

"Yes."

"Is that why you're so…"

"What?" he prompted.

"Hard."

"I didn't think you'd noticed."

She stole her foot from his grip and nudged his thigh, tsking.

He smirked and took up the other foot.

"Is it, though?" she asked. "Why you're so closed off and difficult to read?"

"Life is poker. It's gambles and risks and bluffs, trying to win the pot. Never let anyone know what cards you hold."

"Does that make the baby a chip? Or…?" The anxiety in her voice had his heart swinging out and snapping back into his chest with a sting.

"No," he said firmly. "I'll admit that I had always looked on children the way my parents did. I have a business that needs an heir. Why go to the trouble of building a dynasty if it will die when I do? That's why I pressured you into starting a family."

"Did you?" Her foot twitched in his grip, but he held on

to it, seizing the chance to say things he hadn't been able to say before because she'd been too defensive.

"I did." He saw that now and regretted how blithe he'd been when he brought up having a baby. He'd presumed it was simple. One more thing to tick off the list. "You seemed ready, but I think you were ambivalent, maybe doing it more for me than yourself."

I've changed. I've fallen in love with you.

He'd been thrown by that confession, but he mourned losing that woman and wished he'd reacted differently when she'd said it.

"When it didn't work out right away, you were distressed," he continued. "We couldn't have known it would be like that, but things grew difficult between us."

"In what way?" she asked in a husk of a voice, as though she wasn't sure she wanted the answer.

"You were angry with your body. I was frustrated that I couldn't give you what you want. I like giving you everything you ask for. It pleases me to spoil you. That I can."

"BDE," she said under her breath.

He froze. "You've accused me of that many times. Are you getting your memory back?"

"What? No." A small pulse seemed to cause her foot to tic in his hands. "But I know what Big Dick Energy is and you definitely have it."

"Hmph." He went back to massaging her foot, wondering if he wanted her to get her memory back when this felt like a second chance for them. Rather than a wall between them, they had a blank slate that at least didn't have the difficult passages of their history written upon it.

"Can I ask you something?" Her voice was timid enough to stall his hands again. "How do you feel about your adoption. Like, really. Deep down?"

"I think being adopted saved my life and kept me out

of jail. Mostly," he added drily. "Look, I know it was hypocritical that I wanted us to make a baby. I see now how selfish that was, considering how hard it became on you, but…" He squeezed her foot, feeling as though his lungs were being compressed, pushing out all the air. He drew in a deep breath, refilling them before he admitted, "There's something about knowing our baby is a combination of both of us that pleases me. I don't have anyone, Alexandra. Just you."

He heard her sharp inhale.

"You have your parents," he acknowledged. "But you've never had a good relationship with them. From the night we met, you made me feel as though you only had me. That you needed me as much as I needed you."

"Do you?" she asked skeptically.

"Yes. When we're on our game, we're a formidable team. Having a baby with you, one who has all the best parts of us…? Or the worst," he added with a husk of dark laughter. "Either way, I want that. I want our baby very much."

She was quiet, teeth worrying the edge of her lip.

"And you? How do you feel?" he prompted. "About becoming a mother?"

Her foot withdrew to settle beside the other one. Her upraised knees formed a barrier between them. He watched her fists close and tuck beneath her elbows in a protective hug.

"I honestly don't know," she said with quiet anguish. "I know I should be happy. I know I will love my baby. I already do." One fist moved to the spot between her breasts and she used the heel of her palm to rub her sternum, as though trying to soothe a pain there. "I can imagine holding a newborn, but I can't—I can't picture being a mother."

Her bottom lip was quivering as if she was very near tears.

"Alexandra." He looped his arm around her bent legs and set his mouth against her knee. "I'm sure that will come with time. This is a strange circumstance. It's okay that it's a shock. The baby isn't due until Christmas. You'll have time to process."

"But do you really believe we can be good parents?" She carefully lifted the edge of her mask to peer at him. "Whatever team we were before... Do you honestly believe we were strong enough to sustain twenty years together? And support our child in all the ways we'll need to? What happens between you and me in all that time?"

"We relearn how to be us. And yes, I absolutely believe we will be together for the rest of our lives."

"How can you be so sure?"

"Because I don't lose the things I value."

"I'm not a thing, Rafael. Unless you realize that, I don't know that we do have a chance." She let the mask drop back into place then rolled onto her side, knees still bent and feet jammed against the sofa back. She curled her arm beneath the cushion under her ear and listened to Richard Gere climb a fire escape to rescue Julia Roberts.

With careful management, Sasha had three days of only a leaden headache, not an incapacitating one.

"That's good," Rafael said when they were eating lunch in the dimmed light of the shuttered dining room. "You can come to the gala with me tonight."

"Why?" He might as well have suggested sending her to a work camp in Siberia. "I won't know anyone."

That was a lie, of course, but she was too deep into this bigger lie to say anything different. She couldn't seem to regret pretending her memory loss, either. He was revealing fascinating and sometimes painful things, but she was also able to be more honest about her own feelings than she had ever been before. The other night, she had told him about her ambivalence around motherhood and he'd been very sweet and nonjudgmental.

"People need to see that we're fine, Alexandra."

"We're not fine."

His gaze flashed up to hers. "We're getting along perfectly."

Perfectly was a stretch, but... "Are you going to wear those gym shorts under your tuxedo jacket?" She nodded across the table where she knew he wore gray, drawstring shorts beneath the shirt and tie that appeared on his video chats.

"My trousers will be delivered later today along with a selection of gowns. It's only an appearance," he pressed on when she wrinkled her nose. "We don't have to stay more than an hour, but it will go a long way toward convincing people that nothing has changed."

"Fine," she mumbled. She was going a little stir-crazy, so maybe a night out would do her good.

After a nap and a very subdued session with her stylist, she came out to the lounge in a bronze gown that was decorated with braided piping. It hugged her torso before the metallic silk parted dramatically to expose her left leg to the top of her thigh. Her makeup hid the fact that she'd lost a couple of pounds and still lacked color. She left her hair down, only allowing it to be straightened so it fell in a blunt line from the caramel roots to the brighter highlights of straw and gold at the ends.

Rafael had brought jewelry from the safe-deposit box, so she was already wearing the thick links of a heavy gold necklace and a wide cuff on her upper arm.

"You look beautiful," he said as she appeared in the lounge. It was lit only by one lamp. "I've always liked this on you." He hitched himself close enough to trace his fingertip along the upper edge of the cuff, lifting goose bumps from her elbow to her shoulder. Even her nipples tightened.

He noticed.

She dropped her gaze to his bow tie, cheeks hot.

"Don't be embarrassed. It's always been like this between us. It's nice to see it's still there." He moved his touch to the arc above the necklace, tickling her collarbone, then slid his fingertip up her throat, lightly urging her chin to come up, forcing her gaze to lift to his. "I know you don't remember how good it is, but it is very, very good, Alexandra."

She did remember. It was.

Between her headaches and his cast and their different sleep schedules, they'd been using separate bedrooms, but she yearned for the closeness they'd always enjoyed. She swept her lashes down so he wouldn't see how much, but she was very tempted to lean forward and tilt her mouth up to his.

"Come to me later if you want to. I would like that." He let his straying touch drop from the hollow beneath her ear and gathered his crutches under his arms.

Later. Not now. He always directed and she always obeyed. She was such a pushover where he was concerned.

That agitating thought turned an otherwise velvety evening into an irritation. The fading dusk became fully dark while they made their way to the museum, so she left her sunglasses in the car and regretted it as soon as they arrived inside. The chandeliers were dimmed, but there was a waterfall effect on one wall that she averted her gaze from studying.

The room was noisy, too. Full of glitterati who immediately noticed them. She didn't get a chance to ask for someone to retrieve her sunglasses. They were approached and she was forced to smile as people expressed their concern.

Rafael introduced her to a couple they already knew.

"Alexandra is having trouble with her memory, but otherwise, we're recovering nicely."

"Really!" The woman's voice pitched high with astonishment. "You don't remember our shopping trip in Singapore? While our men were in meetings?"

"I don't." In truth, she was happy to forget this particular woman, especially when she took it upon herself to pass along Alexandra's condition to a mutual acquaintance the minute another couple joined them.

"Can you believe it? She doesn't recognize any of us." She waved at Alexandra as though she was a curiosity, not a person.

Rafael stiffened beside her. "Such a shame, too," he said. "I'm sure she thought the world of you before this."

Oof. Not that she didn't appreciate his coming to her defense, but what had he thought would happen when they started sharing news like this?

She gritted her teeth, thinking it would be a long, painful night when he touched her elbow and said, "There's someone we need to speak to. Excuse us."

The gossipy woman's husband saved Sasha from what would have been a reaction of near violent startlement.

"Casella?" the man asked, looking past her. "That deal is going through, then?"

"Yes." As Rafael's gaze crashed back into hers, she was already gathering up her composure, ignoring the ringing in her ears as she turned to face Gio and…

Yes. That woman dressed like a golden goddess was Molly.

What the *hell*? Why hadn't Rafael warned her they would see them here? *He* didn't look surprised by their appearance.

"Who, um… Wasn't that the name of the man you said…" She frowned, feigning an attempt to place a name as she paced beside him. "I'm trying to remember what you said when you told me about the surrogate. That she was engaged to your business partner? That's not *her*, is it?"

"Molly. Yes," he said with a watchful look in her direction.

"Why didn't you warn me they would be here? Does he know she's—?"

"No."

"Then why—?" They were coming into earshot with the other couple.

Sasha's stomach tensed around a hot ember of anger as she looked for some avenue of escape while keeping a blank expression frozen to her face.

She couldn't risk Molly guessing that she still had her memory. The whole house of cards would come down. She tried to appear bored by this whole event, but she couldn't help studying her friend, searching for signs their baby was still safe inside her.

Molly's gown had an empire waist so any bump under that drape of silk was well disguised. Her ample breasts were likely all that people noticed, especially since they were adorned with the yellow sapphires of a dramatic necklace.

"Rafael. It's good to see you on your feet. Foot," Gio corrected wryly as he offered his hand. He wore a tuxedo with a black jacket and looked positively dashing. Really, it was no surprise that Molly would engage herself to him, not when he was that handsome and she'd already been nursing a crush.

"It's not slowing me down too much." Rafael dismissed his comment as he tucked his crutch beneath his armpit and shook Gio's hand. "And this must be your fiancée, Molly?"

"We've met. I was on your yacht last year, working for Gio. You may not remember." Molly sent questioning looks between the two of them, likely baffled by their silence since the crash.

"I don't remember anything," Sasha lied blatantly. "I have a concussion from the crash and lost all my memory." The farce of the moment was so acute, she could hardly keep her hysterical laughter from exploding out of her straining throat.

Molly gasped and expressed concern, but continued pretending she didn't know either of them, including all of Sasha's biggest and worst secrets. Rafael was acting as though Molly was someone he'd met once, not letting on that she was carrying their baby.

Sasha clung to her fake amnesia, but blurted, "These lights are giving me a headache. Rafael insisted on parading me around like I'm a circus attraction, but I'd like to leave."

Which was exactly what she did.

Rafael had learned his lesson. He waited until they were home before he said, "That was rude."

By then, Alexandra had taken a pain pill in the car and had put her sunglasses back on, but didn't seem to be wilting into a migraine.

"*I* was rude? You ambushed me!" She kicked off her heels and stalked down the hall to her room.

Yes, but, "I hoped that seeing her would shake something loose."

"Like my temper?" She swung her hair to the front of her shoulder and turned, pointing at her spine exactly the way she'd done a thousand times when they had undressed after an evening out. "I *thought* her surrogacy was supposed to be a secret. You said she signed an NDA. What was I supposed to say to her there? Hi, how's our baby cooking?"

"The secrecy is to keep your parents from finding out. If something had slipped out this evening, I don't think it would have got back to them." He lowered her zip.

As soon as the gown loosened, she caught it against her

breasts and swung around to confront him. "I can't trust you at all, can I?"

"You can trust me with your life, Alexandra. You already have."

She choked out a noise of disbelief and walked away, shedding the gown onto the floor and closing herself into the bathroom.

He pinched the bridge of his nose, accepting that it had been a bad move to not tell her, but he really had hoped it would jar her memory into coming back.

When she came out fifteen minutes later, her face was clean and she wore a white robe. She checked as she saw him.

"I should have warned you," he acknowledged. "But that's how I learned to play when I want something."

"Dirty?"

"Yes," he said without apology. "I want *you*, Alexandra. I want my wife back."

She studied him for a long time, mouth pouted in sorrow. Then sighed.

"I will never again be the woman you married. I need you to accept that, Rafael. If that's what you're holding out for, we should call it quits right now." Her somber, rational tone sent a preternatural shiver down his spine. A sort of panic.

"All right. It wasn't just your memory I was testing," he admitted. "I wanted to see your reaction to her." He wanted to pace, but his freaking leg was broken. He had to make do with sitting on the end of the bed and removing the jacket that was causing him to overheat. "It's childish, but I wanted to see if you had the same instant connection to her."

"What do you mean?" Only one lamp burned, but she picked up her sunglasses and put them on.

"I've never seen you take to anyone the way you reacted to her. I mean, I guess your reaction this evening was exactly the same as the first time you met her, since you were rude to her then, too." He tugged at his bow tie, thinking back to how odd that day had been. "You did a quick about-face and decided she ought to be our surrogate. That never made sense to me, but you seemed excited for the possibility so I went along with it. As things progressed, you became very close with her. I'm embarrassed to admit that it began to feel like an affair, even though you were only texting with her. She calls you Sasha."

"What's wrong with that?" She had her fists buried in the pockets of her robe. Her shoulders were hunched defensively.

"You've never invited me to call you anything but Alexandra." God, he felt puerile saying that.

"You can call me Sasha if you want to." She wasn't pandering. She was frowning behind her sunglasses. "Alexandra feels like a stranger who is carrying a lot of other people's expectations. That's what Winnie called me. I kind of hate being Alexandra."

I will never again be the woman you married.

He *would* have to accept that. In fact, everything about their marriage was shifting, partly due to her memory loss, but also because of the baby.

"I'm going to connect with Molly tomorrow." Hopefully without Gio. He should have tried harder to speak with her this evening, to gauge their relationship, but he'd been more concerned about his wife's reaction than the deal he had yet to finalize.

Damn. That was sobering to acknowledge.

"What will you say to her?" she asked warily.

"I'll find out where things stand. Our arrangement was that she would leave her employment by now and stay at the island estate for the rest of her pregnancy. She had talked about your staying there with her. Would you?" he asked, subconsciously bracing for the answer.

She nodded jerkily, mouth pensive. "Yes. I'd like that."

Damn. That felt...bad.

Shortly after their marriage, when Sasha had gained access to the first portion of her fortune, Rafael had suggested this island estate as a good investment. Humbolt had played the stock market—poorly—and invested wherever it served his attempts to be part of the old boys' club.

Sasha had received a lot of her trust in properties, several of which she had sold out of spite, so her mother couldn't use them, but also so she could buy this.

It consisted of a modern villa amid sprawling acres of farmland that not only paid for itself, but produced a profit off the sale of oranges, olives, lamb, and wine. She had fallen in love with it and only wished they had more time to spend here.

Now was her chance, she thought privately, as Rafael showed her and Molly around.

The property gave the impression of being remote, situated up a hill with a view overlooking the sea, but it was a relatively short helicopter ride back to Athens, should Molly need attention. There was also a nearby village where a nurse-midwife had a small practice. It was already arranged that she would come by tomorrow and continue checking on both women regularly. A housekeeper would come by three times a week with groceries and whatever else they might need.

Sasha knew all of this since she had arranged it, but she paid attention as though it was new information. After nearly three weeks of this game, she was clinging to her lie by her fingernails.

Molly thanked Rafael, then excused herself to the powder room. Talk about a pretense! That woman was *definitely* showing. Sasha had about a thousand questions for her, all of them around her relationship with Gio, but she walked Rafael out to the helipad first.

"Maybe wear a hat when you go outside," he said as he searched through the lenses of her sunglasses. "Are you sure you don't want the housekeeper to move in full-time?"

"No, we'll manage." Sasha dug deep to keep this bland look on her face, so he wouldn't know how close she was to breaking.

"All right. I'll—" He released a hiss of pent-up frustration. "I'll try to come back next weekend, but now that Gio has pulled the pin, I have a lot of triage in front of me."

Sasha had yet to get the full story on *that*, too.

Rafael surprised her by ducking his head and stealing a brief, hard kiss that turned the embers of her old yearnings into a conflagration of instant need.

She had barely reacted before he was pulling away, leaving her breathless as he swung on his crutches toward the helicopter.

She stepped backward into the shade, but didn't step inside until the rotors began to turn. Then she watched from the window as the helicopter lifted off, taking him back to Athens. She felt rather bereft as he became a dot in the sky and disappeared.

When she turned away from the glass, Molly was hovering in the archway between the lounge and the kitchen.

"Oh, don't look so stressed out, Moll. I'm faking. The only memory I lost was the actual crash."

"What? Oh, my *Gawd*, Sasha. Why would you do that?" she cried.

Sasha winced one eye closed and patted the air. "My concussion is real and so are the headaches. Keep your voice down."

"Sorry," Molly whispered and tiptoed closer. "But what on earth?"

"I was trying to get rid of my parents. It got out of hand. And things with Rafael became *impossible*. I love him *so much* and he doesn't feel the same." Her eyes began to well with tears of hurt and despair.

Molly, bless her, didn't judge. In fact, her face crumpled.

"I love Gio, too. I told him last night. This morning we had a fight about it. Then he caught me with Rafael and thought I'd been having an affair with him. Rafael explained this is your baby, too, which was hard enough for Gio to wrap his head around. I couldn't tell him *why* I wanted to carry your baby. He thinks it's only for the money, and there are things in his past that make him look down on me for th-that…"

"Oh, Moll." Sasha rushed over to hug her friend. They both fell apart.

Molly held on to her really tight and choked through her sobs, "I'm not sorry, though. Okay? I don't regret anything about doing this. Nothing," she stressed, then mumbled into Sasha's hair, "Except the part where we've checked into Heartbreak Hotel together."

"Really?" Sasha drew back a little. "There's no one else I'd rather be miserable with."

They both sputtered into teary laughter.

Rafael felt like a guest when he entered the villa a week later.

Molly came from the kitchen with a tray of glasses and a pitcher of lemonade. She wore a simple cotton sundress that draped from a high waist to curtain her bump. Her brown hair was in a ponytail. Her face and feet were bare, making her look about fifteen years old.

"Shall we sit by the pool? Sasha's on a video call upstairs, but she'll have heard the helicopter. I'm sure she'll be down shortly."

"Who is she chatting with?" He glanced with dismay at the spiral staircase. He was moving better on these sticks, but would break his neck trying to negotiate those see-through steps.

"Dr. Narula suggested we reconnect with our counselor."

"Is she having trouble bonding with the baby?" he asked with alarm, following her out the doors to the shaded part of the terrace.

"I wouldn't say that. But I don't want to speak for her," she added with an apologetic smile. "Also..." She hesitated, then said plainly, "We talk about a lot of things, but there are things we don't talk about. You, for instance. We only talk about you in very general terms. She told me that you've both had some ups and downs as a result of the fertility troubles, but she doesn't go into detail. I thought you'd like to know she doesn't gossip about you."

"Hmph." He sat and half drained the icy lemonade she handed him. "How are you? How's the baby?"

"The nurse was here yesterday. No concerns." She patted her middle, smiling.

"But you're also speaking to the counselor? Are you having misgivings?"

"Not at all. But after what happened that day with Gio..." Her brow crinkled. "I knew having this baby would change my life, but I thought I could go back to my old life afterward. Now I know that's not going to happen. I wanted to talk that out with her. Have you, um—" She peered at him, asking with a cringe of apprehension, "Have you spoken to Gio?"

"No." Gio had been murderous when he had caught them together. He had leaped to the correct conclusion that his secretary-fiancée was carrying Rafael's baby. The part where the baby was also Sasha's had put him into a tailspin.

Sasha. Rafael had begun thinking of his wife by that name, feeling closer to her when he did.

Molly was staring at him like a puppy waiting for a bite of cheese so he pulled his mind back to their conversation.

"My people have reached out, but he's not answering. I'm sure it will be fine." He didn't believe that at all, but he didn't want to drop a guilt trip on her.

Molly had kept their secret right up until the showdown in the suite. She swore that Gio would keep the fact the baby was theirs confidential, but Rafael wasn't as certain. He'd seen the dark side of humanity. He knew how useful this type of leverage could be for a man like Gio and was working night and day, ensuring that Gio couldn't use this to damage him.

"If you need a job after this, tell me. I'll find you a place," he assured Molly.

"Thank you, but it's not about needing a job. I won't have to work for a long time, thanks to your generosity." She traced a finger through the dew on her glass, brow crinkling. "It's more that I'm the type who likes to know what's coming. Now my future is a big ol' white space. But after the baby comes, I'll spend some time with my mom and sister. That will be good. It will all work out."

He wondered if that practical optimism and quiet confidence was what Sasha liked about her. It was very appealing.

"How are you and Sasha getting along?" he asked.

"Good. Ah, here she is. I knew she would have heard the helicopter. I'll leave you two to catch up." Molly rose with undisguised haste. She faltered briefly as she passed Sasha and waited for Sasha to nod before she entered the house and closed the door.

Rafael noted that Sasha held a tissue in her fist and tried to see past the black cat's eye lenses she wore. "Have you been crying?"

"I was talking to the counselor." She shoved the tissue under her nose. Her mood seemed heavy. Her hair was loose, she wore no lipstick, and her sundress was a simple thing with spaghetti straps and a flecked print of yellow on green. She was still the most beautiful woman he'd ever seen.

"About the baby?" he asked, bracing himself.

"About…" She sighed and said, "There's usually a breeze out at the gazebo by this time of day. Can you walk that far?"

The path was hard-packed gravel so he easily managed it.

"Another week and I should have a walking cast," he said when they arrived in the shaded octagon where there was, in fact, a very nice breeze. There was also a pair of daybeds. The table between held a stack of paperback romances, sunscreen, a hair tie, and the start of some knitting in a buttery yellow yarn.

He leaned on a post so he could study Sasha's profile while she stood at the rail, facing the sea.

"How are things here?"

"Good." She brightened. "Molly felt the baby move. I didn't yet, but we keep trying."

A pang went through him, partly made up of that sense of threat he experienced when she was close with their surrogate, but the anticipation in her face was such a relief, he could only be pleased by this development.

"You're feeling good about the baby?" he prompted. "Less worried?"

"A little." She immediately plunged back to pensive, chewing the corner of her mouth.

"Do you want to tell me about the counselor?" he asked.

"There's a lot to unpack, but the biggest issue is…." Her brow wrinkled with real distress. "I don't know how to make this marriage work if you don't…" Her voice withered.

Don't love me?

Everything in him became gripped with tension. Was he incapable of love? Or merely afraid of it? Maybe if they had weathered the infertility storm without it causing such a rift between them, he might have allowed himself to be more vulnerable with her, but the more she had distanced herself, the less able he'd been to bridge that gap. He was beginning to see that now. Once Molly had come into the picture, he had put up even more walls.

"If you don't know who I really am," she finished in a shaken voice.

It took him a moment for his brain to catch up. Her words pulled him out of his introspection into seeing an easy fix. "I don't blame you for not knowing who you are. I'm enjoying getting to know you. Sasha."

Her gaze flashed to his. "That's the first time you've called me that."

"Do you mind?"

"No." Her voice thickened. "I like hearing it in your voice."

That hit him like such a heart punch he couldn't breathe. Then he noticed her mouth was quivering as though she was on the verge of tears again.

"What's wrong?"

She looked at her hands. "I wish everything could be… where it needs to be, between us. That we didn't have to go through fire to get there. I don't know if we'll survive it."

"Hey." He leaned out and grazed her hand with his fingertips. "Come here."

She warily placed her fingers into his palm, allowing him to tug her closer.

"We have time. Even once the baby is here, we can take as long as you need." He brought her hand to his mouth and kissed her knuckle. "Time is being forced upon us, actually."

"What do you mean?"

"I have some leads in Asia and Australia. Gio is stonewalling. He hasn't dissolved the deal, but he won't finalize it, either. I have to put contingency plans in place, so I'm leaving for a few weeks. I was going to ask you to come with me, but I can see how important it is for you to be here. That it's helping you feel closer to our baby."

"It is, but…" Her fingers clenched onto his and her mouth seemed to search for words.

He wished he could see the beckoning blue of her eyes.

"But you'll miss me?" he suggested, inviting her closer by guiding her hand up to the back of his neck.

She flowed into him and he dipped his head to kiss her as naturally as he always had.

When her other hand splayed against his rib cage, he paused, but she wasn't pressing in protest. She roamed her palm against his side, then slid her hand around to his back, leaning into him until her curves were flat against his front.

His brain turned inside out.

He let his crutches fall and grasped at the rail to keep himself firmly on his feet while he hooked his other hand behind her neck, dragging her that inch closer so he could kiss her the way he'd been needing to since she'd awakened in Rome and stared at him as though he was a stranger.

A jolt of surprise went through her, then she moaned into his mouth and melted against him. One hand went up to the back of his head, where her fingers sifted into his hair. The one at his back slid down to massage his ass.

His body's response—the sliding tension through his

abdomen and the pour of heat into his groin—was stronger than ever.

Her lips opened to invite an even hungrier kiss. He ravaged her, thinking only one thought. How could anything part them when they had *this*? The precariousness between them fell away. Here, with the taste of her intoxicating him, here everything was right and solid and *good*.

When she pressed her hips into his in the most exquisite way, as though she remembered exactly how much he liked that crushing space between pleasure and pain, he groaned and dropped his hand to her tailbone, encouraging the roll of her hips.

She was on her tiptoes, one long, lithe line against him. He wanted to fill his hands with her. Kneel and lavish her with his tongue. He wanted to press her to one of those daybeds and meld them together for all time.

He couldn't do any of those things, not with this damned cast.

He gripped the rail with all his strength and encouraged the rhythm of their grinding hips. The soft cheek of her ass filled his palm and her breasts rubbed his chest and her breath shortened.

This lovely, lovely woman was bringing him to the brink, seeking the pressure of his diamond-hard erection against her mound. Mewing into his mouth. Tensing.

Just when he thought he would explode like a teenager, she shuddered and dropped her head back to release small cries of joy into the rafters above them.

As her whole body went limp, he released her ass—he'd probably left a handprint there—and cradled his arm around her, holding her up while he inhaled the sweet smell of her hair and the knowledge that he could still bring her off without either of them getting undressed.

"I thought…" Her voice was unsteady. She wedged her arms between them. "I thought you were with me."

"I nearly was." His voice was thick with the lust that still coursed through him. He let his hand trace up and down her spine. "But edging myself while making you come is pretty much my favorite pastime."

"I don't understand."

"It's when—"

"I know what edging is," she muttered. "Which one of us are you controlling? Me or you?"

"Both. It's fun to see how long I can last. I didn't think this one through, of course. I'm going to be horny for weeks."

She made a noise of amusement, but her mouth was pouted in thought.

He was starting to resent those sunglasses and the way they made it so hard to read what was going on behind them.

"Help me to that daybed and I'll let you break me," he invited, voice rasped with anticipation.

"No," she scolded, chin dipping so he could only see the crown of her head where her dirty blond roots were coming in. Still, her head canted as she looked toward the bed, as though she was gauging the distance and thinking about it.

"Why not? Worried Molly will see us? It's below the rail." The crisscrossed slats provided a screen that allowed the breeze to float across the lower half of the gazebo but left the beds in shadow. "Or because you don't remember doing it to me before? Because you have."

Tension invaded her that wasn't all sexual. It was reluctance. Resistance?

"Sasha."

Her head came up, startled.

"We don't have to. It's fine." Horniness wasn't terminal. It only felt that way. He cupped her cheek. "But I want you to know that the first time we made love, we were complete strangers. We didn't even know each other's names."

Her lips parted, then tilted between naughty humor and something that struck him as rueful. His heart swerved.

"Do you remember that?"

"What? No." She stepped away and bent to pick up his crutches. "Are you staying for dinner? It's Molly's night to cook. We should let her know if you are."

Slowly, Sasha was coming to terms with things she should have addressed years ago. Or, rather, she was beginning to believe what she had known in her head but hadn't been able to accept in her heart. Her affair with a married man hadn't been her fault. Her "lover" had exploited a troubled teenager and played the victim when his actions had consequences.

Deciding to keep her pregnancy a secret, then placing Libby with Patty, had been the only real agency she'd had at the time. She had taken control of her circumstance and her future to the best of her ability. She shouldn't feel ashamed of the decisions she'd made.

Sometimes she even listened to Molly talk to Libby and felt really good about what she'd done.

Then Molly came out to where she was lazing by the pool and announced starkly, "That was Mom. Gio went to see her. He was looking at family photos and figured it out, Sash. He knows you're Libby's birth mom."

"What?" She sat up, scrambling to keep her sunglasses in place. "Rafael can't hear that from someone else."

"Gio won't say anything. Mom impressed on him that it's not his place. I genuinely don't believe he would do that to Libby. He's met her during our chats and seems to like her. He's not malicious."

Even so, the possibility of being outed hung like a storm cloud over her.

The next time she spoke to Rafael, she asked when he would be home.

"I'll be here at least another week. I was able to get my cast off so at least one thing is going in my favor. Why? Do you miss me?"

She hesitated, surprised at the question, no matter how cocky he'd sounded as he delivered it. He had never asked for confirmations of affection in the past.

But they had started having much deeper conversations, especially now that they were apart. She talked to him about the baby and her growing excitement for its arrival. He said he wished one of his mothers had lived to meet her grandchild.

One night, she asked him why he was so determined to expand his father's business.

"Spite," he replied.

She still couldn't use screens, so his voice was in her ear, and maybe that was why he filled the silence that she deliberately left for him to continue.

"The day my father died, I came into the office to find the local gang roughing him up. He couldn't breathe. I got into it with them and was on the floor myself when I realized he had collapsed from more than a gut punch. They took my phone and yanked out the landlines. I went to three different businesses, but none would call an ambulance. They'd been there ahead of me, intimidating them against helping us."

"That's horrible."

"It was. By the time I got an ambulance to him, he was gone. But I wasn't," he said with grit. "And I made sure they knew it."

The growing openness between them gave her the courage to admit, "Yes. I do miss you."

Every time she spoke to him, she thought, *Come home.*

"I miss you, too. I wish you were here." He sounded tired and maybe something else that she couldn't quite put her finger on. Homesick? "You always charm people's socks off."

"Including yours?" It was a lilt of flirtation she tossed out to lift him from his brooding.

"They're already off," he retorted. "I'm fresh out of the shower wearing only a towel. Why? What are you wearing?" The way his voice dipped into smoky and wicked sent a pulse of temptation deep between her thighs.

She swallowed. "Just a sundress."

"Just?"

"And underwear."

"Are you in your room? Alone?"

She glanced out the window to see Molly was at the gazebo. She hurried up the stairs to her bedroom. "I am now," she said, breathless from more than the climb.

"Don't lock the door. Lean against it and take off your underwear, but leave them around your ankles."

"Why?" she asked, prickling with nervous excitement.

"Because I want you to open your legs as far as you can and imagine my hands are cuffing your ankles. I'm kneeling in front of you and I'm going to lick your fingers as you caress yourself. Tell me when you start doing that."

"What, um…" She felt jittery and naughty and aroused as she let the scrap of lace drop. "What are you doing?"

"Opening my towel and thinking I won't be so selfless this time. I'm going to come when you do."

"Oh." She pressed the back of her head to the hard door.

"Are you touching yourself? Tell me *exactly* what you're doing," he prompted in a velvety voice that rasped across her senses. "I'll tell you exactly what *I'm* doing while I'm there on the floor in front of you."

Her husband had a really filthy mouth, but she seemed to

possess a kinky streak that liked it. Within a few minutes, her helpless sobs were filling the room. He owned her, he really did, even from nine thousand miles away.

But as his groan of completion resounded in her ear, her panting lips curved into a tender smile. She felt close to him, despite the distance. She really did.

"When I finally get my hands on you, we won't leave our bed for a week," he promised in a voice she knew very well. It was the one that often played against her ear when she was basking in this same afterglow.

It dimmed as she waited to find out if Gio would use what he knew, but as time wore on she began to believe Gio really would stay silent about Libby.

Then Rafael called one morning to say, "I rerouted to Genoa."

"What?" she cried. "I thought you were coming to Athens."

"Gio Casella finally picked up the phone."

"I was going to come see you." She had only been toying with the idea, but panic had the words blurting out of her.

"I would love that," he said in a throaty voice. "But if he actually goes through with signing the contract, it will be an all-hands situation while I finally get everything off the ground. I want to give you my full attention once we're together so I'll come to you when I can."

Wait, she thought, but he ended the call.

CHAPTER TEN

HE SIGNED IT.

Gio didn't need this partnership as badly as Rafael did, but if he walked away from this deal, he knew Rafael would find someone else and compete against him. He was a practical businessman so he got over his snit and closed the deal.

Rafael had braced himself for fresh haggling and threats to expose the surrogacy arrangement, but Gio only adjusted some dates to reflect the time they'd lost. He remained frosty, though, not mentioning Molly's name or asking how she was doing.

That didn't surprise Rafael. Apparently, their engagement had been a sham, but Rafael was offended on her behalf and said as much before he left. Probably not his smartest move, but he liked her and thought Gio should have treated her better.

The deal was done, though, creating a proverbial electric fence around his own assets. The growth would be exponential and, yes, he would have achieved his nine zeroes well before the age of thirty-five, which was the goal he had set for himself.

That should have brought him more satisfaction than it did. He hurried back to Athens to get things moving, but he was only irritated by the mountain of meetings and decisions that landed on him. He was usually energized by this type of thing, but all he could think about was carving out time to see his wife.

By the time he was finally on his way to see her, they had been nearly two months apart. This house wasn't a home without her and he wanted her here. She had even offered to come to him, but he wanted to collect her. At twenty-four weeks, the baby was moving enough that he might feel one of those kicks for himself.

Since when had he become a family man? Next, he'd be falling in love.

He paused in changing out of his suit to consider that.

His priorities had definitely shifted, which felt unfamiliar, but not as alarming as it might have a year or even a few months ago.

Sasha's memory loss was still a concern, of course, but they were finding their way out of the rough patch that had plagued them for so long. In some ways, her amnesia served them. It had forced them to set aside their go-to coping strategy of lust—notwithstanding the phone sex—and address the underlying issues they had ignored. He had had to name those issues for her and acknowledge his role in their various mistakes. Things like his remoteness and refusal to share his most difficult memories.

Letting her in felt risky as hell, but he understood that trust was a two-way street. He had to offer it to gain it, so he was letting down his guard with her. She was still a mystery to herself as well as him, but he was getting to know her all over again and, to his eternal delight, was more attracted to her than ever. She was softer these days. More vulnerable.

He felt more protective of her than ever and couldn't wait until they were finally together, with their baby, in their home again.

Her name came up on his phone and he slid to accept the call.

"I know, I know," he said. "I'm grabbing a few things from the house, then I'll—"

"Molly's bleeding," she said starkly. "The nurse is here and the helicopter is on its way. We'll meet you at the hospital in Athens."

"Is the baby—?"

"I don't *know*, Rafael. I don't know why this keeps happening! Why am I not allowed to have a baby?" Her anguish was knife-sharp and ripened by fear, but the words and the old defeat baked within them sent a cold flush through his body.

"Alexandra." He wasn't consciously aware of grasping at that old name, but he instinctively knew that's who he was talking to. "Do you have your memories back?"

"They never left," she cried. "I *tried* to forget, but—"

"You remember everything? You've been lying to me all this time?" It was such a crack in the face, it should have knocked his own memories into another universe.

"Rafael." Her tone pulled back from hysteria.

"No," he said, because he couldn't accept it. Not right now. Not when their baby was in jeopardy. "I'll meet you at the hospital."

He ended the call, so blind with outrage he couldn't form a thought or move a muscle.

"Sir?" Tino asked, reminding him that his assistant had been hovering this whole time. "I heard 'hospital.' Is there something I can do?"

That kicked Rafael's sluggish brain into gear.

"Yes. Tell the driver we're going into the city, not the helipad." He gave him the name of the hospital Molly would be flown to.

Her mother. Somehow his scattered thoughts snagged on the importance of informing Molly's mother.

Rafael wasted precious minutes flicking through old emails until he found her number.

Patricia sounded distracted when she picked up.

"It's Rafael, Alexandra's husband. I wanted to let you know that Molly is on her way to the hospital—"

"I just got off the phone with Gio," Patricia cut in. Tension was evident beneath her firmly controlled tone. "He's in New York and has arranged a flight for us. We're leaving the house right now. He said we should be there in twelve hours or so."

Gio. How the hell had *he* heard about this? Molly? It didn't matter. Patricia and Molly's sister were on their way. That was all that mattered.

"I'll update you at this number?" Rafael asked.

"Thank you. We'll see you soon."

She was a midwife, he recalled. She was likely used to medical emergencies, but not ones that involved her daughter.

Guilt assailed him along with profound worry. He didn't know Molly well, but he liked her. He had to wonder, however, whether *she* knew that his wife had been lying to him all this time?

He would bet any money that she did, given how close she was to Sasha. The thought made him even more furious, filling him with such a sense of betrayal he could barely function.

He stewed all the way into the city. Molly had just arrived when he did. She was being assessed so he was directed to a private lounge.

Alexandra was already there. She wore one of her casual sundresses that buttoned from its square neckline down to her knees. A drawstring at her waist gave it a figure-hugging shape, but it was crushed and one of the buttons had slipped free.

She was ghostly white and froze when she saw him.

Conflicting impulses rocketed through him. He had an instinct to rush forward and comfort her. To comfort himself with the solace of her willowy body leaning into his. Getting to twenty-four weeks had made this seem like a sure thing. To have the rug pulled at this stage would be devastating.

At the same time, he was so angry with her, so bitterly disgusted, he could hardly look at her.

"Your cast is gone."

"I told you it was off. What happened? To Molly," he clarified. "Did she fall?"

"No. Nothing. She felt fine. A little tired, but only because the baby woke her early with a big k-kick." Her voice hiccuped. "We were talking. She was upset about Gio, but she was just a bit weepy, not… Anyway, she stood up and we realized she was bleeding."

Her hand shook as she wiped beneath her seeping eye.

"I called for the helicopter, then the nurse. She flew in with us. She thinks it could be a placental abruption. That's when…" Her voice faded with a fear so visceral, it made the hairs on his arms stand up. "When the placenta p-pulls away…"

"I understand." He couldn't bear it. He might want to shout himself hoarse at her, but he couldn't see straight. This was their *baby*. He crossed to her in a few lurching strides and yanked her against his chest.

She shuddered and clung to him, catching back sobs.

They stood a long time like that, clinging to each other as though cast away at sea. They clung to hope, not relaxing their grip until the doctor came in and confirmed the nurse's suspicion.

"The baby's vitals are strong and Molly's bleeding has subsided, but we'll keep her here on strict bed rest and monitor her closely. Hopefully, we can buy a week or two, but she will deliver early. We've started her on steroids to help the baby's lungs develop. We've also given her a mild pain reliever so she'll be drowsy when you see her. They're settling her in her room now. It won't be much longer."

"Can I ask you to speak with Molly's mother?" Rafael asked the doctor. "She's on her way here, but I'm sure she's anxious for news." He gave the doctor Patricia's number and the doctor left to make that call.

"Thank you. I don't know that I could have repeated any of that," Sasha said.

Or should he call her Alexandra? He didn't know who he was talking to anymore! He felt raw, absolutely peeled down to his core that she had lied to him so cold-bloodedly. For so long, too.

He had known she was capable of deception, but not like this. Not something directed at him. It made her seem like a stranger all over again. Like their whole marriage had been one long lie.

At the same time, she was exactly the woman he knew as she absently pulled the tie from her hair, then gathered it into a fresh bun to resecure it. He'd seen her do that so many times it was imprinted on him as *her*.

"Did Molly call Gio to bring them?" he asked.

"I did. You hung up on me," she reminded him flatly. "And—" She looked with frustration between the kettle and single-cup coffee maker. "God, I could use a drink. I know you're angry about…what I did."

"I'm angry that you enlisted Gio to do something that was my responsibility," he said stiffly. "'Angry' doesn't begin to describe how I feel about you lying to my face for two straight months. Is that what really turned you on while we were having all that phone sex?"

She stared at him through a long, drawn-out moment

of silence, then blinked once in a way that was decidedly withering, but her voice shook as she said, "No, Rafael. I don't get off on power the way you do."

"Kýrie and Kyría Zamos?" A nurse poked her head into the lounge. "Kyría Brooks can see you now, but only for a moment. She needs to rest."

Molly was on her side in the hospital bed, various tubes and wires emerging from beneath the blankets that covered her.

"Moll?" Sasha brushed her hair off her face with such tender familiarity, it struck a knife into Rafael's heart. "You doing okay, pal?"

"Mmm-hmm." She left her eyes shut. "Baby's okay, too, but they're going to keep me."

"I know. Your mom is on her way."

Molly's eye opened. "With Lib?"

Sasha nodded, mouth pressed into a grave line. "Yes. It's okay. I think it will be."

Molly's somber gaze shifted to Rafael.

"I haven't told him yet, but I will," Sasha said.

Molly's arm wormed its way out from beneath the blanket. She wiggled her fingers at Rafael, beckoning him closer.

"I know you're mad at me, too, but…" She reached out farther, insisting he give her his hand.

When he did, she guided his palm to press against the side of her bump. It was a surprisingly firm curve. Through the layer of cotton and the warmth of her body, he felt the slightest nudge against his palm.

His breath was kicked clean out of him.

He swung his awe-filled gaze to his wife and caught such a look of envy and sorrow on her face, it was another punch to the gut. She wanted to be the one to give him this. He knew that. She might have lied about other things, but her desire to have this baby was real.

She hid her torment behind a faint smile, then pointed at Molly's phone on the bedside table.

"Call if you need me. We have an apartment a few blocks away. I'll come back when Patty lands."

"Okay," Molly murmured, blinking sleepily. "It's going to be okay, Sash."

"I know," Sasha said, but when she looked up at Rafael, there was nothing but hell in her eyes. She knew as well as he did that they stood to lose everything.

Including each other.

The apartment in Athens was a one-bedroom flat they kept stocked for occasions when they had a late night in the city.

While Rafael set out some takeout he'd picked up, Sasha pulled on a pair of soft joggers and a long-sleeved shirt, chilled to the bone by the air-conditioning that was staving off the still-hot September temperatures.

She knocked back a shot of ouzo on her way to the table before accepting the glass of white wine Rafael poured her. Absolutely nothing in her was interested in the souvlaki skewers he plated.

"I was going to tell you when you came back to the island, but you went to Asia—"

"And there was no possible way you could have told me over the phone," he said coldly. "Or simply *told the truth* when I asked you in Rome."

Heaviness sat on her heart. It was the heaviness of earned guilt.

"I know I'm in the wrong. I know you'll have a hard time forgiving me, but… You laughed at me, Rafael." The mere mention of it still caused a piercing sensation in the middle of her chest.

"When?" He was ignoring his own meal, pacing with a slight limp, but otherwise back to being the dynamic man she'd married—severely handsome and so muscled and powerful, his stiff shoulders strained the fabric of his shirt.

"When I told you I loved you."

"No, I didn't."

"You did. I said I loved you and you said you thought I was going to say I love Molly. Then you *laughed*."

"At myself. For thinking that," he said impatiently. "That doesn't excuse your making a fool of me ever since!"

"That's not why I did it," she said wearily. "That's why it started. Actually, I was screwing with my parents and it snowballed from there. I—" She made herself stop pacing. Stop trying to find rationalizations.

Stop running from the past.

She turned to face him. She faced all of it head-on.

"When I was sixteen, one of Humbolt's friends seduced me. I got pregnant and ran away to have the baby. I lived with Molly and her mom. They adopted her. Molly's sister, Libby, is my daughter."

He stood so still she didn't think he was even breathing.

She swallowed and folded her arms around herself.

"That's why I was so upset when I couldn't get pregnant. I did it before without even trying. I should have been able to do it again."

"Why didn't you tell me that?"

"I couldn't make the words come out of my mouth." That was the truth, but not the whole truth. She took a shaken breath. "I buried that secret because it hurt, Rafael. It hurt so much that I couldn't look at it myself, let alone show it to you. We didn't share secrets. You said you were fond of me, but was that fondness going to hold up under knowing your wife had an affair with a married man? One with small children at home?"

"He had kids? How old was he?"

"Thirty-one."

"And you were sixteen? That's not an affair, Alexandra."

She flinched, hating to hear him call her that after he'd begun sounding so tender when he called her by her nickname.

"I know, but it wasn't against my will, either. I didn't fight him off. I thought I was in love. Mostly I loved the idea that screwing Humbolt's friend would get under Humbolt's skin. All I really did was give him a reason to call me a whore, though." She rubbed her eyebrow.

"He knew about it? And didn't put a stop to it?" He sounded murderous. "What about your mother?"

"She would never admit she knew. And that's not the point. I got pregnant, but I was a minor. I knew Humbolt would use my baby against me. Maybe they would have made me give it up anyway. Or my mother would have undercut my parenting to turn my child into yet another vapid socialite. Nothing about bringing that baby home would have worked in my favor or the baby's."

"That's the real reason you ran away back then. To have the baby."

She nodded. "Patty took me in and helped me hire a lawyer who got Libby's father to relinquish paternity rights. He also set up a trust for her, but I'm not allowed to reveal he's her father. That's another reason I had to keep the whole thing secret. If the paparazzi learned I'd had a baby, they would go digging. At least the fear that he could be exposed made Libby's father keep Humbolt in check to some extent."

"He didn't keep you out of a psych ward, though, did he? They should both be arrested!"

"You're right. But so many people would suffer if this came out now. Believe me, I've thought about it, but Libby's life would be overturned, not to mention the lives of her father's other children. They're not much older than she is. They don't deserve to be hounded by the press while their parents go through an ugly divorce. Maybe he would try to undo the trust. Humbolt would definitely go after Patty for harboring me. He'd ruin her career, likely make a play for custody of Libby since she's Mom's granddaughter and entitled to a slice of my fortune. I doubt he'd win, but the point would be the pain he caused along the way."

He swore under his breath, then used his hand to scrub across his face.

She didn't know what reaction she expected. Maybe some sort of absolution? Understanding, at least?

The weight of his silence sat like a ten-ton boulder on her heart. They hadn't stood a chance, she realized. Not given all that she'd been hiding. Not when he was a man who had never been taught to trust and she had betrayed the little trust he'd started to place in her.

"That's everything?" he asked with scowl of distrust.

"Yes. The only other thing I ever lie about is my weight when we fly."

"I always tell them to add a few kilos anyway," he muttered with distraction.

"A *few*?" That was literally the meanest thing he'd ever said to her.

"You could have told me this anytime," he said tightly. "Long before this." He swept his hand through the air.

"When, Rafael?" she asked with more defeat than challenge. "When you asked me to have your baby and I thought you'd divorce me if I refused?"

"I never said that."

"It was implied. When we married, you told me you needed an heir. I *wanted* a baby. I want our baby." She waved in the direction of the hospital, trying not to think about how precarious their baby's life was at this moment. "I didn't expect it to become so hard to make one. You take care of everything and I had one job, but I couldn't do it.

I was too ashamed to tell you why I felt like I was being punished—"

"No." He shook his head. "You—"

"No, *listen*," she insisted. "For once. Please. When I saw Molly on the yacht, I couldn't even let her tell me about Libby. It was really hard for me to come this far, to be able to tell you about her, but that's because I never had any trust in our marriage in the first place. I didn't trust *you*."

He sucked in a breath as though taking another body blow.

"I've wanted to tell you so many times, but even when we both nearly died and I asked you if we loved each other, you said that was never part of our deal. Why the hell would I share anything so deeply personal with you after that? I ran away the only way I could, by pretending I couldn't remember anything. I thought that would get us to a clean divorce, but you started telling me things I never knew. Things about *us*. Do you know how many times I thought we were engaged in all-out war when we have sex, because I thought you got off on controlling me? I didn't know you get off on holding yourself back."

"Are you serious?" His jaw went slack.

"And those phone calls, while you were away? I thought you were wooing me. That we were finally growing closer. But I knew it would blow up when I told you I had never really lost my memory so I put off telling you. I know that's wrong. I know it is. But I couldn't stay in the marriage we had. And I don't know how we can stay married now, but—" She began to choke up as fresh anxiety welled in her chest. "Can we— Can we have a truce and not make any decisions until we know—"

She couldn't break down in front of him.

"I need to lie down." She hurried into the bedroom and shut the door.

* * *

Rafael started to go after her, but heard the lock click. He sighed and looked at the forgotten drink in his hand.

He wanted to get hammered out of his mind, but he set the glass aside, too stunned to form a coherent thought. What the hell had he just heard?

His mind began to flicker with random memories that he reevaluated as they came and went. The way Sasha had reacted to Molly arriving on the yacht. The way she had stiffened once, when Rafael had asked Molly about her sister. Molly had spoken with enthusiasm and affection while Sasha had listened politely, but he had sensed something was off.

He remembered their wedding day, when there'd been a handful of strangers present, assembled to celebrate Sasha's engagement to someone else. There'd been a man there who had watched Sasha in a way that had made her set her jaw at a defiant angle. Rafael had hated him on sight and only remembered him because he'd instinctively filed him under "enemies" in his mental register.

He remembered Sasha's agitation when Molly's pregnancy had been confirmed and the way she'd broken down at the twelve-week scan. He had put it all down to her fertility struggles. She was entitled to some ambivalence, he'd thought, but he hadn't had any real idea of the things she'd been through.

He hadn't tried to find out, either.

I didn't feel safe telling you these things.

Talk about shame. He prided himself on looking after her well, but he hadn't. Not in the way that counted most.

On the other hand, if she had *loved* him, as she had said she did, how could she lie to him about her memory loss? She had been angry with him. Fine. But she had kept it up for two *months*. That started to feel like the opposite of love. A grudge.

He was exhausted, but he stayed on his feet, brooding, not realizing he was waiting until he heard her stir a few hours later.

She came out of the bedroom still wearing the clothes she'd changed into when they had arrived. She faltered when she saw he was also still awake.

"They've landed. They're on the way to the hospital." She kicked into a pair of sandals and collected her purse.

He picked up the keys to drive her, not bothering to ask if she wanted him to. They didn't speak again until he was coming out of the underground parking lot.

"My sunglasses," she muttered as she dug through her handbag.

He pulled his own from the compartment beside his visor and handed them to her.

"Thank you."

When they arrived, they were asked to wait in the lounge. Molly was asleep, but her mother and Libby had been allowed to step in to see her. Gio had also been relegated to the lounge. His face and clothes were lined by travel, or was that worry putting tension around his eyes?

Rafael nodded curtly. Their last two interactions had been chilly. All of their communications around their partnership were being handled by their various executive teams.

"Did, um, Patty tell—" Sasha started to ask Gio.

"She did." He nodded once.

"*He* knew?" Rafael couldn't help that his temperature immediately spiked again.

"He figured it out a few weeks ago, after visiting Patty," Sasha said defensively.

Weeks. "Before our meeting?" Rafael directed that at Gio.

Gio hitched a shoulder.

There was no comfort in knowing that Gio could have revealed Sasha's secrets and destroyed Rafael in twenty different ways. Instead, he had signed off the deal in good faith. Rafael ought to thank him, he supposed, but he only felt foolish that everyone seemed to have been in on the lies except him.

"I need air," he muttered and yanked open the door.

A woman was on her way in. She faltered in surprise. She was in her fifties with threads of silver in her brunette hair. Her smile was the one that he'd seen on Molly's face nearly every time he'd seen her.

"Hello, Rafael. I'm Patricia. Call me Patty." She thrust out her hand and returned his firm shake.

"Nice to meet you," he managed, but she was already dropping his hand and sweeping past him.

"Sasha," she greeted, melting with emotion as she opened her arms to envelop his wife.

Sasha embraced her, but looked over her shoulder to the empty doorway, expression haunted. "Where's—"

"Libby wanted to stay with Molly. Can you give her a day or two?" She drew back to smooth Sasha's hair. "It's not just you. She's worried about Molly and upset we didn't tell her about the baby."

Rafael was vaguely aware of Gio ghosting past him and out the door, but he was wholly focused on the way Sasha's face crumpled even as she nodded with acceptance.

His heart folded in on itself. Her agony was so tangibly his, it nearly destroyed him.

This is love, he thought. He wouldn't feel her pain so acutely if she wasn't in possession of his heart. He wanted to go to her and hold her, but she was clinging to Patricia. He understood that that was where she needed to express that particular pain, but it was more devastation than he could witness.

He stepped outside the room and closed the door, then leaned on the wall, trying to ease the fire in his chest with slow, even breaths.

It was hitting him, though, the magnitude of responsibility Sasha had shouldered at sixteen. He had dismissed her animosity toward her mother and stepfather as a spoiled heiress who didn't like to be hemmed in. He hadn't imagined that she could understand his struggles, making adult decisions as an adolescent himself, taking over his father's business, and prying it loose from crooks.

Yet at sixteen, she'd carried a baby in secret because the adults who should have been protecting her had left her as bait for a wolf. She'd found a loving home for her baby, refusing to risk that baby suffering the abuse that she'd endured. Letting go of her baby had been so painful, she hadn't been able to speak about it for more than ten years.

He was so racked with pain on her behalf, he braced his hands on his knees, trying not to be sick.

Italian shoes and bespoke trouser cuffs came into his line of vision. He straightened to see Gio.

"Molly is awake. She wants to see her mother." He stepped past Rafael and knocked on the door, then poked his head in to deliver his message. He closed it again, looking grave. "I've arranged a hotel for Patty and Libby. I'll take them when they're ready."

"*I've* arranged a hotel," Rafael said with annoyance.

"It's one less thing on your plate and..." Gio's cheek ticked. "I'd like to look after Molly's family."

Molly's sister wasn't just *Molly's* family, though, was she?

A few hours ago, when Sasha had relayed her past to him,

all of this had been a story. Now it was real. Real people. Real heartache.

Patricia came out of the lounge and squeezed Rafael's arm.

"See if you can talk her into going home for some rest. I need to get Libby to bed, too. We'll talk more tomorrow." She had such a reassuring air about her, he wanted to catch her back and insist she come home with them.

He slipped into the lounge to see Sasha was on the couch, doubled over her folded arms. She wore a shell-shocked expression, eyes dry, but her face was ravaged by tears.

"Sash?"

She drew back when he tried to cradle her cheek and turned her face away.

"She doesn't want to see me," she said in a voice shredded by desolation. "But I can't walk away from her again. Stand in the hall and tell me when she's gone."

A chasm opened inside him. He wanted to sit down and pull her into his lap. He wanted to walk down the hall and tell that little girl to get her butt in here, but she was only a little girl. A child who had probably started her day by getting ready for school, never dreaming she would meet her birth mother today, or that her sister's life would be in danger. She had been completely ignorant of the fact she had a half brother or sister on the way.

Punch drunk from all the shocks, Rafael stepped out the door and, a moment later, Gio emerged from Molly's room with Patty. She said something in a hushed voice and held out her arm for the preteen who joined her.

Nothing could have prepared him for his first glimpse of Libby. How had he not known that she would be a version of Sasha that was like looking at his wife through a lens that saw back in time. She had Sasha's same long hair and slender build, her graceful profile, and she brushed her hair off her shoulder in exactly the same way. Her eyes were so blue he felt the splash of them when she glanced his direction.

And that expression. When she noticed he was staring at her, her brows gathered into a scowl that asked, *Who the hell are you?*

He was a man experiencing love in its most pure and innocent form. What an impudent brat! He wanted to laugh and cry and say, *Sasha, she's beautiful. She's you. Come see.*

He waited until he heard the elevator doors open and close, then he went in to gather his wife, deciding it was best to say nothing at all.

CHAPTER ELEVEN

SASHA WOKE WITH a vague memory of Rafael holding her until she fell asleep, but the apartment was empty. He'd left her a text that he was at the office and would stop by the hospital midday.

There was also a text from Molly.

Peanut is doing somersaults. Dr. says no change. Mom says I have to stagger my visitors so I can rest. I feel like I'm grounded. I didn't even stay out past curfew!

Sasha texted back.

I'll bring you a cake with a nail file.

She took her time getting ready, since it sounded as though Patty and Libby were already there. Patty had wanted to speak with the doctor first thing, so that didn't surprise her, but the pair hadn't slept much, so they had already gone back to their hotel by the time Sasha got there.

"Libby is mad at me, too," Molly said, trying to mollify Sasha. "For letting her believe my engagement was real." Her gaze darted toward the open door where Gio had disappeared.

"Why is he still here?" Sasha mouthed.

"I don't know," Molly mouthed back.

"Do you want me to—"

"No," Molly said hurriedly. "He can stay if he wants to."

When Molly grew sleepy, Sasha left, promising to come back later. She filled an hour picking up some random things for her—magazines and moisturizer, a deck of cards and a board game that was suitable for a tween. Did she want to go broke buying bribery gifts for Libby? Heck, yes.

Instead, she went home and checked in with her counselor, who said, "Time may not heal all wounds, but all wounds need time to heal."

Ugh. It was glib, but she was right.

She had just missed Patty and Libby when she went back to see Molly, but at least she was able to eat dinner with her, since Rafael had already said he would be working late.

"Do you think you two will get through this?" Molly pried gently.

"I don't know, Moll. What I did was pretty unforgivable, but…" She swallowed. "I didn't mind being married to someone who didn't love me when I didn't think I deserved to be loved. Now…"

"Sash." Molly squeezed her hand.

"Don't worry about us, okay? You're not allowed." Patty was being pretty strict about keeping Molly's cortisol levels down. "For now, the only thing I'm thinking about is you and the baby."

"And Libby?" Molly guessed.

"Yeah," Sasha admitted with a pang in her throat.

"She'll come around. And she'll be nosy as hell when she does," Molly warned with amusement.

Sasha looked forward to it.

Time slowed to a crawl, leaving her too much time to fret about her marriage, especially as Rafael didn't come home until well after midnight.

"Is everything all right at work?" she murmured when he slid into bed beside her.

"Just putting the house in order."

"The house?" She picked up her head.

"Proverbial." He hesitated, then, "No matter what happens in the next week or two, you and I will need some time."

"Oh." She dropped her head back onto the pillow. Her heart stalled, then restarted.

"That's not—I just called the hospital. They said Molly and the baby are fine. Don't worry. Go back to sleep."

She couldn't help worrying. She wanted to ask him to hold her, but they were in too precarious a place. Instead, she waited until his breathing had evened out, then let her hand creep across to rest on his arm before she was able to drift off again.

He was gone again when she woke, leaving her to turn over his words as she waited until she could go to the hospital again.

On the third day of Molly's bed rest, she was in the lounge, waiting for Patty and Libby to leave, when Libby walked in.

Sasha almost dropped her coffee.

Libby faltered, eyes widening in recognition before her gaze darted around the otherwise empty room.

"My mom said there's hot chocolate here."

"There is." Sasha stepped aside and pointed. "It's that button. How's Molly?"

"They're taking her for her scan. Mom's allowed to go with her because she's..." She shrugged.

"Pushy?" Sasha joked.

"Heh. Sometimes." Libby set the cup, then pushed the button. "She sent me here probably knowing you were here, so yeah. I guess."

"You didn't want to see me?" Sasha tried not to let that destroy her.

"I don't know." Libby picked up the full cup, tried to sip and flinched because it was too hot.

"Milk? To cool it?" Sasha suggested, pointing to the refrigerator.

Libby shook her head and set it aside, then looked to the door.

Oh, God. I have to be the adult, don't I?

It wasn't easy when she felt as though she had regressed back to the teenager she'd been the last time she saw her daughter.

"I know Pat— I mean, your mom…" Ouch. "I know your mom has explained as much as she knows about why I let her adopt you, but you can ask me anything you want. I won't be upset."

"Why didn't you come see me?" She folded her arms defensively. "Mom said that you could have."

Oof. Start with an easy one, why didn't she?

"I was afraid to," she answered simply. "I was sad and thought it would hurt too much, and that I might put you and your mom at risk, legally, from my stepfather. Mostly, I didn't feel good about myself and really believed you were better off not knowing me."

Libby wrinkled her nose. "Does that mean you'll stay away after this?"

"I don't want to. Molly and I will always be friends." She couldn't imagine her life without her now. "I'll talk to your mom regularly, too. I'd like to see more of you if you're okay with that."

"Could I see the baby sometimes?"

"Yes! Absolutely! I would love that so much." She was gushing and tried to rein it in. "I know you're angry with me, but—"

"I'm not *angry* with you. I mean, I am," Libby clarified with a scowl. "I'm disappointed that you didn't want to see me before now. I'm mad at *Mom* for hiding that I'm *rich*. Molly didn't tell me she was pregnant and even Gio lied to me about their engagement. He said I could be a brides-maid and everything. Rafael seems like the only person I can trust around here, but maybe he was lying to me, too."

"About what? Did you talk to him?" she asked with as-tonishment.

"We played cards yesterday while we were waiting for Moll to wake up. I asked him if you guys are getting a di-vorce. He said he didn't want that, but that he didn't want to lie to me in case it didn't work out. He said everyone had been lying to him, too, so he understands where I'm coming from. I said it would be really unfair to the baby and also to Molly if you guys got divorced, considering everything Molly is going through."

"Yeah. I know." Sasha rubbed the ache in her sternum and bit back asking her to repeat herself. *He said he didn't want a divorce? Are you sure?*

"I kind of get why Molly wanted to be your surrogate," Libby said in a tone that was reluctantly forgiving. "And I don't really blame you for leaving me with a grown-up you trusted, instead of raising me yourself. I'm going to start high school next year, and I wouldn't want to stop my life to raise a baby. I babysit sometimes and you have to pay atten-tion the *whole time*. I'd rather travel and go to concerts and become a doctor, which takes a lot of effort and dedication."

"It does. Wow. Are you interested in medicine because of what your mom does?"

"Uh-huh. I read her textbooks sometimes. She said Moll will probably have to deliver by surgery, which sounds gross when you read about it, but it saves both the mom and the baby, which is pretty amazing."

It was terrifying, actually, but Sasha couldn't help a rush of pride at Libby's ambition. She probably didn't need to hear this, but she said it anyway.

"I bet you'll make a great doctor."

"I wish I was one already." Libby suddenly looked her age. Young. Vulnerable. Scared, even. "I really hope they'll both be okay."

"Oh, baby." Sasha abandoned her own mug and crossed to hug Libby. "Me, too."

As Libby's arms came around her, Sasha's heart swelled so big it pressed tears into her eyes, but in her periphery, she caught a movement at the door.

Rafael was there, watching them.

This had been the hardest week of Rafael's life and he'd lived some very hard weeks. This wasn't about keeping himself alive, though. At least when the odds were stacked against him in the past, he'd been able to do something. He'd been able to fight, one way or another.

There was nothing he could do to help Molly, though. Nothing he could do to ensure his baby lived. Nothing he could say that would lift the burden of worry off Sasha.

It was horrible. It was torture for a man like him. All he could do was throw himself into work, buying time he hoped they would spend with their baby.

Please let their baby arrive safely. He didn't know how he would survive any other outcome. Sasha would be completely devastated. Everyone would. And he couldn't help feeling guilty that he had brought this about.

I thought I had to have a baby to keep you. That's how little trust I had in our marriage.

He understood that completely now, because he had the feeling their marriage wouldn't survive if their baby didn't. Which devastated him.

He came into the apartment weary from another day of hiring and delegating, analyzing projections and approving action plans. It felt wrong to relinquish this much control, but he had figured out that if he wanted his marriage to survive, he was going to have to fight for it which meant allowing his business to run itself.

"You're up," he said with surprise when he found Sasha sitting in the dimly lit living room, listening to the television.

She clicked it off and removed her sleep mask. "I couldn't sleep. I had dinner with Patty and Libby. Patty thinks they'll make the decision to deliver the baby in the next day or two."

"Oh." He poured a drink and sat down on the other end of the couch.

"She says she trusts the team and that she'll join us in the meeting when they talk about the risks, if you want."

He swore and leaned forward to set his drink on the table.

"She shouldn't have to do that," he said. "She shouldn't be here worrying about her daughter like this. What have I done, Sasha?" He stayed forward, with his elbows on his knees and pushed his hands into his hair. "What the hell have I done?"

"Rafael." She shifted so she was kneeling beside him. She stroked his back. "Blaming myself is *my* thing."

"Don't joke. Not right now."

"I'm not. Not really." Her arms looped around his shoulders as she leaned onto him. The crown of her head rested against the side of his neck. "This was a collective effort. Molly knew the risks. Patty made sure she did. We all went to those counseling sessions and none of us hit the brakes because none of us thought this would happen."

"What if she can't have children of her own after this? What if—"

"I know. I think all of those same things, but at some point, we have to forgive ourselves for not owning a crystal ball. For making mistakes and being human and wanting things that maybe we aren't meant to have."

"I *want* our baby."

"I know. Me, too."

He sat back and gathered her into his lap. She snuggled into him, leaving one arm around his neck, the other tucked against his rib cage. They sat like that a long time, holding each other.

"I wanted us to have a baby because I didn't feel secure in our relationship, either," he admitted with reluctance and shame. "I hate not feeling confident, especially when it comes to you. From the moment I saw you, you consumed me."

She started to pick up her head, taking a breath to speak, but he slid his hand to cup her neck, silently asking her to stay still and let him finish.

"I knew immediately that you could destroy me, so I fought against allowing it." He used his thumb to stroke the soft hollow beneath her ear. "Please remember that you didn't tell me you loved me until I was so jealous of Molly, I could only see green."

"I should have told you who she was," she mumbled against his shirt.

"Yes. You should have. We both should have done a lot of things. We are in a hell of our own making, but you're right. At some point we have to forgive ourselves and each other. We can only move forward from here. I don't want to lose you, Sasha. Not because it would destroy me if you left, but because you give me a reason to live."

She tilted her head back and cupped his jaw, mouth quivering. "I love you. I will always love you, but—"

He slid his thumb to still her lips. "Wait. Let me feel

that." He closed his eyes and let her words wash through him. *Love. Always.*

A helpless sob left her and she buried her face in his shoulder again.

"Love did seem like a liability." He wove his fingers into her hair so he cupped the back of her skull. "It makes you so vulnerable, it's excruciating. But these last days… As helpless as I feel, I am so freaking motivated to kill or die for you and our baby. I didn't understand that love is also power, when you let yourself feel it. When I hear you say it to me, it fills me with strength. With something so right, I'm invincible. Can you please, please feel that, too, Sash? Because I love you. I always will."

Sasha didn't want to weep. She had done enough of that lately, but these were tears of release. Of acceptance. She didn't ask him if he meant what he said. She had to believe that he did. Had to. It was the only way to embark on this new beginning of trust between them. More importantly, she had to believe she deserved his love. It was, after all, a rare and special gift from someone who was very cautious about offering his heart.

"Sash? My love? I know I took too long to say it—"

"Shh," she told him. "Let me feel it."

A choked noise left him, then his arms closed more firmly around her, keeping her safe. Impressing into her the power that he'd spoken of, the way it made her feel valued and centered and right.

When she lifted her head minutes later, she didn't speak or let him say anything. She pressed her salt-stained lips to his and they both moaned with the agony of reunion. It was a chaste, soft kiss of forgiveness that slowly grew into something more questing and generous. It was a kiss that she sank into so deeply, she didn't realize he had tipped her onto the sofa until the weight of his hips were crushing her own.

Still they kissed, letting their love pour into the other. Letting it heal them both. It was a kiss she would remember all the rest of her days. The sweetest most loving of kisses she had ever known.

But the power of their love had other facets. Hot, sharp glints that began to spark and glitter and *need*. As she grew hotter and the insistence of his erection pressed on her thigh, he picked up his head, a question in his ridiculously beautiful eyes.

Her answer was to begin unbuttoning his shirt.

A satisfied growl rumbled in his throat and his chest expanded when her hands crept inside to explore his skin. She kissed the underside of his chin and scraped her teeth against the stubble there.

"Do you want me to shave?" He rasped his palm against it.

"I want you exactly as you are."

"You are deeply, deeply precious to me, Sasha. I'm sorry that I never made that clear."

"Show me now," she whispered.

He did. He undressed her slowly and set worshipful kisses against the skin he bared. He told her how much he adored the tender spots under her breast and inside her elbow and at the crease of her thigh. He said, "I missed you."

"I missed you, too." She wasn't as patient as he was. She pushed at his clothing, arching and moaning at the luxury of his hot, hair-roughened body atop her own. "I want you inside me. I need to feel you."

She wasn't quite ready. It took a moment of shifting and caressing. Of kissing and him saying, "There's no hurry. I'll always be yours."

Then he was deep inside her, pulsing like a heartbeat. He shook and she trembled.

"I pride myself on my control, my love, but I have been wanting you very badly for a very long time."

"It's okay." She petted his back and shoulder. "You don't have to wait for me."

"The hell I don't," he grumbled. "I'd wait the rest of my life if I had to."

That made her smile because in some ways he really would never change, and she loved that most about him.

Of course, he waited. He barely moved while he lovingly fondled and caressed her all over, tracing paths across her skin that left a wake of shooting stars. He kissed her until she was drowning in sensuality, intoxicated by the taste of his mouth and the thrust of his tongue.

Then she realized their bodies had begun the dance of lovemaking. This slow slide and build was them, moving in perfect accord, each drawing the other along the path of ever deepening arousal. He traced his fingers down her breast and she shivered. She opened her mouth against his bicep, delicately sucking, and his breath grew jagged.

In this moment, nothing existed but the two of them. They were utterly attuned to each other, making those small noises of acute pleasure, the ones that bordered on suffering as they fought to stay here, in this glorious place, where they were one. United. Unbreakable.

Then they did break and even then, they were indelibly together.

"I need to tell you something," Rafael said as they were getting ready for their meeting with Molly's team of specialists.

"Oh?" Sasha tensed, distracted. Patty had been right. They wanted to deliver the baby by surgery tomorrow morning and needed to discuss the various procedures, precautions, and risks today.

"I know Humbolt is supposed to hand the reins to you once you have a baby, but he's likely to contest it, so I've put my lawyers onto drawing up paperwork that forces him to move out of your properties. Your mother will continue to receive her support payments and the use of one property, but she can only send you a letter—a physical one that you can choose to open or not—twice a year, on your birthday and Christmas. Otherwise, any contact has to come from you. Humbolt will be forced out of your life completely."

"I…" She didn't know how to react. It had been on her mind that she would have to start the process, but between her real concussion and fake amnesia and worrying about Molly, she hadn't had the bandwidth. She certainly hadn't planned to be so cold-blooded and final about it.

"There's a small settlement if Humbolt goes quietly," Rafael continued. "If he makes one move toward trying to maintain control, I'll sue him for every crime I can think of from mismanagement to child abuse. You can make whatever changes you want. I just needed somewhere to put my anger," Rafael said with a grim curl of his lip.

Sasha didn't need to think about it. The fears that had kept her silent had dissipated now that she had faced them. She had her daughter back in her life and her husband was on her side. She would do anything to protect Molly and Patty, but she had a feeling Gio was also prepared to take up arms in their honor.

"Once a year is often enough to hear from my mother. Otherwise, it sounds perfect. Thank you."

The following morning, for the first time, they all gathered in Molly's room as she was wheeled out for her surgery.

Patricia cuddled Libby on the sofa. Gio hovered like some sort of avenging angel.

Sasha put on a brave face, refusing to think of all those things they'd told her yesterday, but as soon as Molly was gone, she turned into Rafael's arms.

The minutes passed like hours. When sixty had gone by, they all grew restless, eyeing the clock and the door and each other.

Then the doctor walked in.

"Congratulations. You have a son. Molly is in recovery. Things went very well, but the baby will need acute care for several weeks. We'll take you to meet him in a few minutes."

Sasha wilted, held up only by Rafael's trembling strength. Then she had to let go so she could share relieved laughter and hugs with Patty and Libby. Even Gio hugged her and shook Rafael's hand, saying a heartfelt, "I'm very happy for you both."

Then she and Rafael were brought to the pediatric nursery, where they met Atticus. Libby had added his name to their short list and Rafael agreed that it suited their little fighter.

He was under a warm light in an incubator, cradled in a blanket patterned with seahorses. His diaper engulfed his desperately small form. He hadn't had time to put on weight or grow hair. His limbs were thinner than Sasha's pinky finger and wires were secured to his foot and arm and mouth.

"Put on this gown," the nurse prodded gently. "Then we'll set him on you for some skin-to-skin contact."

When Sasha came back from changing, Rafael had his enormous hand inside the incubator. Teeny, tiny fingers were curled in an attempt to hang on to the tip of his index finger. Tears were standing in Rafael's eyes, magnifying the love in them.

"Oh, love," she murmured, ready to dissolve herself. She cupped his face and kissed his damp lips. Then she sat in a rocker and opened the hospital gown, accepting the weightless duckling that was her son against the swell of her breast.

While her own tears ran freely down her cheeks, Rafael fell to his knees beside them. As his warm hand settled on her thigh and his gaze ate up both of them, her heart settled into a state of peace she hadn't known since... Well, ever. Not until now.

This level of happiness was new. It wasn't naive. She knew they had struggles ahead, especially with such a premature baby, but it was going to be okay. Somehow, it would all be okay. She believed that.

And it was.

EPILOGUE

New York, one year later...

"OH, HELLO," RAFAEL SAID, turning in the spray of the shower when Sasha slipped in to join him. "I thought you were still in Patty's room."

"Since tonight is the launch of my own initiative, I feel it would be good manners to show up on time for it."

With Patty's help, Sasha had put together a foundation to raise funds for organizations that offered resources for teen clinics and reproductive care for adolescents. Libby had decided against attending. They had made an announcement a few months ago, acknowledging that Sasha was her birth mother, but Libby didn't want to be the center of attention tonight. Not when she could have her baby brother all to herself.

They saw Libby every month or two, and Atticus always gave her the same gooey grin he gave Molly, who visited even more often. He was still behind his peers in weight and development, but very middle-of-the-percentile when they factored in his due date. He was sitting up, starting to crawl and babbled all sorts of nonsense as he bashed at his toys.

"I got some hot gossip while I was in Patty's room, though," Sasha told him as she lathered her hands and ran them across his chest. "Libby asked Patty if she could home-school so she could spend more time in Europe with us and Molly."

"I'd like that. It always feels like there's a piece missing when she leaves."

"I'm sure Patty feels the same," she said wryly. "Gio wants to buy her and Lib a house in Genoa. Patty's on board, but she has a few clients she wants to stay and deliver first. One is a young woman who's talking about placing her baby for adoption." She lifted her brows to gauge his interest. "Patty doesn't want to get our hopes up, but she said it might be worth our meeting her."

"I'm ready to have that conversation." He paused in running the bar of soap over her curves. "Are you?"

"Yes. Even if it doesn't work out this time, yes." The first months of Atticus's life had been stressful, but he was thriving now. Rafael worked the occasional late night, but he also took lots of half days and long weekends to hang out with her and their son. When Libby was with them, they often spent their time aboard the yacht. Molly and Gio joined them when they could.

"I want another baby so I have a shot at holding my own baby," Sasha joked. "Molly's on her way here, which means the competition for Atticus has increased exponentially."

"Here?" Rafael pointed facetiously at the tiled floor of the shower.

"No, my love. Molly is not joining us for our pregame lovemaking." She slid her arms around his waist, then slithered deliciously against the silky, slippery bubbles that were running down his front. His erection stabbed at her belly. "She can have her own shower with her own husband, if that's what she wants. Between you and me, I think they're trying to make their own little Atticus."

"I wish them all the best," he said sincerely. "But go back to the part about why you joined me." His soapy hands slid from her waist to her backside.

"Nostalgia," she claimed, growing more suggestive in the

way she was rubbing against him. "I looked out at the skyline and was reminded of a party many moons ago, when a very dashing man asked me to dance, then swept me away for the night." She deliberately paused and cast her gaze to the ceiling before teasing, "And a day and another night… What comes after 'debauchery' on the scale of sexual excess?"

"For us? Marriage." Lust and amusement and challenge backed up in his eyes. "Why don't we do that again?"

"Because we have children! Responsibilities. People are expecting us to show up in a couple of hours. I'm sorry, but we'll have to stick with the abridged version." She ran her hand between his thighs, liking the way he caught his breath.

Then he pivoted to press her into the wall.

"I meant marriage, *agápi mou*."

His playful, sexy kiss wiped her brain.

When he let her up for air, she said, "What…um…?"

"Will you marry me, Sasha?"

"I'd marry you every year for the rest of our lives, just so you'd know how important you are to me," she said solemnly.

"Same." He was equally grave. "But I don't need a wedding every year, just one more. Not even a big one, but a proper one, like Gio and Molly's. One with the people we love there with us. One where we promise to love each other for the rest of our lives."

"Rafael." She blinked lashes that were damp from more than the shower spray. "That would make me really happy."

"Me, too. I wish I'd thought of it sooner." He dipped his head to kiss her again. "But you're right about our being pressed for time. I'm going to hit our highlight reel hard and fast, so pay attention."

He dropped to his knees and her laughter quickly turned to a moan of joy.

* * * * *

COMING SOON!

We really hope you enjoyed reading this book.
If you're looking for more romance
be sure to head to the shops when
new books are available on

Thursday 25th April

MILLS & BOON

MILLS & BOON®

Coming next month

ACCIDENTALLY WEARING THE ARGENTINIAN'S RING
Maya Blake

Abstractedly, Mareka registered that they'd cleared the building, that they were out in the square with a handful of people milling around them.

But she couldn't break the traction of Cayetano's stare. His heavenly masculine scent was in her nose. The powerful thud of his heartbeat danced beneath her fingers, his breathing a touch erratic again after his gaze dropped to linger on her mouth, his own lips parted to reveal a hint of even white teeth.

And just like that she was once again thrown to that night in Abruzzo when this foolish crush had taken a deeper hold. When the only thing she'd yearned for, more than anything else in existence, was to kiss Cayetano Figueroa. Who cared that she'd sworn to be rid of this madness a mere…half an hour ago?

Half an hour ago…while she'd been choosing the engagement ring he intended to give to another woman.

Her eyes started to widen. He sucked in a sharp breath.

A camera flash went off, dancing off the diamond ring she'd forgotten to take off and illuminating their

expressions for a nanosecond before immortalizing it in
life-altering pixels.

Continue reading
**ACCIDENTALLY WEARING THE
ARGENTINIAN'S RING**
Maya Blake

Available next month
millsandboon.co.uk

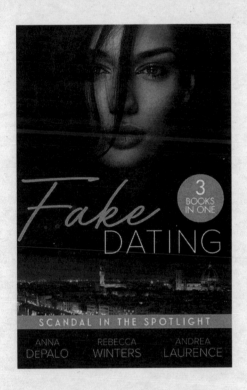

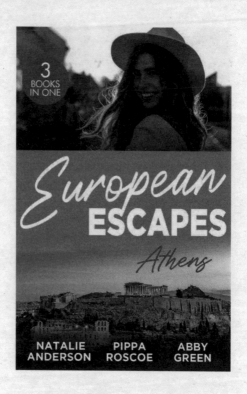

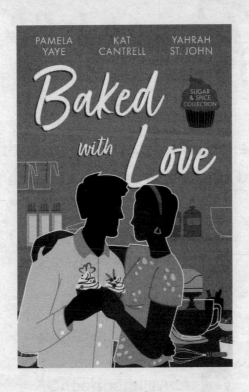

LET'S TALK
Romance

For exclusive extracts, competitions and special offers, find us online:

f MillsandBoon

X @MillsandBoon

◉ @MillsandBoonUK

♪ @MillsandBoonUK

Get in touch on 01413 063 232